WOLVES IN WINTER

Lisa Hilton is the author of four historical biographies and
one historical novel, *The House with Blue Shutters*, which
was shortlisted for the Commonwealth Fiction Prize. She
has made several historical programmes for television and
is a regular art and book reviewer. She lives in London.

Also by Lisa Hilton:

The House with Blue Shutters

WOLVES IN WINTER

Lisa Hilton

CORVUS

Published in trade paperback in Great Britain in 2012 by Corvus,
an imprint of Atlantic Books Ltd.

This paperback edition published in Great Britain in 2013
by Corvus, an imprint of Atlantic Books Ltd.

1   3   5   7   9   10   8   6   4   2

A CIP catalogue record for this book is available
from the British Library.

Paperback ISBN: 978 1 84887 468 8
E-book ISBN: 978 0 85789 709 1

Printed in Great Britain.

Corvus
An imprint of Atlantic Books Ltd
Ormond House
26–27 Boswell Street
London WC1N 3JZ

www.corvus-books.co.uk

To Dominique de Basterrechea, with love

PROLOGUE

Florence, January 1494

HE CITIZENS OF FLORENCE, FAMOUSLY, HAVE LITTLE USE
for light. In this city of white and black, grey and dun and bronze,
only the snowy mountain hump of the Duomo, Our Lady of the
Flowers, surprises with the gaiety of a meadow, its pink and green
façade startling as the sudden space which surrounds it, opening as
it does from the twined, skinny streets surrounding the Mercato
Vecchio, where the grim walled houses hunch towards one another
as though to protect their inhabitants from glimpses of the sky,
which might distract from the business of getting. Light is for
painters, or wastrels; any tremulous sunbeam which steals a cau-
tious finger between the stones is transmuted into gold, battened
down and locked away in chests of iron from the Elba mines.
Stingy, envious, proud Florence, its miserly flesh throbbing with the
hidden gleam of money.

This night, the city is dark as the black ice which paralyses the
river Arno from the Ponte Vecchio along the Bardi embankment.

I

Many years since Florence knew such a winter, so vicious that even the ice-rimed statues seem pinched and emaciated, huddling into the wind that thrashes the snow of the Apennines through the streets, turning the patient saints of the churches to shivering goblins. With the winds come the wolves. Keen, running low, they slip like daggers through the white hills of Fiesole. When the farmers force open their doors to the meagre daylight, their lungs smarting after a night of woodsmoke, they find scarlet mosaics in the snow and cross themselves and close the shutters more tightly, for the wolves are moving. Florence may be a citadel of science, but it is also a city of prophets, where temples to near-forgotten gods lie beneath the busy feet of the merchants. On the night of Il Magnifico's death, a she-wolf howled for hours beneath the city walls. The wolves are moving, and they will bring death with them, from beyond the Alps.

So this night, the streets are empty except for the tiny clatter of dewclaws on the stones of Piazza Santa Maria Novella. Even the beggars who bundle themselves in the wretched shelter of the portico are hidden. Tap, tap. The wolf pauses on the corner of the Via degli Strozzi, turns, a fluid shadow, and begins to trot north-ward, toward the Baptistery, where the great pool in which all the children of the city are given to God is still as lead. Her tail feathers the great carved doors. The gelid marble of the Duomo picks out amber eyes. Audacious, starving, the wolf crosses straight through the piazza, no shadow now, lengthening her stride until she bounds in black flashes of sinew and need, past the chapel of San Lorenzo and into the Via Larga, her skull aflame with the scents of boiled meat, of peppered lard and spiced pigeon, cured pork and creamed chicken, carried from the kitchens and larders of the Palazzo Medici. Saliva hisses on the snow as she noses frantically along the street doors, but this is Florence, and they are iron bolted.

The wolf feels the suck of her empty belly beneath her ribs, lets out a miserable whine, shoves and gnaws, but the doors hold fast. Her black pelt ripples with clutches of want. In the wall beside the doors is a small window, an ingress for messages or alms. The wolf rears her body upwards, stretching her length until her paws rest on the sill. The wooden shutters are loose, their hinges weakened with the contractions of the long winter. The wolf drops to the tamped snow, circles back, gathers the force of the wind in her shoulders, leaps. Her snout strikes the wood, the shutters make a flat thud on the soft drift inside, she scrabbles for purchase, hindlegs and tail beating the air, hauls her bruised weight through the aperture, lands noiselessly, buried. She is inside.

The *cortile* is full of eyes. In Florence, they say that spirits can be imprisoned in statues. In the centre of the courtyard, where the cleared snow shows prints already molten with the new fall, stands a boy; improbably naked save for gaiters, boots and a teasingly pointed cap, his left hand easy on the plump adolescent curve of his hip, his right resting on the hilt of his lowered sword. The wolf checks, he is no threat. A little aside is another figure, not a smooth bronze, but a towering, lumpen creature of snow, planed crystal wings soaring from his back, torso strained about the great serpent which writhes at his feet, jaws agape to strike at him. Already, the lines of the statue are drooping, aged by freeze and thaw. The wolf pays him no mind. The still air hums with scents, but she does not make her way through the loggia to the service quarters on the

3

ground floor, but, head down, confused by her waning need, she follows another trail, which speaks to her blood. Tap, tap. Her claws scratch the fine wood of the staircase, mounting and turning, she moves supple as the lathe, one flight, two. Eager now, along a passage, the glands in her jaw working, wetting the air with her panting, her snout finds a door, pushes slowly until she insinuates herself, drawn by wraiths of desire, into the room.

The room contains a chest, a simple wooden chair, a low truckle bed. Roughly plastered walls, no fire or stove, just a squat iron brazier, its few coals barely disturbing the currents of her breath. On the bed is a child, a little girl. Or not so little, maybe, a spiky starveling thing. She wears a tattered red dress, once luminous silk dulled and shabby, battered knees and soft, narrow little arms protruding. Her spine is held erect, leaving a space between her fragile body and the damp wall. Pale hair, colourless as new straw, obscures her face, which is bent forward over a doll, a stump of a thing, lovemangled, caressed to a grubby chunk of body and a precarious flannel head. The child knows the wolf is there. The wolf hears the stirring of the translucent hairs on her body, the quickening in her lungs, the deepened grasp of her fingers in the puffy cloth. The muscles above the wolf's hindquarters contract, readying her to spring, ears flattening she releases a low growl from the base of her throat.

And the child looks up. Her copper skin catches the flame of the wolf's eyes, drawing them to her face. Eyes green as the depths of the glaciers high in the Apennine peaks, green and unfaltering as the ice that even the August sun cannot move. The wolf cannot find the fear cooling on her skin. Her eyes fix the wolf's eyes, she makes the slightest shake of her head. The wolf shudders along the length of her black body, stilled as quickly as if she had a huntsman's arrow in her heart. She whines faintly. Every nerve in her, drained by days of running, ribs beamed with hunger, wills her to take, to plunge and kill, but she cannot. Head raised, throat exposed, obeisant, she dips her forelegs and shuffles across the boards towards the child. For a moment, gold light melds with green. Then, silently, she turns and trots for the door.

The child waits, her knees drawn up under her chin, wrapped in her thin arms. She sends her ears out from the palazzo, out into the streets of Florence, over the river and up into the hills, until she finds the wolf's heart – and travels with it across the snow at killing speed, bounds longer than her own body, until it slows, slows.

She hears it then, the first quavering howl, and draws back to herself as it is answered, first one, then another and another, the wolves keening for her until the city is encircled with the baying, riding to her over the darkness, and the child draws her quilt about her, and smiles, and sleeps.

PART ONE

FLORENCE

1492–1496

CHAPTER ONE

ALONG WITH EVERYTHING ELSE, THEY TOOK MY name. When I came to the palazzo they washed me in a brass tub in the kitchen, as though I was a fine lady's pet monkey to be picked over for fleas. I would not speak to them, so they turned out my red dress to look for any signs of me. My mother had sewn it for me, cut down from her own wedding gown. It was the finest tabby silk, pomegranate-coloured, so when it turned in the light it was sometimes the rich crimson pink of a sunset, sometimes as bright and crisp as the skin of an orange. The silk came from Kashmir, my papa told me, a mountain place like our city of Toledo, only the mountains were so high only God could see their peaks. My mother stitched her love into every delicately worked gather on the bodice and sleeves. Inside, where my heart would be, she placed a pentagram, and inside that she stitched my name. *Mura*. From the old language, when the caliphs were kings in Toledo. Mura: wish, desire.

They saw my mother's mark, but they could not read it, for it was *aljamiado*, their letters in our first tongue. I can speak Spanish and Arabic and even a little Latin, but I had no words in theirs yet, and I should not have used them if I had. All my words were kept for curses. Mura, my mother stitched, for I was her wish. But I was no longer Mura Benito, the bookseller's child from Toledo. I was *esclava*. Slave. They took away my doll and my red dress and gave me a coarse grey robe, stuffed my feet into heavy wooden clogs. They clipped my hair close to my head and took it away in a kerchief, to sell for a vanity. My brow bound in a black striped linen cloth, I kept my eyes to the ground and became invisible, just another moving cog in the machine of the palazzo. I had learned by then that my face brought trouble. I became *Mora*, Moor, because I am Spanish and they knew no better, even though my skin is not plum-black but the colour of new gold.

The world shrank until it was contained within the walls of the kitchen. I marked the passing of days with the church bells that sounded dimly from the city beyond the thick stone, and with the journeys of thin wands of light that probed through the high windows. I shuffled about, silent except for my newly clumsy feet, performing the simple tasks they set for me. I stripped beans, separating the pink streaked pods from the creamy husks, I washed salt from the muslin sacks of capers unloaded from wagons which brought supplies from the countryside, I picked stalks from spinach. For hours and hours I stood at the stone troughs and scrubbed plate, rubbing it over first with sand, then rinsing in grey, greasy water, until my hands puffed out like fresh white rolls, and then, as the weather grew colder, cracked and reddened like an old woman's. Twice a day I sat at a trestle in the stench of the household's sweat, knowing

I stank as they did, and tried to eat their coarse Florence food. Bland and greasy, everything smelling of pig; hard, dull-tasting bread, murky pea soup, disgusting withered shrivels of pork rind. If I allowed myself to think of the hammam, of black soap and orange flower water and the wonderful feeling of being clean inside as well as out, I knew I should go mad, so I kept my eyes down and did my work and tried to make myself as dull as a pebble.

Gradually, the sounds around me resolved into sense. First objects – cloth, bowl, spoon – then slowly I was able to understand more and more of the speech around me. As I worked, I repeated the words to myself, though I would not speak them aloud.

Mora the slave did not speak.

I learned that the palazzo belonged to Piero de Medici, the son of Lorenzo who was called the great, *Il Magnifico*. There were wonders in the house beyond the kitchen, they said, though I had seen the courtyard and did not think it so very fine. All the business of Florence passed in the palazzo, for Piero was a great man, one of the greatest in the whole of Italy, richer than any prince, for all that his blood was not noble, but tainted with the ink of the counting house. The palazzo was never still. From the moment the street gate opened at Prime until the porters closed it at Lauds there came streams of people, to petition, to plead, to bargain, taking their seats on the wooden benches set into the walls of the courtyard, trying to mind their dignity as Piero kept them waiting for weeks. Clerks scuttled self-importantly back and forth with their account books and abacuses, processions of factors and lawyers, notaries, priests and ambassadors, artists and gentlemen and even bishops passed through to hover expectantly at the foot of the great staircase which the likes of me were not permitted to climb.

Sometimes, ladies came to pay visits to Donna Alfonsina, Piero's wife, who had recently given him a baby son. The kitchen people said that Donna Alfonsina was a proud lady, a Roman princess who thought herself too good for Florence. I did not think that so wonderful, for everything was grey in Florence and the sun never seemed to shine; but the house slaves were affronted – they counted themselves Medici too, part of the family, and so took up their dignity at Donna Alfonsina's disdain. As if she would pay them any more mind than she might a fly, black and buzzing about beneath her as they were. I saw the ladies sometimes, as I crossed to the loggia lugging a basket of fresh linens for the noon dinner. Their bright silks and fresh skins were like sudden rainbows in a cave, so that it hurt me to look at them.

The kitchen folk thought me dumb. At first they tried to rile me, with overset basins, cuffs and slaps I did not deserve. My arms blued with sly cruel pinchings, then when I did not cry out they fell to coaxing, wheedling me into speech. But so long as I was careful never to raise my eyes to them, they would, in time, cease to notice me. That was all I wished. To be Mora the slave and stay safe until I could become myself again.

And that way, a year went by. A year with no flowers or books, no walks in the meadows beyond the walls with the sun setting like pink velvet over the mountains, a year with no scent except the faint lavender rustle of a lady's train and my own sour unwashed body, a year in the finest house in the finest city in Italy and nothing but heaps of greens to look at to soothe the keening in my soul.

At night, lying on my straw pallet in the unsteady peace of the chamber of sleeping women, I mourned. I mourned and I dreamed. I crushed my arms across my chest to dull my breaking heart and I walked the banks of that crystal river beneath Toledo, by buildings of marble as pale and delicate as the first frost on the boughs of the almond trees, and I searched for my mother and my papa.

I wore my red dress that day, the day the world changed. That was all I had of my mother, the thread of her own heart's desire against mine. She named me because she rejoiced that she would have a little girl of her own – wish, desire. She knew she would die of me, my mama. That is why she placed the sign above my heart to keep me safe, since she would never hold me close to her own. But she was with me, my papa told me, she was always with me. If I was ever lonely, or afraid, my mother would come to me in my dreams to keep me safe.

For all the while I was a girl, in Toledo, I pictured my mother like one of the Holy Virgins I saw painted on the wall when we went to Mass, distant and serene, the gold of her hair melding with the gold cloth of her mantle, a pool of sunlight where I could dip my hand whenever I needed. I was not lonely. I had my papa, and he was all the world to me.

My father, Samuel Benito, was a bookseller. Books were his livelihood, and it was books which brought him to his death. We lived in the Zocodover, the ancient market quarter of Toledo, and buyers came to our crooked little house from all over Europe. My father explained to me that in the time of the caliphs, the *convivencia*, the libraries of the Moors had been preserved with all their learning and it was this which made Toledo so important for scholars, a place of tolerance and translation, where *moriscos* like us could meet Jews and Christians as equals, united in respect for the ancient learning of the lands of the East.

My father was not a doctor, but that learning taught him how to cure sickness. Often, after consulting his books, he would take me with him to the slopes above town to gather plants that he stewed and ground to make medicines for the people who would tap at the door after dark. Sometimes they paid him, if they were rich, but many did not. Not that his kindness served him anything, in the end. That last spring, we would go up to the meadows as we had always done, where the new grass was a pale gold-green and the hills were carpeted with crocuses, opening their flimsy violet petals to the ripening sun. He named them for me, set them softly in my hands so that I should know their touch and smell, told me of their qualities and how they might be used.

'We'll never starve, little Mura,' he would tell me, 'for people are always sick, and they are always afraid.'

Fear had come to Toledo by then. Fire and fear and treachery blazed through our city which had once been celebrated for its knowledge and harmony. The Castilian queen and her husband, Ferdinand of Aragon, called out their troops to drive away the infidel, and the city turned upon itself like a rabid dog. Families who had lived for generations as Christians were persecuted as *morisco*, heretics who secretly worshipped the Moorish God. Neighbours whispered against each other in the market and each day the bell of my father's shop rang less often, until weeks would go by when nothing but the sweet mountain breezes stealing in through the shutters disturbed the golden dust on the heaped volumes. My father began to parcel up his treasures and send them away, to merchants in Venice and Paris where the danger was not so great, and at night I would hear the scratch of his pen as he went over his accounts, squinting behind his seeing glass in the light of a single tallow candle, sighing over how long he might hold out against ruin.

My father began to insist that we attended Mass each week in the still-unfinished cathedral, and afterwards he would walk about with my hand tucked into his arm, bowing politely to everyone he recognised, making sure we were seen. Although the bags of rice in the larder slumped and grew thin, and we no longer ate meat except on holidays, I was not afraid. I was glad that my father had more time for me, now that he was no longer at his correspondence at all hours, tracing out the works his clients sought. My papa had always been so gentle with me, so careful and patient. He had fed and bathed and dressed me from a babe, with all the tenderness I knew my mother would have shown; but he had often been weary and distracted, and those nights when his friends came to drink wine and talk with him in the parlour I had known better than to disturb him. Talk, I knew, was his only pleasure now my mother was gone. So, now that my father's friends had left Toledo, and those that remained would greet one another with no more than a swift flicker of eyes as they passed in the streets, my father had time for me.

He began, with increasing urgency, to talk to me of the old learning. He would stroke my hair in the warm light of the stove and whisper to me, as I fell towards sleep, of Zoroaster of Chaldea whose learning was carried to Egypt, where the ibis-headed god Thoth invented writing. How King Solomon had learned to summon angels, and how all the arts derived from the seven principles of grammar, rhetoric, logic, arithmetic, music, geography and astronomy. These were my childhood stories, the names of the *magi* the heroes of my fairytales, kings who travelled on camels over golden deserts, summoning magical creatures from the movements of the stars. Like all odd children, I did not think it odd.

The only time I ever saw my father angry was when I questioned his passion. I was a good Christian girl, I knew my catechism and I asked my father whether it was right to speak of such things, whether this learning was not sinful. He banged his fist on the table with such force that his wine glass jumped to the floor and shattered, and I was so shocked to see the rage on his gentle face that I began to weep. He gathered me to him and stroked my hair.

'I'm sorry, little one. Don't cry. Listen. "Wisdom and knowledge shall be granted unto thee, and I will give thee riches and wealth and honour such as none of the kings have had that have been before thee, neither shall any after have the like."'

'What does that mean?'

'It's from the Bible, Mura. The Chronicles. And none of

these holy murderers with their false trials and their hateful piety know anything of knowledge. It is no heresy to seek to know, to understand the world God created for us. Their torture and their persecution and the fears they spread, that is true evil, because it is the evil of ignorance, and ignorance defends itself with cruelty. Remember that.'

My papa had told me many times how, hundreds of years ago, before the Spanish king El Sabio came to Toledo, the city belonged to the caliphs. And how before that, before the walls and the churches were built, men came here from the north, men who crossed the mountains and mixed their pale hair and eyes with those of the people they found here. How they scratched their runes into the rocks and how a century ago their magic had been collected and sent over the world on pages of vellum.

'That is why our city is so special, little Mura. Many learned men came here and they brought books with them, marvellous books that told of medicines and the movements of the stars. They came from all over the world to study and talk here in Toledo, and some people say that there is another city, under the earth, a magic city with tunnels instead of roads and palaces in caves, and a river as cold and clear as frozen diamonds. If you can go down into that city, they say, and fill a flask of water in the river, then it will make peach trees bloom in winter time and cover the earth with blossom.'

I could never hear enough about the magical city, though my father told me I must not speak of it to anyone but him. He said that some people were afraid of such things, and that was why the city had to be kept secret, because people would try to destroy what they feared. I knew that there was nothing holy in the fires that burned in Toledo in those years, nothing of love or peace. Only ignorance and the love of power, and fear is the greatest weapon of the powerful. I knew that books are feared because their strength is silent, their challenge unspoken. My papa taught me then how knowledge that knows when to stay silent can never be destroyed.

The winter came. I was excited, for my father had told me I was grown big enough to wear my red dress for the Feast of Kings, *Epifania*. I had spent the afternoon carefully painting a gold crown Papa had helped me to cut out from packing paper. He put me to bed early, with a cup of warm milk and cinnamon, stroking my hair and telling me to stay quiet as a leaf. The early winter dark had not yet fallen, but Papa had already shut up the house and was moving uneasily in the dim rooms on the ground floor. Now and then I heard a curse and a crash as a heap of books toppled, and I wanted to laugh at his silliness. Why did he not light a candle? It was cosy in my little bed, which Papa had moved next to the stove to keep me warm, and I was dozing off under the blankets when I heard a tap at the street door and my father's steps going to answer it. The hinge creaked as it closed, and I heard some muttered conversation; it wasn't hard to pick out the husky boom of Adara's curious voice, even though she was trying to whisper.

I liked Adara. I liked her bold swaying walk and the sour-spicy smell of her large bosom when she hugged me. Like many in our city, her skin was as black as a ripe fig and she wore huge hoops of twisted gold in her ears, which she would take out and let me play with as I waited for my father, dangling my feet in the blue-tiled fountain in her courtyard when it was hot or sitting snugly by the fire in winter on a settle covered all over with flowers worked in silk. Adara lived in a fine house with several other ladies, and I thought that she must be very rich, even though she had no husband.

Her name in our tongue meant 'virgin'. I asked my father once why she wore no habit, if she was a nun, and he smiled and said she belonged to a convent of a sort, but that he did no business there. That wasn't true, I said, because he took powders and salves to Adara that he made up in the back of our shop, and I had seen her handing him pesos to put in his purse.

Tonight, though, Adara had not come for almond water or the bitter black paste my father forbad me touch. There was an urgency in her voice that roused me to listen more attentively.

'It's too late,' I heard my father say.

'If you come with me now?'

'No, they have it. They have the *grimoire*. I was betrayed. But you will do as we agreed?'

'Very well.'

'I have packed them for her. It's a poor enough dowry, God knows.'

'I will care for her.'

My father came up the stairs, treading slowly. He carried a candle and my dress lay over his arm.

'It's time to put this on, pretty one.' He smiled, his teeth showing white in the grey of his beard. It makes me lose my

19

breath now when I think what that smile must have cost him.

'Papa, what's happening? Are we going somewhere special? With Adara? The crown isn't dry.'

'Come here, my little love. Something special, yes. Like a pageant. And you will be the most important player.'

Then he told me what I had to do, and opened the shutters wide.

*

It seemed a long time that I waited, hunched on the windowsill. It was icy, and I tried not to shiver, feeling the blood drawing towards my heart and my hands grow numb where they clutched the window frames. They came across the square, as Papa said they would, a line of torches, yellow light glancing on hooded faces and the fat crucifixes chained on their breasts. That was the first moment that I was afraid. The men stopped before our door.

'Samuel Benito. Samuel Benito! In the name of the Tribunal of the Holy Office of the Inquisition, you are under arrest.'

Aside from the river of flame beneath my window, the square was entirely dark. No one would stir, no one would come out to defend my father. Peeping over the sill, balancing the wax flowers my father had wound in my hair with one cold-clumsy hand, I watched him step into the circle of light. He wore his best cloak, but his head was bare. The men fanned out, encircling him, and I saw that those in the front ranks were not monks, as their hoods made them seem, but soldiers, the hilts of their short swords visible beneath the black robes like quartz in a pebble.

'Does this belong to you?' One of them was holding a fat square parcel, which I knew contained a book.

'It did. I sold it some time ago. I am a bookseller, sir.' My father's voice was low and courteous.

There was a muttering amongst the group. I caught the words 'heretic' and '*morisco*', but my father's stillness had unsettled them, somehow. They had expected a fight. He spoke again.

'I trust I am to come with you, sir?'

I heard Adara move into the room behind me. I could smell the oil on the two rush torches she carried. She knelt before the stove.

'Are you ready?'

'Yes.' I spoke from a dream, ensorcelled by the scene outside.

'They will burn the house. We must be swift. No tears, do you understand me?'

I nodded, my eyes fixed on my father as she dipped the torches to the flame in its iron cage.

'Now.'

As the light flared I scrambled up on the windowsill, flapping at the red fabric around my legs. My hair was crowned with a circlet of briar roses, retrieved by my father from a sack of carnival costumes. They were dusty, but from a distance they would seem fresh. My hands were as red as my dress, the palms dipped in my father's precious cochineal. I was to hold them before me, Papa said, and be sure to open my eyes very wide. For a moment, none of the men below me saw that I stood there, then one of the figures screamed, pointing up. The torches with which

Adara illuminated me cast their light onto pale faces as they fell to their knees, crossing themselves.

Slowly, I raised my hands, the dye dripping from them like blood.

'*Demonio!*'

'*Maligno!*'

'*Diablo!*'

I was uncertain what to do now. I cast my eyes around the group. Only my father was standing, his face seeking mine. He smiled once more, and the torchlight caught the flash of white in his beard. He raised his hands to his mouth and bunched them in a kiss, tossing it to me like a fine gentleman.

'Come now, Mura, come!'

I reached for Adara's hand, and as I clambered off the windowsill, I took one last look for my father, but he had vanished. All I could see now in the square was a huddle of cloaks and the swift flash of a swinging blade. Then we were running, banging down the stairs and through the back door of the shop. I could hear them already, beating at the bolts behind us, and I smelled a sharp, crisp scent, which I knew must be the first of the greedy flames lapping at parchment.

In the alley behind the house, Adara lifted me onto her hip and began to run, my hands clinging to her neck, and her flanks working strongly beneath me as she bounded downhill, her strides lengthening fluidly, her heartbeat mounting in her neck against my cheek. I was too surprised to weep. We ran through the empty streets behind the Zocodover, down towards the city gates, past the brick façade of the Santa Maria synagogue, we ran

22

and ran until we came to the door of Adara's house. She staggered, gasping for air, and let me down, but before she pushed me into the courtyard I saw that the sky behind us was no longer indigo but orange and gold and red, the fireworks from my lost home burning briefly brighter than the stars.

CHAPTER TWO

LEARNED TWO THINGS IN ADARA'S HOUSE. I LEARNED that people were afraid of me. And I learned that my papa had told the truth, that my mother would come to me in my dreams. That first night, I lay curled on the floor like a melon rind, hollowed out with shock. When I finally began to sob, Adara was kind. She gave me a sweet, hot drink made of wine and spices and something else that made me sleep for a long time, and when I awoke my skin smelled of orange water where she had washed me and dressed me in a clean woollen robe. My hands were still pink from the dye. I ate flat bread with mountain honey and dried apples, feeling strangely calm, as though I had woken from a bad dream.

'When will Papa come, Adara?'

She too had bathed, though the heavy perfume she wore, rich with rose oil and musk, did not quite hide the scent of her own skin, the salty, almost bitter tang which I had smelled when she carried me away from our house. Adara's face twisted, she looked very sad and confused.

'Not for a long time, little Mura. Those men last night, they were bad men. That's why we had to trick them, so you could escape. Your papa told me you had to be a good girl here with me and when the bad men have gone, he will come to fetch you. Maybe before the summer comes . . .'

I wanted to ask why the men had burned our house, and what had happened to Papa's books, but I half-knew the answer and was afraid to hear it. Adara clapped her hands and a maid came in with a little bundle.

'For you,' Adara said encouragingly.

Inside was a doll; not a stuffed rag, a real one, with a soft body and real golden hair, a pretty wax face and a green velvet dress and cloak. I had never seen such a lovely thing, and I skipped off happily to show her the fountain and the orange trees, just as Adara had known I would.

The red tint on my hands faded day by day, and my papa did not come. Adara made a little bed for me next to the stove in her own room and gave me a pretty inlaid chest of scented cedar wood in which to put my own things, my dolly and my red dress, washed and mended. As time went on I added more treasures: some violet-coloured pebbles from the courtyard, a little scent bottle of red glass with a silver stopper, an inch of brocade I found under a chest. Before I went to sleep I would spread out my marvels and imagine how I would show them to Papa. For a while, I stayed mostly in this room or in the courtyard, chattering to my doll or watching Adara as she rubbed creams into her skin or painted black lines around her eyes, or peeping from the window at the ladies who shared the house.

The ladies got up very late, sometimes after dinnertime, and if the winter sun was shining they would sit in the courtyard, their faces creased and puffy, wrapped warmly in their cloaks, combing out their hair. Adara said I wasn't to go outside when they were there, but I loved to watch them, drinking endless little glasses of tea and slowly waking themselves so their skin brightened and their voices began to rise and chatter like starlings along a wall. A few hours before the sun went down, everyone grew busy. The maids came and went with jugs of hot water or mended dresses over their arms, and the old porter – the only man in the house – jumped up every few minutes to answer the street bell. It was exciting, with packages arriving and the ladies calling to one another and the smell of roast meat and chocolate from the kitchen.

A maid would bring me a plate of supper and I always ate it quietly, sitting on my bed while Adara dressed herself, peering dissatisfied into her silver looking glass, tweaking her chemise lower over her bosom, rubbing another layer of rouge over her full lips. When she was ready, I watched her cross the courtyard and climb the staircase, her loose silk robe trailing behind her. The rooms above were finer than mine, I knew that, with arched windows and benches full of cushions; and though the shutters were closed to the winter air I could hear music and laughter and smell sweet, smoky incense as it drifted through the cracks into the chilly night. As Adara left she would tell me to get into bed, but I would creep out from under the covers, clutching my doll, and watch the visitors arrive. Sometimes they came alone, purposeful, their faces muffled; sometimes they were in groups of three or four, already staggering a little with drink and making loud jokes, banging one another on the shoulder and tripping over their swords. They were men, gentlemen, and I knew they were rich because every morning when I woke I would see a little purse of coins stuffed under Adara's pillow as she slept on through the morning light.

In a while, though, I grew restless waiting every day until Adara awakened, and one morning I too climbed the stairs to the rooms above the courtyard, which each evening seemed so gay and happy. The room I entered was not the grand, golden chamber I had imagined. With the sun stealing in through the shutters I saw a long table covered in wine cups and plates of congealing meat. There was a full chamber pot underneath and the horrid smell of wine and urine was worsened by a pool of vomit next to the fireplace. On the stained floor was a discarded glove, the pale leather soiled and yellowed. I put it on, pretending I was a beautiful grown-up lady, and trying to conjure the chattering glow of the night into that dismal room, when I heard a clatter behind me. One of the maids had come in with a broom and a bucket.

Usually, I hardly saw the maids. They were *esclava*, their skin purple-black like Adara's, dressed in plain grey wool dresses with white headscarves. When they brought my food or tidied Adara's room they barely looked at me, but this girl was standing still as an icicle, gaping, her hands frantically crossing and re-crossing her breast. The spilled hot water steamed as it spread across the dirty floor. I went to help her pick up the broom, but she backed away from me and I heard her footsteps pounding down the staircase. I could not understand what had startled her. I began to creep back down the stairs, fearing Adara would scold me if she knew I had broken her rule.

As I passed the kitchen quarters, I heard loud exclamations, the same words I had heard that night in the square, '*maligno*', '*demonio*'. Was this something to do with what had happened to my papa, with the men who had come for the book, with my strange disguise? Why did the slave think I might hurt her? I made my way back to Adara's room, feeling very lonely. She was still sleeping, one hand bunched under her chin, soft snores rustling in her throat. I picked up her looking glass from where it lay amongst a huddle of jars and combs and carried it to the window. I had not often seen myself in a glass, but there was nothing strange to me in my appearance. My skin was coppery-coloured, like many people in Toledo, and many people in the city too had green eyes, though not so bright as mine. My hair was unusual, true. I had never seen anyone with hair so light and clear as mine, but I knew the reason for that. I had the blood of the northmen in me.

It didn't matter that I didn't look quite like other children, my papa told me. It meant I was special. When he washed me in warm water scented with rosemary and dried me carefully with a bleached linen cloth, he told me that I was a true child of Toledo, the city where all magic and learning were mixed. They were my mother's people, he said, the northmen who had come to Spain even before the time of the caliphs. The Moors called them '*al madjus*', in their Persian language – 'fire-worshippers' – and from there we had our Spanish word, '*mago*'.

He told me of conjurers who could change their shape to run

28

with the winds and shift the storms that carried the dark birds of their longships; who spoke with the old gods through the blood of sacrifice. They were cruel, proud people, he said, fearless. When they fought, it was easy to believe they had magic in them, so wild were they, so reckless. And beautiful, he said, the most beautiful men the people of the caliphs had ever seen. There was a book by a Moorish traveller who had journeyed up along the rivers to Rus, at the peak of Europe, and his stories were full of awe at these fair giants, their white skin inked all over until it gleamed like green glass, who carried longswords as heavy again as a man, who could fight without armour, or even a shirt, for the cold could not touch them.

Their god was Odin. He had two pet wolves, Geri and Freki, who brought good luck to those who saw them. They left some of their magic behind in Toledo, along with their pale hair and light eyes, like my mother's hair, my mother's eyes, which were also mine. So I carried a little of their strangeness in me and one day, my papa said, we would sail away together, on a ship, to their lands of ice and forest where bonfires blaze at midsummer and the sun never goes down. And maybe my mother would be waiting there, and she would bind flowers in my hair and take my hand to dance.

I could still be comforted, back then, by the memory of my papa's stories. I smudged away the tears, took my doll and pattered out into the courtyard, pulling the hood of my robe over my face. The old porter was wrapped in his cloak, snoozing, and didn't see me as I stretched up to unlatch the street door. I felt strong, defiant. I knew the way home well enough from my walks with my father. All I had to do was make my way towards the tower of Santa Maria and I would find myself in the Zocodover. I was happy again, now that I was outside, though it felt strange to be alone in the streets, and I soon reached the market. For a while, I wandered amongst the stalls, feeling as though I had been away a long time. My nose twitched at the smell of *manchego*, and I stopped to stare at a heap of little partridge laid out on a trestle, their delicate grey breasts soft and quivering in the morning breeze as though they were still alive. I wished I had a coin in my pocket for a fresh *magdalena*, to squeeze the almondy sweetness of the cake between my teeth. No one noticed me amongst the housewives and servants jostling with their baskets, and I skirted the edge of the square until I came to where our house had been.

It was only then that I truly understood. Of course our house was not there. They had burned my father's books and our house with them. All that remained was an ugly heap of blackened timbers and the staircase, tottering crazily amongst the rubble, leading nowhere. The space of the ruins seemed pathetically small. How could this have been my home, where my papa had his shop, where I played and did my lessons and watched the mountains from the window that was vanished as though it had never even been there? I felt sick. Suddenly, coldly, I knew that my papa would not return for me, as Adara had promised. He was never coming back. I began to cry again. I felt panicked, tiny. Clutching my doll I began to run about howling, 'Papa! Papa!' until a woman with a bundle of laundry and a washboard on her back stooped to touch my shoulder, peering into my smeared face.

'What's the matter, little one? Are you lost?'

I pushed back my hood and held out my arms to her, my sight blurred with tears. But she did not pick me up and carry me home. She dropped the washboard and the clang disturbed the buyers around us.

'Santa Madonna! It's Benito's child!'

Suddenly there were people all around me, pulling at me, shouting. The woman pushed me away so roughly I fell down and began to crawl away from her, my sobs shocked back into my throat, choking me. I was so small. I had never known the quickness of hatred, or fear, or the knowledge that came to me now — that if I did not escape, these familiar people would hurt me. A gobbet of spit landed on my neck, a booted foot caught me beneath my elbow, sending me sprawling again. All I could see were cruel, twisted faces, cruel hands reaching for me. I squirmed to my feet and began to run, still holding tightly to my doll, the bitter burned smell of the black beams of my home mingling with the bodies of the crowd.

I moved so fast that for a brief, almost joyful moment I felt as though I were flying, and then I became aware of a silence behind me. I came to a halt, heaving great swallows of air into my chest, and then I turned around. No one had followed me. They stood there, huddled together, gazing at me. And then I recognised that smell on them, that thick, acid reek pushing out from their pores: fear. I took a step towards them, and they shrank from me in one movement like a wave.

They were afraid of me.

I raised my chin and cocked my head to one side, a play-act

31

of listening. It seemed as though I could actually hear the troubled patter of their hearts. Suddenly I wanted to laugh. My doll was in my left hand, dangling against my hip. I raised my right, thumb tucked around my middle fingers, index and little finger raised like two horns. *Cuerno*. The sign of the devil. I gave them the sign of the devil, and then I *did* laugh. I laughed in their faces, and turned my back on them, and ran for my life.

*

Adara swept into the courtyard in only her chemise and took me by the arm so hard that her varnished nails dug into my flesh.

'Where have you been?'

I tried to speak, but I was gulping back sobs, shuddering, barely able to breathe.

'Did anyone see you?'

I managed to nod. 'I went to the marketplace.'

Adara dragged me back to the room, her face grim.

'You are to stay here, do you understand? Or I'll lock the door on you.'

She left me. For a long time I stared stupidly into space. My papa was never coming back. Then the tears came again, kindly, and I wept until I fell asleep, bundled on the floor, with a strange peacefulness that came from knowing I was alone.

*

The year turned. I crept about the room and the courtyard, playing listlessly with my doll whenever Adara was there. I stroked the mark my mother had made against my red dress, I

32

watched as the turning sun from the high narrow window fetched out the colours from its folds. Without my papa's lessons, our walks and visits, the days seemed hopelessly long. Somehow, I knew better than to ask Adara where my father's books were stored, but it was not so hard to find them. There was a storeroom behind the kitchen-house, stacked with jars of oil and preserved lemons, and here was kept my papa's trunk filled with his books.

As the first heat of spring began to mount, the household maids rested in the afternoons, so I could prowl about unhindered by their mutterings. I removed one book at a time – just the smaller, lighter ones – and carried them to the courtyard, hidden inside my cloak. So long as she could see me, Adara paid me little attention now and so for a time I could read and read. In truth, I understood little of what I traced from the pages. Sometimes the book would be in a language I did not understand, sometimes it would be filled with page after page of strange diagrams and numbers, but my papa had taught me well, and even just the scent of the pages, their soft, dusty touch, made me feel a little closer to him. I whispered the odd words to myself, ran my fingers along the dancing signs of our old tongue. It soothed me, and the hours passed much faster.

'Quite the little scholar, aren't we?'

Adara was standing over me, her powerful body blocking the light.

'How dare you steal?'

'I'm not stealing. These are my papa's books. My books!'

She snatched the volume from out of my hands and I feared

she would tear it, but she held it away from her body like a live thing.

'Do you know what a heretic is, Mura?'

'Yes. Someone who does not follow the teachings of the church.'

'And you know what they do to heretics?'

'I think so.'

'They burn them. They tie them up and burn them until the flesh melts off their bones and their eyes burst like figs. Would you like that, Mura? Would you like that to happen to you?'

I was terrified. Her face twisted with hatred, like the faces of the men who had come to take my father, like the people in the marketplace.

'But my papa is a good man! He told me there was nothing bad about his books!'

For an answer she had the porter whip me with his belt until the blood ran from my back and put a huge padlock on the trunk. I had never in all my life been struck. Then she dragged me to our room and pushed me onto the bed, the sheets clinging painfully to my flayed skin.

I think it started to grow in me then, a little seed of hating. I was not to let the servants look at me, I was not to walk abroad, I was not to read my own books that my father had left me. I had tried to be quiet and good and I had been beaten. She would be sorry, I would make her sorry. I lay on my stomach to spare my back, biting at the sheets with rage. And then I must have slept.

*

I dream of a city. A city of spires and domes and palaces, but ruined and broken, with huge buildings sliding into the mud of a stinking river, as though giants have begun to make homes there but grown tired and wandered away. A teeming city, where delicate music dances through the nights across filthy alleyways, and the sound of laughter and the clatter of silver plate mix with the nightmare cries of the lost and the dying in the streets. There is a woman before me. I can see only the back of her red silk dress and her bright gold hair coiling down it. She stretches out her hand to me, and in the touch of her fingers I know her, my mama.

We take a step, and then it seems we can fly, floating over the city, the two of us, seeing it all at once, like birds. Below us, through the darkness comes a train of mules, laden with heavy sacks, and in the dream I know that the sacks are filled with gold. We approach a window with a single candle burning in the night. Bells are ringing everywhere, the streets are full of torches and movement, but in the window stands a man, quite still, his head turned to one side as though he is listening for something far away. He is a young man, I feel, though in the dream his face is covered by a black velvet mask. His lips are cut as fine as a statue's; a warm mouth, a greedy mouth. His clothes are black too, so that he blends with the shade behind him, and when he turns away to speak, only the high blade of his cheekbone is visible in the light of the little flame. He speaks my tongue, Castilian, but the dream shifts before I understand his words.

A dream of shadows. Grey and black and purple in the folds of the night. We are amongst them, sometimes, my mama and I, the cold earth hard beneath us as we run. Miles and miles we cover, hungering, never tiring, every sense alert in the cold air for the throb of blood in a living thing close by. We do not heed the rain or the snow, our muscles moving smoothly, strongly, through wet black forests and across icy screes of rock. I know a wild delight, a joy beyond thought: only the mad pleasure of the hunt and the lure of the kill.

Sometimes I am myself, Mura, standing alone with the walls of a high city behind me. They come to me silently, their eyes glowing amber in the dark. I stretch out my arms to them and as I do I feel kinship, the warm tug of recognition, like a skein of silk wrapped around my body. It stretches back, far back to a place where there are no villages or people – only the forest and the shadows, and the moon overhead, watching where dark blood blackens the ground. I am of them and not of them, I hear them and I call them and I am never afraid. I stand above them as they feed and I feel a presence near me. I will see her face now, in the dream, I will see my mama's face that I have never seen – but as I turn she is gone. I try to call out to her, my wolf-mother, but she is away with them, running with the wind. Instead I see the young man, the masked man, with that strange half-smile on his face, somewhere beyond the shadows, waiting for me.

*

When I woke, I was calm again. I had seen her, and she had left me something like a medicine, something to take away the pain of being alone and helpless. That little seed of hate: a gift from my mother, a gem of ice, a northman's diamond with fire in its cold heart. I could find it, and I could make it smoulder.

36

I peeled my stinging body from the bed and tried the door. Locked. Adara had gone up to meet her gentlemen. Shadow-soft, I pattered across the room and opened the box where she kept her jewels. I filched one of the silver pendants she hooked through her ears and then I tugged at the hem of her sheet where the linen was worn until a little piece came free. I squeezed painfully at one of the welts on my raw back until I had a bead of blood in my palm, then I dipped the metal hook into the blood and drew a pentagram on the scrap of cloth, just like the one my mother had sewn into my dress. I knew why she had put it there now – I had read enough in my father's books: silver and blood, to bind a demon.

CHAPTER THREE

LITTLE FOOL THAT I WAS, I THOUGHT MY CHARM HAD worked. As my skin healed, Adara grew kinder. She rubbed my wounds with a sharp, astringent salve and as she ran her hands over my body she told me that she was sorry, that she had promised my papa to keep me safe, and that she had to protect me. I did not quite believe her, but I wanted to, so very much. Something bad must have entered into Adara, I thought, but I had made it go away. She even promised to take me to Mass, if I was a good girl and did not meddle with what I did not understand.

The house was closed on Sundays. The ladies slept even later than usual, their rooms shuttered against the pealing bells that fluttered across the city, until early evening, when they emerged smoothed and scented to quarrel across the courtyard like a flock of jays, glimpses of turquoise and scarlet flashing beneath sober Sunday cloaks, no paint on their faces but their hair elaborately coiled beneath starched linen coifs, pearls plunging enticingly into hidden bosoms.

'Are they going to church?' I asked Adara. She laughed and said yes, though I couldn't see that it was funny.

'But they are all dressed up. Like a play.'

'Yes, little one, and they are the actresses. You'll see, Mass is a fine marketplace.'

'So we shall go too?'

'Not today, little one, not just yet. Think we're going to have a visitor instead. We must get ready.'

I wondered who it could be. Someone important, I thought, as we walked over to the hammam. Toledo was full of bath-houses, some of them just wooden shacks with a brazier and a bucket, others with deep tiled pools fed with icy spring water, where the shock of the cold stole the breath from your steamed body. Adara's house was so fine that it had its own bath, reached by a wooden walkway that led round the kitchen-house, built in whitewashed stone, a steam room, a washing room and a resting room, all thick with heat and the scent of coal tar and orange blossom essence.

I left my dress in the resting room and followed Adara's naked behind to the bath. I couldn't help comparing my own thinness to the luxurious roundness of Adara's body, her heavy, conical breasts, the rich curve of her dark belly with a furze of tightly curled hair at the fork of her legs. After we sat awhile in the delicious heat, Adara helped me to use the soap and pumice, then we went to the washing room and poured bowls of water over ourselves until our skin was sparkling and polished. Adara took a long time massaging almond oil all over her body and showed me how to do the same, then she used her own silver comb to work through my hair and spread a muslin cloth over my shoulders so the oil should not stain it as it dried. I felt a strange mixture of happiness and sorrow as she tended to me. This was what my mother would have done, we would have walked to the bathhouse together each week with our fresh clothes in a cloth bag, and she would have washed me and combed out my hair.

'Come,' she said, handing me a clean white tunic. 'Now for your visitor.'

'Papa!' I cried out, and knew as soon as I did that my swift flash of joy was mistaken.

'No, little one, not your papa,' she said soothingly. 'Someone who wants to meet you.'

There was a lady waiting in the courtyard, seated on a settle by the fountain. From the evidence of the silk cushions that had been brought out, and the respectful way in which the maids served mint tea from the finest chased silver jug, I thought that she must be very important indeed. I curtsied and said good evening as politely as I knew how, mindful of what my papa had taught me, and cast my eyes down meekly as the lady and Adara spoke of the weather and the busyness of the city and the problem of maids, in that way that all ladies do, everywhere. I peeked up at her from under wisps of my floating hair. She was black skinned, like Adara, but where Adara's skin was so smooth and tight it looked set to split, her face was pouched and marked with black pocks. She was so fat she wheezed like a lapdog and the heavy jewels that covered her fingers seemed to ooze from her flesh like resin from a tree trunk. She stuffed a whole plateful of pastries into her mouth, one after another, as she chatted and nodded, brushing the crumbs from the precipice of her black silk bosom. When the pastries and the polite remarks were done she told me to stand.

'So this is she? The little changeling?'

'Quite so.'

Her fat hands reached towards me, the flesh of her finger-pads moist on my collarbones. I tried not to wrench away.

'Just slip your little tunic off a moment for me, dearie.'

I did as she asked, though I was old enough to feel ashamed, there in the courtyard, with the twilight air chilly on my bare limbs. She peered at me.

'Hmmm. Special. Not for everyone, that's for sure.'

'You can go to our room, Mura. Supper will be ready. Say goodnight nicely.'

Like all children, I loved to hear myself talked about, but Adara's room was too far away for me to catch the rest of their conversation. The other ladies returned as they were speaking, and through a chink in the shutters I watched them gathering round the fat lady, smiling at her remarks and dipping their heads as she reached those questing hands to pinch a cheek or pat a haunch appraisingly. Adara followed her to the porter's lodge, and I could hear better.

'She won't turn then?'

'No, the father thought not. That's why he begged me to keep her.'

'She might do very well then, very well. There's them as likes that sort of thing.'

'Worse luck for us!' Adara laughed.

'In a while then.'

Adara accompanied our visitor respectfully to the street door and I turned to my supper, feeling tired and deliciously clean, and safe in the knowledge that Adara would take care of me, as she had promised, as my papa had wished.

The lady came again at the end of the spring.

Even in the city we could smell the almond blossom in the valley. The maids brought baskets of pear-shaped loquats from the market; their creamy yellow flesh sherbety and delicious. I was scooping one out with a spoon when the lady came into our room with a bundle in her hands.

'Well, Mura, look what I've brought you! Now you just put these on and we'll fix you up a bit. Come along now.'

Adara was standing behind her and the two of them watched me appraisingly as I struggled into a pair of soft plum-coloured breeches and a delicate lawn shirt. The clothes were not new – if I looked closely I could see they had been carefully mended – but they looked very smart, for all that they must have come from a rag-seller's cart.

'The hair,' said the lady.

Adara held out a pair of iron tongues.

'Stand still, now,' she said as the room filled with a smell of scorching. I felt the bounce of curls on my shoulders.

'That'll do. There, look. A proper little angel.' They both laughed, but I didn't feel happy. I felt scared.

'Now you go along with Adara, and mind you do just as she says.' The lady settled herself comfortably on Adara's bed with her cracked heels scratching in the counterpane.

Adara held my hand as we crossed the courtyard, but we did

not go into the big room on the first floor, which was already full of the sounds of music and laughter. We went upstairs again, to a smaller chamber, where there was a table nicely set with a figured cloth, wine and fruit, and a wide bench with yellow silk cushions. There was a gentleman waiting. He was quite an old gentleman, with a grey, flabby face showing over a dark cloak. When he smiled his teeth were greenish stumps.

'Here we are, just as I promised!' Adara had pushed a laugh into her voice, though her fingers were tight and damp around mine.

'Now, Mura, I'll be just along outside. Mind and be nice to the gentleman.'

She left us. I had no idea what I was supposed to do, no idea of anything except that I did not want to be alone here. He stood up, a big man, sloppily built. He reached out and took one of the curls that hung around my face, fingering it. I tried to keep still.

'Would you like to sit down?'

I sat on a cushion and he seated himself next to me. He put an arm round my shoulder. I could smell him, the rich stink that hid under his arm. I felt the loquat rising acidly in my throat.

'Look, I've brought you something.'

He handed me a top, a wooden spinning top with a little red leather whip.

'Thank you,' I said flatly.

'Wouldn't you like to play? Try it.'

Obediently, I squatted down on the floor and tried to remember the trick of the game. The silence behind me was thick. After a few strikes I had it turning, I concentrated on the flash of the red whip. There was a rustling sound.

'Very good, very good.'

The top clattered to the floor as I turned. His hands were buried in the cloak, moving in a strange jerky way. He looked very silly.

'Sir? Should I . . . should I carry on, sir?'

'Come here,' he gasped.

Then those arms were round me and he was pushing me down among the cushions. I turned my face from his breath and tried to struggle free as he fumbled at the breeches, trying to pull them off. I felt something against my bared thigh, a hard, wet thing, I was crushed by his weight, he was pushing against me. I tried to cry out but my mouth was stopped with yellow silk. His hands had found my bare flesh, probing and squeezing, and when I tried to wriggle free he panted, 'Yes, good, good.'

Then a sudden razor-slash of pain, as though he were ripping at my skin. The dust in the cushions was choking me, he was grunting and writhing. A foul drop of thick drool crawled into my ear.

I didn't know what he was trying to do, but I would not let him do it, I would not. Behind my eyelids came the memory of my dream, of my mother and the wolves running, free, savage. So I turned my head and bit his hand, as hard as I could, gagging as my teeth met over the bone and my mouth filled with his filthy blood. He screamed, I staggered up, gasping and retching as his boot caught my knee and I fell, hitting my head against the table. I heard the bang of the door, and then the floor came up to meet me, where the little top lay on its side.

44

When I awoke I was a prisoner. The fat lady was gone, our room was dark. I tore off those hateful clothes and threw them in a corner, then pulled and banged at the door, but no one came. Eventually I put myself to bed, not caring to look any more at the lights across the courtyard. They left me like that for some days, only two whispering maids unlocking the door to pass in a plate of food and take away the pot. I wondered what Adara would do to me now. Would she turn me over to the men who had taken my father? Would I be beaten again and sent back to another gentleman, now that I knew what was wanted of me? The thought of it made me retch. What had that bulging hag called me? 'Changeling'.

All I wanted was to sleep, so that the dream would come to me again. In the dream I was strong and free and fearless, but awake I was just myself, skinny, pitiful, abandoned me. I thought then that I must be cursed. My father had spoken to Adara about me. He had said that I would not change. Was I to blame for what had happened to him? *Maligno*. The startled look on the face of the slave, the steaming water spreading towards me like a pool of evil. Was that me? I scrabbled for my little charm under Adara's bed, but it was gone. Had the maids swept it up with the dust and hairballs? Or had Adara taken it, to show to the Spanish queen's priests so that they would burn me? Would they believe me, if I told them what the man had tried to do to me? It was not my fault, none of it was my fault, but then why would I be treated like this if I was not to blame? I was ill-wished, I thought, bad luck, and I could not escape it.

*

45

One night, Adara came in earlier than usual. She stumbled as she passed inside and let out occasional giggles as she relieved herself in the pot and flopped onto her bed. There was a knock at the door and Adara fumbled up again, poking a taper at the stove to light the lamp.

'Oh, what now?'

'Gentleman for you,' the porter's voice.

'Tell him he'll have to come back tomorrow,' Adara chuckled. 'I'm indisposed.'

'May I speak with you, madam? I can pay.'

A stranger now, a foreign voice, speaking Spanish with an odd, jerky accent. Adara opened the door, putting her hand to her hip and looking out into the darkness with a scornful expression.

'What do you want?'

'I want news of Samuel Benito.'

I knew that if I was to learn anything I must keep very, very still. I pushed the air slowly out of my lungs, although my heart was leaping in my chest.

'What do you know about Samuel Benito?' hissed Adara, opening the door wide and pulling the stranger towards her by his cloak. I was desperate to look, but I knew even a twitch of my eyelids would betray me.

'Don't be afraid, madam. I'm not from the Holy Office, I'm just a bookseller.'

'I don't know what you're talking about.'

'I think you do.'

I heard the bedsprings squeak as Adara sat down. 'Go on.'

46

'I come from Genova, madam. I had business with Benito, for many years. I come to Toledo every year, and this time I found his shop gone, destroyed. As you know. Don't trouble how I found you. People talk. Samuel was good with medicines, was he not? You bought mercury from him.'

Adara's voice changed. She was respectful, even wheedling. 'If you like, sir, you can see for yourself that I have never needed such things.'

'You are kind, madam, but I haven't come for that. I want what Samuel left with you. Don't worry, I'll give you a fair price.'

'I know nothing about any books.'

'Did I speak of books, madam?' Adara's breathing quickened. She had made a mistake. 'You have the child.'

'I took her in out of the kindness of my heart, an orphan.'

'Very commendable. But I heard about what happened that night. A pretty piece of conjuring. The description is in Solomon, the *Almandal* if I remember.'

'I don't know what you're talking about.'

'No, perhaps not. But the Holy Office will, if I choose to tell them that you assisted the necromancer Benito to spirit – hah, a good joke – to spirit away his child?'

'What do you want?' Adara's tone was surly.

'As I said. Samuel's remaining merchandise. But I imagine you are much occupied, madam, with your-er-profession. I will take the books as well as the child.'

After that, the world changed again. The next day, Adara woke me early and told me I was going on a journey, a long journey, with a kind man who would take care of me. I tipped up my chin and looked her in the eye. I knew all about her 'kind gentlemen'. She fussed around me guiltily, tying up my little chest, wrapping a warm shawl around my shoulders, tucking a twist of candied orange peel into the pocket of my robe, but I could hardly bear to look at her. My papa had trusted her to take care of me. I did not speak a single word to Adara, or to the book merchant.

I was perfectly, perfectly silent through the days and days of journeying to the coast, jolting along in the cart next to my papa's trunk, through a countryside filled with the soft air and heavy green of summer. I did not speak even when I saw the sea at Valencia and the huge ships my father had told me about, nor during the voyage, which ate a season on the waves with the dull blur of land to one side and the shifting glass of the ocean to the other. I did not speak when we came to Savona which the book merchant said was in Italy, and the tongue around me was strange and not strange, sometimes like Spanish and sometimes like nothing I had ever heard. I did not speak when I was taken to a house on the wharf and a woman bathed me, dressed me in my red dress and combed out my hair. They took me to a long hall where groups of scared-looking women stood, whispering to each other in our old tongue as brightly dressed men considered them and made marks on slates. I did not show that I understood their words, because I knew what was happening; and when I was told to put back my shawl before one of them, I gazed at him with all the fury I could summon, so that he stepped back from me and muttered something to the bookseller. I watched my price pass between their hands, and took no leave of him.

I did not speak all the time we journeyed across the warm plains of this new country, nor as we came under the walls of Florence, nor as we passed the great church when I wanted to cry out – for its colours were of *marzepan* on carnival day, soft pinks and greens that seemed to call for me from Toledo; the only bright things in that cold city.

In the *dormitorio* of the palazzo, I sunk my teeth in the straw mattress as I came to waking. Every morning, I lay there, soaked and trembling, until the yellow light of dawn brushed across the ceiling and I remembered who I was. Not Mura Benito, the bookseller's child from Toledo. Not Mura who could wish up wolves and far away cities, mirages conjured in the stove-light for a delighted little girl. Not Mura safe in her little room above the shop. I was Mora, the slave. Mora, the ugly orphan who was fit only for whippings and the whispered desires of foul old men, so each morning, I put aside my dream wanderings, and I kept my eyes down.

I did not want, I did not feel. I sought the little ice-shard that was all I had of my mama, now, and instead of longings, I conjured hate.

CHAPTER FOUR

MAY, AND FLORENCE IN ITS BOWL OF HILLS BEGAN to vibrate with gathering heat. As the evenings grew longer, the benches set into the walls of the palazzi filled with people, talking, eating, shawled women at their needlework with children scuttering at their feet. As the sky turned from gold to purple, the torches would be lit in the braces at street corners, and candles would appear behind the linen screens covering the windows, and then the sound of singing filled the city – the *stornelli* beloved of the Florentines – until those thin, sweet songs were replaced by the chiming of the bell for Lauds. This was the signal for householders to cover their fires and throw out their slops, carefully secure the doors of their shops and obediently shut themselves in until the first hour next morning. Even kitchen slaves might take advantage of these brief hours of fresh air, and imagine themselves in a garden, if they had the wit.

I did not. I still shuffled through the days locked in my carapace of bitter loneliness and longing, living only to search for my mother through my dreams. Until something happened that made me see I could find something, somewhere in the city, that might get me free.

There were three of them. *Esclava* like me, a little older than I, all mouse hair and watery blue eyes in fat moonfaces, bought from the Venetian trade. We slept beside one another every night. They were always gossiping and chattering, though they did not know I could understand their talk. I knew they went with the lads from the kitchens, allowing a pinch on their bared soft breasts, or more, before the curfew rang and the steward came round with his lamp. Gropings and fingerings, coarse words and grubby giggles. Perhaps I would have despised them if I could have roused myself, but I tried not to think on them, I tried not to think on anything. They felt it, though, my contempt, and they turned on me. At supper, my dish of beans and lard would be accidentally knocked to the floor, so I would have to scoop my meal off the floor or go hungry. One night I found the pot had been tipped over my sheet. I had to shiver through the night in my clothes, with the straw poking at my skin, then carry the stinking bundle to the laundry in the morning, and get a box on the ear for fouling the linen. It was strange, but it became almost a distraction to me, through the long days, paying them no mind, containing each slight, each piece of bullying, adding to my store of hate. Sometimes I felt I would burst with it, and felt an odd pleasure in pressing it down, in stopping up the rage inside of me.

Every week, before Mass, we were permitted warm water to wash with. I did not look at them as they stripped, I breathed through my mouth so as not to catch the scents released from their chemises. When my turn came at the basin I dipped a rag gingerly into the water, trying not to look at the horrible scum of greasy tallow soap and floating hairs, and rubbed it quickly over my neck, under my arms and between my legs, crouching with my back to them and my own chemise bundled over my shoulders. Suddenly, it was snatched away. I turned, trying to cover myself with my dripping hands.

'Ugh, look at that.'

'*Che brutta.*'

'She's got nothing.'

'*Poverina*, no wonder she's too ashamed to speak.'

For a moment, I thought of hurling the copper basin at them, or of pressing its unfinished rim against one of their fat throats until the blood ran. I was twitching to do it. I tried to stare them down, but they wouldn't stop.

'Don't you ever want to do it, Mora?'

'Don't you want to feel what you've got, up there? But you can't, can you?'

'Disgusting.'

'Deformed, she is. Shall we tell?'

They sniggered delightedly. They were creeping towards me. I thought they would push me over, slide their hands over me like vines. *Mind and be nice to the gentleman*. I could hear my own breath, high and rapid. I thought I would explode. Then just as quickly they grew bored, the bells were tolling for Mass and they began to plait their hair, shuffle into their skirts. Carelessly, one of them threw my chemise at my feet. I felt as though cold water had been dashed in my face. Was this what I would become if I stayed here? Would that be me in a year or so, tormenting some poor new creature, grateful for an onion-breathed boy groping under my skirts? I saw our chamber with its truckle beds and the motes of dust drifting between the beams suddenly as sharp as a jewel. This was not what I was, it could not be. This would never be my home.

As I trailed behind the Medici servants to San Lorenzo that day, I looked about me, at this world to which my grieving had blinded me for so long and I felt redeemed. I had so nearly been lost, I thought. I had not listened to what my mother tried to tell me as I slept. I would not spend the rest of my life working out my strength until I was so useless I had to be grateful for a coarse robe and a bowlful of scraps to mumble by the scullery fire. I would not. Something was waiting for me, I was certain of it, and I had only to calculate and consider how I might get away to find it.

Behind the palazzo, on the San Marco side, there was an irregular space in the wall, left there when Piero's great grand-father had pulled down a whole block of buildings to build his new house. Two long stone benches were set at angles, coming to a point where a dusty chestnut tree shaded the corner with its ever-yellowing leaves. The kitchen people were absurdly proud of this tree, 'our tree' they called it, and they guarded the privilege of sitting in its patchy shadow jealously. There were, it seemed, hardly any green places in the city, so to be a Medici servant under a Medici tree was a fine thing indeed for them. As the evenings warmed, they made a holiday of it after the day's work was done.

The customs of Florence about the separation of men and maids were strict; one bench for them and one for us. The first night, I was happy to sit with my bundle of clumsy needlework, happy to sit at all and feel the strain of a day on my feet easing out of my muscles. As usual, none of the other women tried to include me in their gossip, none of them even looked at me. The next night, I went to sit a little further away, towards the corner of the street. The night after that, I walked just a little way out into the wide sweep of the Via Larga, dominated by the forbidding walls of the palazzo. And on the fourth night, I set myself free, alone in the streets of the city. So long as I was back for the first chime of Lauds, when we would be counted back through the gates of the palazzo like so many sheep, I realised that no one would miss me at all.

For the first time, then, I was grateful for my ugly servant's dress, for it made me invisible. I tied my headcloth more firmly round my forehead to contain the scraps of silver hair which were beginning to grow again, and I moved at a deliberate dawdle, a slave on an errand making the most of her time. At first, my wanderings had no purpose. I had been confined so long to the kitchens that I had almost forgotten the pleasure of moving for its own sake. For that first year, I had been so listless with sorrow I had seen no further than the tips of my clogs. Now, as I walked the city, I began to come alive again.

The first time, I made my way along the Via Larga, a short distance to where the space opened up around the Duomo, the great cathedral, surprising amongst the dull bricks of the narrow streets that wound so tightly a man could span them with his arms. In the evening, the steps of the church filled with people, 'taking the mountain air,' they said, for the coolness of the stone. It was nothing like a real mountain, but I could see how one might think it of that huge humped dome, rising as high as the hills on the horizon. From the Duomo, I found my way to the old marketplace, where braziers were lit to fry up messes of tripe and entrails, sharp with rosemary and stuffed between tranches of saltless Florentine bread. I was disgusted by the sight of spurting white flesh, and astonished to find my mouth watering at the smell. I discovered the huge square in front of the Signoria, the government building, though I knew enough even then to know that the palazzo with its high tower was only a façade: the real power lay behind the doors of the Medici palazzo. I walked to the riverbank and watched the bruise-coloured waters of the Arno flow beneath the statues of the Trinity bridge and the crazy, jumbled-together houses of the Ponte Vecchio.

As I walked the city, I began to pay attention to its configuration, to the different moods of its districts, to the chatter and gossip I heard as I paused to take a drink of brackish, ferrous water from a fountain or appreciate the shade of a crowded loggia. Until I left Toledo, I had never thought of the future, except as children do – that vague, unimaginably distant country where I should be a grown-up. Now, passing from a broad piazza to a street of dark little shops, I was searching. Each evening, I tried to go a different way, as far as I could before the ringing of the bells for Compline reminded me of the other servants beneath their sorry tree.

One evening, my walk took me to a church in a poor neighbourhood, the Oltrarno on the southern bank of the river. On every street was a stand covered in tiny wicker cages, each one housing a cricket, each fiddling a love song, bringing to these busy streets the calming throb of a country twilight. The Feast of Crickets was a Florentine tradition, an old festival from the time before the month of May belonged to Mary. It was the sort of thing my papa would have liked, and I was bending over a pile of cages, wishing I had a copper to take one back, when I heard a hissing voice.

'You, green eyes. Come over here.'

I was startled. My first thought was to run, that it was someone from the palazzo, that I should be whipped. The voice came from a pile of rags in the corner of the church porch. Then I saw a head, bound in a red cloth, and a bony arm beckoning me.

'Come on, I won't hurt you.' The voice was cracked and reedy, an old woman, though the turnip-like face inside the cloth looked sexless, it was so wizened. There didn't seem much to be frightened of, so I walked over to her.

'Who're you then?'

I was so surprised that I went to answer her, but I had been silent so long that all that came from my mouth was a hoarse croak. The creature nodded sympathetically.

'Dummerer, are you? All the better, for them's as got the gift. I'm Margherita, hee hee, Suora Margherita to those what pays. Let's have a look at you, then.'

She had my headcloth off before I saw her hand move, and I

felt her bony fingers raking through my hair. I was disgusted, but she seemed so fragile that I was afraid I should hurt her if I pushed her away.

'Pretty good, pretty good. Won't have the boys after you, will you? Now, you sit down next to me, here, and have some of this.'

She scrabbled under the rags which covered her body, sending up a foul whiff, and pulled out a white linen napkin, delicately embroidered, which she unwrapped to show a glowing coral of quince paste. Her dirty fingers tore it in half and passed a piece to me. I closed my eyes as I sucked at it, the first sweet thing I had tasted in so long, but she must have seen the surprise before the greed.

'Don't go thinking as I stole that! Oh no, my little onion, that was given me, along with all sorts of other things. I've got all sorts of treasures under here, hee hee.'

She was obviously mad, and smelly, and coarse-minded, but she spoke to me as though I was there, as though I was something more than a slave's gown and a pair of working hands.

'I was watching you. Servant, are you?'

I nodded.

'Out where you shouldn't be?'

I nodded again. I sensed that she would be disappointed if I tried to speak.

'Well, you come along back here tomorrow, if you can. Would you like to earn yourself a few florins? For your wedding box! Hey, you, Nennis!' She was calling to the man with the cricket cages.

'You give one of those to my new young lady. Brighten her up a bit. A good noisy one, mind.'

I pulled my headcloth back on, bewildered, as the man obediently selected one of the cages, no bigger than his palm, reached up the church steps and handed it to me. As he did so, the bells began, and I grabbed at it rudely, knowing I should have to run half across the city.

'Off you go then; mind and come back now,' called Margherita as I headed off, my clogs in one hand and the frail cage held carefully in the other. As I ran through the emptying streets with the little creature chirping, I realised that I did not have nothing after all. Whatever had caused my father to do as he did, whatever frightened my old neighbours in the Zocodover, whatever the crazy old woman had seen in my face, that thing was a kind of power. And it was mine. I stretched the muscles of my thighs, my bare feet moving smooth and easy over the stones, running as freely as I did in my dream of shadows. For the first time since I left my papa's house, I felt almost happy.

People fear what they do not understand. The morning after I met Margherita, I woke in the dormitory to find my poor cricket's cage crushed about him, his hard crust of a body smeared to an ugly green–grey sludge by a heavy clog. I tried to scoop up the mess, for I knew I should be punished for dirtying the floor, and as I was scraping his last, pathetic home into my hands I heard a giggle behind me. I dropped the wreck of the cage in the brimming slop bucket where it stank in the corner of the room and went down to my work.

That night, and the next nights for weeks, I made my way across the river to Santo Spirito while the other servants stitched and gossiped. Margherita, I learned, was a great deal more than a mad old tramp. She was one of the wise women of Florence, respected and consulted throughout the city, like Suora Domenica, or Donna Ciliego, who lived like Margherita in the church porch of Santa Maria Annunziata. Margherita produced a sort of costume for me from her inexhaustible heap of rags, a silver silk scarf which she arranged loosely about my neck and shoulders to show off my hair, and a necklace of polished coins which she said came from the time when Florence belonged to the Etruscans. When I was dressed, we would sit in the porch, munching companionably on whatever delicacy her visitors had left for her, and wait for the clients to arrive.

'You're my green girl,' she explained the first evening, 'my little wood-nymph, eh, *ciccia*?'

I was still puzzled as to what she wanted from me, how she thought I could help her. After we had waited a while, a woman set her hand cautiously on the pilaster of the porch, as though she were trying to knock. Despite the still-sharp heat of the evening, she was wrapped in a heavy brown cloak, but beneath it I could see the hem of an apricot-coloured mantle and the tips of embroidered silk slippers. Not a woman then; a lady. Her face was mostly concealed, but I could make out her anxious dark eyes, sore-looking as though she had recently wept. She looked surprised to see me and went to draw back her hand, but Margherita patted her rag pile invitingly.

'Don't worry, my dear. This is my new assistant. All the way

59

from Greenland, where the sun always shines and the ice never melts. See that hair, those eyes? Her mother was from the forests of the north, where the trees stretch for months and her father – *hee hee!* – her father was a werewolf! Don't mind, don't mind, just my little joke. She's deaf as a post and dumb as a basket, ain't you, *ciccia*?'

She nudged me sharply with her elbow. It seemed very stupid, but I could see the lady watching me intently, so I tried to put on a suitably vague expression.

'But she can see, my little mooncalf, she can see, oh yes. Now, dear, you tell Margherita what the trouble is.'

The lady leaned forward and whispered urgently in Margherita's ear. Margherita began nodding sympathetically. 'Oh he has, has he? Oh, the pig! Pigs, all of them. Three months married, you say? And him carrying on already? Oh, you want to know, do you? Well, a wife's got the right to be sure. Don't want him bringing home anything nasty, do we? Now, let's see what we can do.'

She scrabbled in her smelly bedclothes for a while before triumphantly producing a little velvet purse from which she extracted two stones, one green, the other blue.

'Emerald,' she announced, 'all the way from India, and a sapphire from the court of the Shah of Araby! Which is it to be, mooncalf?'

Even I could see that the stones were more pebble than gem, but I felt I knew what Margherita wanted as she proffered her fists to me. I closed my eyes and mumbled some incoherent sounds, which in truth was as much as I could manage.

Blind, I tapped Margherita's left hand.

'Sinister!' she crowed. 'Now dear, you take that home and slip it under his pillow when he sleeps. Any stinking vice that's in him'll cloud the stone, see, and then you'll know for certain. Mind and bring it back now, tomorrow evening sharp.'

The lady scrambled to her feet, stowed the stone in her purse and took out a coin, which she gave to Margherita, making us an awkward bow of thanks before stealing away. Margherita waited until her shadow disappeared in the direction of the Carraia bridge before confiding in me.

'Oh, you'll do, *ciccia*, you'll do very well. I knew it, first time I saw you. Gives it more of an air, see? A change. There's an idiot boy over at San Marco prigging half my business.'

She saw my look of confusion as I gestured towards where the lady had gone.

'Oh dear, I know. Out all night at the *bagnio*, sure as sure, her man. Well, maybe she can keep him at home before the watch has him. A kindness, dearie, a kindness.'

In all the time I knew Margherita, I was never certain of how much she believed in her 'kindnesses'. That her clients did, I was sure, for it soon became clear that the Florentines deserved their reputation for superstition, but I never quite decided whether Margherita was a charlatan, a fairground trickster, or something more. Sometimes it seemed as though she did not quite belong to the everyday world, as though her distracted ramblings were not eccentricities but messages from another place. But as soon as I began to believe in her a little, I would see the sharpness in her eyes when she bit on a coin, and change my mind, thinking that after all it was merely harmless cunning.

She was certainly popular, which suggested that her pronouncements and remedies had some effect. People of all kinds came to her. Sometimes it was an anxious mother, too poor for the apothecary, who wanted a remedy for an ailing child, sometimes a portly merchant wanting to know the most auspicious time to set out on a journey, sometimes a labouring man who thought his apprentice was stealing from him. Mostly, though, Margherita dealt in love.

Love, as I saw it then, was to do with lack and money. Love was the pain of mourning, as I mourned my papa and, more dimly and sweetly, my mother. Or, it was money – Adara's business. Margherita's clients seemed to see it much the same way. They lacked, they yearned, they wept and they paid. And it was as well that Margherita believed me dumb, for I learned more from those anxious confidences of what happens between men and women than I had ever perceived in my brief period as a tenant in a whorehouse, and the knowledge shocked me beyond words. So many ways for the flesh to ache with desire, so many ways to profit from it. An elderly husband anxious to please his young wife was prescribed cow dung beaten up with fresh eggs and white wine, a servant girl whose sweetheart had taken up with another was advised to steal a lock of his hair, soak it in her menstrual blood and hide the charm beneath his bed for a month. Margherita's clients believed she could make wayward lovers return, indifferent lovers fond.

She dealt in consequences, too. A betrothed bride anxious that her fiancé should not learn she had gone too far with an earlier beau? Margherita assured her that her virginity would be restored with alum boiled in linen. A harassed mother of ten who could not bear to bring another mouth into the world? A scraping of a mule's nail melted into the wax of a sacred candle and placed on her body when her husband came to her in the night should ward it off.

None of the remedies Margherita recommended were in the least like the medicines my papa had so carefully prepared after consulting his books. I could not believe that any of them truly worked. But so long as I made my silver necklace jangle and looked wisely into the distance; so long as I made a dumb show of choosing a charm from her hands or tracing the line of a beloved's fate in an eager palm; she and they were happy. As was I, for each week Margherita would give me a silver florin, which I tied in the corner of my skirt and smuggled silently into a hole I had worked in my pallet at night.

I had begun to have a plan, a real plan. At the end of the summer, I calculated I would have a stock of money enough for a suit of plain clothes and a carter to carry me away from Florence. It was so easy to slip away each evening and one night I should simply not return. I doubted that I was valuable enough in that great and complex household for anyone to care for my loss anyway. I had no thought of where I might go, or how I should live, but the thought of escape was enough to sustain me through long days in the sweltering kitchens. My dowry of books was gone, stolen and sold by Adara, but I could read and write, I knew Spanish and Italian: I should find something, somehow. I dared not count my coins at night, for fear the chinking would alert those three pairs of spiteful blue eyes, but I thought of them, each solid weight another step to freedom. For a time, my dark dreams were suspended by hope.

As midsummer drew near, the evenings grew longer. Amidst flurries of preparation, sweating and swearing from the servants, Donna Alfonsina had finally left Florence with her son and her new baby daughter for the cool of the hills, but the palazzo remained busy. Unusually, Piero de Medici had remained in the city. The courtyard still thronged with Medici familiars, and I often recognised Messr Bibbiena, Piero's secretary who ordered the household, passing to the great staircase with a stern, urgent expression.

Something had entered the palazzo that summer, something that groped with cold, probing fingers into the upper regions of the house, seeking to clutch Piero in its chilly fist. I listened more intently than usual to the talk in the kitchens and the laundry, but the world of the slaves was so confined, contained within the tiny limits of the offices and those brief moments of leisure beneath the tree that we servants might well have been as mute as I feigned each night with Margherita. I sensed that something had changed. I felt the same rage I had experienced on the Genovese ship that brought me to Italy – I was no more than a mote of dust, swirled about in the robes of the great and shaken off where they would. I never understood the forces that moved me. I *wanted* to understand what was happening in Florence, but the coins Margherita gave me were too precious for me to dawdle on my nightly walks to Santo Spirito in the hope of overhearing the citizens gossip as they gathered on the benches. I could hardly ask questions, for my dumbness, which I had adopted in fury, was now my most precious disguise. Yet there *was* something awry in the city, a hint of suspicion and fear that I recognised from my last months in Toledo; and angered as I was by my own insignificance, I was determined that this time I should protect myself.

With the long evenings, I grew bold, relishing my freedom from the confines of the palazzo. The gates were barred at the last bell, but I discovered a way to prolong my absences. Set into the wall near the porters' bunk was a tiny window, for putting out alms, or receiving supplies in plague times, when big houses were shuttered down to keep quarantine. I found I could wriggle through it, small and slight as I was. It was hard to hoist myself up the wall outside, but I had always been light and agile and my muscles were lithe and taut from the hard work in the kitchens. If I wanted to return after the bell, I would push the shutter ajar as I left the courtyard and work my fingers above the wooden lintel when I returned. I was not afraid of the porters – rough men who spent their evenings in the taverns and slept it off in the lodge – and even if I were discovered I didn't imagine I had anything worse to fear than a whipping. The thought of a few minutes of pain did not deter me. It was a strange way to learn courage, I thought ruefully; that it comes when one has nothing one cares to lose. But I was never caught.

As the city emptied during the suffocating heat, business grew slow. One evening, Margherita and I had sat a long time in the porch, with no clients to serve. As the sky turned from bright blue gold to a soft purple, she stretched herself, sending up the

usual foetid whiff from her nest, and asked me if I was hungry.
I nodded. There was plenty of plain food for the servants at
the palazzo, but I hankered after the savouries I smelled in the
streets each night.

'Come on then, mooncalf.'

She tottered to her feet and arranged herself for travel,
which took quite some time, as all her oddments and mysteries
had to be stored in two sacks, which she pushed into a corner of
the porch. Presumably no one would dare to steal them. As she
stood, it occurred to me that I had never seen her legs, but she
set off at a sort of bounding hobble, and I was surprised to find
I had to trot to keep pace with her. We turned to the left, slap-
ping at mosquitoes as we followed the river along the Borgo
San Frediano until we reached the city gate, which Margherita
circled around, taking us up a rise covered in scrubby trees,
where the city wall ran flush against the steep hillside. We
climbed laboriously up the slope and descended on the other
side, leaving Florence without passing the gates. As I picked
my way along behind her, I could smell woodsmoke and roasting meat and hear music, a reedy piping with a drum beneath
it.

'Nearly there, *ciccia*,' Margherita encouraged.

We arrived at a scene from carnival. Three shabby wagons
with tattered streamers were drawn up in a circle, with placidly
cropping horses staked to rings beyond them. In their shelter, a
fire burned on a flat rock, tended by a man whose massive shoulders and thick black beard distracted me for a moment from
noticing that he had no legs. He was seated on a low wooden

trolley with little wheels, which he manipulated dextrously with strong hands, turning himself this way and that to baste a line of rabbits turning on a spit. On the ground beside him sat two young women, wearing colourful cloaks over men's breeches and shirts. A thick-necked dwarf in a soldier's jacket was idly turning cartwheels around them, flicking tiny spurred boots into the air. I had seen dwarves before – they were popular servants for grand people in Toledo. Two more men, long nosed and grey eyed and alike as reflections in a looking glass, were mending a pair of metal hoops with wire, as though it were usual to carry out such work in nothing but red satin drawers. The music came from another man, whose eyes were bound by a black cloth to advertise his blindness, puffing into a long metal pipe and keeping time on a tambour with a drumstick held between his bare toes.

They all looked up and greeted Margherita, but glanced suspiciously at me.

'Come on, *ciccia*, come on now. Show yourself!'

Cautiously, I put back my headcloth to reveal my coin crown, my hair, my eyes. At once the two women came up to me, pawing at my skin, even tweaking a tuft from my scalp as though to check it was real. Close up, I could see how pretty they were, slim and golden haired, their breasts provocatively visible under the lawn of their grubby shirts, and I was suddenly conscious of my own meagre limbs, my chest as scrawny as a pigeon's. I lifted my chin and caught their expressions as the firelight lit up my eyes.

'Where did you find her?'

'What can she do?'

Margherita was settling herself by the fire, chuckling, reaching for a flask of wine from the trolley man.

'Oh, she's a good 'un. Dumb, but she's got it, she's got the sight, haven't you, my green girl?'

One of the girls leaned towards me, mouthing loudly, as though I were a simpleton. But her expression was kind.

'I am Annunziata. This is Immaculata. You?'

'I told you, dears. Dumb as a statue.'

The others came up, even the trolley man trundling over to courteously kiss my hand, introducing himself as Casinus. The twins were Chellus and Gherardus, and the blind musician Johannes. The dwarf approached, and I tried to make my expression friendly when he bowed to me, the buttons on his toy-soldier coat glinting, and gave his name as Addio.

'What my mother said when she saw me, young mistress,' he said solemnly, twisting back suddenly so that his lumpy face appeared between his knees. 'A dio to that one!' I smiled.

'Come on then,' hooted Margherita, swigging busily, 'ain't you going to give the girl a little show?'

The girls exchanged glances with the twins, then stripped off their jackets. Johannes paced carefully back to his drum and began to beat out the tense, regular rhythm of an expectant heart. Chellus and Gherardus dragged over the hoops and set them atop each other in a figure of eight. Addio went first, taking a run and hurling his compacted body through the upper hoop, landing bent over, nose to knees, followed by the girls, one after the other, landing on top of him. Then the two men swung over, catching at the girls' elbows and raising them, slowly, impossibly, until their bodies fanned out like branches either side. I could see the thickly compacted muscle of their torsos, admire the strength and control it took to hold their bodies to such a disciplined line, but before I had a chance to applaud, they flip-flopped over, pulled Addio from beneath their feet and inserted him into the lower hoop. They produced scarlet whips from their breeches and began to spin the hoop. The dwarf whirled round inside it until he became like a hummingbird, buttons and spurs flashing. The twins, wrist to ankle, locked their bodies into another hoop and made circles round him, rolling over and over like a crazed astrolabe, until Annunziata and Immaculata leaped in, raised the hoop with Addio inside it gripping the rim, and held it high above their heads. He flipped his body upwards like a leaping fish, swivelled, caught the rim, repeated it a second time, a third; and then he landed in the hoop in a crouch. In a flash, Chellus and Gherardus dived through the hoop, their heads barely missing him, and the girls held it side on, like a picture frame, their own flushed faces peeping prettily in on either side.

I had never seen such a thing. I was dazzled by their skill and clapped as hard as I could, grinning with delight.

'Good, aren't they?' asked Casinus, as we moved to sit by the fire.

I nodded as vigorously as I could, but there was something sad along with the pride in his tone.

'No work here, though. We're moving on.'

I wanted to say politely that I was sure such talented acrobats could make all the money they wanted, but I minded and held my tongue. As we picked at the rabbits, smeared with a sweet, spicy *mostarda*, and cleaned our hands on soft, charred flat bread that Casinus pulled from the embers, they talked with Margherita of the changing times in Florence.

'You're well off, mistress,' said Addio to Margherita, 'there's always plenty as'll pay for charms, discreet like, but we can't work without a public.'

'And they won't have us any more,' added Annunziata indignantly. 'Called us whores, if you please! As though we were *puttane* who can only stick their legs in the air!'

'You'll be glad of what I've brought you then, dears,' said Margherita, taking a last gulp of wine and getting to her feet. I heard the chink of coins in Johannes's lap. 'Where are they? Come on, mooncalf, you too. I'll be needing you.'

Puzzled, I followed her to one of the wagons, where the twins pulled aside a leather curtain, releasing a powerful musty stink. They unlocked a slatted wooden grille and held up a lantern. I gasped and jumped back against Margherita's steadying arm. Inside the wagon was an ape, and next to the ape, a bear. And next to the bear, a wolf.

'Don't be afraid, *ciccia*. Sleepy, they are.'

Cautiously, I peered into the stinking space. Each animal was held by a short, thick chain, allowing no more than a few inches to move its head. The ape's eyes were open, staring at us in a disgruntled fashion, but the bear, a poor mangy thing that looked too thin for its patchy fur coat, was so still it might have been dead. My heart lurched with pity for them. The wolf had stretched out along the width of the wagon, its hindquarters bunched against the grille. The head was buried in the forepaws, but it was not sleeping. The very tips of its ears twitched minutely.

'We drugs 'em, see, when we travel,' said Chellus apologetically. 'Has to keep 'em quiet.'

Deftly, Gherardus slipped a leather muzzle over the wolf's jaw, then undid the collar chain, fastening it to a longer one. He tugged and the animal came awake, getting slowly to its feet and then dropping heavily out onto the turf. I caught a whicker of fear from one of the horses. Margherita had produced a pot and handed me a rounded, blunt knife.

'Give him a scrape, that's my girl,' she whispered, 'you give his skin a good old scrape. Right under the fur now.'

She showed me, rubbing forward with the knife and then scraping it against the lid of the pot.

'Brings it on, see,' she hissed, 'boil it up nice, swallow it down, and hee hee, no more baby. There's ladies in Florence who pay good money for Margherita's special tea.'

She was quite mad, I thought, but with all those expectant eyes on me I didn't dare disobey her. I laid my hand on the wolf's warm flank, feeling the coarse hair on top and the unexpected softness of the under pelt.

*

And there it was. He recognised my touch, I knew it. That skein of silk, twining into me, binding us together. I felt his heart, I heard

71

his breath. Without knowing why I did it, I bent forward over the splayed bone of his shoulder, as high as my head, and hummed softly in his ear. Somewhere, far away, I could hear Margherita's voice, 'I knew it, I knew it. My good girl, my shadow child,' but there was nothing near me but the scent of him, the coil of his strength under my hand. I tried to speak to him, to tell him not to mind, that I would not hurt him, and that I knew what he longed for, for the stretch of his body over the ground and the wild flight and the sweet salt of warm blood on his tongue. Slowly, I began to work the knife along the thick skin of his neck, delicate, so as not to startle him—

*

And then one of the horses neighed and reared, mad with fear at the scent of him in the darkness, and he came awake, snarling under the muzzle and bolted, the chain snapping taut and pitching Gherardus to the ground. The acrobat hung on, as the creature ran for the wood, battering the man's body over the stony ground as the other horses picked up the panic and suddenly the air was full of screams as the troupe ran to calm them.

'Help him!' yelled Chellus in my ear.

Only Margherita was calm, looking at me steadily.

'You heard.'

I took a few staggering steps, but I knew it was useless. Beyond the firelight, the wolf had turned, swiping at Gherardus with his strapped jaw, pawing at him to drop the chain and release him. I was afraid to call out, but then I knew that I didn't need to call.

Send him your anger, your rage, your hate. Summon him to you, calm him with all you know of captivity, of longing, of constraint. Let him see the ice in your eyes and the silver wind in your hair. Let him see the forest in the blue wire of your veins. Have him come back to you out of the dark, but let him know it is just for a little while.

*

I found the flame in the wolf's eyes and held it. He stopped butting his head at Gherardus. I trotted up gently and took the chain from the fallen man's hand, stooped and sank my face into the thick reek of his pelt, searching for the beat of his heart tight against my own. Then I led him back, quietly, to where the others were waiting. The girls moved past me to tend to Gherardus.

'Phew-ee,' breathed Addio, 'where d'you learn that then?'

'I told you,' giggled Margherita exultantly, 'she's a clever one. Deep like a spring she is, oh yes!'

'Well, if ever you need a job, missy, you come to us. Never seen anything like it.'

I tried to smile, shook my head to clear the dream. This was part of the gift, my mama's gift. Her people, my people, the fire-conjurers, the wolf-worshippers of the north. It was in me, in my eyes, what Margherita called 'the sight'; it had called me through my dreams and rescued me – from the hateful old man in Toledo, from the palazzo kitchen. I shook my head again. And then I was just me, Mura, my lips still spicy with rabbit, my tatty fancy dress scarf unravelling down my back. But I didn't feel lonely any more.

CHAPTER FIVE

ARGHERITA WAS DOZING, HER STUBBY FEATURES covered in what looked like an altar cloth. No matter how the sky blazed, she never seemed too warm. I was half-asleep myself, lulled by the thick air and the soft cooing of the doves in the bell tower above us. I had seven florins now. In a little while, perhaps when the summer ended, there would be ten. Ten, I thought, was the sum I needed. I was dreaming, imagining myself in Venice, a floating city of books, or on a boat, the breeze rippling across my skin, bound for Constantinople, for Kashmir . . .

I started at a soft touch on my arm, and as I opened my eyes I almost cried out before I remembered myself, for the face bending towards mine was one I recognised from the palazzo. A boy with a thick crop of reddish hair under a faded blue cap, and a face as speckled as a brown egg. Where had I seen him? Trotting through the courtyard with piles of papers – he must be a clerk's assistant. Although my throat was suddenly icy with fear I thought hurriedly; there was no way he could recognise me in my silvery disguise, no way that he could associate the wise woman's companion with one of the creeping, grey creatures of the household. I stared blankly into his face, which looked friendly and somehow amused, and nudged Margherita awake.

'What's is to be, Messr?' she asked, her voice sharp and bright with the hope of a profit. 'A charm for a midsummer's night, eh? Though you're a bit young for that, shame on you, hee hee! What's it to be?'

The boy looked behind him and inclined his head before stepping back respectfully as a tall, slouching figure emerged from the violet shadow of the porch. The coldness, which had begun in my lungs, spread through me and I began to shiver, my hands shaking until I twisted them tight together in my lap. The tall figure whose broad shoulders momentarily obscured the sun seemed to be the young man from my dream. As in the dream, his face was hidden by a black velvet mask. I watched as his full, sensuous mouth curled into the same anticipatory smile. I sucked the musty air that rose from Margherita's rags slowly, deeply, trying to calm myself with its comforting odour. Although the man was plainly dressed and wore no sword, Margherita sat up straight and addressed him almost reverently, with none of her usual bawdiness.

'How may it please you that I help you, Messr?'

The man handed her a scrap of parchment.

'I want you to tell me what you know of this, Suora.'

Margherita squinted at the inked characters and turned the paper about. Of course, she could not read. I held out my hand to her. If she was surprised at this sudden skill in her mooncalf she had the sense not to show it. I read to myself silently.

'The cross of God's anger rises from Rome. The black cross hangs over Florence. Repent, oh Florence, while there is still time. Clothe thyself in the garments of purification.'

I nodded to show that I had understood what I had read. A warning: anger, purification. I screwed up my eyes to stop the sharp memory of the soldiers in Toledo. This was part of the shift I had sensed in the city's atmosphere, the words like those I half-remembered from the hushed talk in my father's shop, when the Spanish queen sent her men to my home to stir up blood and fire as her god demanded.

'It was in the *tamburo*,' the man spoke again, his voice calm and deep as though he were trying to control it. I knew of the *tamburo* from Margherita's conversations with her clients. The drum in the cathedral piazza was a depository for anonymous letters where people could inform the magistrates of their neighbours' vices; petty, spiteful things usually, dropped by cowards after dark. The man repeated the words to Margherita in a whisper.

'What does it mean? Is it true?'

Margherita recovered a little of her showmanship.

'Well, Messr, my girl here has the sight, you see, the gift? She'll see the truth in it, if there's truth to see. What she could tell us if only she could speak! Her mother was a mermaid, you know, from beneath the frozen lakes.'

'Tell me.' He had cut her off, irritated by her nonsense. I took the paper in my hands again, and looked into his face, into that smooth blackness.

*

77

I plummeted into my dream, wrapped in velvet night. A she-wolf howled beneath a city wall, and under the howling I heard deep, rasping growls. I saw two great golden beasts, lions, tearing at one another's throats until the growls were choked with blood that streamed like a banner across the sky, spreading over the outline of the city that I saw was Florence, the mountain of the Duomo swelling over it. Through the blood pierced a sword, a gleaming sword, which became a bolt of lightning, juddering through the night towards the dome until it struck and, in my dream, the crack splintered the sky and brought me back to my senses, gasping like a landed fish.

*

'Well?'

I rootled in the pile of rags beneath me, my hands encountering strange shapes and repellent softnesses, until my fingers closed around something, something I must have known they would find. I brought the object out and the three of them craned to see it. A wooden ball, smudgily painted over in gold. Perhaps it had fallen from the carving of a litter. It sat in my palm, rolling slightly, and as it turned we all of us saw a crack, a break in the wood where it was coming apart. The man reached for it and as he took it up it divided, one half falling to the marble floor with a dull little thud. It was hollow. I didn't wait to see their reaction, I knew that I had to get away.

I jumped to my feet, scrabbling at the headdress and the foolish necklace, ducking my head into the shadows, shaking off Margherita's grasping hand. I didn't care if the man would give me a coin, he'd had his answer. I didn't understand what I had seen, but I knew enough to be afraid. I ignored the calls of Margherita and the boy, did not stop moving until I was safely back under the tree, my head covered, my eyes down. It would be my last night in the palazzo, I decided. There was savagery coming to Florence, as it had come to Toledo, but I was no longer a child, I would outrun it. Seven florins would have to be enough.

My days always began with a jolt of pain. The moments before I woke were the cruellest, those few half-conscious minutes of peace when I believed myself still in my bed in our old home, and that I would breathe the smell of raisins and new bread and the tobacco musk of my papa's sleep. Then the swift recognition, the deep ache that brought tears to my unopened eyes. That next morning, though, I could feel my mouth curve into a smile. No more dreams. I had seen the man in black, I had understood that I must leave.

It all seemed so clear, like a story in one of my old picture books. I lingered a little, enjoying the first sun reddening the inside of my eyelids, telling the story over. My father had known that my strange looks would play on the superstition of those who accused him of heresy. When Adara failed to protect me, my mother came to me, as he said she would, and sent me the strength to escape the palazzo. The man in black would bring me the sign. It seemed so simple.

I was disturbed by a tiny clatter, an unmistakeable clink. Too late, I glimpsed the back of a grey skirt disappearing in the doorway and I knew before I had reached my hand into the hollow in the straw beneath me that I should find it empty. I flew down the stairs, hunching my robe over my head, stumbling down to the courtyard, where the three of them were waiting, sneers prepared on their faces, their yellowed teeth bared in the falsest of smiles. For a moment, I simply stood and stared at them, unable to believe that they had stolen all my money – all my hope – from me. Then one of them, the tallest, held out her hand and laughed, rubbing her thumb against her first two fingers in the sign of money. All the shock and pain eased out of me then. I felt suppleness in my limbs, an energy that stretched through my sinews to my fingertips, and in seconds I was on her.

I had never fought before. I had seen drunken men brawling late at night after carnival in Toledo, and a year in the kitchens had witnessed several scrappy catfights amongst the girls. But this was different, no clumsy male blows or flapping, feminine scratching and hair pulling. I was going to kill her. I was going to tear out her throat with my teeth if I had to. I caught her a blow on the underside of her jaw with my fist that took her down and another that knocked her head back against the tiles. The weight of my hurled body shocked the breath out of her and I rammed my elbow into her face, splitting her snub nose like a melon. I could hear shouts around me, but I was conscious only of the smoky scent of the blood that spread over her face, dripping down her neck and staining the stones beneath us. I had a fistful of her hair in my hand and was bringing up her head to crash it down on the stones when another blow sent me sideways, clear off her whimpering form, landing me on the side of my face so my ears rang and burned. I closed my eyes, for a few moments full of a strange, wounded pleasure, and when I tried to open them my right eye smarted and couldn't see. The other eye stung with blood – mine? As I peered about, I saw a collection of clogs – the servants out to jeer us on, I thought – and then a pair of boots. Polished leather boots. As the thudding of my heart quietened, I was aware of the terrible hush around me, as though the air was still with shock.

'What in the devil's name is this? How dare you?'

I knew before I raised my head. I knew that voice, and I knew the owner of those boots. For a moment I wanted to lay my head against the warm flags and laugh. I believed I had never seen Piero de Medici, but the young man last night in Santo Spirito had not been the masked creature of my dreams. The pain in my head was stronger now, dizzying me. My headcloth was lost, I was exposed, I lifted my eyes.

'You.'

I didn't care what happened to me. I did not fear being whipped and turned out to beg, but I knew it would be worse than that. I crawled to my feet and attempted a tottering curtsey. Without the mask his face was handsome, brown hair falling to a finely worked linen collar. I watched him. First would come confusion, and then fear, and then I would be finished. I knew his secret, I knew he was afraid enough to come sidling to a crazed soothsayer, and I knew he could crush me like a cricket beneath those fine Spanish boots. I waited, wearily, for the order. Perhaps he would have me taken as a witch, to burn as they burned heretics in Toledo. I didn't care. A voice broke our dumb tableau.

'Messr Piero, Messr Piero, sir?'

The boy I had seen at the church, the clerk who had shown Piero where to find the wise woman. He was panting, as though he had been running hard.

'Begging your pardon, Messr Piero, but Maestro Ficino says it's her. The bookseller's child.'

The brown curls on Piero's neck shifted as he wheeled his head in surprise, but that was all I heard, because then the dizziness came again and the stones of the courtyard rose once more to meet me.

*

I awoke in a forest. Slender, elegant dogs picked their way through an undergrowth figured with bright flowers, leaves curling around their paws. Then I saw that what I had taken for trees were lances, stretching upwards, carried by vividly dressed men on plump horses, except they must have been riding underground, for there was no sign of sky. I raised my arm and saw it was draped in the red silk of my mother's dress, and then I knew that I had died and I was waiting by the riverbank under the streets of Toledo, for my parents to come and find me, so that we would walk together amongst the flowers.

'She's awake, sir.'

The boy. I was not dead then, but as I raised my head, I saw that I had come into another world.

'Drink this.'

Wine, warm and sweet with cinnamon, as Adara used to give me to make me sleep. I was lying on a great high bed, soft with a patterned silk that seemed to wander like a meadow from what I now saw were paintings on the walls. The air smelled of beeswax and lavender. The cornices on the door, so far away, were a medley of enamelled woods, all colours from black to the palest pearl. I was in the palazzo, the palazzo I had heard of, but never seen.

'Can you hear us? Can you sit?'

I pushed myself up on my elbows, feeling the silk of my dress tight under the arms. I must have grown, working down there in the kitchens. There were three of them, grouped about the bed, Piero, the boy and an old man, a dried up creature who gazed at me avidly as though I was a precious thing he wanted to steal. He spoke in Castilian, and I wondered for a moment whether I was in Florence after all.

'You came with the books. The Toledo books?' I could hear that he was forcing his voice to be kind, and that it came strange to him. Always the books; the books that took my papa from me, the books Adara sold me for. The old man was scrabbling in the sleeve of his robe, a worn robe, I noticed, more like a servant's than someone who would be allowed into Piero's chamber, for I supposed that was where I must be. He produced a folded paper and held it out to me. It was a picture, a picture of myself. I stood framed in the window of our house, my dress and my hands inked vivid red, my hair waving wildly above a crown of roses. At the top of the drawing were some words. I traced my finger along the letters.

Angel.

'You can read?'

I nodded, still dumb. Piero and the boy were watching us both now, this odd exchange, both of them leaning forward on the counterpane like gawpers at a fair.

'This, this vision? You saw this. Your father did this?'

I opened my mouth. Inside my head I heard my papa's voice, telling me to be brave, just as he had done all that time ago. At first, no sound came. I swallowed hard, feeling their impatience. I knew that if I could not find the words then it would be the kitchen and the beans forever. At best.

'Yes, sir. My father. Samuel Benito.'

*

I wore my red dress on the day the world changed. They came for the book, and they took my father. The cold air was on me, the smell of Adara's body as she held me close, the steady rhythm of her footsteps, carrying me here, carrying me to Florence.

*

The old man's voice brought me back to myself.

'You saw this?'

I was confused. How could he know what had happened that night, why had that picture been made? Why that word, 'angel'? Then I understood. The old man did not *know* what he was seeing. He thought my father was a conjuror. He thought he was seeing magic – so I answered carefully.

'I did, sir.' Which was no more than the truth, after a fashion.

The old man turned to Piero. 'I told you, I knew it!' He was gleeful. 'It is she, the child I told you of.'

I had given him something, something he wanted to believe. I was glad then that I had never cared to learn the names of the kitchen folk, for as I lay back amongst the clean silk cushions of Piero's own bed, I knew that I should not be returning there.

*

So my world changed once again, supple as a shining fish tossed in one of the cook's pans. The old man's name was Maestro Ficino. At first, I had no idea of the importance, indeed the eminence, of my new friend, this short hump-backed creature, whose thin frame, long soft hands and tatty robe made him a very caricature of the absentminded scholar. All I knew was that I possessed something he wanted. Later, ruefully, I realised that my father would have gladly given all his books to spend a single day in Maestro Ficino's company.

As with Margherita, I was uncertain of what it was I had that he clearly yearned for; but I had learned from her, and from Adara before that, how desire was the only currency worth bargaining with . . . and just like Margherita, however vague my notions of what I could offer, I could feel his hunger for it. Perhaps then I became a true Florentine, for desire is worthless unless it can be transmuted into value.

I was moved to a room of my own at the top of the palazzo, and along with my red dress, which I clung to even though the hem almost showed my knees, I was given my old doll. And a wooden truckle bed and a chair, and a box like the one I had at Adara's house, though I had no treasures to put in it and thought

85

it would be wisest to keep the theft of my lost seven florins to myself. A maid, her mouth screwed into a prune of disapproval at my sudden elevation, carried up a box of cut-down clothes, and I chose a blue cloak of soft wool to cover my shabby frock, though it was far too hot to need it. I was no longer to eat with the slaves and house servants, but would take my meals in the sala, the huge room behind the courtyard where Piero dined every day with twenty or thirty of the most important men in Florence. I was seated far away, of course, at the end of the table in a huddle of goggling clerks and pages, but still I could share the delicate dishes, artichokes and eel and thin slices of liver cooked in sweet wine, with white manchet bread to soak up the sauces. I wore the cloak to cover my battered face, though no more had been said about the fight, and it seemed as though my enemies, along with all the other familiar faces from the kitchen, had quietly disappeared, so great was the distance between the people who occupied this same space. Although I had so recently been one of them, they were so dingily unrecognisable to me now, when I came across them, that as time passed I almost let myself believe I had never been one of their number.

In the daytime, Maestro Ficino occupied the study on the half-landing of the great staircase. There was another *scrittoio* in the house, behind the *antecamera* where Piero slept and conducted his private business, but this room was more like a treasure house with cabinets filled with tiny drawers to display jewels and gems, books bound in gold, and a huge cameo bowl. A room for display rather than for studying – which, after a few days of observing Piero at closer quarters, I decided summed

86

him up quite well. Maestro Ficino's room was different. It reminded me of my father's house, with piles of books mingled with mortars and alembics, jars and bottles, and ceramic pots of cinnamon, white sugar, attar of roses, giving to the whole, as soon as the thick door was opened, a mysterious, inviting smell of vellum and spices.

That first morning, I saw that the young clerk, already grubby with ink, had been set to copying a book I recognised. Maestro Ficino ignored him, but it was all I could do not to snatch the worn green-tooled cover from his hands. My father's books were here, in the palazzo. They had been here all the time. For a moment I saw him holding it close to his face in the candlelight and I almost groaned with pain. I concentrated on chivvying the last of the almonds I had secreted from the breakfast table from the pocket of my cloak, scraping the fine membrane from the nut and crushing its sweetness between my teeth to taste my home again.

'Have you seen this book, Mora?'

Maestro Ficino, was holding it out to me, eagerly, as he had done the day before. I was bewildered.

'The *Corpus*? The *Corpus* of Hermes Trismegistus? This is my own translation, *Pimander*.'

Suddenly my confidence in my new position fell dizzily away. This was a test, and if I failed it, the kitchen and the salt caper berries beckoned forevermore. I was at a loss, I looked around the room as though the dusty piles of words would show me an answer. Then I caught a glimpse of the boy, seated in the window bay. His cap had slipped off revealing a bright tuft of coppery hair and his freckled face was focusing urgently on me as he nodded his head.

'Yes, sir. I have seen it. In my father's house.'

'Your father was a follower of Aristotle?'

I began to agree, but the frantic bobbing of the curls allowed me to shake my head in time.

'Oh no, sir. Not a bit.'

And so it went on. He questioned me for an hour, and each time the boy in the window provided my answer. He spoke of Solomon, and the seven divine arts, of a monk called Michael Scot who had studied in Toledo hundreds of years ago, of divine beings and heavenly configurations, while I shook and nodded like a marionette, grateful that my hood concealed the frantic gesturing of my eyes. As I answered, Messr Ficino scribbled on a linen tablet, dabbling at his thin lips with his thin fingers, murmuring 'good, good, excellent' until my head ached with the tinny reek of rose oil and dust and the skin under my arms prickled with anxiety. Eventually, when I agreed that indeed, my father concurred in the belief that celestial bodies were capable of imparting their powers to terrestrial matter, he reached for a volume and began to leaf through it, concentrating so absolutely that for a long while the only sound in my room was my own breathing and the scratch of my saviour's pen. When he looked up, he seemed surprised to see me there and waved his hand absently, his eyes wandering back to the page.

'You may go now. We shall speak again tomorrow.'

I wandered outside the palazzo, since there was no one to stop me now. The despised tree seemed rather inviting. I sat down and bunched my knees under my chin. Although I had grown taller, I was still as ribby as a street cat. I thought of walking over the river to find Margherita and astonishing her with my newly discovered powers of speech, and that made me remember my poor little store of florins and my thwarted plan of escape. It seemed pathetic. Anyway, perhaps I wouldn't be permitted to walk about by myself, no Florentine lady could be seen in the streets without a chaperone. But I wasn't a lady; I didn't know what I was. Another treasure for the Medici collection, like Maestro Ficino? Or was I to return to the world of cellars and pantries, leaving the palazzo once a week for Mass and a glimpse of the dull Florentine sky? I could run, I supposed, even yet; but I had nowhere to go and nothing to go to except a heap of rags and a crazy woman in a doorway. I was bewildered, disconsolate. I had understood so little of what happened in Toledo, and since then I had kept myself alive by deliberately *not* thinking. I was ugly and scarecrow-headed and there was no one to care for me. Hunched in my cloak, I made myself small and silent once more, and in a while began to weep.

'Well, here you are.' It was the boy again, his face washed, looking even younger without the inky shadows.

'Cecco. Cecco Corsellini.'

'Mura. I am Mura Benito. Thank you for helping me.'

'You don't know anything, do you? How old are you?'

I thought. I had been ten when I left Adara's house, and I had not minded the days since then. 'Eleven, I think. Maybe twelve by now.'

89

He looked at me appraisingly, at my bony ankles sticking from my too short gown.

'No one would know you were a girl, anyway.' He seemed to find this satisfactory. 'Come on then.'

'Where are we going?'

He made a deep bow from the waist, like a real gentleman, and held out his hand. 'To the finest seller of baked apples in all Italy, of course.'

As we passed along the walls of the palazzo, Cecco pointed out the symbols set in stone around the portico, a diamond relief with a pattern of feathers and lumpy little globes.

'They're the *palle*,' he said proudly. 'Palle. Balls. The symbol of the Medici. From when they started the bank. The palle are like the little weights they used on the scales to balance the money.' He lifted his head and proclaimed, '*Chi non se volta a esse colle palle gli fie rotto la testa e le spalle*. In other words, if you don't support the palle, you'll get your head broke. We're Medici, see?'

'Not really.'

'Just as well I'm here then.'

Florence was beautiful that day. As we wound our way through the straits of the Borgo de Greci, Cecco kept up a stream of information and it was as much as I could do to trot beside him, staring about me, while he explained that his family lived in the *gonfalone*, or district of the Golden Lion, where the Medici supporters congregated . . . that his father was a notary, connected with one of the big Medici estates, but he had plans for his son to become a scholar and sent him to school, where

Maestro Ficino had noticed him – oh, and had I tried a hot tripe roll? . . . The paintings on the walls of the Signoria were of enemies of the Medici who had plotted against them, he continued, and in this bell tower there is a painting of Daedalus by Giotto – did I know who Daedalus was, or Giotto? . . . Piero was nothing to his father Lorenzo, everyone said so . . . Florentines hated all foreigners and foreigners hated them, because they had the best artists and architects and poets in the world – did I know who Botticelli was? – which is why Donna Alfonsina was so unpopular with her proud Roman ways . . . Had I tried the sweets from the nuns of San Nicola, who made comfits for the Medici? . . . This is the bench where Buonarotti had quarrelled with da Vinci – did I know who Buonarotti was? . . . Cecco was learning Greek and would go to Constantinople once the Pope won it back from the Turks, because that was where all the great learning was and then he would have his own room in the palazzo like Maestro Ficino.

At least I had heard of Constantinople, but Cecco was not impressed.

'God's a dog if I can understand what Maestro Ficino sees in you. You're an ignoramus.'

I was shocked at his swearing, but I knew he was only doing it to show off, and that made me like him better, for it meant he was nervous too. The apple stall was to the east of the city, at the foot of the Ponte Rubaconte. I sat on a big stone close to the water and batted off the mosquitoes while Cecco scrambled up the bank. He returned juggling two fat apples, stuffed with ricotta and honey and raisins, the smooth cheese delicious against the scorching, floury flesh. For a while we scooped and slurped, puffing our lips round each mouthful to cool it. I felt braver. Cecco wiped his sticky mouth on a dockleaf and looked me in the face.

'How did you get here then? After that business with the angel?'

'My father gave me to a woman to look after me when they . . . when they took him. But she sold me.'

'I know. I've seen the account books. They paid fifty florins for you, Maestro Ficino bid it. Well, for the books, really. He thinks you can help him.'

'But how? I don't understand what he wants from me.'

'Well, it's not just because you're so funny-looking. Sorry. He thinks your father could raise demons, he wants to do it too. And he thinks you know how, 'cept you're too dumb to see it.'

I wasn't sure if I could trust Cecco, but it would come out soon enough.

'It was a trick. What my father did back in Toledo was just a trick, to save me.'

'Well, I wouldn't let him know that. Besides, I saw you in the church, remember, with old Suora whatsername? You put the wind up old Piero good and proper. It was a clever move, that, hiding the palle under those filthy old scraps.'

'Messr Piero thought it meant something?'

I knew, though. That same creeping coldness was reaching into my throat as I remembered the hollow golden ball, how it cracked on the stones. The symbol of the Medici and their power.

'I'm no witch!' I stammered hastily. 'That was nothing –

92

Margherita is just a fortune-teller. It's wrong to even think about such things. They burn people for less, in Spain.'

'Not here. In Florence there's this monk. Savonarola?' Cecco shook his head despairingly at my blank expression.

'Well, he's very powerful. Some say he's a fanatic, others a prophet. But old Lorenzo, Piero's father, had him brought to his death bed just to be sure. So this Savonarola tried to say that Maestro Ficino was a heretic, that his learning was ungodly, but all the scholars in Florence supported him because Maestro Ficino wrote that driving out evil spirits was holy work, and that learning how to do it was true Christian scholarship. So those hounds of God, the Dominicans, were left chasing their tails.'

Wisdom and knowledge shall be granted unto thee, and I will give thee riches and wealth and honour such as none of the kings have had that have been before thee, neither shall any after have the like.' The grim faced priest, the man struggling for his last breaths on the bed, the howling shadow beneath the walls.

'But magic is wrong, surely? Anyway, I can't do anything magical. My father just made it look like that.'

Cecco considered me. His face was so young, gawky, the planes not settled into their lines, but his smile was so open and his freckled skin so cheerful that I could see in a while he would be handsome. His face was pleasing to look on. Not like mine.

'I don't believe you.'

I thought of my dreams, of the shadows, of my father's stories of the world beneath the city, of Margherita's reedy cackle as she told her poor gulls I had the sight.

'Maybe.'

'Well, you've got a lot to learn if you're going to keep him happy. And I don't mind helping if you promise to stop howling the whole time.'

'Alright,' I smiled.

'Besides,' he added, a note of admiration in his voice, 'you may be a fool and a cry baby, but I've never seen a girl who could fight like you. A proper she-wolf.'

He pulled me to my feet and we began to walk slowly back to the Via Larga, our faces turned up to the silver sunbeams which alighted on the austere façades of the palaces.

CHAPTER SIX

S O CECCO BECAME MY GUIDE THROUGH THIS STRANGE
new country that was the upper world of the palazzo. He showed
me the statues, Judith cutting off the head of the tyrant
Holofernes, David the naked boy in the courtyard, so beautiful
that even in death the feather of defeated Goliath's plumed
helmet snakes suggestively up his bare thigh. The great staircase,
which had represented the horizon of my world when I belonged
to the kitchens, was reduced to a thoroughfare I pattered up and
down as confidently as if I were a true Medici. Once we even slid
all the way down its polished, pompous length. We chattered on
the outdoor benches, tracing their delicate walnut intarsia with
idle fingers, as Cecco proudly explained the history of the family
– how they were so rich that they were known as God's own
bankers, how all the princes of Italy revered them and how,
thanks to the Medici, there had been a time of peace and wealth
in Italy such as had not been seen since the days of the Romans.

I did not quite believe him. I remembered Piero's anxious
face on the church porch, the prophecy from the *tamburo*, that
image of a cold shadow clawing at the heart of the palazzo. As

summer slowly freshened into autumn, the house was as busy as ever; but in the streets there were rumours of complaints against Piero, of scuffles between Medici clients and their critics, and almost every day there were messengers from Milan, with talk of an alliance made by the Sforza duke with the hunchback king of the French.

There was much talk too of the monk Savonarola, returned from preaching in Bologna where he had dared to criticise Donna Ginevra, wife of the Bentivoglio lord, as a painted whore. Savonarola spoke of fires and scourges that would overtake Florence, of God's revenge that would descend on the city from over the Alps.

And I dreamed my dream of the young man in the velvet mask, looking out over the teeming night city, and each time I dreamed it seemed he turned his head a fraction closer, as though next time, next time, I might see the source of that lazy, patient smile.

Each morning, I went to Maestro Ficino's *scrittoio*, where he perched behind his desk, huge as all Medici furniture seemed to be huge, with Cecco working away behind him, never giving a hint that we were friends. As the old scholar talked and questioned, I realised how much I had absorbed from my papa in those quiet days – that, in fact, I understood much of what the Maestro spoke of. My papa had believed in the practical qualities of things, that certain plants or spices could be used to cure people, but that their powers, their properties, were in turn influenced by the stars, and that if one knew this, one could shape and control nature itself.

And from my mother I knew other things, vivid in my dreams and as clear and real as my memories of Toledo. Some of them I tried to describe to Maestro Ficino, who listened avidly. I told him a dream of tall, fair men, beautiful men, their bodies wound all over with strange blue markings, who came in long ships with fires at their prows. The Maestro nodded and scribbled as I spoke of the northmen, the fire-worshippers. He took a slate and scratched out three triangles, arranged in a larger triangle and asked me if I knew what that was, the mark of a victim to be sacrificed to Odin, the name of the old Northern god. So I told him of a dream where I had seen these marks, inked on the bodies of men and women who dangled from the trees of a forest where I walked, swaying like great fruits, so many that they made a forest of their own. I told him that I dreamed of strange shapes, a sort of writing, etched into the palms of these men. I began to understand that he believed the key to his searches was in the old magic, as he called it, the magic that the northmen had brought with them to Spain, and that this was why I, and my father's books, were so precious to him. He spoke of sorcerers, drunk with the power of magic which they called the *seid*. They could cross into the lands of the dead, these conjurors; they could see the future. So I told him what I believed he wanted to hear, whatever it would take to keep my new place in the palazzo, but I did not speak much of my dreams of wolves, of my mother or of the black man, for those things seemed too real to me to be consigned to the fond fancies of his notebook.

When I considered what Maestro Ficino had recognised in

me, I knew that Margherita had seen it too. Her *grullo* tales of wood ladies and mermaids suddenly seemed to make sense, and there appeared little difference, to me, between her harmless conjurings and the more august researches of the Maestro, for all that hers were cast from a bundle of rubbish and his with the latest instruments that scholarship could provide. She too had believed in the powers of nature, like ginger in crystals to heat the blood, that a menstruating woman would cloud a mirror, that vinegar could cool a husband's temper or asparagus rouse him to ardour.

Why then had Piero de Medici chosen to go to Margherita in his fear instead of his household *magus*? I saw little of Piero, and what I did see I could not like. I saw that he was lazy, that he left most of the work to his secretary Bibbiena, and a roomful of scribes; that he was vain, caring more for ordering new clothes to show off his fine physique; and that he was proud, believing the Medici to be as great as his wife's family, the Orsini, who had been grand in Rome for centuries while the Medici were no better than peasants in the marshy countryside of the Mugello. Oh, he liked to play the scholar, determined to show the world he was as great and discerning a critic of the new arts as his father Lorenzo had been. But I could see his eyes wandering when he came to discourse with Maestro Ficino, trying to catch a glimpse of his latest velvet coat in the reflection of a brass bowl; and I pitied my teacher then, for I saw that for all their learning, the scholars of the Medici household were just another sort of slave, bound to their books for their living as I had been bound to the greens and the sacks of capers.

Why then had Piero indulged Maestro Ficino in his protection of me? I should have liked to speak to Cecco of these things, but it never seemed to come out right. His worship of Piero was as complete as his conviction of my own odd specialness, however much I tried to convince him that I knew nothing, could do nothing. In Cecco's mind, the fact that Piero had needed me made it so. And I knew that I *was* strange. What was it that had so frightened the people in the marketplace, that had convinced my father I could execute the trick that bought my life, that made Adara so keen to abandon me? And I thought of the travelling people and the poor, sorry wolf, and how I had made him come to me.

One afternoon after dinner, when the house was quiet, I stole tentatively into Donna Alfonsina's rooms. She and her ladies would be resting, I thought, and if not I could invent an errand – for though I saw her often, sweeping like a proud ghost through the palazzo, she did not know me. All of us in the household moved on our own trajectories, like clockwork dolls, crossing paths occasionally but always proceeding along our proper course. Her chambers were on the floor above Piero's, a long suite of painted rooms glowing vivid as a jewel box. There was a scent of apple wood from the fire and fine incense, and my feet moved silently, cushioned by a thick crimson Turkey carpet. Other carpets were spread along a table and benches, their colours picked out in a row of silver basins ranged on a shelf. There were several books, embroidery frames and instruments scattered about, and I smiled at myself that I had once thought the salon above a brothel in Toledo a palace. Everything in this warm, luxurious space hummed quietly with money. In the corner of the antechamber was a huge mirror, from Venice, I thought, the city of water where the most beautiful glass in the world was made. Standing before it, I took off my cloak and my old red dress and my shift, and looked at myself naked, as I had never done before.

I was a poor thing, that was for sure. My hip bones and collarbones poked out, I could work my fist in the gap between my thighs, though I turned my eyes shyly from the smooth place between my legs. I was all straight lines and angles. I knew enough from my time with Margherita of some men's desires, that they preferred their own sex to the other, though my mind shied away from those foul moments with the gentleman in Adara's house. I was a between thing, I thought, and that was why they had dressed me as a boy. 'Changeling', they called me. Well, I thought, there was time for growing, and I tried to find my papa's voice, my papa who had told me I was beautiful, special. He must have loved me very much, I thought, to say such things with the evidence of my ugliness plain before his eyes. I sighed a little as I dropped my shift over my meagre limbs and thought I would pay a visit to Margherita. Perhaps amongst her 'kindnesses' there might be something to make a girl into a woman. Besides, I had meant to visit for a long time, ashamed of myself that I had neglected her. At dinner, when we were served a sweet *frittata* with candied cherries, I cut off a slice and wrapped it in a cloth for her.

Winter was coming on and the lost heat of the summer was almost unimaginable now that the city had sunk in freezing, icy mist. I made my way to Santo Spirito through a ghost city, the fog so thick and white that the streets vanished a few yards before me. Only the lanterns in the tabernacles at the corners – lighted early to guide the bumping, cursing citizens – helped me down to the river. Margherita was not there, nor was there any sign of her precious heap of smelly treasures. I thought perhaps the chill had driven her away, to a snugger roosting place, and I looked around me to ask after her, holding my drooping slice of omelette like a torch. A barrow man came up out of the mist, the heavy wheels of his laden handcart almost crushing my boots, and I jumped back, recognising the cricket seller who had handed over my gift that last spring. I asked him politely if he had any news of Suora Margherita and he answered me twisting his cap, taking me for a young lady in my new clothes, not recognising the shock-headed sprite in the gaudy necklace who had kept company with the wise woman.

'If you've come to ask something of her, miss, it's too late. She's been gone a month or so now.'

'Gone where, if you please?'

'Hell, I imagine, begging your pardon. Or the Bargello at least.'

I knew of the dungeon beneath the fortress of the Bargello. Cecco had told me about the tiny cells there, the prisoners who wasted away for years without a glimpse of sunlight.

'But why? What had she done? She meant no harm.'

The man leaned towards me and tapped his nose confidentially.

'Enemies in high places, miss. It was Piero's men what came

for her, curse him for a tyrant. You could try Donna Ciliego, over at Santa Annunziata, I've heard she's very good.'

I stared after him as he heaved his barrow across the deserted piazza, vanishing into the thick whiteness. Margherita had known Piero. She had known, as I had not, the significance of that little shattered ball. And perhaps the Medici fortunes were doubtful enough for it to be unwise even to let a crazy old conjuror who lived in a doorway speak freely. Poor, poor Margherita. I regretted that I had not sought her out sooner, but I knew well that I was too insignificant to have done anything to save her. I saw too that Piero was ruthless, and that his fear would make him cruel. As I trailed back to the palazzo, I thought angrily on how little we mattered to the great people, who thought human beings could be owned and discarded like broken tools.

I told Cecco that I thought Margherita had been locked up, but he refused to believe it. She would be back with the swallows, he told me, and said I should not mind it.

'Besides, it's not Ser Piero's fault,' he said stoutly, 'the people are stupid. They want tournaments and feasts and all suchlike nonsense, and because Ser Piero can't pay for that they go listening to that creep Savonarola.' *Piagnoni*, he called the Florentines, snivellers.

Piero was unpopular in Florence. There were many who resented the Medici merchants who had set themselves up as princes. And the city was threatened, Cecco said, by the Milanese and the French.

'Why Milan?' I asked. We were sharing the sweet omelette, there seemed no point in wasting it.

Cecco sighed and rolled his eyes. He enjoyed reminding me of my ignorance. 'The Duke of Milan is a halfwit. They say he lives in filth, with only his dogs for company. Milan is ruled by his uncle, Lodovico. They call him *Il Moro* – moor, like you.'

The idiot boy, he explained, cared nothing for his position so long as the uncle kept him supplied with pleasures; but his wife, a princess of Naples, who certainly did care for her dignity, was outraged that Lodovico's son was treated as the heir to Milan rather than her own boy.

'So the King of Naples is planning to march to Milan to protect her honour and make good her rights,' said Cecco. 'And Il Moro has asked Piero to join with him against Naples.'

If Piero was not loved, nor did he have the money to buy fear. The vast Medici vaults, to which all the kings of Europe had once been in debt, lay empty and cobwebbed.

'What have the French got to do with it?'

'Just as well for you that one of us has ears on his head. The French have a *claim* to Naples. They can make an alliance with Milan, give the dukedom to Il Moro, and put their own king on the throne. They say he's a hunchback, the French king.'

Thresholds are special places. Between inside and outside, public and private; the border between safety and danger, between different selves. Everywhere in the palazzo, the door-ways and lintels, ledges and stair-treads were carved and decorated with stories for those who traced them over the stone. I had seen already how the house was divided, how the kitchen folk were invisible to the family who lived above. Only the faintest of traces showed where their treadings had crossed, just as deer and boar make tracks through a forest and never quite meet. I had known the kitchens. The streets were a second world, where I walked with Cecco, gobbling saffron cakes and raisins, a world of sober clad merchants who moved with the pulse of money through the stony gunnels of the city's veins. We saw scrawling in the alleyways – 'People and Liberty'.

As the streets grew clogged with snow, there was hunger in Florence. More and more penitents turned out to hear the preaching of Savonarola. Florence was a city built on sin, he claimed. The Medici had tried to wash their usurers' wealth in beauty, transferring their wicked gold to the statues and paintings which made the city famous – but was it not a sin, Savonarola asked, that the rich should walk in scarlet, drunk on the imagined perfections of their hired artists, whilst the poor starved beneath the walls of their treasure houses? The sword of God, he railed, would descend from over the Alps, slicing off the diseased limbs of Italy like a surgeon's blade.

Piero's, of course, was the greatest treasure house of all. The palazzo was another world, bright yet untouchable, where I glimpsed Piero in his court of power, and the *scrittoio* was the last, a *hortus conclusus*, a walled garden, Maestro Ficino called it, shut off from politics and money and the business of living, where all that mattered were the spirits of the books. A garden, he said, but I thought it more like a bird's nest, a bundle of steal-ings, with my master pecking at his manuscripts like a greedy magpie. He paid no mind to the news from Milan, or the stories of the French, or the fresh talk of the streets, nor yet to the passage of the envoys on the staircase beyond his door. He would forget to eat, Cecco said, if his plate was not pushed in front of him.

While the other worlds of the city moved through their thresholds for wealth or places, or simple hunger, Maestro Ficino governed each moment of his day by the stars. He wanted to cast my chart, and grumped when I told him I could not remember my birthday. He had been born, he said, with Aquarius nearly square to Mars in Scorpio. 'Saturn set the seal of melancholy on me from the beginning,' he explained. Those born in the first month of the year were inclined to an excess of black bile, to be removed by warm spices and bleeding (though for himself he found that wine cured it better). This was his little joke, he gave it every day at dinnertime, and I was always sure to smile, for I saw that he was a kind man in his way, so gentle and refined.

He questioned me over and over about my father's books, for his plan, he said, was to gather together the greatest collection in the world of the writings of the philosopher Plato, and translate them into Latin to continue in the glorious tradition of Piero's father. Plato was the last of the line that had come through Trismegistus to Orpheus to Pythagoras to Philolaus, names that I had absorbed even through my sleep as my father and his friends talked around the fire. I did not see that Maestro Ficino cared too much for the glories of Piero, nor much for the good and true properties of things – for healing, like my father; rather, he cared for what was beyond them.

The only power that interested my master lay between the stars and the things of the world – properties, he called them –

which bound the celestial and the terrestrial. He was an accomplished musician, believing that the soft stirrings of his harp might echo the movements of the planets: Jupiter was 'earnest and sweet', Venus 'wanton and soft'. All this he showed me on his charts, to teach me. He had me mix scent for him, heating rose oil and dried jasmine flowers, to burn in a pure alabaster perfume-cup, and brew white sugar and cinnamon, as being the pure foods that would help him lift his mind to the spirits. While Cecco copied and sighed, and blotted his freckles with ink, I measured and stirred and listened, so far as I could follow him.

Like my father, he believed that there was nothing sinful in knowledge, that witchcraft was a coarse word, and that seeking the divine alignments of the elements was the most proper pursuit for scholars. I hope I was an apt pupil, difficult as I often found it to follow his thoughts. It was agreeable to be there, soft work; and when he set to reading or making his notes on the letters that came daily from all over the world, I set to my own learning. I repeated the names of plants and herbs, tracing their pictures in his diagrams of bright-coloured ink, learning how they should be treated to bring out their kindness. We sat thus for hours, each day, but still I was always glad when he waved his hand to dismiss me and I could set out with Cecco under the gateway of the palazzo to that other world beyond.

Gingilassi. It was a Florentine word, a word I liked. It meant to waste time, hang about doing nothing, and that was my favourite thing to do, to wander about with Cecco when we were released from the *scrittoio*.

'You wait,' he was saying one evening, 'Ser Piero will see for those Frenchies. They'll never care to come against a Medici.'

Piero was hesitating against the offers from Milan, for Florence was presently allied with Naples. The whole peninsula, Cecco said, was waiting to see which way the Pope would turn. Cecco puffed out his chest the way he always did when he said the Medici name.

'You're always creeping up to him.'

He elbowed me cheerfully in my skinny ribs.

'Ow! You are too!'

We were walking quickly, to keep off the cold, we had come a long way up the city, near to the church of San Marco.

'I'm proud of it. Palle forever!' he said.

'What are you saying then?'

We turned to see who had spoken. There were a group of them, standing about in a doorway. Boys a little older than Cecco, scrawny and tough-looking. Hungry-looking.

'I said, palle,' Cecco repeated, 'and proud of it. What's it to you then?'

I patted his shoulder. 'Cecco, it's late, I think we should go home.'

'Shut up.'

I didn't like it. I didn't like the way they eyed us, the fineness of our Medici clothes. Their jerkins were tatty and they had no boots. We were a long way from the Medici *gonfalone*, in this part of town.

'Come away.'

I tried to hurry him, but as we passed before them a stone caught Cecco's back. Another and another.

'Freedom, that's what *we're* for. We're no Medici arse lickers.'

Cecco tried to keep walking, but one of them came up behind him and hooked his foot about his leg so he fell. I went to help him, my hood slipped off my hair.

'It's her. The witch! Ficino's witch!'

They were around us now, pushing us tight together. I began to be afraid.

'We've heard about you. There's witchcraft going on in the palazzo.'

I looked about frantically, hoping that one of the *Oresta*, the magistrates who kept order in the streets at night, might be passing, but there was no one. They made the sign of the *malocchio*, the evil eye, pointing their fingers at us. I thought quickly, there was no way we could fight them. I put my head up and gave them my eyes straight.

'I'll tell my master of you,' I said. 'And do you know what will happen?'

They were silent, just boys after all.

'If I say so, he'll fetch out a fresh corpse from the graveyard at Fiesole. And it will walk down through the streets at night, and it will find you.' Quick as a cat, I shot out my hand and grabbed the hair of the nearest one, twisting a clump of it away in my hand so he screamed. 'It will follow the thread to you, like this,' – I drew out a hair between my fingers – 'and you'll wake in the night and its rotting breath will be in your face and then it will sink its teeth into you, for they are hungry, the dead. And you can scream and yell all you like,' – I kicked out contemptuously at the boy who hunched over beside me – 'but no one will hear you, for the dead are silent. And they'll find you in the morning, all ready for the grave. Shall I tell my master, then?'

They were moving away from us now. It was almost too easy.

'Yes,' shouted Cecco, 'that's how they do things in Toledo.'

'Shut up, you'll spoil it.'

I stared them down until they reached the corner, then I stretched out my fingers and hissed at them, and they scattered like pigeons. Cecco was staring at me, astonished, even a little fearful.

'Is it true, Mora? That was really good.'

'*Scemo*. Of course not. I had them, though, didn't I?'

We ran home, laughing all the way, our good boots loud on the cobbles.

*

That winter, the wolves came to Florence. They ran low through the shuttered gunnels, hunted, starving. At first, they took the lonely ones, the poor creatures who hunched in rags in doorways and ditches, then they grew bold and slid into houses, nosing their prey through cellars and stairwells, so that the last sight a wakened sleeper saw was the glow of their amber eyes in the darkness. I dreamed them, I dreamed them all. I dreamed the she-wolf who howled at old Lorenzo's dying. She came to my chamber but I was not afraid, for she knew me as one of her own. Wish, desire. She was my wolf-mother. I dreamed I heard the thump of their hungering blood, and smiled; for I had the light of the forests in me, and the black man watched over me. They sang me to sleep, my sweet shadows, and I placed no light in my window, as poor fearful snivellers did. I dreamed them and I knew I should not be harmed.

*

So the ambassadors went back and forth, and Piero prevaricated, and in Milan Lodovico Il Moro declared for France. In exchange for the confirmation of his ducal coronet, he would send his soldiers down the spine of Italy and take Naples for Charles, the crook-backed king of the French. And Piero commissioned a snow statue in the *cortile* from a young man named Buonarotti. A whimsical conceit of a thing, as though to show that the Medici had no need of marble to make their greatness known. To squander a winter's worth of bread on a caprice was his response to the sword that Savonarola dangled over Florence. It was the prior of Santo Spirito, they said, who had taught the young sculptor his anatomy. Nor did they miss the defiance of the gesture – that Piero would take the Dominicans' artist and put him to work on a trifle.

But Buonarotti surprised him. Perhaps Piero thought that his protégé was malleable, that he would produce something curious and flattering and pretty. For a whole day the slaves shovelled snow in the courtyard, compacting it into a huge block with their spades, and the boy, who could not have been more than twenty, had them build a series of shelves around it, with torches in the brackets so that he could work by night. We slept that evening to the faint scrape of his chisel and in the morning it was there. St Michael the Archangel, Michelangelo, stooping to cut the throat of the writhing serpent grasped in the clutch of his arm, the straining power of his torso an affront to Piero's airy dismissal of the spirit abroad in the city.

This is might, it seemed to say, this the lock which fate will hold you in, and you can try to wriggle free, but you will never escape.

Maestro Ficino shuffled down in his tatty robe to gawp with the rest of the household, not even minding his bare feet, clucking and muttering at what his master would think. But Piero could not allow himself to betray any emotion but pleasure as his servants drew back to let him see the marvel, and the young man beside it, his face flushed with cold and triumph after his long night's work. It stood there then, this wondrous thing, a reproach to Piero's attempted insouciance, until the thaw reduced it to a dripping, shapeless lump; but by then Piero had other matters to contend with than the conceit of a cheeky sculptor.

The Florentines believed that spirits could be imprisoned in statues, that their makers could cast ill wishing into the stone, and though the statue was gone by spring it seemed that after all, Savonarola's predictions would come out. He had cast himself as the avenging angel of Florence, and the Medici power was trickling away in the meltwater of the Alps.

CHAPTER SEVEN

AT THE END OF HOLY WEEK, THERE WAS TO BE A BALL at the palazzo. First came the ceremony of the carriage, which Cecco rushed me to Mass to see. All the fires in the city had been extinguished since Good Friday, and now the flame in the Baptistery would be relit with the spark of the stone chips from the Holy Sepulchre itself, brought to Florence by the first man to scale the walls of Jerusalem. The crowd was so thick that Cecco hoisted me on his shoulders so that I should not miss the spectacle as a curious mechanical dove was placed in an iron war chariot, of the ancient Florentine design. This year, defiantly, Piero had ordered that the chariot be filled with gunpowder. The square was quite silent as the orange spark hissed along the fuse, everyone waiting to see if the spark would take, which would promise a good harvest after this cruellest of winters. For a moment there was a crackle as the flame caught, and then I was thrown to the ground as Cecco lost his footing and stumbled, shoved backwards by the surge of the crowd away from the deafening blast. I scrabbled at a cloak to tug myself to my feet, in time to put back my head and see the grey spring sky come alive with a volcano of colour, my ears ringing with the delighted roars of the crowd. Cecco was grinning, a smudge of bluish powder on his cheek.

'Did you see, Mora, did you see it? Isn't it wonderful!'

I smiled back, more pleased by his pleasure than my own.

'And see, I'll dance with you later, too. We'll dance in the spring, eh?'

As we walked up the Via Larga, Cecco took my hand. We had to push our way through the gate; it was so busy with carts delivering provisions, a troupe of splendidly raggedy tumblers, and three sheep being driven complainingly to their doom. I remembered Margherita's tumblers, wondering where their travels had taken them, if they had struggled through another lean season. I was lucky, I thought then. After all I had endured, I had come safe to this place, to this city of marvels, I would see a ball, and warm in my own was the palm of my friend.

Attentive to the complaints in the city, Piero had declared that the spring ball would be an open affair. Any Florentine who could muster a decent costume should be admitted. Disgusted, Donna Alfonsina departed for the country with her children and women, as soon as she had heard the Easter Mass – which was, perhaps, Piero's true intention. I had never been taught to dance, I should make a fool of myself if I tried, but all the same, as I washed my face in rosemary water in my attic room, with the sounds of the palazzo preparing itself beneath, I couldn't help but feel thrilled, like any girl, like a *real* girl. My red dress, I admitted ruefully, was much too short and shabby, but I had another cut-down gown, in dark blue, and with my hair hidden under a white linen cloth I thought I might look, if not well, at least not shaming.

I went down early, by the servants' way, for though Piero was keen to show himself a man of the people, the great staircase was of course reserved for the grandest guests. The *cortile* had been tented over in yellow silk, which made a wonderful light as the torches picked up its warmth under the dimming night sky, and tables ran along each side, displaying the subtleties over which the convents and confectioners of Florence had laboured for weeks. Here was the church of San Lorenzo, the Medici church, reproduced in gold-figured marchpane and here a green sugar-meadow filled with tiny meringue statues. Here a tower of caramelised virtue, holding fast against a company of tiny knights, their costumes as bright and intricate as those who rode the walls of Piero's chamber. And here a mountain range, in the coal sugar eaten at Epiphany, with a column of scarlet soldiers winding up it only to fall into a ravine where a group of plum-cake lions already held the first of their victims in cochineal jaws. The French. This was Piero's solution then: gaiety and beauty and splendour should drive them out. As I looked, the familiar cold tingle of my dreams stole across me.

*

Night. I stand wrapped in a cloak, waiting by the window of a huge room. The darkness smudges the plasterwork mouldings, so that this space, which has been all made of playful light, seems menacing, more like an ancient fortress than this perfect palazzo, so high and delicate that its pale stones might have been wrought for a fairy city. At the table, upon which a single candle flickers in its tall silver holder, sits the man in black. As ever, his face is masked, but I can make out the power in the breadth of his shoulders beneath his velvet cloak. His wrist is delicate, elegant in a black leather gauntlet as he moves his hand to summon forward the two men who wait at the end of the hall. When they speak, I know by their voices that they are Florentines; I can hear the golden Italian of Tuscany in their voices. The man's voice is low, its quietness containing great anger, or perhaps a simulation of anger.

'I am not pleased with your government. How can I trust you, how can I be sure you will not attack me? You must change your government and pledge to support me – for I have no intention of letting this state of affairs continue.'

The older of the two Florentines answers him. 'Florence has the government it deserves, and no other power throughout Italy keeps better faith with its people.'

The other adds that Florence has the protection of the King of France. The king has ruled that no incursions be made into their territory, they await six thousand men.

'I know better than you what the French king has in mind,' says the masked man. 'If you rely on France to defend you, I suggest you will find yourselves deceived.'

The candleflame glints on a huge ring forced over one of the leather clad fingers: a ruby stone, its dark depths drawing the light. I have seen this jewel . . .

*

115

'Mora!' Cecco was dragging at my sleeve. 'What are you doing, mooning here? You look half-asleep! Come on.'

He pulled me urgently through the crowd, whispering the identities of those he recognised. At the loggia we had to stand back against the wall, almost drowned in a lake of crimson silk skirt as a party of ladies made their way towards the staircase. At their head was a beauty who knew it, nothing of the customary Florentine modesty in her countenance, her head imperious on a long, slender white neck roped around with black pearls, pearls the colour of her huge plush-lashed grey eyes.

'D'you see her,' hissed Cecco gleefully.

'The dark haired one with the pearls?'

'Donna Alba. She's Piero's mistress.'

'Mistress? But he has a wife,' I answered stupidly, still fuddled from the memory of the daydream.

Cecco gave me a pitying look.

'I forget, you're as innocent as an angel. I'm hungry.'

We ducked into the sala to stuff our pockets with hot pork rolls, chewy and musky with sage, and then ran through a miasma of scent and music to the long gallery on the upper floor where Piero was receiving his guests. He was bowing to Donna Alba, bent over her hand, his eyes raised flirtatiously to her haughty gaze. The crowd closed around us and Cecco motioned me to follow him beneath the feet of a credenza. I felt a splinter graze my knee as we wriggled along the dusty tunnel, re-emerging at the other side of the room. Cecco peered eagerly at this beautiful, scandalous woman. So there we were, our heads goggling out like double gargoyles, when a pair of young men stepped towards the couple and the younger of the two attempted to take Donna Alba by the hand.

'Giovanni and Lorenzo,' whispered Cecco.

I knew the young men. They were Piero's cousins, descended from a junior Medici branch, but even as the wealth of the chief family was in decline, these two had made a fortune dealing in grain and now people said they were even richer than Piero himself.

'The lady is engaged,' Piero was saying.

'Indeed she is,' replied Giovanni, his tone polite but his face arrogant, 'to me.'

Donna Alba sent her grey eyes between the two Medici men, clearly delighted to be the subject of such a prestigious quarrel.

'It's spring, Giovanni,' added Piero condescendingly. 'There'll be plenty of girls who'll be happy to have you as a partner.'

'Quite so, sir. But Donna Alba shall dance with me.'

'I think not.'

By now the whole room was hushed, the guests no longer even pretending to ignore the scene. Piero took a step towards Giovanni, drawing himself up, all the pride of the Medici in his gait, but Giovanni did not recoil.

'This is my house, sir.'

'For how long?' Giovanni sneered.

Piero's hand shot out and cuffed the boy across the face. It was a gentle blow, as one might pat off an unruly dog, but of course that only made the insult worse. I could hear Cecco holding his breath beside me. For an endless moment, Giovanni stared at Piero, a flush of rage darkening his features, his hand playing awkwardly at his right hip. His brother Lorenzo stepped forward and placed a warning hand on his arm. Giovanni recovered himself, with effort, and made a brief bow.

'Of course, cousin. How could I so forget myself?'

Signor Bibbiena, Piero's secretary, signalled frantically to the musicians, and Piero handed Donna Alba forward. The other couples lined up, but the measure had not begun before Lorenzo had pushed Giovanni from the room, their boots sounding above the hum of the pipes.

'Oh my,' said Cecco, 'oh my. There'll be trouble now.'

Had any other man committed such an insult, Giovanni di Pierfrancesco de Medici would have called him out to fight. As it was, he was dishonoured because he could not in duty challenge the head of his family. The powerful have two methods for dealing with trouble. To cozen and charm, to bribe and beguile until the wound is healed over, or, having made an enemy, to strike him down at once. Was it that image of crumbling strength in his courtyard that goaded Piero to choose the second?

*

Time stretched like a lute-string. Through another summer the city broiled beneath smudged skies. Each day the peg turned, tighter, tighter. I was no longer summoned daily to the *scrittoio*, Maestro Ficino was closeted all day with Piero and the candles burned in his chamber long into the night. Tighter, tighter, until by September the very breath of Florence seemed to hum with the tension.

I wandered the streets with Cecco, disconsolate, idle. The only life in the city appeared to be among the astrologers, who set up on street corners and filled their purses with the coin of fake omens as the people, usually so bustling and busy with getting, turned bench-whistlers, their shop shutters closed to the beat of the sun, their minds skidding between doom and the false hope peddled for florins. Through the streets came trails of children, led by one of Savonarola's black hounds, solemn in unbleached linen, their hair roughly shorn, holding out baskets into which housewives tossed their hoarded finery. They sang as they marched, vanishing and reappearing like puppets between the curtain of the sun's glare and the cast iron shadows of the streets. Tighter, tighter.

And then the string snapped, and the wolves came over the Alps, just as the monk had said they would.

The French were in Milan, in Pavia, at Piacenza, they were crossing the Venetian territories towards the border with Tuscany.

'Come on, Mora, get up! They're here!'

Cecco was in my attic room, stumbling over an old thick sword bound with a bright sash wrapped several times round his narrow boy's waist. His face was bright and excited, like a child on carnival day.

'What do you mean they're here? The French?' I leapt out of bed in my shift, it didn't seem to matter since we were all to be murdered.

'No, not in Florence. At Fivizzano. The messenger's downstairs, with Messr Piero. They sacked the whole garrison.'

He drew his hand slowly, with relish, across his throat. 'Come on!'

'Where to? Besides, you look ridiculous. Where d'you get that?' I grumbled, peeved that Cecco, his exuberance usually kept so earnestly in check within the palazzo, was behaving like – well, like a boy. And he had not noticed that I was a girl and that it was improper for him to be in my chamber.

We banged down the stairs, past a line of gentlemen who were hissing and gesticulating frantically amongst themselves, their faces unshaven and wan in the early light. The courtyard was full, all the house slaves exclaiming and chattering, hardly paying any mind even to Donna Alfonsina, who stood embracing her brother, the white linen of her nightgown falling softly over the armour that covered his chest. Men heaved heavy chests for the cart that stood at the gateway, the cooks were rushing out with bundles of provisions, steam still rising from new bread.

'Messr Paolo goes to Sarzana,' hissed Cecco. 'The Orsini troops are mustering for Florence.'

'How do you know? Scribbler.'

'Exactly. So you can shut up. I know because Ser Piero was writing letters all night with Maestro Ficino, I was *scribbling* away. So then I went home and my uncle gave me his sword, so there. And I have an important message to take, do you want to come with me or not?'

I nodded, my bad temper forgotten in the excitement.

'You'd best leave that, all the same,' I said gently, 'if we're in a hurry.'

Reluctantly Cecco unstrapped the sword and laid it under a bench. He grabbed my hand and we were out in the streets, running with no care for propriety, giddy with the unreality of it all. After the frantic energy of the palazzo, the city seemed frozen, the streets empty, only a few groups pressed together in the church porches.

'Cecco, what has happened?' I panted.

'You should see it from the walls. Whole caravans of people, running from them. They say all the girls have been shut up in convents already. Rapists, they are, the French. Not that *you* need to worry.'

I felt my temper rise again. 'Stop it! It's not funny! Besides, they won't come here, because Ser Piero won't let them.'

'What if it's not up to him any more?'

It seemed that it was not. Cecco's message was for Messr Lenzi, one of the richest and most important men in the city. Florence needed money, Piero said, money to pay the *condottieri* who would man the forts on the frontier, and even the Medici coffers were not deep enough to pay. But even now, Florence would not give up its gold, and when Cecco took up Lenzi's answer the household heard Piero bawling with rage.

The French were at Vigetano, they were moving on Pisa. And the broken lute-string of time skeined the city, looping itself around the house on the Via Larga and tightening like a noose. The quarrel at the spring ball, that disdainful slap that Piero had dealt his cousin Giovanni, was duly paid out. The brothers, Lorenzo and Giovanni, sent messages to the French king to claim that the Medici were finished in Florence and that he would have their support. This the whole household knew, for Piero screamed louder at their treachery than he had done at Messr Lenzi's refusal.

In her Roman way, Donna Alfonsina insisted that carts were loaded with linens and tapestries to be sent to the Medici house at Cafaggiolo, where Piero insisted his unruly relatives should retire; but the fine lawn sheets were barely unpacked from their lavender-scented wrappings before Giovanni and Lorenzo had escaped their polite exile to join King Charles. The French were at San Stefano, they were at Pontremoli. And then, Piero too was gone.

He left quietly one morning, dressed in his plainest clothes, like the merchant his father and grandfather had always pretended to be. Without him, the palazzo collapsed into the lassitude which had overtaken the rest of the city. Donna Alfonsina kept to her room, the household gathered on the bench by the tree to whisper and speculate. For two days, Cecco did not come. I took my courage to find Maestro Ficino in the *scrittoio*.

'What is it?' he asked irritably, looking up from a pile of papers, for all the world as though the world beyond his books was not ending. 'Oh, you, yes, Mora. Well?'

'Please, Maestro Ficino, I wondered . . . That is, I thought you might perhaps tell me what is happening?' I feared he would rebuke me for impertinence, but he looked at me wearily.

'I had hoped, Mora, that perhaps you might tell me.'

I considered a while. 'I have – I have those dreams,' I said at last.

'Dreams?' he asked eagerly.

'I have had them since – well, before I came here, Maestro. I don't know, but I'm afraid it will go badly for Ser Piero.'

'You have had visions? You have been visited?'

'No, Maestro, nothing like that. I just – dream.' I spoke to him then of the omens, the beasts fighting in the sky, the burning sword, the shadows crossing the mountains, even the small shattered ball, broken in my hand in the church porch.

'Why did you not speak of this to me before? I did not bring you here to stay dumb. God knows you wasted enough time with your play-acting in the kitchens!'

'I'm sorry, Maestro. Please don't be angry. I didn't understand, I haven't ever really understood. You have been very good to me, you and Ser Piero. But I thought it was the books you wanted, my father's books—'

'No, you little fool, it was you! I had them search for you, buy you, but I was told they had brought the wrong slave. I had merchants out of Savona seeking you a year before your brawling found you out.'

'Maestro, forgive me, but I don't understand.'

He scrabbled through the papers on his desk, but as he made to speak, a servant entered with a message.

'Ser Piero is come, Mora. I must speak to him quickly.'

*

Piero's guard wore deep scarlet, the Medici colour. Their swords clinked against their spurs as they swung into their saddles. We came into the courtyard as they clattered into the Via Larga, and

Maestro Ficino was buried in a crowd of supporters who fell in behind them, shouting 'Palle, palle!' I glimpsed Cecco trotting proudly among them, his red hair brighter than ever under a scarlet cap. The broad man next to him must be his father, I thought. I tried to make my way towards them, but the crowd was too dense. Every now and then I paused to stand on tiptoe, to check for the sight of the cap, hard on the hooves of the rear-guard's horse. Maestro Ficino was calling in his creaky scholar's voice, 'Wait, wait!' but Piero was already gone.

'I'll follow them, sir,' I threw over my shoulder, then I was swept up into the roar of noise and pounding feet. We twined our way to the Piazza Signoria, which had already filled with young men and boys, the faces of a few old women bobbing among them like wizened apples in a barrel. This crowd was silent, though, sullen, and the cries of Piero's supporters gradually fell away until the only sound was the tread of the horses as they approached the gate of the Signoria. But the gate did not open.

Piero sat easy on his horse, still and erect, as cool and handsome as if he had stepped down from the walls of his chamber. Indeed, the whole of Florence seemed to be there, captured like *maquettes* arranged ready for a painter's brush. Nothing in Piero's countenance betrayed the fact that for the first time in his life, he had been disobeyed. Then the door opened, but the threshold remained barred. The sentry's message passed through the crowd like a breeze over a wheat field. Piero might only enter alone. He was to disarm and make his way into the Signoria like a petitioner, through a side door. Piero's supporters in the crowd got up a few cries of 'Shame!' but they rippled away as Piero stayed like a statue on his horse.

More and more people were arriving in the square, the crowd was pressing and beginning to surge, I had lost sight of Cecco and was anxious for him. Stooping and twisting, I worked my way back through the crowd to the corner of the Cione loggia where I joined a group of watchers squashed together precariously on the outer pedestal. Eventually, the gate opened, but again Piero did not enter. He dismounted and spoke to a group of men, he was refusing what they asked, I could see it in his face. The gate slammed shut. Moments later, the first toll of the huge city bell, the *Vacca*, rang out over the city.

The sound exploded in the crowd like the crack of a whip. As I clutched for what purchase I could, I saw a swarm of men surround Piero, who was struggling to mount his horse. I could not understand what had changed, how Piero's command over Florence had collapsed so utterly, but then I fell down amongst the rushing boots, and could think only of how to force my way through, to find Cecco, to reach the palazzo.

Stones began to fly, bodies staggered around me, my arm was crushed beneath a running foot. Blind with terror, I half-hunched, half-crawled my way through the press of bodies, trying to follow the edge of the piazza where it would meet the Via Larga. I heard the rally of the Medici supporters – 'Palle, palle!' – and hoped that Cecco was safe. Then I was clear of the square and running, just as a crash of hooves behind told me that Piero and his supporters had also broken through. I pressed myself against a shuttered *bodega*, flattening my body against the deadly charge, the animals' flanks all but brushing my face as they hurled past. I tried to fall in behind them, but as I turned I saw that the way was blocked by a horrible mass. Twisted figures, braying faces, tumbled gargoyles, all screaming, '*Liberta, liberta*!'

My hood was lost, I was bewildered, I thought perhaps I ought to run, run as far as I could until I crossed the river, then I felt a hand on my arm and saw Cecco's face, blood on his forehead where a rock must have caught him.

'Mora! Come!'

He pulled me into an alleyway, one of those Florence runnels where the sun never touches the flagstones. The air felt as cool and thick as water. We squatted, gasping, the shrieks of the crowd seeming suddenly far away, mounting as they passed and then falling as they raced for the Signoria.

'Cecco, what's happening? You're hurt!'

He pushed impatiently at his brow, where the clotting blood dulled his hair.

'It's nothing. We need to get home. You can come to my family's house. We'll be safe there.'

'Safe from what? I don't understand.'

'They say that Piero went to the French king, that he offered them Pisa and the fortresses if he would leave Florence alone.'

'So why are they so angry?' I asked stupidly.

'He's not a king, Mora. He had no right. The Signoria refused to receive him. The Medici will be finished in Florence, now.'

'But how?' I thought of the palazzo, of its treasures, of the statues and the paintings, of the army of slaves, the coffers of gold. How could Piero be finished?

'It doesn't matter. Giovanni de Medici is calling himself *Il Popolano* now, they're already tearing the palle off the walls of the houses. We have to go, Mora. Can you run?'

'Of course I can.'

He looked at me and grinned. 'Of course you can. We'll get away, Mora, you'll see. We'll go with Messr Piero and when he comes back to fight for Florence, I'll be with him. Come on.'

There was no need to run. We walked quietly out into the Via Larga, empty and littered as though a carnival train had passed. All the houses were closed-up tight. We saw no one as Cecco led me eastwards into the heart of the 'Golden Lion' district. His home was on the Via delle Ruote, the Street of Wheels, near the church of Santa Caterina, a quiet area with no shops, just a few weavers' workshops. Several of the houses seemed fine, as though gentlemen might live there, but even though we had crossed just a few streets, it was a world away from the palazzo. Outside one of them stood a man on a ladder, chiselling away at an engraving above the door.

'Papa!'

The man was almost knocked down as the door opened and a woman rushed out, followed by a gaggle of little children, all crying Cecco's name and all with his same bright red hair. Cecco's mother held him tightly, exclaiming her thanks over and over that her son was safe, whilst his father stood by almost shyly, smiling quietly.

I saw the raw stone above the doorplace, half of a weathered Medici ball not yet chipped away, and realised that the news of Piero's fall had spread even to this quiet part of the city. I curtsied politely to Signora Corsellini when she asked me to step inside, but I was terribly conscious of how his little brothers and sisters stared at me.

We entered the house. It was neat and brightly painted, though sparsely furnished like most Florentine dwellings. Cecco's father glanced quickly down the street before carefully bolting the door, enclosing us in a smoky atmosphere thick with the scent of bean pottage. Cecco's mother served the soup and thick floury dumplings stuffed with *bietole* and ewes' cheese. We gobbled them down. All the time we ate, Cecco's mother touched her son, exclaiming over his wounded head, making up a poultice, stroking his sleeve, his cheek. She shooed the children into an upper room and suggested courteously that I might like to rest. Obediently, I lay down on the settle that made one of the room's few pieces of furniture, and dozed to the sound of Cecco's voice describing the events in the Signoria, the riot, the rumours that Piero had capitulated to the French. So peaceful was that little home, so warm and stuffily snug, that I slept awhile, exhausted by all I had seen. When I woke, I saw a circle of eyes around me. The children were watching me, solemnly chewing at hunks of bread and lard.

'Are you a witch?' asked one of them excitedly.

I pretended to consider.

'Yes,' I answered eventually. 'Shall I turn you into a toad?'

They screamed and ran away to hide in the corners. I

grabbed a twig from the log basket and pointed it like a magician's staff.

'Whoosh! And you're a pig!'

They giggled and we began a game, each of them pretending to be a different animal, me 'magicking' them into ever more extravagant shapes, dragons and lions and turtles. We jumped and romped and even Cecco condescended to join us as a bear and then a rhinoceros. We played until the thickening of the shadow beyond the shutters told us that night had fallen and I helped Signora Corsellini to wash the little ones before she took them away to bed.

'Don't mind their teasing, dear,' she told me kindly. 'We're odd enough ourselves, goodness knows.' Her face was as plain as a saucepan beneath her carroty frizz, but I thought her the sweetest of women. She gave me a shift and a blanket and told me I might spend the night in their parlour. Before the family settled down for the night, everyone knelt down and Cecco's father said the Ave Maria, then we all prayed that God would protect the Medici.

'Goodnight, Cecco,' I said as he took his tallow light to follow his parents to the sleeping chamber. 'Thank you for letting me come here.'

'It's not what you're used to, is it?' he asked shyly.

'I think you're lucky. And I am too, to have you as my friend.'

'Go on with you.' He blushed until his cheeks matched his hair. I don't know what made me do it, but I leaned forward and kissed him quickly on the mouth.

'What d'you do that for?'

I turned away, ashamed. 'I'm sorry. I meant nothing.'

'No, it's alright. See, I'll give you one back.' And he did, brusquely, his lips wet against my face.

So I watched the dying embers of the fire until I slept again, and thought that someone had kissed me.

CHAPTER EIGHT

AT DAWN, WE RETURNED TO THE PALAZZO. ONLY THE scent of smoke suggested Florence was still a city of living beings, stirring behind their barred doors, for we saw not a soul as we made our way westward towards the Via Larga. No carts were drawn up in the street, no anxious line of petitioners shuffled their feet in the blue light of morning.

'They're gone, Cecco. I know it. They're gone.'

'Shut up! Ser Piero would never do so. As if he'd creep out of Florence like a thief!'

Yet the gates of the house swung wide and the courtyard was empty. We walked through an enchantment, a silent palace of treasures that belonged only to us. The kitchens were empty, the stoves cold, only a few limp flour sacks cast aside on the floor to show us that the kitchen folk had made away with what they could carry. Slowly, we climbed the staircase, heavy with silence, and made our way through the upper rooms, all vacant, shimmering in their lost loveliness.

'They're gone, Mora, they're really gone.' Cecco was

bewildered, everything that made sense of his world had been taken from him.

'We must leave too, now. There's nothing for us here. Let's go, please.'

'What about Maestro Ficino. The books? He'll need his books.'

I had forgotten my master, I had failed him again. Our footsteps sounded horribly loud as we made for the *scrittoio*, where the Maestro was desperately trying to cram a few more volumes into a bulging sack, far too heavy for him to lift.

'Last night,' he panted, 'they left last night. The best were packed, but my books, my books' – his voice rose to a wail of grief – 'I must save the books!'

'Save them?' I asked stupidly.

Then I heard it. A great roar, swelling so that the walls of the palazzo vibrated with the rage of it, rushing on us like a storm. Ficino's hands dashed frantically amongst the papers.

'They're here. Children, save yourselves, run!' The first crash of shattered glass told me that they were inside, come to wreak their revenge on the fallen Medici tyrants as a steady chant '*Liberta! Liberta!*' built beneath us.

'No!' screamed Cecco, as he ran for the door.

I tried to stop him. I tried to pull him back. I thought we might go through the attic rooms, out onto the roof and hide until they were done. It was gold they wanted, not blood. But he was too brave, and too loyal, and all I could do was stand petrified in the doorway and watch him as he ran for the staircase, his arms spread out before him as though he could calm them. Then I had to look as that great crowd surged upwards, armed with a thousand greedy red mouths, yelling for Medici gold, a forest of staves closing over him, hands clawing him down, pulling at him as he tumbled.

'Palle!' he yelled, 'Palle!', his defiance turning greed to hate.

They turned in on him, striking out with their boots, so the last thing I saw before the mob swallowed him up was the bounce of his bright hair against the marble, his blood spattering brighter still, a second or two, on the pale stone.

I slammed the door, breathless. I could not think of what I had seen.

'Help me,' I spoke. Together, Maestro Ficino and I heaved the huge desk against the wall. The door was tried, rattled as we held our breaths, they passed on, baying in their frenzy.

'They'll kill us, Mora,' he whispered. 'When they see this, they'll kill us. Savonarola's fanatics will have us burned.'

I cast my eyes quickly around the room, the books, the instruments, the jars of spices and ointments. He was right.

'We could wait. Bar up the door better and just – wait.'

'They'll burn the palazzo unless the French king gets here to stop them.'

Above us, we heard the chanting, the smashing, as cabinets were toppled and hangings ripped from the walls. I smelled wine, they had got at the cellars.

'Then I'll get us out,' I said fiercely.

His face brightened and I wondered for a moment if he expected a conjuring trick – a flaming angel from Toledo come to carry us through the window.

The window! It overlooked the street, a narrow thorough-fare running off the Via Larga. I scrambled up onto the ledge and gingerly parted the shutters. Craning precariously to the left, I could see that the main street was packed with bodies, shoving to and fro, many of them trying to make away with bundles, others pushing forward to get at the spoils of the palazzo. But beneath us, the street was empty. Too far to jump; we would be dashed to pieces from this height. I could not help remembering how I had stood, so bewildered, on another windowsill, with another fearsome crowd below me. Then, sickeningly, I thought of that bright blood on the staircase just a few feet away.

There was time for this. I would live, we would live.

Desperately, I cast my eyes around the street for inspiration. There was a flurry in the stream along the Via Larga. A wagon being backed into the side street, the horses stamping and protesting, their heads held by two women. A second wagon, then a third, squeezed cautiously into the tight space, the faded colours of their awnings almost buried in the November mist. *The troupe.* Crazily, I thought that my old friend the wolf might even have heard me in my moment of need, might have sensed the shuddering fear in my heart with his own.

'Annunziataaaa! Immaculataaaa!' I bawled in a scream that tore at my throat. 'Here, up here!'

Maestro Ficino may have thought I had taken leave of my wits, but I did not care.

The women turned about, wondering where this ungodly noise was coming from. Then one of them looked up and I pushed back my hood, leaning as far as I dared from the casement, hoping that my hair would show in the dim light. If Annunziata was surprised to see Margherita's dumb apprentice wailing like a banshee from the most dangerous building in Florence, she had the sense not to hesitate. She raised her arms to me, questioning. I pointed, down, then raised two fingers. She nodded swiftly and eased her way round the head of the horse to the next wagon, beckoning. In moments she, Immaculata and the twins had shinned up the creaking awning, their hands at their lips in a warning.

'We will need money, Maestro. What is there of value?' I hissed.

'The books . . .'

'The books are lost. Quickly. Little things. The ivory clock, the little gold sundial. Cinnamon bark, peppercorns, anything, hurry. Fill your pockets and do as I bid.'

He hopped about like a crow in his flapping robe, trying to move quietly, though the orgy of wrecking about us quenched any sound we could make.

'Very well. Now take the stool, yes, climb up here where I am. Do as you are bid.'

His good old face was terrified yet he obeyed me awkwardly. I wriggled past him and shoved at his slippered feet to boost him onto the sill.

'What is this? Who are these people?'

'We will die if you do not do as they say.'

'But they tell me to jump!'

'Then they will catch you. Or you'll die anyway. Go!'

135

'I cannot.'

Behind me, I sensed a lull in the fury. They were calming now, questing about for what more they could despoil. They would try the door again in moments. I stood on the stool and shoved my head through Maestro Ficino's robe. Chellus and Gherardus were planted, legs apart, on the struts of the wagon top, the girls on their shoulders, leaning together to make a cradle of their arms. I saw what they meant, but my master's face above me was white with fear.

'I cannot do it.'

'Forgive me, sir,' I said. 'I'll save the *Pimander*.' Then I pushed him with all my strength.

I did not wait to see what had become of him. I dumped the books from his abandoned bag and rifled through until I found his precious translation. I wanted to take more, at least to find something of my father's, but one book was already heavy against my breast. In a moment I had the door open, pulled down my hood and shouted, 'Here! In here! Sorcery! Here is the devil's work!'

I flew down the staircase before their feet could find me, keeping my eyes ahead, whipped out of the gates and turned right. I dived straight between the shafts of the backed-up wagon, knocking Addio from his seat at the reins. From far above came a fluting chorus of shattering porcelain. They were in the *scrittoio*.

Addio was setting a green cap jauntily over one eye.

'Well, mooncalf,' he said. 'You're surely full of surprises.'

'The way is too narrow. You won't back the wagons through.

136

We have to go forward, as fast as we can, to the river, away from the Signoria, to the Prato gate.'

'Found our tongue, have we?' But he was smiling, I could see he loved the thrill of it. He stood up at his full little height and yelled, '*Popolo! Liberta!*' at the top of his lungs as he brought the reins cracking down. I joined my voice to his, and that is how we left Florence, swinging through the streets at a canter, crying out in pretended joy.

*

By the time the little hunchback king rode into the Piazza Signoria with his lance on his hip, we were at Careggi. Quite recovered from his odd circus adventure, and much restored by the safety of his *Pimander*, Maestro Ficino had directed the troupe to the Medici villa in the hills, a day's journey from the city. We would be safe there, he said reassuringly. Whatever was happening in Florence, the *contadini* of the Tuscan countryside loved their Medici masters.

He was wrong. We smelled the wet fug of burning wood before we saw what had become of the villa. No one came to challenge us as the wagons drew up in the courtyard. The body of the building stood, charred and blackened, but one wing had collapsed and the high loggias, whose balconies I had seen in my dream, were buckled and sagging, their fine-wrought stonework swinging like laundry where it had not already crashed to the walled garden below. They had been here, too.

Maestro Ficino rushed straight to the library to see what had become of the precious books, while Annunziata, Immaculata and I looked out what dry kindling we could find for a fire in the gaping kitchen hearth. They had been very kind, asked me no questions, had not sought to discover what sorrow lay on me as we crawled through the dank bare landscape, but that night, when the beasts were attended to and we had scraped up a soup of herbs and soaked black bread, they asked me what I would do.

'You can come with us,' said Addio. 'We'll go south. Get out of this damned damp. Maybe as far as Naples.'

'The French will be there first,' put in Gherardus.

'And they'll want entertaining, won't they, the conquering heroes? We'll be rich.'

'You are welcome, Mora,' added Immaculata gently. 'Truly welcome.'

I thanked them, but I would not go. I was *esclava*. I could not risk them being charged with stealing Medici property. Wherever Piero was, I belonged legally to him. Besides, I would not bring ill luck upon them, as I did all who tried to care for me. My mother had loved me, and I killed her with my arrival, my papa had loved me and died that I might keep my life. Margherita was rotting in a cell, or starved to death for all I knew and Cecco – I could not think of Cecco . . . yet of course I thought of nothing else. How his knuckles inked his forehead when he sighed over his work, his hand in mine in a bright spring street, the taste of ricotta and apple foam, the pride in his voice as he told me what it meant to be a Florentine. I bit my lip and gnawed at my fingers until they bled to squash down the thoughts.

After the troupe had stayed a while, helping us to restore order in the tumbled rooms, gathering fuel and what poor supplies had been left, we said goodbye. I watched them on the road until they vanished from sight, the draggled streamers on their wagons showing bravely. I had no stomach for an adventure on the road. I would stay and mind my master, who cared for nothing but his books, so that I could not bring him harm.

*

The nobility of the famous republic dressed themselves as Frenchmen to greet Charles and the cries of 'liberty' were replaced in San Giovanni with '*Francia! Francia!*' They set fireworks to dazzle his bulging eyes and stilt-walking giants to muddle his big lolling head with all the refinements of the most civilized city in Italy. For all that the city tried to turn this charade of welcome into reality, there were fights and woundings and rapes in the streets, and it was the French, they said, who had sacked the Medici palazzo, even as the good Florentines surrounded it with guards and sent the clerks to make an inventory. All this we had in a letter from Signor Bibbiena, who was one of the clerks.

Maestro Ficino wrote to Cecco's parents, to tell those poor people what had befallen their son. How he had been brave and loyal to the last, as though that could comfort them. He offered me the letter, and a fresh pen to add my own words of condolence. I took it to my chamber, but I could not bring myself to write a word. Was I not the curse that had brought such terrible sorrow on that simple cheerful home? I could not bear to imagine Signora Corsellini's plain sweet face all crumpled with grief, or the dignified quiet with which his father would bear it; those tumbling, happy children with their brother gone. I had seen how proud Cecco's father had been of his son, the scholar, the hope of his family, who had died in a dream of faith to a man who barely knew his name. It was my fault, my fault. I had boasted to Maestro Ficino that I had the sight, and I had not even been able to prevent Cecco's death; we had been saved by fairground tumbling, and the loud voice of a girl who had conned money from the credulous by feigning dumbness. Cecco had been my friend, my true friend, he had even kissed me, and I had not saved him. He had died and I, who did not deserve it, lived.

I was glad that those first weeks were so hard, glad to have the ache of hunger always inside me, glad that after a day of hauling and fetching and cleaning I fell into a dreamless sleep in the nest of rags I had huddled together for a bed. That we had nothing did not seem to trouble Maestro Ficino. He did not mind the biting chill, nor the sorry messes of flour cakes and rotten cheese I scrambled together to feed us. By dint of an energy which surprised me in the old man, he made a snug place for himself in a little chamber off the library, where once I had rubbed the smoke stains away we saw that the walls were all set with coloured stones, a bright spring landscape which contrasted sharply with the endless grey without. He scavenged amongst the emptied closets and toppled cabinets and produced a collection of treasures. Such books as remained; a wonderful cup set in ivory, made of a single polished shell; a many-sided sundial in painted wood; an astrological chart in gilded leather with an ebony rim which he told me was ancient work, Arabic work such as might have come from Toledo.

I cared nothing for it. I wished to learn nothing more from him. I wished only to make myself as numb as I had once been in the kitchens of the palazzo, and I wondered what had become of the folk there, now they were fled, and often wished myself among them. Better that I had never been found, never been brought to the *scrittoio*, for then Cecco might have lived.

Maestro Ficino set himself to writing letters, searching out news of the family. He found a lad from the village along the hill to carry them and a nag to carry him. By and by, the people round about sought to make amends for what had been done to the villa, or perhaps they were merely afraid of a time when Piero might come to his own again, for I began to find little offerings laid out on the kitchen threshold, a few eggs, a loaf of new bread.

I thought it unlikely that Piero would ever return to Tuscany, even less so that he would remember his precious scholar lost in the countryside. He was at Bologna, he was at Venice, Donna Alfonsina had torn the rings from her fingers to pay him an army, but the Medici jewels were locked up in the Signoria and the French had taken what the Florentines had overlooked. And when the hunchback king marched on to Rome, God called on Savonarola, the monk of San Marco, to govern Florence, that it might be a righteous city, cleansed of the taint of the Medici tyrants. All this we learned from the letters that trickled in from the Maestro's correspondents all over Italy, but I paid scant attention.

To work and then to sleep and to bring no trouble was all I thought on.

CHAPTER NINE

THE DAYS WENT BY AND I BARELY SPOKE TO MY master. I tied my head in a cloth and went to the woods each day. There were mushrooms and garlic root for eating, and I found other things, some of which I had seen on my walks with my father. I gathered comfrey and alder to soothe the skin, dock and fern, radish root and fennel bulb, rosemary and sage, hyssop and mint. I went down to the vegetable gardens and saw that they could still flourish, when the spring came, that there would be figs, perhaps white peaches and rose petals for cordial. There was a fountain in the *cortile*, a naked boy holding a fish, where I gathered water lilies to stew the roots into a tea which staved away dreams. It gave me a bitter smile to think that once I had sought refuge in sleep. I scoured out the larder and set my herbs to dry there, so that gradually their sweetness covered the lingering stench of smoke. Careggi was more silent than a convent, but the peace did not soothe me. If I moved every moment I was awake, and swigged at my swamy tea like a *barbone* in a tavern, then I could check the remorse; but in the few moments between lying down and the opiate's curtain falling, my head was wild with ragged, unbearable screams.

A cart arrived, laden with boxes and bales of linen. Maestro Ficino came to me in the garden, his eyes dancing with excitement. I was prodding at the claggy yellow earth with a hoe, trying to dig a runnel to plant cabbage seeds.

'Ser Giovanni, he's coming! Look, he has written, he says he is coming here, to Careggi.'

I remembered the young man at the ball, Piero's cousin, who had betrayed him. I supposed he would be master here now.

'Well, I hope he brings some supplies. There's next to nothing for us, let alone a fine gentleman's servants,' I said sourly.

'Yes, yes of course, Mora. I'm sure Ser Giovanni will set everything to rights. But do you not see? He is coming, he will bring books, instruments. It will be like the old days. I shall go on with my work!'

I had heard plenty of the old days at Careggi, in the time of Piero's father, when a whole academy of scholars filled the villa, where the talk was all of Plato and magic and the old learning. I was sick of it.

'I'm glad for you, sir, I'm sure,' I answered, like a proper servant.

'No, Mora, you do not see. There was not time in Florence, I found you too late. I told you I had brought you for a reason.'

He was moving towards me, with an odd look in his eyes.

'What? What reason?'

His gaze moved along my body. I had put away my old draggled red dress, it was hardly decent and I feared to spoil it further. I wore a pair of breeches I had found in the stables and

144

a torn linen cloth tied about me like a shirt. The copper skin of my ankles showed above my boots.

'I will explain everything to you, Mora. But first, if you would,' his old voice grew wheedling, 'we should go indoors. I would have you undress.'

I thought he had run mad. And then I thought I knew all about that, and there would be no yellow silk cushions stifling me this time. I picked up my hoe and held it in front of me.

'For shame, sir! Do not come closer to me, or I shall strike you, I shall do it! And I'm sorry I saved you, I should have left you to burn.'

My eyes were brimming with hot tears, I could not believe that my quiet master should use me so. I was angry, so angry that I wanted to tear at him with my teeth. Maestro Ficino looked puzzled, then he stepped back with his eyes full of pity.

'You do not know? Mora, I am sorry. I had thought . . .'

'Thought what?' I yelled. 'Thought what? You take me and you keep me like a fairground creature and I work for you and I understand nothing and Cecco, Cecco.'

I was weeping now, sobbing with fury, and he reached out a tentative hand and touched my shoulder.

'I am truly sorry. Come, I mean you no harm, Mora. No harm. Come and I will explain to you.'

Warily, I followed him upstairs to his little library, still brandishing the hoe in front of me. Iron. Good for binding demons.

My father had known what I was. He had seen it in me, even when I was a tiny girl, Maestro Ficino said. I knew nothing as he had sought to protect me, but he had written of it, and his

145

letters had been copied to Ficino himself. He would have had me read them, had there been time, but they were lost now, trampled under some Gascon mercenary's foot. My master said he had been searching for me ever since the drawing of the Toledo angel had been seen in Italy.

'The *Almandal*,' I said, 'I heard him speak of it. The man who came to buy me.'

'Your father had very little time,' Maestro Ficino replied, 'but he knew what he was doing. The *Almandal* is ascribed to—'

'—Solomon,' I said wearily. I was tired of it, so tired of his mysteriousness, his belief in things which changed nothing. What stupid conjuring trick could bring Cecco back?

'Well done. For the invocation of angels, their names written with a silver stylus on a wax tablet. They manifest as children, in red garments, their hands blood red, crowned with roses.'

'So you know it was not real. Cecco thought—'

'Poor Cecco. He was too young, he was not so learned as he liked to think, poor, poor lad. He told you I wanted to summon angels?'

'Something like that.'

'I sent for you, you and the books. But I was away at Pisa when you came and since you would not speak they could not make out who you were, they thought you were bought as a house slave.'

'And slaves are invisible.'

'It is true, I should have taken more care to seek you out. But then I was so busy with my studies. It was not until Cecco saw you and recognised you as the wise woman's assistant—'

'He told you that?'

'But of course. Still, I needed to be sure. I had you speak with me, and it seemed to be so. Your father taught you much better than you think, Mora. I was ready, but then—'

'—the French.'

'Yes, and I thought my work would be destroyed.'

'Margherita. Her name was Margherita. She was good to me. But what she did, it was just cunning, cunning and a little knowledge of herbs, nothing more. She had no learning. Piero locked her up, you know. She didn't deserve that, either.'

'Indeed. But she saw in you what your father had seen.'

He was speaking in riddles, round and round we went.

'Seen what, Maestro? Please be plain, seen what?'

'It is delicate.'

I looked at the hoe, my foolish weapon, and wondered if I would have to use it after all.

'You might be a source, Mora. A key.'

I was losing my composure again.

'Maestro, if you do not speak plain I swear I shall beat you until your old bones rattle. Sir.'

Samuel Benito, Toledo bookseller, had advertised around Europe that his daughter was a freak, a changeling true, a monster. A between-thing, neither male nor female; hard and smooth where I should be soft and hollow; maleficent; cursed indeed. And when they came for him, the soldiers of the Inquisition, he calculated quickly that his conjuring trick would scare them off. But dressing me as he did also conveyed another

147

meaning – one that he hoped would allow me to be found. That, and my dowry of books, would explain who I was and make me precious indeed to the scholar who was lucky enough to get me.

That scribbled pamphlet I had seen in Florence, which I thought was sensation, a crude thrill for ignorant people, was full of signs for those like Maestro Ficino who knew how to read it. The flowers in my hair? The *eiresione*, the hermaphrodite's crown of flowers. The cochineal on my palms? The blood which one spilled in fallow fields when girls gave up their maidenheads on Midsummer's Eve, a sacrifice to make the soil fruitful, in the old way. The pose he had me take, staggering there in the window place, arms outstretched? The alembic, the contrary cup of the alchemists, the source of the Philosopher's Stone. Such an elegant key, my clever father had prepared, so learned, so witty. So Maestro Ficino had seen the drawing and read the letters, sent out the merchants stocked with Medici money to bring back his prize and I wished to every God I had ever heard named that I had stopped my mouth and stayed hidden in the kitchens.

I dropped the hoe so it clattered on the floor. My master watched me, and in his avid eyes I saw that he believed it. And I thought it might be true.

I thought of the crowd in the Zocodover, the startled maid. *Maligno.*

I thought of the hammam at Adara's house, of her hands passing over me, caressing, appraising. Of the fat old woman, who thought she might turn a fine profit from my strangeness. *Mind and be nice to the gentleman.*

148

I thought of my three enemies in the palazzo, how they had snatched off my chemise to stare and sneer.

I thought of my reflection in Donna Alfonsina's mirror.

I thought of Margherita. *Won't have the boys after you, will you?* And Cecco's sweet little brothers. *Are you a witch?*

And then I made myself think of what I touched when I washed or squatted over the pot. A nubble of skin like a bean in the place between my legs. Underneath, all smoothness. *People fear what they do not understand.* I had thought myself cursed, and I had thought right.

I wrapped my arms around my shoulders to stop the shaking, feeling the delicate bones beneath my linen, like folded wings. I could not cry. The troupe had been right, too. I belonged with them, a curiosity like Addio, a deformed thing like poor stumping Casinus.

'They should have killed me. They should have drowned me at birth like a kitten,' I spat.

'They would have done once, in Greece,' said my master placidly.

'The dreams I have?'

'A sign, a sign of what you might become.'

'Shall I grow a beard then, and you can show me at the fair for a florin?'

'Do not speak so lightly. It is a precious thing, a great thing. Come, sit. I will try to tell you.'

I could not listen. I jumped up and ran from the library, out across the grounds and into the woods. I ran until my breath scraped my lungs and my legs shook, stumbling and falling, heedless of the thorns and the goring branches that awaited my eyes. I listened for that fluid sliding rhythm of the ground beneath me, to run until I was lost in it and beyond pain. But I staggered clumsily, ripping at a torn trunk as it came up to meet me, slicing a deep cut in my palm. I paused and licked at it and rubbed my blood over my face. Then I sank down against a trunk and howled until my crying seemed a thing apart from me, a thing of the darkness of the forest, throbbing through ferny hollows and treetops. Gasping and whining until I came back to myself, panting and sore, I knuckled my eyes and they filled with dirt.

I would never marry, even if I could find a man willing to bed something as ugly as me. I would never have my monthly courses. I would never have a husband of my own, nor feel the plump, satisfying weight of a babe in my lap. If Cecco had known what his lips touched, he would have retched. I was a foul, unclean thing. I thought of my little cabinet of herbs, and how I believed I might make cures and be useful, and live quietly. I felt empty, scraped out inside with the loss of something I had never yet known. I saw now why my father had tried to teach me of the northmen, and their magic. Had he not told me that the *seid* was the gift of between-ones, those who slipped like shadows between the spaces of the world? *Mooncalf*, Margherita had called me, *mermaid*. Both things and not-thing. Nothing.

*

I went back, of course. I went back because I had nowhere else to go and winter was coming on and it was Careggi or starve in the forest. No one would ever want me now except Maestro Ficino, who had not even noticed my absence. I sliced off my hair with a kitchen knife, and stitched myself a clumsy shirt from a sheet. So, when Giovanni de Medici came, he found the old scholar and his boy slave, his apprentice. Just as Cecco had been. Ser Giovanni brought house servants and grooms and horses, and looked to set himself up as master at Careggi, since there was none other to challenge him.

Piero de Medici was fled from Florence, an outlaw with a ransom of four thousand ducats on his head. Savonarola, the monk of San Marco, claimed the French king as the instrument of God's justice, come across the mountains, just as he had predicted; to crush vice and exalt virtue, make straight all that was crooked, renew the old and reform all that was deformed. Charles installed himself in Piero's emptied palace and demanded one hundred and fifty thousand ducats as the price of the city's safety. If the Florentines did not pay, he proclaimed, he would sound his trumpets and put the city to the sword. The Florentines, who always cared more for gold than for honour, refused him. If he would sound his trumpets, they declared, they would ring their bells – and their defiance was successful, for the king turned his army on to Rome. With their money secured, they were willing to let Savonarola have a care for their virtue, and make him a greater tyrant than ever Piero had dreamed of being.

I feared that some of the mouths who travelled with Ser Giovanni might recognise me from the palazzo, but all had been so turned about since Piero's fall that none of them even thought on me. The talk was all of Savonarola, who had decreed that Florence must fast for its sins, and of those children of his I had seen parading through the streets. The 'Blessed Bands' they were called. They were hollow-eyed now with hunger, gathering books and pictures and all that had made Florence gracious and learned. The Dominicans rewarded them for spying on their own parents, reporting a game at cards for a few coins here, a treasured length of lace locked up in a marriage chest there. They carried olive branches and red painted crucifixes around the Signoria and, much to Maestro Ficino's disgust, it was said that angels had come among the people, to redeem them and bring them back to God.

'He called upon the people to put to death anyone who called for the restoration of my family,' Ser Giovanni explained. 'The palle are gone from every house in the city. Even my own.' He had the decency to look ashamed. 'We are called Popolano, now.'

'There are those who try to stand against him,' he went on. 'They throw stones at the bands and make a racket when he goes out to preach, but he is loved by many. They say that he will make Florence a new Jerusalem.'

There was a Venetian merchant who had offered a fortune for certain pictures; they made an effigy of him and set it atop a tower of scent bottles and gowns, fans, jewellery, looking glasses, velvet bed canopies and silk stockings, and fired it all. They burned words too, poems and plays and philosophy, anything that might distract the people from their duty to God or let them dream a while on something rare and beautiful.

'They seek magic books, Maestro. Books are silent heretics, they say.'

My master put his head in his hands and groaned. I thought of Cecco, of how proud he had been that ignorance and superstition would never govern in Florence. At least he had not lived to see his beliefs in flames.

'And what shall you do, sir?' asked my master carefully.

'The city grows hungry. They will need grain, and they will pay for it. I shall stay here and keep quiet and see about it, when the time comes. I am writing to the Countess of Forli, who has lands in the Romagna, great estates of wheat. I think she will be willing to sell.'

A silence fell. There was a fire burning in the library now, and wine and fruit on the table.

'And I, sir? As you see, it is more urgent than ever now that I continue with my researches.'

'You are welcome to stay as long as you wish, Maestro. I know of the high regard in which my uncle the great Lorenzo held you. I should be honoured if you would remain here at Careggi.'

So after all that had happened, it seemed that very little had changed. I spent each day with my master, shut up with the books, while the Duke of Milan turned his coat again and leagued with the Pope and the Venetians to drive the French out of Italy. Thus I heard the name Borgia for the first time. Borgia, the Spanish Pope. They said he had bought the papacy with a mule train of silver. They said he was debauched, a murderer. They said he knew the old arts, the black arts, that each night four or five men, bishops and prelates and others too, were found washed up in the river of Rome, and that no one dared speak for fear of poison. For all that he was a Catalan, the Pope claimed that he loved Italy, and would surrender his tiara rather than bow to the French king. Charles's army persuaded him otherwise, and that winter the gates of Rome were opened to them.

So skilful was this Pope, so subtle and beguiling, that Charles rode on to Naples believing that he would receive its crown from the Pope's own hands. Yet while he played the gallant with a whole chapbook of beautiful whores, and his men bit the very fingers from the women of the city just to have their rings, the Pope was scheming against him. By the summer Charles was chased out of Italy like a journeying dog, biting first one and then another, all his looted treasures left behind and his great army laid about with the pox.

Careggi seemed enclosed, marooned beyond the currents that were reshaping Italy. Only Maestro Ficino's correspondents brought us news of what was happening beyond the hills. In truth, though, my master cared very little for the tides that washed these armies up and down the peninsula. He cared little for the Pope and his Holy League or the Duke of Milan. His thoughts were all for me. He had me read to him from his own tracts on alchemy, and the Philosopher's Stone. I had heard of this from the mountebanks who thronged the street corners of Florence before the coming of the French, and I wondered why my master should concern himself with such things. He explained that this was no vulgar search for gold. He was not chasing after magical dreams of wealth. Rather, he sought a heavenly and spiritual substance, which could transcend nature itself and bring all things to their best, most perfect state. It was no chimerical phantasy, he said, but a sober possibility of Nature. It was not a stone, quite. Its appearance was a powder, almost impalpable to the touch, sweet tasting and fragrant, dry yet unctuous, capable of tinging a plate of metal. It was named 'stone' because its nature was so fixed as to resist fire.

'It is the father of all miracles, Mora, combining all the elements in such a manner that none will dominate, but rather produce a *fifth essence*, a glorious, spiritual gold. That is what we are seeking. That is why I needed *you*.'

His belief in it was so fervent that I could not help but be convinced. He was a great scholar and I knew so little. He thought that I had been brought to him by design, to help him; and I was so dull and sorrowful and disliked myself so for the twisted thing he had shown me I was, that it seemed my duty to do so. What other purpose could there be for me?

He talked and talked, and I tried to listen, though often it bored me and my mind would drift away. More often, though, it frightened and disgusted me. He did not mean to be unkind, my master. Indeed I think he even felt affection for me, so much as he could feel it for anything that was not written down in a book. But day after day, as he theorised and consulted his charts, I felt like a surgeon's specimen, pinned down to be sliced apart and the pieces served up for my master to scrutinise.

It would take many, many years, he said.

I would grow old at Careggi, I thought. Imprisoned by walls

of paper, as from the first, in that drawing of the flaming child in Toledo.

'"*Prima materies*,",' he read to me, '"corresponding to the synthesis of heaven and earth, to the spirit and the body, it contains all metals and all colours and engenders itself . . . the Philosopher's Stone, which is identified with it, is represented by a crowned Hermaphrodite."'

That, I supposed, would be me.

'"*Adamus philosophicus*,",' he went on, '"is double-sexed, because though he appears in masculine form" – where is your gown, Mora? – "he carries within him his wife Eve. That it may be realised in the mystic alembic" – you that is – "the magus" – myself – "enquires into the synthesis of contraries, as fire–water, sun–moon. The union of brother and sister elements, as reconciled in a medium which partakes of both natures, symbolises this return to the most ancient of unities."'

My master said it was natural and right that I should be humble, but he mistook me. I did not wish it to be true. I did not wish to believe that I should never be a woman, but there it was, concealed beneath my breeches, no dark hot place between my legs, but only that secret skin I blushed to touch. I came to hate my flesh so much that sometimes I thought of taking a knife to it, to cut out the pain.

As my master believed the planets to govern all the movements of the world, so Mercury amongst them was most apt to his purpose. We spent many nights shivering up in the broken loggia, where hatred of Piero had left us a fine observatory. My master watched the sky through a curious glass of his own devising, and I slowly turned blue as he tracked their movements through the dark, the three male planets, the three female, and Mercury, my planet, which was both and neither. Mercury, quicksilver, the liquid metal which can melt gold and regenerate it, mercury which can dissolve into all things like the shimmer of a peacock's tail. Sometimes, in the books, Mercury was shown as a breasted youth, sometimes as a naked girl, all smooth and flat like me, the *coroi*, my master called her.

When he judged the alignments to be correct, we would seal off the library with sheets of white linen and scent the air with perfume. Seven torches had to be lit, for the seven planets, the floorboards sprinkled with vinegar. My master bemoaned his lost harp, and his gemstones, for sapphire, he said, was very strong in the summoning of Mercury. I was to sit in a chair and my master placed a garland on my head as tender as a bridegroom, giving me a flower to hold in one hand and in the other a piece of unicorn's horn which had flown through the air with him to safety from Florence.

It never came right. No hovering phoenix appeared in the air before us as my master cast and chanted, no constellations of silver and gold for him to pluck from the air like fruits. I asked him once if he was not afraid that what we did was sinful and that a demon might appear before us, but he chided me for foolishness. Though no one could have looked more foolish than he, as he hopped around a heptagram dripped in candle wax on the floor with his robe hitched up and his bony ankles showing, so that for all my sadness it was as much as I could do not to laugh aloud.

'We must go on, Mora. I am an old man, I have not much time left. The calculations were not clear, I need more time.'

He had me sit up at nights copying descriptions of our attempts until my head ached and my eyes could not follow the letters before me. Then I would open the shutters so the fresh wet air of the hills came to me, and wish myself anywhere but closed up here with my dismal duty. Could this be what my father had meant me for? Then I thought on what I was, and saw that he was right, for what place could there be in the world for one such as me? Where else was there for me to go?

CHAPTER TEN

I HAD BEEN NEGLECTING MY LITTLE STORE OF HERBS since Ser Giovanni's arrival. I was so shy of everyone now that I barely ventured into the kitchens. But as it turned out, I was glad I had kept them, for when harvest time came Ser Giovanni was struck down with the gout. As the Holy League fought its last battle against the fleeing French, Ser Giovanni was confined to his chamber, his leg and his temper both aflame. He was no longer the proud, arrogant young man I had seen at the Medici ball. He had been quick to adapt himself to the times, and wise to retreat to Careggi. Fine manners and learned conversation were no longer respected in Florence. Now, Ser Giovanni played the country gentleman, meaning to make a fine profit on the sale of Popolano grain. He was out in the fields each day, until the humours mounted in his limb, swelling his foot until it bulged and shone like an overripe cherry. From the library we could hear him roaring at his men, furious that he could not be amongst them to oversee the gathering of the crop.

'It will pass,' said my master, irritably, 'they are all plagued with it, the Medici. I remember Lorenzo and his father giving audience from their beds in the *cortile* of the palazzo when they were struck down.'

'May I go to him, sir? I might perhaps help?'

'If you must, if you must, but hurry back, Mora. I want you about my translation of Psellus.'

Ser Giovanni had his foot propped on a stool before the window, anxiously scanning the sky for signs of rain. He had a little dog on his knee, and he winced at its every restless stirring.

'What is it now?' he grumbled. 'Oh, you. What's-your-name. Well?'

'You might let the dog go, sir. It will do no good. Here, I will lift him down for you.' Folk believed that the heat of an animal could draw away the pain, but I knew it to be useless.

'I have something else for you.'

'I want none of Ficino's meddling. What do you get up to in there anyway, closeted up with him? You should be out working with the other boys.'

'I do my master's bidding, sir, as do they,' I answered smartly. 'Here, I have made a poultice for your foot, a plaster of crushed fern, cooling, that would numb the skin a little and stop it breaking. And here, if you can take this with a little water perhaps. I do not think wine is good for what ails you. Celery root, boiled down. It will ease you.'

It did, and he was glad of it. In three days he could ride out and watch the carts roll back high with wheat for threshing. He commended me to my master, who grumbled when next I was summoned to attend to a maid in the kitchen, who had cut her arm on a rusty chafer and feared it would creep into her blood.

My master complained more and more as almost every day a message would come for 'the 'pothecary' to bind a bruised hand or bring a fever down. I was as glad as he was irritated, for it meant at last that I could go out with a basket into the warm air, so fresh after the stifling confinement of the library, to gather what I found and be alone a little. My head felt so thick with Latin and ink, it was a relief to pull off my cap and feel the sun on my shorn hair, to crush blackberries into my mouth and stretch my limbs on the road down to the village. I spoke little, but I smiled and tried to make myself pleasant so that soon I came and went like a familiar between the farmhouses and the offices of the villa. Like a plant that has been spliced but still yearns to grow, I felt myself knitting together a little – coming right, or as right as I would ever be. I liked the freedom of my shirt and breeches. Sometimes I ran just for the pleasure of it, and even felt young, sometimes, as I had a right to.

Ser Giovanni knew that I could read and write, and asked my grudging master that I might accompany him on his rounds of the land as a clerk, to take down how many carts of grain could be filled, and what it would fetch, and the profit that would be in it. I had never sat upon a horse, but I found I loved it, it came easily to me.

'You have good hands, boy,' Ser Giovanni said to me once as we trotted towards the villa at sundown.

It is a lovely time of year to be in the country, when the fields are empty but the shade is thick under the late summer canopy, when the air smells of dust and honey. From a distance, Careggi did not look ruined, the winter rains had cleaned the pale marble of the façade and there was smoke from the kitchens. I was hungry, I hoped there would be pea soup and rabbit for dinner, stewed with lettuce and capers.

'I am Spanish, sir,' I said carelessly. 'They say that we have a way, with horses.'

'Spanish? I thought you came from the palazzo?'

'I was Maestro Ficino's pupil there, sir. And then we came . . . here,' I finished stupidly.

He said no more, just kicked up his horse ahead of me and I went back to thinking on the rabbit.

The harvest was good that year. Ser Giovanni received news from the Countess of Forli, whose plentiful estates to the south would feed Florence that winter. He was never anything less than Medici, Ser Giovanni, for all that his new name and his support of the French had spared him Piero's end. He and his brother had wheedled their way back into the favour of the Signoria. They were appointed buyers for the city, and there would be money in it for the brokers. Once the Careggi grain was gone to the mills, my master grew crosser than ever, for Ser Giovanni had him turn clerk too, going over the Countess's figures. Caterina, her name was, signed in a looping sprawl at the end of her secretary's letters, sealed with an odd device of two serpents with little figures held in their mouths. One could make out their flowing hair in the red wax. It was a Sforza device, as the Countess was niece to the Duke of Milan who had brought the French king into Italy that he might have the coronet for himself.

Late in the autumn, Ser Giovanni left for her city of Forli, to entreat with her himself, leaving me to trail after Maestro Ficino in Cecco's place. My master was outraged at the indignity of it: that such a scholar as he should be reduced to scratching out sums on a slate! We entered the figures laboriously into the account books each evening, and if my master found it beneath him, it was melancholy enough work for me too; every stroke of the quill reminded me of Cecco, of my poor lost friend. It was as much as I could do to stay the tears from dripping down my nose and spoiling the parchment. He felt it, my master. He let his pen fall idle and I had to coax him to take up his work. I thought he could feel the cold of winter coming on in his bones, reminding him of how little time he had to complete his great work, though for myself I was not sorry it had been put off. I had had more than enough of mercury.

I tried to distract him by asking about the Countess Caterina. There had been talk amongst the stable lads when Ser Giovanni rode off, that she was a beautiful woman, and a scandalous one, and I was eager to learn more of her. I would fetch a hot posset from the kitchens and we would sit there, gossiping like two old wives.

'Tell me about the Castello, Maestro.'

My master's face softened. Since there was no one at Careggi with whom he might discuss his learning, he took some pleasure at least in telling me stories.

'Caterina is a Sforza, Mora. You must never forget that. The Sforza were the finest *condottieri* in Italy – they have warrior blood, and you see that it came out in her, for all that she is a woman.'

'What happened?'

'She was married to a nephew of the Pope, Girolamo Riario. When the Pope died, there were many in Rome who wished to deprive her family of their rights, and she rode out, great with child, you know, with armour over her gown, they say, and she took the Castel Sant'Angelo, the papal fortress, and held it against them until she had her due.'

'And then?'

'And then her husband, a hateful fool of a man, was murdered in their palace at Forli.'

I knew what happened next. How the Countess had taken unspeakable revenge on the treacherous people of Forli, how she had her enemies dragged from horses round the city square, their houses burned, their innocent children hurled down wells. Neither women nor priests were safe from this bloody virago.

'They said Riario's body was so riddled with stab wounds it resembled a sponge,' continued my master, 'and that his killers threw it from the window into the piazza. And then Caterina's executioner—'

'Barbone,' I breathed, thrilling like a child at the terrifying Turkish name. He smiled indulgently.

'Quite so, Barbone. Well, when Caterina captured the culprits, this Barbone hanged them from those same windows and had the corpses hurled down—'

'—where the crowd tore them apart like lumps of meat,' I finished gleefully. 'And then? Tell about the children, Maestro.'

My master huddled deeper into his cloak and sipped at his posset. I could see that he was far away, on the walls of that little city, watching the confrontation that had already passed into legend.

'So, the rebels who had murdered her husband wanted to depose Caterina and set up one of their own in her place. But she tricked her way into the fortress, the Rocca of Ravaldino, and stood there on the battlement to defy them. And they dragged her children out before her and threatened to put them to the sword if she did not submit.'

'And then?'

If I didn't know better, I might have thought that Maestro Ficino was blushing. 'You understand this is not suitable for, um, for the ears of a young person?'

'It's me, Maestro.' I risked a little familiarity. 'We are scholars together, no?'

'Well,' he leaned forward, whispering. 'And then, all defiance, the Countess lifted up her silk gown and she showed them her woman's parts and scorned them, and said that they might murder her children, for she had the mould to make others.'

I gasped with delicious shock, as I always did at this part of the story.

'But they did not?'

'No. Just like the Castel Sant'Angelo, she defied them, and she had her will.'

From the sniggering in the stableyard, I heard other things. That Caterina had lived like a princess in Rome, that she was a beautiful lady with an eager eye for a strapping young man, and that where her eye was pleased, she pleased herself.

'Fancy your chances, do you?' they teased each other.

165

'Not likely!'

For after the death of Riario, Caterina had taken another husband, a low-born man named Giacomo Feo, with whom she had a child. The people of Forli were shocked at such a disparagement, and they plotted to murder Feo when he was returning from hunting. Caterina's own elder son, it was believed, was amongst the assassins. And again the streets of Forli ran with blood as the virago took her revenge.

'And they say that Messr Giovanni's looking to replace him.'

'Rather him than me! Let's hope he wears his breastplate to bed her!'

I was drawn in by this talk, though I knew they should be ashamed if they thought that I was not quite one of them. What kind of woman could Caterina be, to take such magnificent and appalling risks? There was a saying in Florence: 'If you wish to live as you choose, you should not be born a woman in Italy.' The women of Florence lived closeted and quiet, yet this Caterina seemed as reckless and powerful as a man. I was fascinated by her, joining in the speculation that there was more than business between Forli and Florence.

When Ser Giovanni returned, though, it was not as an expectant bridegroom. He came storming into the library, where I sat writing as my master dictated from Scot's *De chiromantia*.

'This has to stop. All this. Now.'

My master plucked at the sleeve of his gown. 'I do not understand you, sir. Why do you disturb my work?'

'Your work? Your precious work will have us all burned if Savonarola has his way! Where's the girl?'

166

'The girl?'

Ser Giovanni reminded me of Piero at that moment, lordly, imperious, all Medici. He recovered himself and respectfully asked pardon.

'I have a letter here, from the prior of San Marco himself. It came to me at Forli. I have ridden through the night.' I could see, his handsome young face was drawn and there were yellow hollows beneath his eyes.

'I have no fear of the Dominican, sir. I have come against him before. He knows that my studies are the Lord's work, just as his prayers are.'

'He tells me I have been harbouring a sorcerer. That you are . . . conjuring devils and Christ's own mother knows what. The Signoria will not stand for it! We are Medici, remember, they want no continuing of Lorenzo's ungodly ways.'

'Was it not Savonarola himself who waited at great Lorenzo's deathbed in this very house?'

He breathes, slowly, resignedly, waiting for the end. With each breath, the wolves run across the mountains. They stream through the passes, fluid as wine, I taste their hunger. Each breath surges them onwards. Faltering, the man raises his hands to the priest who stands grim beside him. His hands draw the sign of the cross above his breast, the she-wolf raises her snout and howls.

'He writes that you have a familiar. A Spanish witch. That she spirited you out of the palazzo. Well?'

I looked helplessly at my master, who hemmed and mumbled and scrutinised his sleeve.

'Spanish?' he turned to me. 'Spanish? Ficino, I demand you

tell me what abominations you are practising here or so help me I will have you in the Bargello by nightfall and none of your sainted scholarship will save you from the fire.'

There was nothing for it but the truth, or a version of the truth, at least. I was sorry for my poor master, he was as much a slave as I at that moment. He had nothing but what his reputation and Medici charity had given him, and Giovanni could turn him out to beg his bread on the roads if he wished it.

'There is no harm in it, sir. She was a servant in Ser Piero's house, I saw she was intelligent and taught her. My apprentice was . . . lost, when the palazzo was attacked. I brought her here, we came with some travelling people and I thought it better she change her gown, for safety you understand, the French were on the roads. That is all.'

'So you are the girl?' He looked at me as if he were seeing me for the first time, and it struck me again how invisible we were to great people, how we only existed if we made trouble. Piero had lost plenty by that blind arrogance.

'Yes, sir. They called me Mora, at the palazzo.'

'Mora the apothecary. And where did you learn to heal? These are Spanish arts you have practised upon me and my household?'

'No, sir. I know what my master has taught me, from his books.'

'She is special, sir,' interrupted Ficino eagerly, and I burned with shame, willing him not to boast of our labours.

'You are too kind, master,' I put in hurriedly, glaring at him. 'All my poor knowledge has been gleaned from your wisdom.'

Giovanni paced up and down, the spurs snapping at the floor. 'I am sorry, Maestro. But I must ask you to give up your pupil. I have a use for her, and her skills.'

'You cannot, you do not understand. We are coming close!' I was astonished, I had never thought my master cared enough for me to shout.

'If the Signoria thinks that I am harbouring a sorcerer, the Dominicans will have you burned. And I shall lose my contract with Florence and we shall all be ruined. Do you understand me? You are most welcome to stay here and continue at your studies, but I can have no talk of witchcraft at Careggi. You must give her up.'

I was so sorry for my master in that moment. Whatever I had thought of his work, I had been honoured to be in the presence of such learning, and he had sheltered me. It was what my father had hoped, that a scholar who could read his key might protect me. What would Ser Giovanni do, if he knew what I truly was? He would turn me over to Savonarola and they would duck me in the Arno.

'She is nothing, sir, a slave. Why should you trouble yourself about her?'

I would forgive him. I would forgive him though his words went through my skin and squeezed around my heart. He had said no more than the truth.

'I wish to present her to the Countess. She is much interested in herbs and medicines. I will take her with me when we leave for Forli.'

PART TWO

FORLI

1496–1499

CHAPTER ELEVEN

W̲E SET OUT ON A BRIGHT MORNING IN DECEMBER.
I rode astride, comfortable in my boys' breeches and warm
cloak. Ser Giovanni had given me a good horse, a young chestnut. I shared his delight at being freed from his frosty winter
stable as his long strides covered the frozen ground. Ser
Giovanni was travelling as a merchant, not a Medici prince. His
clothes were as solemn and drab as even the fanatics of Florence
could wish, but his doleful appearance couldn't quite disguise
the light of happy expectation in his eyes. The closer we drew to
Forli, the more apprehensive I became, though the crisp bright
winter sun shone and Giovanni was in an exultant mood, singing
snatches of *strombelli* to himself and kicking his horse into a
gallop wherever the path lay clear. He, at least, was not fearful,
and when, bivouacked around the fire at nights, we heard the
wolves singing, nor then was I. The others might huddle closer
to the fire and draw their daggers near, but at night at least I
could believe I was riding towards a new life, free of old books
and rituals and the endless scratch of the pen that never let me
forget what I was not. The crying of the wolves brought back my

dreams of my mother, and I fancied again that she was bringing me safely to the Countess, away from the ghosts and griefs of Careggi. I was eager to see this extraordinary woman, I would try hard to please Caterina, I thought, and serve her well.

Forli, when we reached it after four days of hard riding, seemed at first a charming place. As we walked the horses slowly down the pass, I could see over the city walls to a circle of gardens, where cachi fruits, plump and orange-coloured, gleamed against leafless branches in the sharp winter light. Two rivers crossed the plain, and there were several water mills turning, whilst within the oval of the walls I could make out the roofs of fine palaces and churches, and a tall campanile adorned with a huge clock, such as I had never seen before. It wasn't until we drew closer to the principal of the four gates that I made out the hideous human skulls, draped with strands of hair and leathery flesh, impaled on posts to remind newcomers of what would befall those who were disloyal to Forli's countess.

We came into the broad piazza, with a church at either end, and I felt another shudder of disgust when I saw the Palazzo Signoria, blackened and abandoned, which the Countess had deserted when her first husband was murdered. I remembered Maestro Ficino's description of the people falling on the corpses of the murderers like cannibals. Yet there was no dark place on the stone flags to show where such horrors had taken place, and the stallholders and housewives in the market looked clean and cheerful, prosperous. It was difficult to imagine them as a howling mob of flesheaters. More difficult still to imagine the beautiful woman who greeted us in the inner courtyard of the

Ravaldino fortress as a creature of vengeance and nightmare.

The Countess of Forli was not young, perhaps in the middle thirties even, and her skin was a little lined. But that skin was the whitest I had ever seen, and her eyes, heavy-lidded and turned up at the corners, were amber-coloured, playful. Unlike Ser Giovanni, she was formally dressed, in a blood-coloured gown tightly laced and low across the bosom, the sleeves slashed to show a mantle of cloth of gold. She wore gold at her neck and her wrists, and a single huge ruby in the hollow of her throat that picked up the glints of gold in her loosely curled hair and those jewel-like eyes. She stood very straight as she moved forward in welcome, and made a half-curtsey to Giovanni – a perfectly balanced gesture of courtesy, which yet displayed her awareness of her higher rank. Maestro Ficino had told me that when she ruled in Rome like the Pope's own daughter, she had been presented with basins full of jewels so precious that they could have bought all the treasures of the Medici. But the woman before me would have seemed like a queen in a peasant girl's shift, so secure was she in her own powers to command.

Giovanni pushed me forward. I was conscious of how dirty my face and clothes were, and awkwardly uncertain as to whether I should bow or curtsey, dressed as I was. I removed my cap and make an awkward bob. I anticipated the usual expression of surprise when the Countess's eyes fell upon my face, but she remained cool and distant as her gaze travelled over my countenance.

'This is the child you told me of? Ficino's pupil?'

Giovanni nodded.

'Thank you. What . . . rare looks.'

'Mora.'

'You are welcome to Forli, Mora,' she said graciously, but she was already turning away. 'Your journey must have been most wearying,' she remarked to Giovanni.

'Indeed, Countess.'

'Then perhaps this evening we will dine alone.'

Behind me, I heard one of the grooms snicker. I did not see either Giovanni or the Countess for the next three days.

Perhaps a Sforza lady felt more at home in a fortress, for after the murder of her first husband, the Countess Caterina had never returned to live in the city. Instead, she had built a new palace within the curtain wall of the Ravaldino fortress. To my eyes, it still looked like little more than an armoury, certainly nothing like so grand as the Medici palazzo in Florence, nor even so refined as the ruin of Careggi, but the people of Forli were proud of it, naming it the 'Paradiso'. In case they ever forgot her power over them, though, the Countess had ordered the prison to be moved against her house where it connected by the *cassero* with the fortress – named, of course, 'Inferno'.

Within, the house was comfortable and graceful. The great sala was covered with frescoes, with tiled floors in deep blue and pale yellow which, with their airy designs of fruits and flowers, made me think of Piero's *scrittoio*. Beyond the house was a walled garden, most beautiful, with some fine statues, avenues of fig trees, and, to my great pleasure, a well-stocked herb bed. I wandered too in her hunting park, where it bordered the *cittadella*, the enclosed space for troops and weapons, discovering a pretty green summerhouse planted round with trailing roses. In truth, I had little to do those first days other than accustom myself to my new clothes. Once Ser Giovanni's servants had left, Caterina had a gown made up for me, much better than anything I had ever worn, of a heavy pewter-coloured damask with a green velvet cap that almost caught the glow of my eyes. I supposed that she would think of her new slave as a fashionable thing, like her *moresca* perfume holders, twined in silver minarets and studded with pearls. I had been so used to the freedom of my boy's clothes, at first the gown felt constricting, the tightly laced bodice leaving me breathless; but in a while I grew used to it.

The Paradiso was filled with beautiful things. It was clear that the Countess had always lived amongst beauty. The wellhead in the courtyard was of polished Verona marble, the loggia carved with foliage and animals and set with alabaster figures. Countess Caterina ate with gold spoons with her devices chased elaborately in their handles, the Sforza serpents writhing as she turned her hands. She drank from an enamelled ivory chalice, her gowns and linens were stored in painted caskets, the tapestries on her benches and tables were the finest silk, so heavy it took two men to lift one. Above all, she seemed to love mirrors. In her crimson-draped chamber a curtained recess held a looking glass of deepest ruby Venice-ware, with fat gold cherubs playing round its rim. I peeped at myself in that, and in the reflections of the polished silver basins in the sala, in the ivory hand-mirror that lay on the Countess's marquetry table, in the gilt-work night mirror with lamps set into its frame which stood by her high bed. And very foolish I looked; I might have been back in the porch of Santo Spirito, with my crown of coins, such a gewgaw I was, with my collarbones poking out like razor clams and my copper skin darkened from the sun of the Careggi countryside.

I was almost sixteen, but my chest stayed stubbornly flat and my hips and thighs were as narrow as a child's. I had been glad to pass for a boy at Careggi, but somehow it hurt more to remember what I was – and was not – here in this elegant house, surrounded by the beautiful possessions of a beautiful woman. I wondered if my mother would have pitied me, and loved me despite it all. I wished I could at least be plain, dull skinned and mousy haired and ordinary, but in my grey dress with my mop of white hair I looked like an icicle from a pantomime, an imp. When I began to attend on the Countess I was conscious again, as I had not been for so long, of the whispers and giggles that followed my progress in her wake. I tried to smile, and not seem too proud, and I was too ugly for any of the Countess's other maids to be jealous of me.

From the first, Caterina herself was kind. Because I was Ser Giovanni's gift, his learned Spanish slave, she had me attend on her. I had been so little around women, I feared that I should be clumsy. But it was not difficult to brush out her hair while she sat at her glass and gazed at herself like an oracle, nor to hand her a basin of rosewater to clean her face, or the gold pot of alum distillate that she rubbed into her skin to keep it so white. I soon felt quite the lady's maid, though it did not escape me that my own odd looks were a perfect foil to her own flourishing beauty.

And perhaps that was why she liked to keep me at her side when she gave audience to the Signoria in the fine apartments of her son, for whom she ruled Forli as regent. But it was dull work, all the same, for all that the things I handled were so lovely. I was glad, when Ser Giovanni returned to Careggi, that the Countess had time once more for what she pleased to call her 'experiments'.

The Countess had built a blue-tiled *farmacia* for her work, and here I felt at home. What knowledge I had I owed more to my father and my own gatherings at Careggi than my studies with my old master, but she found me as adept as I was willing. I was glad to be at work again, for so long as I had tasks to complete and make me feel useful, I felt lighter. Each morning, I would walk into the town to collect the Countess's orders from the spice dealer, Signor Albertini, and from the convent of Santa Maria della Ripa. Whilst the Countess attended to her business, I would prepare the pestles and mortars, the jars and instruments according to her own instructions, and then, about an hour before dinnertime, she would appear and we began. As soon as the Countess learned I could write, she gave me the task of transcribing her successful 'experiments' in a ledger. I explained that I had little Latin, but the proper names she dictated herself and for the rest I did my best with what I knew. It was a hodge-podge language I invented, but we could make it out.

That summer, naturally enough, we made beauty remedies. I boiled betonica root in oil and cooled it with rosemary as a tonic for the face, I mixed ampoules of aluminium sulphate with rosewater and juniper essence, which the Countess showed me how to distil, then beat into egg whites. A drop rubbed into the face and neck whitened the skin surprisingly – soon my sunburned face had taken on the colour of warm cream. We boiled cuttlefish in white wine to make tooth powder and a paste of cloves, nutmeg and sage to sweeten the breath. Ivy leaves stewed in water filtered through ash made a wash to lighten the hair. I combed it through and we sat together in the garden whilst I read to the Countess from Marullo's poems as her hair, streaming almost to the ground as she lay in the shade with her head propped on a cushion, brightened slowly in the sun.

If there was any doubt that Madonna Caterina was in love with Giovanni, her talk to me dispelled it. She questioned me about Careggi, about what he did and who visited him, about what he liked to eat and how I had cured the Medici gout. I answered her shyly at first, but she had a way of making my hesitant remarks seem fascinating. She told me of her own first visit to Florence, as a little girl, when her father had been Duke of Milan. They had travelled with five hundred soldiers, a hundred knights and fifty grooms, all in the Sforza livery, each leading a warhorse saddled with gold brocade, with gold stirrups and silk-embroidered bridles. She had been carried into the palazzo to be received by the Medici ladies in a brocaded litter, and been shown all its treasures. I told her about the snow statue, and the *scrittoio*, and how sadly I heard that Florence was changed. I asked her of Rome, which Cecco had always dreamed of seeing. The most magnificent city in the world, he called it. She smiled, and her eyes slid to the ground. It was splendid, she said, the palaces and basilicas, the cardinals with their great trains, the pilgrims from all over the world. But she had never cared for it, she admitted, it was Florence, ever since that first visit, which was the city of her heart.

In the autumn, Ser Giovanni returned, with a train of sixteen mouths, and it seemed as though he had come to stay for good. When I left the Countess for my truckle bed in her anteroom, I knew that the door to Giovanni's apartments would open softly, and that he would cross the sala to spend all night in bed with her. I stuffed my pillow over my ears and longed for my lily-root tea, for the sound of their love was hard for me to bear. It seemed cruel that I should suffer as all girls that age suffer, when unlike them there was no prospect of my greening being cured with a wedding. I clamped my knees together and ground my teeth and in the mornings, glimpsing myself while my lady was at her toilette, I thought I looked uglier than ever.

The Countess, though, seemed to grow more beautiful by the moment. In the mornings she was flushed and lazy, her ruffled curls tumbling into the lace of her chemise where it slipped off one rounded shoulder. She grew a little plumper each day, her skin as rich and smooth as junket, her belly a soft, quivering mound beneath her bodice, her breasts pushing upwards above her gown. With Giovanni there, she left off the severe colours she had been used to wear as the stern governess of Forli and dressed in violet and yellow, rose damask and cloth of silver, setting off the heightened colour in her cheeks. As I held out her chemise, she would pinch at the fat on her thighs and claim to despair at the rounding of her hips, but I could see from the way that she ran her hands over the contours of her body that she was pleased with what she saw. And at supper she would take a sweetmeat from Ser Giovanni's own hand, crushing it between her reddened lips, relishing it greedily.

With Giovanni's return, we made other remedies in the *farmacia*, receipts that reminded me of the prescriptions old Margherita had handed out. Castor oil and crushed red ants were the ingredients of one potion whose purpose the Countess, giggling, had me disguise in our book with a series of coded letters.

'Have you had a sweetheart, Mora?' she asked me suddenly.

I was surprised. It was the first time she had spoken to me of myself, of my own life.

'No, Madonna.' I could feel the blood rising in my neck.

'Would you like one?' she teased.

'No, Madonna. I'm content as I am.'

'Well, perhaps one day we'll find you a good husband,' she said gently.

I screwed up my face to keep back the tears, pinching the scuttling insects, enjoying the cruelty of dropping their tiny oozing corpses into the bubbling liquid.

'As I said, Madonna, I am content as I am,' I managed to force it out.

'But I have upset you. Come, tell me why. Are you not happy here in Forlì?'

'I am quite content.' But even as I said it, the tears were running down my face, tears for Cecco and my father and my ugliness, for all the losses and strangeness of my life. And before

I remembered myself, I gabbled out the story of what had become of my father, and how I had been sold away from Toledo, and how I never wished to love anyone again. I had no thought for her station, of how improper it was for me to speak to her thus, I simply wept, and talked, and in a while I began to feel a little better, as she listened gravely, never interrupting me.

When I was quieted, she said to me, 'I was married very young, you know.'

I watched her face. People will tell you things, if you keep silent long enough.

'I was just twelve. His Holiness wanted Imola, my city of Imola, for his nephew. They were nothing, the Riario, fruit sellers from Liguria until Sixtus won the papal throne. And then he wanted to found a family, a great dynasty. He went to the Medici to raise money, but was refused, so he came to my father, the Duke, and it was agreed. Imola would be my dowry. It pleased them both, I think, to feel that they had cheated the Medici, and I would have a great marriage. I think my father meant well, but he did not consider – I was too young, so very young, and my husband was not a kind man. They hated him here, you know, and in the end they killed him.'

I composed my face gravely. Everyone knew of the killing, and of the Countess's revenge.

'Did you love him, Madonna?' I asked.

'Never,' she hissed savagely, 'he was a fool and a coward. I am a Sforza, and he was no better than a market trader's brat. It was my blood they needed, as much as my money.' She laughed bitterly. 'God knows, I showed them what Sforza blood is.'

She looked away, and I wondered if she was remembering the dark stains on the flags of the piazza, those rotting corpses strung up to prove her Sforza will.

'So you see, Mora,' she continued, recovered to herself, 'there are worse things than having no husband. They say that if you wish to live as you choose, you had better not be born a woman in Italy, but I think we do very well here, nonetheless, no?'

She smiled a true smile then, a delicious, wicked smile, and reached out to brush the last of the tearstains from my cheek. 'You can always open your heart to me, you know,' she said smoothly, though I knew that our confidences were at an end for the present.

I turned back to my work, and as I stirred and measured I thought of her, wondering that she could show so calm and gentle when she had such steel in her heart. I was glad all the same that I had not told her that I had not, quite, been born a woman.

CHAPTER TWELVE

We WERE WALKING THROUGH THE PARK TO THE loggia, on one of the last bright days of the year. Countess Caterina walked ahead on Ser Giovanni's arm, a new gown of silver damask trailing carelessly behind her. There was no secret now as to what was between them, it was talked of openly in the town that the Countess would take another husband before the season turned. The ladies arranged cushions and unpacked baskets of cake and jam, setting out the picnic on linen napkins, one of them began to pluck at a lute. I stood by demurely, eyes to the ground, holding the Countess's reticule in case it was wanted. The ladies' voices carried high and clear in the warm air, which had the first whisper of winter dampness in it, a lower note, like the occasional rumble of Ser Giovanni's deeper voice as he joined the conversation. I thought we must look like a painting, gathered so, and tried to make the time pass by imagining which classical allusion a painter might take as his theme for a lady and her lover enjoying a sylvan feast. In any case, I thought glumly, I should always be the servant, standing attentively in the background.

It was soon to be All Hallows Eve, and the ladies were frightening one another with stories of ghosts and spirits, as the light turned from gold to grey.

'There was a woman at Modena,' one of them was saying, 'who had a priest as a lover, and they conjured demons together.'

'I heard that if you fill a glass bowl with oil and honey and set it before a tomb the spirits will come out to eat on All Hallows night,' giggled another.

Ser Giovanni suddenly noticed me, in that way great people have, as though they were surprised by the appearance of servants, like actors who had stepped through a curtain.

'Come ladies,' he said, 'this is childish talk, when we have a real scholar amongst us. A scholar who knows the magic of the East, eh, Mora? What should we do if we want to see a ghost?'

They turned their heads to me, some with a little quiver of distaste. I did not like to be noticed by them. I did not like the sound of that slave's name before them, I did not like their white skins and their light eyes. I could see the Countess watching me sternly.

'Please, your honour,' I began shyly. 'Maestro Ficino, whom the ladies will know is a very great man, teaches that there is a sympathetic relationship between terrestrial materials and celestial bodies. If the harmonies are aligned, as in the musical properties of the seven planets, then it is possible to speak with the spirits. We would have to purify a room, hang it in white and seal it, sprinkle it with rose vinegar, and then—'

'Thank you, Mora,' the Countess cut me off. My face burned. I was pompous. I did not know how to make charming conversation. Ser Giovanni looked embarrassed. I had failed him.

'There, there is another way,' I gabbled. 'We need laurel leaves, to write on.'

The Countess nodded indulgently at one of her women, who scampered off to rummage in the garden. I took a pen from her reticule and squatted down to show the ladies what to do.

'See, we write the name so, of the spirit we want to see. It has to be a secret, write the name of the person you want to see.'

Some of the ladies looked thoughtful, others tittered, but they all scrabbled for the quill.

'And then we hold it up to the sun, like this.'

We stood in a line, facing westward.

'So now, when you go to your beds, the spirit will visit you in your dreams.'

The ladies laughed, squinting excitedly at their leaves.

'But you mustn't tell, otherwise the magic won't work.'

'Then I hope you have chosen your ghosts wisely,' said the Countess dryly. 'Come, it is growing chilly.' I caught Ser Giovanni's eye, and hoped that he was pleased with his gift.

Next day when I drew back the curtains of the tester, the Countess's gold eyes were waiting for me accusingly.

'What did you mean, Mora, by that foolish game with the leaves?'

'Nothing, Madonna. Excuse me. It was nothing, just to amuse the ladies, you know. To do it properly . . .'

'I know, one needs amulets and incantations and heavenly lyres,' she was smiling, her sternness was a game.

'So you summoned your spirit, Madonna?'

'I did, and most gratifying it was. My husband,' she stretched luxuriously, her hair tumbling from her cap, 'was quite pleased to have a little excursion from Hell. And I to send him back there. Thank you, Mora, I slept excellently.'

I did not believe her, how could I? And yet I was glad, so glad that I had pleased her.

'If you like, I could cast a chart for you. Maestro Ficino taught me well.'

'And what might you see?'

'Oh,' I said slyly. 'Weddings, and such things, you know. Venus riding on a stag with her hair all unbound, holding an apple and a flower garland. Love. Abundance. Those things.'

'Is that so? Well, we shall see, shall we, little witch?'

Witch was not a good word. Witch was a word of howling crowds and spitting priests and cells and flames. Witch was the thin line trodden by Margherita and her kind, who took refuge in madness. Witch was what we had fled, my old master and I, when I pushed him out of a window in Florence and made him fly to the ground. *Maligno, demonio*. But in her pretty mouth it had a sweet sound, not 'Moor', not nothing, but a name made just for me.

The turn of a season is an odd time, a perilous time. As the winds shifted and grew colder, changing the pressures of the air, Caterina's youngest child, Bernadino, fell sick. I had seen little of her six children. Of those she had borne to her first husband, the eldest – the Pope's nephew, Ottaviano, who one day would rule Forlì and Imola – was training as a soldier, whilst her second boy was in orders, and her daughter, Bianca, already betrothed. Bernadino was about six, the child of handsome, low-born Feo. Feo had been as hated in Forli as Riario and, like Riario, the people had murdered him. The Countess had wreaked terrible revenge upon them for their act.

The younger boys had their own household within the Paradiso, where my lady would visit them each day, and I never went there until a maid was sent for me in the *farmacia* to tell me that the little boy lay ill with a high fever. The Countess's 'experiments' were not merely for her own amusement. In the old-fashioned way, she doctored her family and her servants, noting the success of her cures as my father had done, as I had done at Careggi. Yet she was gone to Imola with Ser Giovanni, to see after the last of the grain harvest, so there was a mutinous look on the maid's face; I could see she resented that I was being called to the Countess's place.

Bernadino lay on a daybed in the nursery, with the shutters closed and the fire banked high as he sweated and trembled with the sickness. The nurse stood by with a wetted cloth, smoothing his brow under damp gold hair the same colour as his mother's. Though his eyes were glassy and far away and his face was wan, I saw that he was a pretty child. I put my hand to his temple and to the fluttering throb in his wrist and asked the maid when it had come on.

'He had a fever three days ago, but very slight. It had gone by evening.' Her voice sounded close to tears, she was terrified that she might lose her place or worse if something befell the child while his mother had left him in her care.

'It is quartain then.'

The fever that creeps into the blood from wet marshy places, attacking every third day. Many are brought low with it in Italy, and whilst a grown person may wait out the cycle, I knew it could be fatal for little ones. There was a seed my father had used to bring it off, swertia, ground with cloves and cinnamon; but I doubted I could find such a thing in Forli. It grew in the high mountains of the East, where the silk for my mother's wedding gown was made. Gentian was close to it, I would need that, and lemons, basil leaves, black peppercorns. I sent the maid to the kitchens to ask after the fruit. She brought it to me in the *farmacia*, where I was roasting a spoon of alum on a metal plate. I ground it with the pepper and basil, and mixed in water and lemon juice, adding a spoonful of honey to help the child swallow it down. I sent the nurse away.

'I will sit with him.'

Just a little after he had taken the mixture his brow cooled and his pulse settled. I changed the pillow beneath his head and watched him sleep, wishing I knew some childish song, such as a mother might sing, to comfort him. I opened the shutter a little to clear the air in the room and looked out across the walls at the city. I might be peaceful here. I might tend to the Countess and work in the *farmacia* and wait quietly when she rode out hunting. I might walk to San Mercuriale and light a candle for poor Cecco's soul. I felt the warmth of the fire spreading into me, and contentment came with it. I knew I should never forget what I was, but I might grow a little more comfortable with it, grow to believe that here, perhaps, was a place for me in Forli.

So I sat and dozed through the night, making sure to administer the medicine at the sound of the first bell, and when I woke again there was the boy, bright eyed and laughing in his mother's arms, she all flushed and muddied from the fast ride from Imola, and covering her son with kisses.

Mora Buona, she called me. Good Mora. But I liked *little witch* better.

*

One day my lady came to me as I was sorting her chemises for the laundress, running my hands over the delicate lawn, looking for tears or stains, and placed her hands over my eyes.

'What is it, Madonna? What's the matter?'

She was giggling like a girl, delighted with herself.

'Come, Mora. I have a present for you.'

I had not had a present since Adara gave me my lost doll. I stumbled before her, she guiding me so I did not fall. We passed through the sala, down the stairs to the hall where I smelled roasting meat from the kitchens, out into the cold air. We crossed the courtyard, slick with wet, then turned towards the stables, passing through a door into a place which smelled not of leather and animal sweat but clean and crisp, of soap and mint.

'Look, Mora, look!' She clapped her hands and when I saw what was there I began to cry. She had made a little room for me, with a settle and a table and a fireplace. There was a quire of paper on the table, and an ink bottle and a box of quills. A package of books in oiled canvas, sealed with red wax. She danced around, showing me what she had sent for from Florence and even Venice. The smell as I unwrapped the parcel was of my papa's house and I cried all the harder, half in sadness and half with joy. There was a candlestick and a box of real wax candles for when the winter days grew dim, an astrolabe and a cushion for my back.

'Are you pleased, little witch? See, now you can cast your spells in peace!'

She was teasing me and I laughed with her as I went on my knees to thank her for her goodness to me. I was quite overcome. I was full of pride. I had a *studiolo* all of my own. I thought I could write a letter to Maestro Ficino, to tell him how I did, and that he would be proud of me that my learning had brought such credit. I should sit in my own room, on my own seat and wait for a letter in return. I could read and read, and learn Greek even, and write to scholars in far away lands as my papa had done.

That winter, I thought that the dreams, the black dreams, had finally vanished, replaced with visions of a future where I should be safe. I had my own room, here in the Rocca, and it did truly seem a paradise to me. I was full of plans for what I should become, I thought even that I could send for one of the little Corsellini boys and have him to a student, so grand had I grown in my own eyes. No one laughed at me now, and if there were some puzzled, jealous words from the Countess's ladies I did not care for them, for she cared for me. I thought I was precious, as my papa had told me, not for some old man's fancy that my deformity made me a mystical prize, but for myself, for what I knew and how I could use it. For the first time since Adara carried me through the streets of Toledo, I felt valued and safe.

But then the comet came.

*

For weeks after Twelfth Night, a blizzard enclosed Forli in an eerie snow-cloud, the roaring of thunder muffled by the incessant soft fall. We were cosy and merry enough in the Rocca, though. The Countess kept the *cittadella* provisioned permanently for siege, and we were glad of it as the drifts banked up against the walls. There was music and dancing each evening in the sala, and now I was no longer so awkward and fearful I quite enjoyed watching the ladies as they darted and spun. The Countess and Ser Giovanni would retire early to her apartments to discuss their business. The grain accounts, she said, needed a great deal of attention. If the townsfolk were gossiping, her little court in the Rocca were mindful enough of her authority to confine themselves to no more than knowing looks and smiles. Towards the end of the month, the snow cleared, but the sky darkened from the grey of a goose's wing to the black of a raven's, so that we had to light torches even at noon, until the day when the countryside was lit up by a series of explosions, a giant's firecrackers – and then even the Rocca shook as the comet struck on a hillside just beyond the walls.

The Countess sent militiamen with shovels to clear a path that she might see for herself what had happened. She insisted I ride out with her to inspect the site where it seemed all the people of Forli were gathered, fearful as to what the comet's appearance might portend. They held up fragments from the fall as we passed, some three sided, like cracked iron, others as large and lustrous as the Countess's own famous pearls. The impact had hollowed out a great pit, as large as a house, into which the snowdrifts were already subsiding.

'What does it mean, then, Mora?' The Countess was turning to me, her tone light, but her gloved hands were playing tensely with the fur collar of her mantle. I wondered what answer Maestro Ficino might give.

*

The rain is lashing the walls of the Rocca. Darkness, except where the booming guns find their targets and howls go up from the walls as figures collapse into invisibility. Then fire, its orange glow silhouetting the swarming, desperate figures on the ramparts as the guns pound on, until suddenly the wall sways and bellies, the great stones seeming to hover, suspended for a moment in nothingness until their weight brings them down and the fortress splits apart like an egg, bleeding fire. From the breach walk two men and a woman, her spine proudly erect, her dress smeared with smoke and blood. Caterina. Her hair hangs forlornly down, plastered by the rain, but she holds her head up and does not look back at the dark shapes, firelight glinting on their drawn swords, who swarm like ants into the crack. The man beside her attempts to take her arm- in support or in possession – but she shakes him off and continues, her amber eyes blind with grief. Behind her, the second man, a dark blur in the darkness. Until the fire from the walls catches his face, the brim of the black hat hiding his eyes, but the mouth visible, smiling, a glint of teeth as white as the pearl on his collar. Him.

*

The dream had come to me so quickly that I staggered a little, dizzied with it.

'I think it means nothing, Madonna. These things are much more common than we suppose. Maestro Ficino would say—'

'It is an ill omen.'

I closed my eyes, trying to blink away the image of the man in black following the Countess from the wreck of the Rocca.

'If you'll forgive me, my lady, I think not. Iron has many properties. It can bind spirits, drive away curses. Perhaps if the fragments were to be gathered together, blessed, this might bring good fortune,' but I was babbling, and we both knew it.

'It is an ill omen.'

'Yes.'

The Countess ordered that all the pieces be collected together, and declared that she would have a monument made to them in marble at the church of San Mercuriale. But that winter the rains fell and the floods came, and though bread was sent out from the Rocca, there were many who starved in Forli, and many more who blamed not the comet but the Countess for defying its warning.

My dreams returned, haunting me as I worked in the *farmacia* or combed out the Countess's hair or tried to lose myself in my studies. I thought again of my mother and the charm she had worked into my old red dress – she'd had the sight, and knew what it meant. And sometimes I saw myself, standing in the window above the Zocodover, the light streaming out behind me and my hands gleaming red, and I thought of what I was, and how I was cursed. I thought perhaps I should run away, that it was me who would bring bad luck to the Countess, but I pushed it from my mind. I was happy here, and besides, I knew now that however far I ran, the shadow of the man in black would find me.

CHAPTER THIRTEEN

HAD PROMISED MY LADY TO CAST A CHART FOR HER wedding, and I dearly hoped that she would take Ser Giovanni as her third husband. He was a Medici gentleman born, and surely the people of Forli would love him for his handsomeness and his fine manners and his Florentine gold as much as they had hated the others, men who they had taken from her with murder. When she had me take the maids to the gardens to gather white and yellow jasmine and heavy-scented tuberoses to garland the pavilion, I was glad, for I thought that they would be betrothed and that her city would celebrate with her. I thought that with a strong young husband at her side, her lands and her family would be safe. Yet there was no proclamation of the wedding, no exchange of letters and gifts and no great people arriving to feast at the Rocca. There was only the Countess in her nightgown before dawn on a late summer's morning, bidding me rise and help her to dress; a walk across the silvered parkland, our feet making deep prints in the dew; Ser Giovanni waiting in the summerhouse with a monk fetched from the convent; and a ring that passed from his hand to hers and then to mine, for I was her witness and I was to keep her secret safe.

There was talk, of course, that the Countess was secretly married, but I kept my countenance and held my tongue, letting out her bodices and lacing her less tightly, but it would not be long before her belly showed the world what she still denied. Her uncle, the Duke of Milan, would be sorely angered, she told me, if he learned that she had married without his permission. Forli was too isolated, too weak without the protection of the Sforza. When Il Moro sent an envoy from Bologna to sniff out the rumour of the marriage, my lady put on her widow's weeds, draping herself in heavy black, and Ser Giovanni kept his own room. The rumours of love between them were lies, said my lady sweetly; her Medici guest had prolonged his visit to see about the harvest for which Florence hungered, and to avoid the trouble which had befallen his family there. There would be no new marriage, she claimed, that her uncle did not choose for her. The sala at the Rocca glittered with all her treasure of plate and she murmured as she served the envoy's wine with her own hands in a gem-encrusted cup that she was a poor widow, who counted on the goodness of the Duke to protect her. Ser Giovanni made it plain that he was no lover of the French, and sent his loyal respects to Milan. My lady, meanwhile, wrote a pious letter to Savonarola in Florence, expressing her wish that he would assist her to come closer to God. The Florentines bought another huge consignment of grain and ten lions were ordered for the hunting park of the Paradiso; the envoy departed no wiser and I thought the Countess must be very clever, to get what she would have from all, and commit herself to nothing.

It pleased her, as her time drew near next spring, to walk the walls of the Rocca, looking down over the *cittadella* and the town. After the child was born, she would build a new house outside the city, where the air would be fresher in the summer, and where she could retire when the time came for her eldest son to govern.

'Or perhaps we shall go to Florence, Mora. It is so long since I visited. Should you like that, to see Florence once more?'

I did not care much for the idea of Florence, but so long as she said 'we' like that and turned her eyes upon me so gently, I think I should have followed her anywhere. Or she would speak of the child, a boy, we were both certain. He would be her seventh, and sure to be a great man.

'He shall be a soldier, certain,' she said, 'a true Sforza warrior.'

She told me of the first Sforza duke, the greatest *condottiero* of Italy, and how his mother had trained all her children, even the girls, to fight like Roman gladiators. The Sforza were Tuscans, like the Medici; the finest soldiers in Italy were Tuscans.

'He shall have warrior blood on both sides, Mora. The Medici claim one of Charlemagne's knights as the founder of their line.'

'Truly?'

She laughed. 'No, not truly. But a better story than money grubbing in the Mugello marshes, no?'

The baby came in April, on a night so filled with stars that the sky looked like black sequins in a cloth of silver. It was an easy birth; the child slipped out like a fish, and bellowed and grasped his mother's hair so that even in her pains she laughed and kissed him. When he was washed and had been put to her breast, she told me to carry him to the window, to bathe him in the starlight. Our shadows fell on her pillows. 'I'll call him Lodovico,' she said softly, 'for my uncle of Milan.'

Men like my old master were so dedicated to detecting the auguries of fate that they overlooked its most obvious manifestations. While Piero de Medici was playing the prince in Florence, the statue he commissioned in snow from Michelangelo was thawing quietly to nothing in his own court-yard. The struggling figures of the angel and the serpent collapsed gently into an embrace, drop by gelid drop his power was melting and he never troubled to notice. So my lady chose to celebrate her last son's birth that spring and rejoice in the bright stars that heralded his coming, allowing them to eclipse the memory of the comet. I went to my books and tried to work diligently with my compass and my astrolabe, but she barely gave a thought to my researches, lost in milk and the sweet-hay scent of her baby boy, a true Madonna. Each day, her messengers brought news, and I began to see that the new baby's fate would not be determined by the planets but, like all the people of Italy, by Rome.

I dreamed of wolves again. Huge black wolves, streaming down a mountainside, slavering, savage. I dreamed too of a great bull, rampaging through the farmlands of the Romagna under a flaming sunlit sky. The devices of the Borgia, the bull and the flaming double crown of Aragon. I dreamed I saw a palace where the bull walked docile between the streaming rays on the walls, ridden by Cupid. I tried to warn her. I explained, as though to a child, that the Borgia bull must be tamed or it would ravage and put the countryside to fire, and she listened to my child's stories with her head on one side and her amber eyes the colour of the Aragon sun and told me that my dreams were very pretty and that she ought to have me whipped for lying, for what could a slave know of the great game of politics?

I was ashamed then, and dared not tell her of my other dream, of the Rocca all aflame and she led out captive, like a pagan queen, through her ruined city. She believed herself indomitable, Caterina. She had her sons and her young Medici husband. She was beautiful and beloved in her cities of Forlì and Imola, and her uncle was the lord of Milan. Had she not held the Castel Sant'Angelo against her enemies? Had she not defied those who rebelled against her and scorned their threats to murder her children and triumphantly revenged herself? Had she not lived as it pleased her, for all that she was a woman? She was a Sforza. What need did Caterina, Countess of Forlì have of the counsels of her maid, cobbled together from eavesdropped dispatches? So I held my tongue and dandled her baby and kept my place. But I wish I had not.

I heard him called a sorcerer, the Borgia Pope. He had cozened his power from the devil himself. I did not believe greatly in the devil, he was not someone for whom my master Ficino had much time, but then nor did I believe in the powers of sapphires and unicorns. People fear what they do not under-stand, true; yet my lady thought she understood the Spanish

Pope too well. He had long been her ally, and she saw no reason that he should not remain so. In the days of her first marriage when she had queened it in the Holy City and Alexander VI was Rodrigo Borgia, the Catalan cardinal, they had been friends, such friends indeed that Borgia had stood godfather to Caterina's first son, Ottaviano. And had he not restored the Riario palazzo in Rome to Caterina once the papal tiara was on his head, receiving her ambassadors with honour and giving a cardinal's hat to her uncle Ascanio Sforza? And now, had he not just offered his own daughter, Lucrezia, as a bride for his godson? And Caterina practically laughed in his holy face.

They quarrelled about it, the Countess and Ser Giovanni. I was as eager to listen to their talk as I had been to avoid the sighs of their lovemaking, though it grieved me to hear them at odds.

'It would be unwise to offend him, my love.' Ser Giovanni's voice was soft and reasonable. I heard my lady pacing their chamber in the darkness.

'He is a Sforza! Would you give our son to a Spanish bastard?'

'Ottaviano is Riario's son, too. We may have need of Rome, in time. And the younger boy is married to a princess of Naples.'

'Sancia of Aragon?' my lady hissed scornfully. 'A bastard married to a bastard. And she is Cesare's whore.'

I knew that name. Cesare Borgia was cardinal of Valencia, the lover of his own sister-in-law and, it was whispered, of his own sister too.

'Would you have my son polluted with incest as well as bastardy?'

She spoke of the scandals of the Pope's children, the same as I had heard whispered in the stables and the kitchens and the marketplace. Of Juan, Duke of Gandia, the second of those beautiful, dissolute siblings whose body had been fished out of the Tiber, a sponge of stab wounds. And everyone knew, but no one said, that it was Cesare who had put him there.

'He will have Cesare renounce the cardinal's hat. He has sought Carlotta of Naples for a bride, and Federigo of Aragon gives out that a Borgia will do for his bastard but not his own true born child. Is a Sforza to stoop where a Spanish interloper will not bend?'

'They say that she is beautiful, the girl.'

'She is a whore! I had it from Mantua that she had a bastard to her own father, hidden away in a convent. Has she not shamed my family enough?'

Caterina might say that a Borgia bastard was no wife for a son of Sforza blood, but this Lucrezia had been married to a cousin of the Countess, Giovanni Sforza of Pesaro. Lucrezia's father and brother insisted on a divorce, forcing Giovanni to claim that he was not enough of a man to make the marriage true. I thought the Countess might pity her a little; for all she was the Pope's daughter she remained the pawn of her father and brother, to be pushed passively across the chessboard of Italy where they willed it, just as Caterina herself had been.

'They are calling her a virgin still. She's the laughing stock of Rome.'

'We must think. Why did His Holiness take his child from Pesaro and offer her to you?'

'So that her children will rule Forli and Imola. I will not have it. I want no more papal meddling in the Romagna. Ottaviano will marry where I choose, and I do not choose a Catalan whore for my son.'

All the gentleness was gone from her voice. I heard the woman I had been told of, before I came to Forli – defiant, fearless, bowing to no man's will. Ser Giovanni was no match for her. So the Countess of Forli wrote to the Pope most politely that she did not think that her conscience could accept a divorced woman for her son, even one whose chastity had been so vigorously proclaimed as Donna Lucrezia's, and she wrote to her uncle of Milan that she cared too much for Ottaviano to entrust him to a whore and a poisoner.

There was no more talk of Rome. Nor did the Countess seem much concerned with the new French king, Louis XII, who had taken his throne the same month that she declined the alliance with the Borgias. Florence was allied with France and Forli with Florence. There was no cause for anxiety. More pressing was the Florentine's war against Pisa, which Piero de Medici had so carelessly thrown away to another French king, and which Giovanni was determined to help them take back. That spring, the Lion of St Mark flexed his muscles, and news came that the Venetians planned to move into the Romagna in support of Pisa. Forli would remain neutral, but Caterina had obtained a *condotta*, a paid mercenary post, for her son Ottaviano, and like their Sforza ancestors, he was now obliged to turn out his men. Giovanni, she insisted, must accompany him. The Florentines ignored her increasingly urgent requests that they garrison the mountain passes. Caterina temporised with the Venetians, proclaiming that her neutrality was unaffected by the fact that she was sending her son to fight on the other side as a business arrangement, yet she grew more and more anxious, and had the walls of the Rocca inspected and reinforced.

Giovanni was ill the day I bade him farewell. The gout, that plague of the Medici, was grieving him and I had prepared a medicine of lime paste to ease the pain in his leg. He thanked me and bade me have a care for his son.

'I'll be home in the autumn, Mora. And perhaps we will go to Florence again, now that the mad monk is where he should be, eh?'

The priest who had burned the treasures of Florence had perished that year in the flames of his own ardour. The Florentines who had so joyously gathered up their wigs and rouge pots, their perfumes and trinkets, their books and their paintings and cast them all into the fire now crowded to the Signoria to see Savonarola himself consumed by the blaze. His very bones had been reduced to ashes and scattered on the waters of the Arno, and the people cried 'liberty' once more. But I could not rejoice with Giovanni at the thought that the Medici might have their own again. It was the Pope in Rome who had brought about Savonarola's end, always the Pope behind it all, and I saw him as a fat spider, squatting in his palace, spinning a web in which all Italy would flail and stifle.

'Will we see a Medici in Florence again, Mora?'

His tone was teasing, yet I sensed the need in his question.

'I make medicines, sir, not predictions, as my lady the Countess reminded me. God speed you safe home.'

I stood on the walls of the Rocca and watched until Giovanni and his column of men were obscured by the dust from their horses' hooves. He seemed a boy to me, peacocking in the chased silver armour my lady had ordered him from Milan, a boy playing at war and greatness, who had no care or knowledge of the conflagration that awaited him. And how could I warn him, when I had seen it only in my dreams?

Giovanni did return home that autumn – but to Florence, not to Forli. And he did not ride at the head of his men, a Medici champion, but in the plain wooden coffin of the soldier he had never truly been. All summer he had sickened and failed, though he wrote daily to Caterina, reassuring her of the news from the field, even as the Venetians drew closer, anxious to hear when Il Moro would finally send the troops he had promised from Milan. Not until September did his letter reveal his illness and urge the Countess to come to him. Though we rode hard for Bagno, Caterina arrived only in time to hold him in her arms as he left her. We remained in Bagno just long enough for the arrival of Lorenzo, who came to transport his brother's body for burial in the Medici chapel in Florence. The Countess spent her time in prayer until his arrival, but when he was announced she rose from her knees and greeted him with the same regal haughtiness she had displayed on our arrival in Forli two years before. Lorenzo offered her no condolences, and beyond the merest words of convention, nor did she console him for the loss of his brother. The marriage had created no family affection between them. She did not wear mourning, and on the ride home she sent her men before her with her own standard and that of

Giovanni. Whatever her grief, she kept it to herself, and I barely heard her speak in all the three days of the journey. There could be no bloody revenge for Giovanni, no public quarterings to assuage the violence of her misery. His death was not to be spoken of. I wondered how it should go with her then, into what conduit her rage should pour, but I did not dare to offer her comfort, for what comfort might I offer, I who had never loved or been loved?

So we returned to the Rocca, and much of that winter was spent by my lady in correspondence, with her uncle of Milan, with the Venetians. She began to send out her jewels and her plate to dealers in Rome who could supply her with money to pay troops. Something had shifted in Caterina, the loss of Giovanni had hardened her. The woman she had been was giving way to something else, something ruthless and warlike that it pained me to see. That soft, contented flesh which had enfolded her began to fall away, showing the planes of her face sharp, and though she looked beautiful still, there was something fierce and wild in her face now.

When she was not in her *scrittoio*, she rode out for hours, galloping away her grief so that her horses returned broken-winded and covered in foam, and the grooms complained. Nor was this enough to calm her. I had thought that with Giovanni gone it might ease her to have me to sleep in her chamber, but my truckle bed was set up in the anteroom as usual, and still I heard the soft click of the door to her rooms night after night. I did not know which of the young men about the court visited her when her doors were closed, and nor did I care to, but what I heard – and I could not help hearing – was far removed from the joyful cries of her lovemaking with Giovanni. It was not love I heard then, but desperation, as though in the poundings of a young man's body Caterina sought to bludgeon herself into quietude. Some nights the straining of the bed, the slaps and gasps, were so loud that I felt my face burn in the darkness and wrapped my ears in the coverlet for shame. And yet I was not sorry that I heard it, for the savagery of those cries spoke to me in a manner which the idea of pleasure never could.

With the spring, Il Moro's ambassador, Signor Orfeo, arrived in Forlì. Despite a season's worth of pleading, no troops had been sent from Lombardy, and as the Countess hissed furiously at the nervous Milanese when they dined together for the first time, her uncle appeared to believe that she could defend her affinity with words.

'Will your master's pretty phrases hold my walls against the French?' she demanded furiously. 'Will his assurances feed my men and buy my powder when Valentino calls out the Romagna? And my uncle is a fool if he believes that this *beast* he unleashed on Italy will not turn upon him once more. Do you hear me, a fool!'

Signor Orfeo stared at his plate, his eyes shifting anxiously in the candlelight. It was true that all Italy was speaking of Cesare Il Valentino. Louis of France was determined to claim his rights to Milan through the Visconti heritage he shared with Caterina – and, they said, to reclaim the Kingdom of Naples, which Charles VIII had briefly held when he came over the mountains and destroyed the Medici. The key which would unlock Italy this time was Valentino, the second son of the Pope, married to a French princess in return for the annulment of the French king's own marriage, and promised the might of France to make himself Duke of the Romagna.

'I am sure there is no cause for alarm as yet, my lady,' Orfeo replied smoothly.

'Alarm? Alarm? Then what do you make of the fact that the Borgia in Rome has declared my right to Forlì forfeit and transferred it to Valentino? That when I sent my legate to the Vatican offering to pay the tribute I owe, and God alone knows where I can find three thousand fiorini, he was not even admitted into the presence! Get out, Signor Orfeo! Get out and ride to my uncle and tell him that he is lost, as I am lost, unless he acts now.'

Signor Orfeo did not look especially discomfited. Indeed as he rose to his feet he fixed Caterina with a lecherous stare, his eyes hovering on the ruby between her breasts.

'Naturally, I am disappointed, Countess. I had hoped to enjoy rather more of your famous . . . hospitality.'

There was a sharp retort as Caterina flashed out her hand and slapped his face. He staggered a little, bewildered, reaching for his cheekbone, which was dripping blood where her ring had caught it. Some drops spattered the pale flesh of her neck. Then, with a smirk on his face, he made a bow and retired, closing the door of the sala softly behind him.

For a moment the Countess stood transfixed, as still as an icon, until her body rippled as though beneath a wave and she sank to her knees beneath the weight of it, her shoulders heaving. I could hear her murmuring through clenched teeth, 'I will not, I will not,' so I went to her and touched her and tried to raise her up. But her body was too much for my slightness, so instead I stooped, and for the first time I rocked her in my arms while she wept out the torrent of grief and rage. As I pressed her against me, I wept too, for everything that had been taken from me, and everything I would never have, for my papa and Toledo, for Cecco and Giovanni, for the life that stretched so tenuously before me, until we collapsed, exhausted, our faces pale and smeary.

'Come, my lady,' I whispered. 'I will mix something to help you sleep tonight.'

She took my hand and held it a moment, soft in her own, and briefly I could see the girl she had been: young and frightened like me, motherless, sent amongst strangers. Then her spine straightened and she pulled herself to her feet.

'Thank you, Mora. This – this weakness has passed, as it must. I am better now.'

'At least you had it,' I murmured under my breath.

'What?'

'Love, Countess. You had love and you have your children.'

I feared I had been impertinent, made too much of the moment, but her face was ruefully kind.

'Yes. From the stars to the cemetery, no? I had it. You are a good girl, Mora. And I will take care of you, as Giovanni's gift to me.'

I said I would take her necklace, to clean it while she rested. I helped her into her nightgown and brought her a dish of camomile tisane, laced with dried comfrey, which had her breathing calm and regular in a few minutes. Then I went to her chest and took out one of her muslin petticoats and slit a thin swatch of fabric from the hem. I rolled it around the necklace until the few spots of blood from the ambassador's face were absorbed. Then I went to the image of the Virgin in its alcove in her bedchamber and quietly, slowly scraped a little of the gold leaf onto the cloth, then I wound it round tight like a ring. I pushed my truckle bed a little away from the wall and into the space I tilted my candle, carefully tracing out a pentagram with the wax. I put my sewing knife to the pad of my thumb and squeezed out a drop of my own blood, crossing the cooling wax with a 'V'. I put my charm inside and there it was, hidden, an amulet against what was coming to Forli. And then I sat and stared at the wall until my eyes slipped closed of their own accord and I was too tired to dream.

CHAPTER FOURTEEN

THE LAST SUMMER OF THE CENTURY WAS HOTTER than anyone had ever known. The sun sliced through the thick air like a dagger, turning the trees and the fields a dull bronze, and with the heat, the plague came to Forli. Ever swift and practical when her own was under threat, the Countess was busy, relieved to have a distraction from her mourning and the seemingly endless wait for news of the French, doing all she could to protect the people from the pestilence. The city gates were closed and the town divided into sectors, each supervised by doctors she had summoned from Cesena and Faenza. The afflicted were separated from their families, transported on carts to the convent of San Mercuriale outside the city walls to be cared for by an order of poor nuns. If their relatives chose to accompany them, they could not return for a month. Plague homes were destroyed, and while the sickness raged, no one was allowed to pass in or out of the city. Thus the Countess kept her people safe, and though they grumbled foolishly at her strictures, there were fewer deaths in Forli than anywhere else the plague had invaded in those torrid months.

I was occupied in the *farmacia*, mixing cures under the Countess's direction and noting them in her book of receipts. I brewed fennel-root tea, to clear the skin of the fat purple buboes that exploded on the bodies of the sick. I ground red coral to keep their hearts beating strongly. The powdered waste of a dog, dried first in the sunlight, then boiled in broth of meat we found excellent in bringing down fever, though it was hard to persuade patients to swallow the stinking soup. Caterina had all her tapestries and curtains rolled away and the Rocca scrubbed out daily and scented with lavender and rosemary. This way we were not afraid that the sickness would take us. Strangely, it was a happy time – we were busy, side by side amongst the clean flasks and the sharp scent of herbs, and I was proud that the Countess trusted me with her powders and the pen. Wearing unbleached linen gowns that had been boiled in lye I thought we looked like sisters, or nuns, maybe, working quietly together. For a few weeks, until the disease died down, we were insulated from the world, untroubled by the summer storm that was waiting to break over Italy.

Yet when finally the gates were opened, I thought again of my dreams, of the Borgia sun blazing over the fields of the Romagna, for the messages that awaited Caterina had only one subject, Valentino. The French king had had his papal decree, so that he might divorce and take to wife his own brother's widow. No longer a prince of the church, Cesare was now Duke of Valentinois, and his father had had the letters of congratulation from King Louis read aloud in the streets of Rome, though the students of Paris had rioted at the ignominy of the match. Now the French were preparing once more to cross the Alps, to take the Sforza dukedom from Il Moro, and Valentino was to command them. Already the Countess's uncle, the Sforza cardinal, had fled Rome, whilst the Neapolitan prince who had been persuaded to marry Lucrezia Borgia had abandoned his pregnant bride, since the Pope had surrendered the cause of Naples to become the court chaplain of the French.

From all over Italy, the Countess's couriers poured out news of Valentino. No Italian, they said, but a Spaniard, a black eyed, black haired, barbarian Spaniard. He was handsome, claimed the Venetian ambassador, the most beautiful young man. His face was scarred and spoiled with the Spanish pox, said the Mantuan envoy. He was a coward who hid behind his father's cassock, he was a great soldier who fought bulls on horseback. He was a lecher who had naked courtesans dance for his pleasure in the very shadow of St Peter's, he was worse than a lecher, having eyes only for his beautiful sister Lucrezia, his lover had been a Turkish prince. He dressed so magnificently that even his warhorse wore a red silk cloak, adorned with gold roses worked thick as a man's finger, the collar he had worn to meet King Louis was a blaze of diamonds worth thirty thousand ducats, he travelled with five hundred servants. It seemed that as soon as one looked for Valentino he vanished, as supple and tricky as a wolf, but one thing was certain, and that was he was coming.

And amidst the rumours and whispers another ambassador came to Forli. I was always at Caterina's side now, though I was careful to look no more than her foreign slave when she received or dined. I was part of the formal retinue of her state as

Countess, an accessory, like a gown or a carefully, carelessly placed manuscript, designed to display her wealth or her knowledge. But when I saw the knobby-headed little clerk from Florence, nervously twisting his cap in the Countess's sala, I started and had to stop myself from grabbing at her skirts. I had seen him before, I had dreamed him. In that white palace, floating high above the mountains, the bony planes of his face etched out in the light of a single candle while he spoke urgently to the masked man. Before I heard the softly aspirated consonants of his Tuscan accent, I knew it was he. Machiavelli, his name was. I stood there as mute as I had been in the Medici kitchens, whilst another stone of Caterina's toppling fortress was wheedled out of place.

Ottaviano was no longer contracted to fight for Florence and Caterina had determined to send her men north to Milan to aid Ludovico Il Moro in the coming struggle against the French. The Florentines wished to renew the contract, as they too would be threatened if Valentino broke the Milanese. But the Countess prevaricated.

'I always like what the Florentines say,' she told him, 'as much as I dislike what they do.'

Thinking to secure her own defences, she offered to renew the *condotta*, on the condition that Florence promised in return to come to her aid should Forli be threatened. But the little clerk was calm and stubborn and would not give his word, and after a week he went back empty handed.

So when the news reached Forli that Il Valentino was in Milan, and that his French troops had used the great mould of the statue of my lady's grandfather for target practice, she and I knew, at least, what was coming. It was to have been a wonder they said, cast by Maestro da Vinci, the great *condottiero* towering above his city on his warhorse; and now, in October of that year 1499, it was reduced to so many pellets of clay. Caterina's spies in Venice had sent word that the Borgia cardinal had appeared a month before, with a coded letter from Valentino to the Signoria in which he informed them that he intended to have Imola, Forlì and Pesaro. The Venetians tried to stall, claiming they would have to consult with King Louis, but no one believed that Valentino moved without the consent of his new royal cousin. Even as the baked armour of Francesco Sforza shattered in his castle yard, a legate came from Rome to inform my lady that her rights to her cities were forfeit to the Pope, as the census was not paid. It was a trick, they both knew it, as she had offered the money, but still the pretence of civility was maintained.

The Countess received the legate in the walled garden of the Paradiso, splendid in a crimson gown lined with silver and all that remained of her Riario jewels. I attended them, pouring sweet wine into the green Venetian glasses she had brought from her wedding trip, and read the paper as calmly as though it were an inventory of grain from the *contada*.

'You will tell His Holiness that I will have the honour of writing to him on this matter.'

'Of course, Countess.'

'And I beg the honour of remembering the health of His Holiness in my prayers.'

She kept her countenance until he was ushered away, then

fell back in her seat, pallid, panting. Her hands squirmed in her lap like eels, the rings twisting bruises into her palms.

'It has come then, Mora.'

'You will write to Florence, Madonna?'

'Of course, of course, though they will fail me. They will lie down like whores for the French as they did last time.' She got to her feet impatiently. 'The park must be razed. At least we'll be able to see that jumped-up bastard in his French feathers.'

'Madonna, there may be something else to be tried.'

I did not contemplate the magnitude of what I thought to do. What mattered, the only thing that mattered to me, was saving Caterina. My dreams and their warnings had been proved useless over and over, but my knowledge was real. I knew about sickness and how it worked, how it could creep into the blood, how it could move invisibly until it was too late. So that night, while my lady sat up in the Rocca with her papers and her lists, I slipped down through the city to the walls, where the guards had been warned to let me pass. I took the road out from Forli, and after twenty minutes walking in the moonlight, came to the convent where the plague victims had been sent to die. The bell was tolling Lauds as I reached the buildings, and I could see the pale gowns of the nuns as they crossed to the chapel. I thought of Florence, and how my journeys through the city had always been marked by the chime of bells. For a moment I was afraid I should be discovered, that the nuns would raise an alarm, but I waited until I heard the murmured drone of the office, then I closed my eyes and thought of the shadows. I should move like a shadow, like a wolf, like Valentino, and I should not be found.

The pestilence had withdrawn, but the Rocca received reports that a few cases still endured at the convent. I had never visited the hospital before, and I was glad of the lamp bracketed to the wall of the lobby. I was gladder that the nun who attended the ward was sleeping on her chair, her face obscured by a cushion that smelt as though it was stuffed with sweet herbs. The long room was cool and clean smelling. None of the wooden truckle beds were occupied, though. I passed through, and gingerly opened the door at the end, peering into the dispensary and a small chapel until I found a second door giving onto the courtyard. I moved slowly over the packed earth, towards a low, light-coloured building. I could smell the fresh lime on its walls and I paused at the door, half-hoping it would be locked, but it gave easily and I stepped into the mortuary. I told myself I was lucky, for those who die of plague are buried immediately, and the poor creature here must have gone after twilight, gaining an extra, useless night above the earth. I had a candle and a tinder-box, but I was afraid to strike it, less for my fear of discovery than for what I knew I must see.

The corpse lay shrouded in coarse linen on a table at the end of the room. I had a horrid fear that as I approached a crabbed dead hand would shoot out to grab me, but I forced myself forward and held the light to the bound face. The dead look dead immediately, not calm and sleeping like effigies on tombs, but dead merely, irretrievable. The face drawn in and collapsed, the lolling mouth secured with linen bands, the perceptible reek of deep, deep rot. As though a few mutterings and scrapings of holy statues could raise them! I stared at the sexless face with its coin-

218

shuttered eyes for a few moments to calm myself. Then I began work. Using an old pair of gloves, I drew two thin cloths of fine blue water silk from my bag and turned the body onto its side, unfastening the tapes at the neck of the shroud, glad that my fingers did not have to make contact with the cold flesh. A man, from the shrivelled muscles of the back and flat torso, though the skin was so covered with congealed buboes it was barely possible to tell. Carefully, I rubbed the cloth over the gaping blisters, surprised to see that they still released fluid pus, pushing the silk into the wounds until it was thoroughly soiled. Using the space left by the body, I spread a packet of letters with my lady's seal on the table, and wrapped them tightly in the cloths, squeezed the roll into a cane tube of the sort used by couriers to protect their messages, then broke the end from my candle, heated it and sealed the tube with tallow. The gloves I would burn as soon as I came to a quiet place on the road. I wished I could ask for his name, so that if my plan worked my lady could reward the poor man's family, but all I could do was mutter a prayer over him before I slipped out again and made for Forli.

I told myself that I was an instrument, that as a slave I was not responsible, but the idea had been mine, formed in those weeks in the *farmacia* when I prepared the medicines against the plague as Caterina had taught me, and tried to consider how it could pass so quickly between the sufferers. I knew what would come to me if I were found, that nothing would await me but fire at best, but I was unafraid. The church had taken my papa, the hounds of God had driven Maestro Ficino from Florence. And the church turned on its own, on Savonarola, on Caterina who had once been a princess at the court of Rome. I had spared barely a thought for God since I had left Toledo. I had never questioned whether I believed. It seemed to me that the priests with their flummeries of incense and incantations were as misguided as my poor master in his search for alchemist's gold, as poor Margherita's eager buyers, anxious to twist their fate with a useless charm. There, on the road to Forli with the soft autumn darkness all about me, I knew that if I believed in anything at all it was the dark gods of my long ago ancestors who had my allegiance; the spirits of the northern forests who recognised and rejoiced in the savagery of death. That was all the power I would ever need. I felt cold then, as cold as my green eyes, as cold and cruel as the Mura who played with shadows in the half-world of my dreams.

My plan did not work. My lady had the walls of the park pulled down, the orchards beheaded and the beautiful, delicate green pavilion dismantled. The Florentines temporised, the carts rolled through the streets of Forli towards the Rocca, the overseers went out to the farms for supplies. Florence declared neutrality, my lady inventoried her goods and looked over the armoury, her captains drilled the garrison and the weeks went by with no news, or too much. Valentino was moving on the Romagna with his Swiss mercenaries and Gascon gunners, Ottaviano left for Imola and the leaves fell. In Rome the Pope lived. I was certain that when his greedy Borgia hands unwrapped the letters of submission wrapped in those poisoned cloths the boils would appear on his body as black as his heart, but the Forlivese were always a stupid and a cowardly people, and my lady's messenger to the Vatican, Tommasino, confided my scheme to another servant. His secret was barely whispered before the pair found themselves in Sant'Angelo, and His Holiness's Spanish torturers had it out of them before the canister was even unsealed.

I had feared Caterina would be angry at my failure, but when the courier came with the news that the Countess of Forli's attempt to assassinate the Pope was the talk of Rome, she merely smiled a little grimly and said that there would be no quarter for her, then. Abandoned by Florence, knowing that the Rocca could never hold out against the force of those legendary French guns, Caterina was nonetheless happy. Her Sforza blood was up, and she appeared as lithe and straight as a goddess as she strode the boundaries of the *cittadella*, with a breastplate strapped over her fine gowns and a hawk on her gloved wrist.

'If I must perish,' she said, 'then let me die like a man.'

Despite her fighting words and the rigour with which she oversaw the preparations, there was a sense of girlish anticipation to her, as though she longed for Valentino's coming. I noticed that while she worked all day, even hauling supplies down from the carts in her own arms as an example to the men, she nevertheless washed her hair in lemon juice and combed it out each night, and that beneath her gauntlets, her hands were moist and fragrant with the rosewater lotion I prepared for them.

Imola fell to Valentino at the end of November. The French guns breached the walls of the citadel, and though the *castellano* held out for a week (as well he might, since my lady had his wife

221

and children safely hostages at Forli) his resistance was, as she said contemptuously, more a matter of mere good manners than of honour. From the walls of the Rocca, we watched what seemed the whole of the Romagna in flight, the road crowded with carts and weary figures carrying bundles or children, trudging pathetically south. I pitied them in my heart, these poor people who paused to pray in roadside shrines as though the Church herself was not the author of their misery, but my lady felt only disgust for those who fled. Nevertheless, she set me to packing the goods from the inventory that she wished to send to Florence for safety, her silver basins and ivory boxes, great chests of linens and fabrics, her walnut bed and her gold and pearl crucifixes. She seemed to find satisfaction in the idea that though Valentino might kill her, he would not have those Borgia hands on her precious mirrors, her tapestries or even her gilded sewing scissors. Sadly, I bundled up my own books and instruments and added them to the cart.

What hurt her most was sending her youngest boy away. Since his father's death he had been known as Giovanni, for the Countess's secret, lost husband. At a year old, he disdained to crawl and clutched his way determinedly round his nursery, toppling the chairs and bawling furiously if the nurse tried to keep him still. I cried as I packed his little clothes into a trunk, with another case of medicines from the dispensary. He seemed so tiny, so fragile in his innocent cheerfulness that I could hardly bear to think of him sobbing for his mother who might never come to him again. He was to go to his uncle's house at Florence, where he would be safe, and I drilled the girl into remembering what must be done if he should fall ill. I stitched a charm into the breast of his gown, his name inside a pentagram. As I worked the cambric with my tiniest stitches I thought of that other charm, gathering dust beneath my bed, and I knew as sure as the future is contained like an insect in amber, that it too was useless.

CHAPTER FIFTEEN

NTIL IMOLA, THE COUNTESS HAD BELIEVED HER-
self beloved by her people. Had she not fought for them, fed
them, sheltered them from disease? She chose to forget that she
had also slaughtered them, made beasts of them, that she had
never been one of their own, and that her pride – her cursed
Sforza pride – had refused the Pope's alliance when it was
offered and brought Valentino down upon them. When Imola
surrendered, she saw they were no longer to be trusted.

In early December, she met with the councillors of the city,
who advised her to flee. Why could she not do as the King of
Naples had done, as her own uncle of Milan had once done, and
leave the city, sparing the citizens the horrors of war, and wait
until Valentino had passed through the Romagna before coming
to an agreement? She could save herself, they argued, and she
could save them. The Borgia Pope was old, and the effects of his
dissipations would soon tell on him. It could not be long before
he died. Of natural causes, they delicately implied. But Caterina
would have none of this. If she had to sacrifice herself, she declared, she would do so. She was prepared to fight until the end.

The Forlivese had no stomach for such talk. The Council gathered them in the piazza and reassured them that they had private word from Valentino that if the city should only submit as peacefully as Imola had done, there would be no violence. They sent their leader, Niccolo Tornielli, to inform her of their decision. He came to the gatehouse, bareheaded, scrunching his cap into a miserable rag, and told my lady that despite all her care and protection of them, the people of Forli would not rise for her. They were not prepared to close the gates against Valentino; they wished to be absolved from their oath of allegiance to their Countess. He could not look my lady in the eye, but waited there, like an admonished child, stumbling over his words. My lady showed no anger, there was no time for anger. She came close to him, so close that I knew he could feel the hiss of her breath cooling his skin.

'You recall, do you not, Signor Tornielli, what happened here in Forli after my husband the Count was murdered?'

He nodded, still avoiding her gaze.

'Then you may tell the people that I absolve them from their oath. They may ring the bells of San Mercuriale for Valentino, if they choose.'

For a second, relief spread across Tornielli's countenance. 'Thank you, Madonna'.

She leaned closer and her voice was cold as steel. 'But tell them this also, that they had better go on their knees to Valentino now for mercy, for when I prevail, they shall see none from me.'

Caterina had the cannon of the Rocca fired over the very heads of her treacherous citizens. They too were her enemies now. The Rocca was provisioned and ready, there was nothing left to do but close the gates for good, shutting out those they had been built to protect. The people of Forlì might do what they would, but for the Countess's small court and her five hundred soldiers there could be no resolution. She had bound us to go to the death.

The storms came on the day Il Valentino left Imola for Forlì. The air until then had held some of the heat of that raging summer, sharp and bright, as warm as harvest time by noon; but that day, the middle of the month, it thickened and grew sluggish, the sky obscured by a dingy veil of heavy cloud. My lady had been prepared for some time now, and this new stillness in the air, which gave resonance to even the merest twitch of a leaf on the poor remaining trees in the barren parkland, tightened our anticipation to an unbearable degree. I recalled Florence in the months before Piero fell, that sense of time constricting like a noose. Nothing moved, and yet the space around us was tense, pregnant.

The Countess paced the walls of the Rocca, her head bowed. The garrison sprawled amongst their idle weapons, playing round after round of listless dice, the brief clatter of bones on the parapet like rats' claws, scrabbling their way into our dulled and aching heads. Dinner was served in the sala, stripped of its fine cushions, not even a carpet on the table, but none of us could eat. Our hands moved like separate creatures amongst the dishes whilst our senses were cast towards the windows, alert to nothing but the approach of a horse. I asked my lady's permission to leave the room, but she barely acknowledged me, waving her fingers to accede to my dismissal. I gathered my cloak about me and climbed to the top of the tower. The two waiting guards scrambled swiftly to their feet when they saw me, their faces avid for news, but I shook my head and moved away from them, looking out behind the city to the hills.

I closed my eyes and listened, but though I watched there a long time, there was nothing. When I came to Forli, the wolves had sung me there through the nights. Beyond the frill of grey rock which marked the heights, the country was empty. It had been too warm, I thought, they were not yet hungry enough to come near the plain. I told myself this, but part of me believed that they were spreading, circling out to the high slopes, knowing what I could not. I propped my back against the wall, feeling the cold stone through my cloak against my spine and hunched my head on my knees. No sound, silence enough to hear the passage of the clouds.

*

I am in the cathedral of Florence, huddled amidst a mass of bodies in the dim candlelight. My sight is blocked by the crow. Only by straining my head back can I sense the vastness of the church under the dome. The faces of the men and poor old women who wait for Mass are sharp boned with fasting, for the friar has prescribed bread and water five days a week, that God might divert the French beast to plumper pickings. As we move forward into the plain of the nave a skinny youth sways and staggers like a drunkard, clutching for an arm to break his fall, but those around him turn away, as though to help him would taint them with his weakness. I think again that this is a mean city, crabbed and grasping, and that for all its magnificence there is no charity in this church. I push forward and find a place close beneath the lectern. As he comes from the sacristy, a silence falls, so that in this huge place there is only the sound of the slap of his sandaled feet on marble. His face is almost hidden beneath the black hood of his robe, but as he passes me I turn my eyes sideways to catch his beaky profile, his full lips incongruous in the stern face.

'Behold!' cries Savonarola, and his voice, for all that it is thin and peevish, is full of a compelling certainty.

'The Sword has descended; the scourge is fallen, the prophecies are being fulfilled. Behold, it is the Lord God who is leading on these armies. It has come!'

As he speaks, the crowd begins to murmur and sway, mechanically crossing themselves, clacking at rosaries like a gaggle of chickens. And then, hovering in the space above the pulpit, I see it: a huge sword chased in silver, with the sun's rays streaming down its blade and a bull being put to death, the flowing blood curving back into the pattern of the sword to form a motto. I squint my eyes, but I cannot make out the words. The crowd behind me melts away, I am alone with my vision now, and the sword twists on its vicious point, dancing for me. Then I see the name 'Divius Caesar' engraved into the hilt. Caesar. Cesare. The monk is right and he was wrong. The wolf that will come over the Alps, the sword of God, is not hunchbacked, simple Charles, or his strutting, arrogant cousin Louis, but the Pope's own warrior. Cesare.

*

When I woke, there was a rider below the walls of the town. In the moment that I saw him, the bells of the Rocca began to toll the warning of invasion, echoed in moments by the churches of the town. A rush of footsteps on the staircase and the Countess appeared, two of her captains panting behind her. She leaned over the parapet and watched the horseman pass the Schiavonia gate. The city was so still that we could hear the hoofbeats as clear as if they walked beneath us. It stretched so long, that moment, the last seconds before the Countess of Forli embraced her fate. Time held, stretched, a few more instants before a clap of thunder, fit to split the Rocca in two, burst above us, and the sky turned in an instant from turgid grey to black, with the hiss of the rains sounding on the tiles in the time it took for our pupils to open to the dark.

'How apt, Mora,' my lady smiled, a real smile, the first I had seen for weeks. 'Like a country masque, here the thunder, and now the devil himself.'

For the next hours I trotted behind her as clumsy as a convent *serbanza* let out for her first court ball. The garrison moved behind her skirts like dancers, heaving the guns into position, lining up the powder kegs under the protection of the loggias, weaving the measures of my lady's defiance along the walls of the citadel. The roar of the storm and the continuous tolling of the bells were deafening. Then Caterina gave orders to begin the bombardment of the town, every report from the guns reverberating in our thudding hearts. The thunder and the cannon kept pace with one another for that night, and the next. Neither the rain nor the barrage from the Rocca gave any quarter. I had thrown off my torpor – the torpor that had held the whole garrison suspended for the time of waiting. Now I could be busy again. In the *farmacia* I had brewed a cauldron of mallow root, mixed with rosehip syrup to help it down. The potion causes the heart to beat more strongly; it would keep the men alert. Every few hours, as the soldiers changed their positions, I went among them, dispensing spoonfuls like a nurse to the newcomers to keep their senses sharp. My lady had ordered that no wine be given out just yet, the time for that would come.

On the third day, Valentino rode beneath the San Pietro gate and into Forli. The Council sent out twenty-five horsemen to greet him, assuring him that the city would submit to occupation without a single blow of the sword. In response, Caterina trained her guns on the tower of the campanile. The rain and the smoke from the guns obscured the view from the walls, but beyond, in the countryside, we could make out the massed ranks of the soldiers who accompanied him, a black swarm on the sodden hills. Ten thousand, came the reports, twelve thousand, fourteen. Like a mist, the swarm formed into a column and trailed towards the walls. The piazza was so dark that the torches were set alight in their brackets, and they illuminated the figure on a white warhorse, surrounded by his French courtiers in crimson and cloth of gold.

Always, it seemed to me, Valentino moved within his own prism of light. The rain was as hard as ever yet as his bearer carried the Borgia standard into the piazza, the streaming comet's tail of the pennant stretched itself into the sky and made a tunnel through the cloud, so that the tall, erect figure on his white horse seemed captured in a luminescent spiral, a valedictory light, as when the last ray of a sunset recalls within it the fact of night. The guns were silent. Our ears had become so accustomed to their punishing boom, that it made the quiet seem enormous. The garrison stood silent too, along the walls of the Rocca, surrounding my lady.

The approaching figures came up into the square, the suck of the sodden ground muffling their steps.

'Look at him,' sneered my lady, 'the Catalan bastard come courting.'

Valentino too was dressed in crimson, wetted to the colour of dried blood, the cloth of gold lining to his sleeves drawing the lemon-coloured sunlight towards him. His face was obscured by a soft cap of the same tissue, a white feather curling coyly over his cheek. He was too distant to make out anything other than the soft set of his broad mouth. I watched my lady's face, I watched her take in the ease with which he sat his horse, the movement of his hips languid in time with the push of its shoulders, the taper of his waist and the spread of his back under the tight cloth. Despite their treacherous submission, the people of Forli had not turned out to greet their new ruler, so it was a solitary figure which circled the square three times, slowly, his lance resting at his hip in the conqueror's gesture, reclaiming the fief for St Peter. It was so quiet. I knew I ought not, but I thought he was beautiful.

*

In Florence I had seen two paintings: the soul in purgatory and the soul damned, both framed in ribbons of gold. In the first, a resigned figure cast up suffering eyes to the rays of what I supposed was Heaven, in the second the same figure was a howling gargoyle, mouth agape, eyes swollen in frenzy, flanked by two horned demons with lolling tongues. Maestro Ficino said such stuff was nonsense, that it played only upon the fears of the ignorant, who had not been taught that the soul's essence communed with celestial entities, that spirit was too subtle to be confined by demons and pitchforks. So I thought that I did not believe in Hell. I think, though, that if my master had stood there that day on the walls of the Rocca, and seen it all as I did, he would have changed his mind.

The Forlivese had believed Valentino would be merciful, but he had made no such promises for his French troops. The cross in the piazza was their first victim. The revered statue of San Mercuriale – venerated by the people for generations – was torn down and dragged ignominiously around the square. Within hours of their arrival the roofs of the city were smouldering under the ceaseless rain. The streets were black with French locusts, one after another workshops and warehouses were looted, so that we heard glass smashing and the thud as beams fell to the fire.

'They'll be at the wine shops next,' remarked one of the Countess's men.

He was right, and for a while a grim calm fell on the city as the barrels were broken out and the troops swarmed in huddles to drink. We waited there, mindless of the soaking, gelid rain, helpless, watching. I pulled at my lady's sleeve.

'Look, they're moving up, to the convent.'

The height of the Rocca gave us a clear view over the whole city, with the nunnery of Santa Maria enclosed within the walls on the north-eastern side, so close, it seemed, that we might have reached through the mizzle to pluck a leaf of ivy from its walls.

'Turn the guns,' she ordered.

The Countess had seen battle before. I did not know whether she wanted to fire Forli's beloved convent for revenge; or whether my lady hoped to give the sisters a kinder fate than that she knew awaited them. For a few moments, the cannon smoke obscured Santa Maria as the shot found its target. The tower of the nuns' chapel swayed drunkenly, then slowly, hovering a moment in the sudden space beneath it, collapsed. The upraised arms of the Virgin, toppled from her niche, lodged in the walls as her veiled head crashed to the ground. Roaring with rage, they went on.

'They will have barred the doors?' I asked.

'Surely. All the maids of the city will be inside,' she replied, her mouth set tight.

But the doors might have been sculpted in butter for all the protection they gave.

I wanted to stop my eyes when I saw them dragging the women through the town, the nuns in their dark habits and the lighter dresses of the girls, their hems already smeared with blood. They brought them praying and weeping across the city, right up to the walls of the Rocca. We could hear them, above the gunfire, the steady murmur of the nuns, calling on the

Mother of God to save them, the screaming of the girls, calling on their Countess to save them.

'My lady, we might open the gates.'

'We can keep them off long enough to get the good sisters inside.'

'No.'

'My lady—'

'I said no. Do you challenge me?'

She had done worse, I knew. This was not the first time she had stood on the ramparts of her fortress, defying those who came against her, this was not the first time she had closed her ears to pleading and her heart to pity.

They herded them together, perhaps thirty or so, surrounding them with a wall of staves and bayonets. Then one woman was dragged forward, falling to her knees, her white head cloth slipping into the mud, her face washed bright with the rain turned up to us, desperate.

'It is Suora Cecilia.'

I knew her, I had seen her often when I went to the porch of the convent to buy herbs and dried fruits for the Countess's *farmacia*. Sometimes she would put aside a twist of candied rose petals or cherries in a paper for me. A kind woman, her pale face gently laced with wrinkles. She had taken her nun's name for the saint of music, she told me, because her greatest joy was offering her voice to God when the sisters sang the orders. That voice had sung Matins this morning and now it was cracked and broken, calling again and again on her lady to save her. They pushed her down in the filth and her shift rose up, exposing the soft flesh of her thighs that no one had ever seen. Then a blow from a boot silenced her, and they began.

I had never seen Venice. I had often wondered about it, that city on the water where all the wealth of the world passed through. I had heard of the women there, those prized and beautiful creatures whom even kings would beg for a night of favours. They had a custom there, that if one such woman betrayed the man who had her in his keeping, his friends would take her, one after the other, to punish her. Seventy-five was the longest any of them had lasted, I heard, amidst the sniggers of the grooms back in Careggi. It took six until Suora Cecilia's body lay broken in the mire, but as they pushed the others forward, one after the next, I could not bear to count. The Countess could not fire on them, even had she wished to, they were too close to the foundations of the walls, and they knew it. She stood it out, my lady. She had warned the people of Forli that they would have no quarter. Even as I hid my face in my cloak and sickened groans of the men about us were drowned by the whoops and cheers of those below, she watched, looking down, her countenance as calm as the statue of the Madonna which lay shattered in the street.

Hell came to Forli that day. One by one they took them, and those that lived were left to crawl away in the dark. They took their clothes and burned them, and left them to creep away naked with nothing to cover their shame. There were not many, I think, who wished to live. When, at last, it was done, I was flensed inside, scoured out with weeping. I begged that I might be allowed to go down, with my bag of medicines, to go amongst them and see what I might do to help. I should not have cared if they had taken me too; I should have gone gladly, if it meant I could give some succour to those poor damned creatures.

'There is nothing to be done for them, Mora. Forli had made its choice. This is war.'

I did not care if I angered her, I did not care if she dashed me from the walls with her own hands.

'For shame, my lady, for shame.' I tried to stare her down, then I turned my back on her and walked slowly to the stairwell. I could feel her eyes on my back as I left her.

'Mora.' Reluctantly, I went back. She bent her face down to mine then, her hand on my shoulder was trembling.

'I cannot bend, Mora, I cannot. But it does not mean that I cannot feel.'

That evening, in the Rocca, we danced. With the bodies in the mud outside, we danced. For the troops in their miserable encampment in the park, it was a sorry Christmas feast. But my lady had platters of roast meat sent out to them, and despite the driving rain insisted that the shuttered windows of the sala be opened, so that the light and the sound of the lutes and the scent from her Moorish incense burners might drift through the night to the Palazzo Numai, where Valentino was lodging. None amongst us had any stomach for it, yet the Countess was implacable. That night, and the nights that followed, we would be gay, that the sound of our rejoicings should reach Valentino's ears and he would know that she cared nothing for him, that every day the Rocca would be relieved.

From dawn to dusk, the guns bombarded the city, then as it

grew dark my lady would send for me to dress her and reappear in one of her finest gowns, silver or azure fringed with gold, for all the world as though she were still the Pope's beloved daughter and not his enemy. We lined the window seats with the plate spared from the carts to Florence. The Countess ordered us to place candles and mirrors against it, so that the rich gleam could be seen by the wretched souls in the streets below, whom the French had forced to pin white crosses to their remaining pathetic rags as a sign of the occupation. Caterina still believed that the Rocca would hold, that Florence or Venice would send troops, but as the year looked set to turn, even as she danced proudly over the wreckage of her city, I sensed that in her heart, she knew she was alone.

CHAPTER SIXTEEN

ON ST STEPHEN'S DAY, WE AWOKE TO SILENCE. THE storm and the fire from the French guns had stopped, and our skulls rang with the quiet. There was no word from the town, though the scouts on the ramparts reported that the lines were still drawn up to the south and north-west of the Rocca. The Countess bade me accompany her to the *farmacia*, where we spent a morning of ghostly peacefulness, preparing a mix of egg yolks, sugar and Brionia water, to smooth and whiten the skin. It astonished me that she could appear so tranquil, and I asked her if she thought that Valentino might have reconsidered.

'No, Mora,' she answered grimly. 'But then all the more reason to make the best of it. I don't want to make an ugly corpse.'

Towards noon, as the mixture was cooling in a china pot and we were cleaning our hands with scraps of muslin, a maid came to inform the Countess that a messenger was positioned on the main drawbridge.

'Dress me,' muttered my lady, and we hastened to her rooms. I laced her hurriedly into one of her finest gowns, scarlet tabby with a gold mantle, and she added her sable pelisse, scrabbling in her jewel chest for her ruby pendant. Caterina paused before the looking glass, tweaking at her hair beneath her working linen cap, before loosening it and arranging it becomingly over her shoulders. The glance she gave herself was one I had not seen in a long while – expectant, satisfied, flirtatious.

'They're lighting up the city, Madonna.'

From the window, I could see a train of torches, illuminating one by one the climb to the Rocca.

'How festive,' she replied sardonically, rubbing a layer of rouge over her lips. 'Shall we?'

I followed her out onto the ramparts above the gatehouse. I saw how she set her shoulders so as not to tremble with the cold. Below us, he waited on his white horse. Like Caterina, Valentino was dressed in red, an elaborate gold-frogged doublet beneath a scarlet cape, soft leather boots with gold spurs, and a huge soft hat with white eagle feathers that he swept off as Caterina stepped forward. I hung back, hovering with the guards in the doorway, so that I could only see the colours of him, his face obscured by the Countess's body and the rise of the wall.

'Caterina, Countess of Imola and Forlì?'

'Monsieur le Duc.'

Their voices carried easily in the still cold, the Countess spitting the French title with courteous contempt.

'I come to ask you, madam, if you will not render yourself peacefully into my protection, as your uncle of Milan chose to do. Forlì is no longer yours to command.'

'I will not.'

'I have a guarantee, from His Holiness the Pope, that you will be compensated with another state, where you may live quietly and honourably with your children.'

'I care not for His Holiness's guarantees. And this is not the first time, Monsieur, that I have defied threats to my children.'

'Then, madam, I will make you repent of this foolish pride.'

'I repent, sir, that I ever trusted in the protection of the Pope. I repent that there is no longer justice in Italy, so that the Pope might declare untruthfully that I have failed in my obligations to him. And I trust that Christ, the protector of innocents, will defend my cause. I have no need of your guarantees.'

'But madam, I will have Forli, in spite of your cause.'

'And I shall die for it like a man, sir, if I have to. I wish you good day.'

They were so well matched, the two of them. They might have been speaking in a ballroom, or a play, old hands at the game: he, gorgeously dressed and supplicating, she the proud virgin on a tourney tower. I recalled the subtleties at Piero's spring feast, long ago, a marchpane lady and her sugar knight.

The next day, as though to remind Caterina of her glory days in Rome, Valentino sent the cardinal of San Giorgio, her nephew by her first marriage, with another offer from the Pope. He came puffing up on his mule, greeting her pompously, calling her 'cousin'.

'You are no cousin of mine, sir!'

He rummaged amongst a pouch of papers and held one up that she might see it.

'His Holiness offers four thousand ducats, Countess. A

pension that he will pay to you every year, if you will leave his state in peace.'

'Forli is mine!'

'And a safe conduct, see here, and you may remove all your possessions unmolested.'

'What has he given you, Raffaele? How much to betray your family? Or did he promise to hurt you less next time he shoved his holy staff up your miserable arse?'

There were gasps of shock from the watchers, but I knew my lady, my courteous, perfect-bred Sforza lady. She was enjoying this.

'If you will reconsider, Countess—'

'I'll consider nothing, you wretched catamite. Is there no end to your villainy that you would hide under the Borgia's cloak to save your own sorry skin? I spit on you, do you hear? I spit on you and your false and shallow heart.'

And she did. She sucked up a gobbet and plopped it over the wall, right on his bald holy head, cool as an urchin firing cherry stones. The cardinal took out a handkerchief and slowly wiped his brow, mindful of his state.

'You are most unwise, Countess. You are a woman, you can understand nothing of His Holiness's mind.'

'I understand his sacred greed all too well, Raffaele. Get you gone, and pray that you don't meet your uncle in Hell. I will have none of such dishonest dealing, none of it. The Borgia is a thief and you are his gull and I curse the day you were born a Riario.'

Again and again she refused. At length, the cardinal kicked up his mule like a chastened schoolboy, while the Countess wept with rage and recalled the vengeance she had taken for her Riario husband, of how Forli had swum in the bloody tide of her anger.

To her defiance, Cesare responded by declaring the Countess an outlaw, with a price of five thousand ducats on the head of her corpse, and ten thousand to any man who could take her alive. Caterina drew up her own proclamation, which she had read into the winter silence from the walls of the Rocca, offering an identical ransom for the Duke. They moved against one another like accomplished chess players, each wryly mirroring the other's advance. There was almost laughter between them, as though this really were an elegant game, as though Forli were not burning, as though the stench of corpses did not carry to the Rocca on the winter air, creeping into our apartments even though I lit the purest Persian incense to keep it out. And the princes of Italy watched the play, and sent letters applauding the Countess for her gallantry, and no one came to relieve us. But the net, the long ago plot of the spider Pope, was slowly, irrevocably, fastening us in its mesh.

Caterina was growing desperate. She had the guns trained on the Palazzo Numai, she sent a squad of guards into the city in the night to attempt to kidnap Valentino, whose French soldiers cut them down at the very foot of the Rocca, and sent their heads back as a gift the next morning. Valentino's men were digging into the foundations of the fortress, attempting to deviate the springs that gave us water, Caterina turned the guns on them. The earth beneath the battlements became a hideous puddle of blood. The surviving citizens, huddled around their pathetic fires in the remains of their homes, repented of their cowardice and of having submitted so easily to Valentino. Each day, they saw their Countess on the ramparts, her breastplate fastened over her gown, going among the soldiers to rally them. They whispered of her that she descended into the city at night, flashing a Turkish scimitar, taking her silent and stealthy vengeance on those who had betrayed her. Notes arrived from the town, declaring love for the Madonna of Forli and begging her forgiveness, but Caterina cast them into the fire. She was pure Sforza now. The hardening I had seen in her at Giovanni's death was complete. It had sculpted her like granite. She thought no more of her children, or her people, or of me, or even, I thought, of victory. She thought only of the battle, giving herself over to the urge for blood with more passion than she had ever known in the arms of her lovers.

In the last days of the year, hope arrived. The Florentines sent forty men, who had made their way south disguised as pilgrims journeying to the jubilee celebrations at Rome. It was not the four hundred that they had promised, but they were admitted to the Rocca and swiftly set to the guns. They told the Countess that Giovanni's brother Lorenzo was sending a mission on her behalf to make peace with the Pope. From Milan came news that Ludovico Il Moro had formed a pact with the German emperor and was preparing to retake his city from the French-appointed regent. If my lady could hold Forli until Il Moro had Milan, Valentino would have to withdraw and ride north to fight for his French masters. Caterina was quick to spread the good news amongst the men, and insisted that the music and dancing continue nightly in the Rocca, that Valentino might know she was not cowed. Yet I knew that in her heart she was preparing herself for the end, and that, in part, she welcomed the crisis that would come.

And I? I could not be afraid, for I knew I should live to witness Caterina's humiliation. I had seen the end; I knew how it should go. My only hope was that the man in black, whoever he was, would allow me to remain with her, to serve her in her grief as I had done in her happiness. I thought then that I knew my destiny, that my fate had not been cast in the marketplace at Toledo, or in the Medici palazzo, or in the hills of Careggi. I thought that I could choose, and I chose Caterina, because I came to know, in those long days in the Rocca, that I loved her.

On the last day of the year, the French hanged a twelve-year-old boy, a pharmacist's apprentice, claiming he had tried to poison one of their commanders. They burned the body in the piazza, except for the head, which they mounted on a pole and paraded through Forli. They nailed his right hand to the door of his father's house, and that was the end of 1499. Valentino's patience turned with the year. The Countess continued to taunt him, sending out rumours that he could not pay his troops, that the French king would abandon him, that the Pope had disowned him. For her part, she declared that she would not leave Ravaldino until her fortress and her own body were in pieces. So Valentino moved his guns from the north-west wall, behind which lay Caterina's rooms, to the south-west, where the belt of the ramparts joined the massive central tower. The cannon no longer ceased at twilight. Valentino was in a hurry. For ten days the artillery fired at the Rocca without cease, pounding the walls night and day.

Caterina's ladies shut themselves in the sala, weeping and praying, or staring dumbly into the space that was shattered every few moments by the relentless thunder of the guns. I had never been much amongst them, first for shyness and later as I had my duties in the *farmacia* and my study to occupy me. Nor did I care for their talk, for it was all of beaux and letters and gossip, of who they liked and who they thought to marry. Such things could never be for me. They were not Forlivese, but Roman too – one could hear it in the nasal twang of their quick chatter. They were all girls of good family. One was a cousin of Donna Alfonsina, Piero's wife, who once, I supposed, had been my mistress in Florence. They talked of what would happen to the republic now, if the French and the Borgia triumphed. Of how Piero was become a sot, idling his days between the tavern and the gaming house, loudly proclaiming the treachery of the Florentines to anyone bored enough to listen, and how Donna Alfonsina still conspired for him, that the Medici might return to their lost palazzo. I had always thought them slight creatures, who cared for nothing more than fine clothes and the latest poems, yet I pitied them deeply now, when even old scandal failed to liven their tongues. The French, they said, were gallant, they did not harm well-born women, but none of them could forget what had become of the sisters of Santa Maria and they bewailed the callousness of their mistress, who had not seen fit to send them south to safety.

The guns went on and on. The very earth beneath the Rocca

trembled with it. It was unendurable, save that we had no choice but to endure. The Rocca had been well provisioned, but supplies ran very low, the salt pork was gone, there was no white bread. We lived on eggs and boiled beans and dried spinach, the men had gruel and cheese. No dancing now, no pretence that we should be saved. No messengers could come near, we had no idea if Milan or Florence intended to make good their promises, and it was only the Countess, with nothing but the force of her Sforza will, which kept the garrison from opening the gates to the enemy, for no mortal could withstand that chaos without running mad. I tried to forget that I needed to sleep, to eat. I worked frantically in the *farmacia*, concocting every cure I knew from our dwindling stock of herbs and ointments, passing among the men to dispense what little comfort I could.

At first, they had been sanguine. There was food enough, and fuel, and they were better off than the benighted souls beyond the walls. Under the endless pounding of Valentino's guns, their will was broken. They went to the guns like dumb beasts to the plough, and slept in their boots where they stumbled back in the *cittadella*. No stories, no games of dice or cards. The Countess said they might have wine now, to give them courage, but the older ones soaked it up mechanically, cup after cup, and the younger men were dull and fuddled, swaying in disbelief as one by one their companions dropped from the walls amongst them. I thought I had seen the worst when they dragged Suora Cecilia out beneath the ramparts, but maybe the devil's own work was nothing compared to man's. I saw one fellow's neck shot away so his head plopped into the hole between his shoulders like an egg into a cup, his mouth still babbling his surprise. After one barrage the *cittadella* was filled with scattered limbs, like a child's forgotten game of spillikins. Another man lay quiet under his blanket for days, and I thought him healed until the stench grew too strong and I pulled away the covering to see his heart beating raw in his chest in a lattice of maggots. I understood my lady better then, for once one has seen such things pity becomes dangerous. Those who grieved went out of their wits, raving and laying about with their swords so that we had to shut them in the dungeon beneath the house – the prison my lady had named the Inferno. There was not time even, in those early terrible days of the year, to bury the dead. The French guns dug their victims' graves and they were left to rot where they fell.

*

The corpses called out the wolves. I was half-dozing, fully dressed, on my truckle bed in the antechamber. The slow whitening of the room showed me it was almost dawn. Caterina, who seemed not to need rest, was already out on the walls. I had clamped the bolster about my ears, so numbed by the noise that they barely sensed the guns, which still jolted my body alert with every report. Still, I heard them, calling to me through the sinuous muddle of my dreams.

The passages of the Rocca were deserted, the women at their vigil in the sala, every man on the ramparts, and it seemed strangely peaceful as I passed along the east front, taking the twisting stair that led to the curtain wall, enclosing what had once been Caterina's lovely park. My senses were scraped so raw that the cold of the stone beneath my feet rasped at my skin and I flinched from the icy wet of the walls. The air was full of sleet, which would warm in a few hours to the black rain with which Forlì had been cursed since Valentino's coming. At first I could hardly make them out, their sodden coats melding with the ground beneath. I no longer knew if I slept or woke. I rubbed my hands over the frozen, bruised plums under my eyes, and the churned mire beneath the ramparts was alive with them, ears flattened back against their heads, misted with the steam of their panting, silent. They too were waiting.

I managed a rueful smile at the sight of those yellow eyes, feeling in the pull of my skin against my cheekbones how thin and worn I had become. It had been weeks since I had gazed over the Countess's shoulder into the looking glass. I stood there, and we watched each other a while. The flames of their eyes swirled from gold to purple to green. I could have drowned there, I was so weary. I thought that it would have been so easy to walk a little further, to climb down through the sleet and let them take me. They starved. The French had long ago emptied the mountains of game, there was not a sheep or a cow living within leagues of this infernal place. So many times I had dreamed of them, I thought I belonged there, that they had come for me. But I shook my head, no, staggering on my feet, swamy and ill with fatigue.

'Thank you,' I told them. 'It won't be long, now. Wait, and you shall eat.'

*

I came awake to the sound of the walls of the Rocca falling, and they were gone.

It seemed to take me hours to reach my lady. I knew I was awake, yet my limbs seemed to move through the sluggard syrup so familiar from dreams, my muscles refusing to draw me on. I was blinded with the sleet and the acrid fumes that filled the fortress. When I rubbed my eyes clear I could see two great breaches in the walls, their innards pale and gaping in the first winter light. There were figures moving up the hill, bringing the beams and ladders that were to carry Valentino's men inside. I groped and staggered my way back along the wall, following the passage around to the central rampart. The Rocca was as frenzied now as it had been empty before, the waiting women shrieking, rushing for the courtyard to hide themselves in the outbuildings, guards running up from the encampment, unstrapping their swords, everywhere the blows of the guns. Caterina was in her apartment, a yellow tunic under her breast-plate, her jewel chest splintered on the floor before her, cramming the pockets of her gown with gold and diamonds.

'Help me now, Mora. Gather what you can and tie it up. Then put these on.'

She flung a bundle at me. My old boy's clothes.

'My lady—'

'Don't argue.' Her voice was brisk, savage, but her eyes were sparkling and her lips were full and wet. 'You've seen what they do to women. You'll have a chance dressed like that. Do it and follow me.'

I fumbled at the ties of my gown and bodice and hunched the

shirt over my shoulders, using my petticoat to bundle up a rainbow of gems. Caterina was working at a chest in the corner, unwrapping a skein of black silk.

'My father's sword,' she said, holding it to the window so the blade caught the light, a huge heavy warrior's sword that she handled as easily as though it were one of Giovanni's wooden toys. 'I carried this with me to Rome when he was murdered, I carried it to Sant'Angelo. The Sforza sword.' She brought the blade to her lips and kissed it at the hilt.

'Should we, should we pray, my lady?'

'Too late for that, little witch. Besides, I have hopes that I shall see the Borgia Pope in the company of his master.'

She would fight like a lioness, I saw, she would not be cheated of her vengeance. And yet still, she had a care for me. Watching her, so brave, so impossibly proud, I do not think it would be too much to say that I worshipped her at that moment. I would have followed her anywhere. I fancied I could feel the wolves outside the Rocca coming close to me, that their magic was in both of us. My fear ebbed back and the flame of it touched me to life, the flame of my people, I thought, the fire-worshippers from the lost forests of the north, so I was filled with a great rush of exhilaration, a swoop inside me at their fury and their love of the kill. I called them to me then, in a prayer of my own, and I followed her.

The scaling ladders were set up against the walls and the guns finally ceased, though the roar of the men as the French fell upon them was equal to the cannon. The moat was full of flailing figures. Trying to escape the merciless French swords, some of the troops had tried to swim the moat, and found their end instead in the weight of their armour. My lady's captains waited for her on the narrow walkway between the living quarters and the fortress.

'Fire the magazine,' she called as she came up, the unsheathed sword in her fist.

'It's madness, my lady, it's too late.'

'I said, fire it.'

It was her last, magnificent act of defiance. The force of the explosion threw us to the ground, and suddenly the whole of the Rocca was in flames. Even the men battling desperately on the bridges were shocked into temporary truce by it, incredulous, astonished. The whole of Caterina's hoarded arsenal, her stores of powder and saltpetre, brought the massive central keep down in seconds. I felt a rush of air pull over me as the wind was sucked into the vacuum. For a moment, there was silence, broken only by the thud of falling stone, then the French lines ranged on the Forlì side broke and surged forward, screaming for victory. Caterina sprang to her feet, backing to the wall, the sword held out before her.

'Get out if you can,' she hissed at me. 'Get out and get to Florence. Take the jewels for Giovanni. Go!'

'I will stay with you,' I whispered. 'I won't leave you.'

She gave me a last grim smile. 'Call me up a storm then, little witch,' as she turned to face the first of them.

The rain did begin to fall, then. My hands slithered on the wet stone as I crept into a newly blasted hollow in the battlement. I could not fight for her, I could barely lift a sword. It was not safe, nowhere was safe, but I thought I might as well die there as anywhere. The French assault backed, gathered, came on like a tide, hundreds of men of the garrison were cut down a heart's beat from my perch, but my eyes were all for the Countess. She swung her sword as true as any man, fought her way through pools of blood that became lakes, giving back, giving back, but still swinging, so that when the fighting moved to the north she was left with just a handful of men around her and I could slip down and stand to her side.

We gazed upon it, the battle of Ravaldino. The French came and came, no matter how many of them fell, they pressed forward. Then there was one sharp, guttural cry and a howl came up from the lines.

'*Les loups!*'

So I was not the only one who saw them. They were real. They slipped between the smoke and the mist of gunpowder like vengeful spirits, dealing death as sure and swift as the Sforza sword, mad with the pleasure of it. A huge man came up the ladder beside us, a Swiss giant, his shoulders bordering the breach. His teeth were black in his mouth, in one hand he carried a dripping bayonet, in the other a severed head, its lips still horribly twitching. I screamed and pressed back, then in one supple bound a wolf was on his neck and he crashed down beneath us. For one crazed moment, I did believe that it was my doing. I thought I had truly summoned them – the *seid* was amongst us, the wolves could turn them back, Caterina would prevail. The French were faltering, falling back. Behind the lines their commanders, bewildered, cantered their horses over heaping bodies, screaming them on.

I think I said it. I said, 'They are here for us, Madonna.'

I think she looked at me, her eyes levelling with mine where she knelt, spent, bracing her hands on the cross of her father's great weapon. There was a bruise on her cheek, her flesh split and pouring. I think she shook her head. Then the wolves vanished like a flight of arrows, bolting again for the hills, and the space of their going was filled once more with death.

My lady remained on her knees, she bowed her head and her hand moved across her bloodied armour in the sign of the cross. Finally, she was praying. I could still have run then, but I knelt beside her and waited until she had finished the Ave. Cautiously, tenderly, I pushed back the sodden strands of her hair, the heat of my own tears burning against the icy rain. I lifted my eyes to the man waiting quietly, a little to the side of us, and gave the slightest of nods, a quick affirming glance of my eyes. He stepped forward. Caterina took a deep breath, her ribs pounding under the torn fastenings of her gown. Her hands on the sword danced like insects, but her voice was low and clear as she pronounced the words she had sworn no man would hear from her living lips.

'*Signor Duca, io sono con te.*'

The French commander took her gently by the shoulder. Courteously, he helped her stand. As we descended the staircase, we passed the Countess's ladies, surrounded by Valentino's guard. She did not acknowledge their deep curtseys. Her face was all begrimed with smoke, the rain cut rivers in it as we passed into the courtyard where I had seen her first, so powerful, so beautiful. We walked slowly through Satan's own meadow, bright with flowers and bubbling springs, down to the gatehouse, where a figure awaited us, quite alone, a hat pulled over his face against the storm. My lady stumbled a little, righted herself, setting her shoulders straight, and reached for the chain at her throat.

'That's him, Mora. Give him this. As a token, tell him.'

I could not see Valentino, I thought my lady must be confused. This man was just another soldier, plainly dressed.

'Sir?'

My voice was choked with tears and powder, the ruby like a coal in my hand.

'Sir?'

And he turned and in the light of the burning fortress, I saw him. *The fire from the walls catches his face, the brim of the black hat hiding his eyes, but the mouth visible, smiling, a glint of teeth as white as the single pearl on his collar. Him.*

I had thought myself free. I thought that I could choose my fate, but it had only been waiting for me, all along. I was cursed, I could not run. All the time, he had been waiting for me, the man in black, that cruel smile curled on his soft mouth, the devil who would destroy Italy. Valentino. Cesare. The man in black.

I could not speak. I heard Margerita's voice, *Dummerer, are you?* I was mute as once I had feigned to be. I could only hold out the jewel and watch as his black leather fingers spidered across my palm. He barely glanced at me, looking to Caterina as she was led forward.

'I thank you, madam. I trust you will accompany me now?'

'Ten thousand ducats!'

A French officer was forcing Caterina to her knees, his sword at her throat.

'Ten thousand, or I kill her now!'

In one movement, Valentino had the sword ringing on the flagstones and his own blade at the soldier's neck.

'You'll have your ransom. Forgive me, Countess. Allow me.' He held out his hand to raise her and she, trembling, allowed him.

They led her down to the city, with the fires blazing up behind her and the rain in her bedraggled hair, just as I had seen it.

CHAPTER SEVENTEEN

N THOSE FIRST DAYS IN THE PALAZZO NUMAI, IT
seemed that my lady was broken. She would have no one near
her but me, and to me she did not speak, except to bid me close
the shutters. Forli was no longer hers, thus no longer of interest. The Countess of Forli slept as the French slaughtered her
entire garrison, save those who had made a bridge of the corpses
of their fellows and escaped across the moat. She slept as the
Rocca was stripped bare in the cruellest riot that poor battered
city had yet seen. Horses, arms, furnishings, everything was
taken and the French quartered their prisoners in search of
swallowed gold. Through that night and into the next the
slaughter continued, but the Countess was numb as a toad.

I learned from the maid who brought us linen and water that
Caterina's ladies, at least, had been saved through Valentino's
protection and sent on to Rome. Not that she seemed to care.
She did not wish to know what had become of her people, or
even of her things, or to write to her children, or her uncle,
though ink and parchment were brought, or to have me wash
and dress her, though a bundle of gowns as fine as anything she

had ever owned was sent as a gift from the Duke as though he too had known all along that the Countess would be his prisoner and had them ready. She would not eat the delicate foods Valentino sent in on his own plate, nor rouse herself to send it away. She merely sat, with her knees beneath her chin in her filthy tunic, staring at the wall and worrying at her eyes with her grimy fingers, as though she might pull their lids apart to another reality.

My heart ached for her. I tried to cheer her, to interest her in the heaps of letters that arrived hourly. I spoke to her of Florence, where I was sure we would be allowed to return, that city of her heart which she had not seen since she was a small girl, but she seemed not to hear me, and in a while my own twittering voice sounded foolish, and I too fell silent. I longed to open the window, to walk a little beyond the confines of the room, but if I moved to do so, she would quietly lay a hand on my arm and I knew I might not. I wished that I had taken her at her word and taken my chances with the French troops and the road to Florence, but it was too late. In truth, I too was afraid of what lay beyond the door – not the ravaged streets of Forli, where the soldiers still howled drunkenly; but Valentino. For, now my dreams had reached their source, they vanished. I had thought I had the sight, like my own mother, like poor Margherita, I had taken it as part of me, even as a gift to compensate for my deformity, but it was gone, quite gone, and my sleep was as clear as that of an exhausted child.

In the long hours that I watched over Caterina, I sorted through my memories, piling them like pebbles, one here, the other there. I scrabbled my hand between my legs and ran it over my closed flesh. That was true. I scrabbled in my memory beneath Margherita's rags and saw myself drawing out the palle beneath Cecco's astonished eyes. That was true. I rooted through my dreams and saw that they had come about, that I had seen Piero's fall, and Caterina's. I had brought back the old wolf at the troupe's campground. That was true. And they had been there, that night at the Rocca. So why, when I tried through those endlessly short winter days, to send out my voice to the hills around the city, to make the wolves come again, were they gone? None of it made sense to me, except the futility of my fantasies that I would ever escape. So if my lady was beyond weeping, I was, too. I had been taken once from my burning home to be locked up in a strange place in the clothes I stood up in, and here I was again, no better or wiser than that frightened girl long ago in Toledo.

Each evening, a message came from Valentino to ask if the Countess would take supper with him, and each evening I refused for her. The month was nearing its end when word came that we were to be moved to the Palazzo Paolucci, where the French command was lodging. At least my lady submitted to me now, though she maintained that silence that I understood so well. What use are words when everything has been taken from you? But she allowed me to bathe her in warm water and scent her skin with attar of roses, to comb out and braid her hair and lace her into a soft gown, which hung a little loose at the waist and hips. She was not to go out as a prisoner, but as an honoured guest; the French sent an escort of guards and even a trumpeter, as though she was an ambassador rather than a trophy of war. We made the short walk across the city in twilight, through empty streets. Those who still remained in Forli had barricaded themselves in their houses, and though the ravages of the French could be seen on every side, the town seemed curiously peaceful. The Countess kept her eyes to the ground, she would not raise them to the skyline where the blackened hulk of the Rocca loomed above us.

As we came into the piazza we heard shouts. A group of drunken soldiers had cornered two young girls, dragging them, leering and stumbling, towards San Mercuriale. The girls' cloaks were torn from them, they clutched their gowns pathetically over their breasts and then, as we watched, one of the group took his dagger and slit their chemises, exposing their naked skin. That, finally, wakened something in the Countess. Even as the guards rushed over to discipline the men, she screamed. Shrieking, her arms flailing wildly, she tried to break away, and when one of the men held her arm she fought him desperately, kicking and writhing. It took three of them to subdue her, sobbing hysterically on her knees, as I rushed to her side and held her hand tightly.

'Please, Madonna,' I whispered. 'Please, not here. Not where we can be seen. Come, now.'

She clung to me, as she had done once before. I knelt awkwardly to support her weight, stroking her shoulders and hair to soothe her until the storm of weeping had passed.

'You must be brave,' I told her, 'you mustn't let them see.'

She calmed, I helped her to rise, settling her gown into place, glaring furiously at the smirking guards.

'My lady was unwell,' I said loudly. 'It is the shock of the night air. But she is better now.'

'Blasted wildcat,' muttered the guard who had restrained her, sucking at his arm where she had bitten it.

'You will know your place or regret it, sir,' I answered stoutly. My lady composed herself and continued walking, her head held high now. I shuddered at the cries of the soldiers, unchastened and jeering, prowling the piazza for another victim.

We were greeted by Monsieur d'Allegre, the representative of the French king who had heard my lady's submission. He offered refreshments, which the Countess refused. Nor would she speak, nor send me away, though Monsieur d'Allegre addressed her first in Italian, then in French, then, despairingly, in schoolboy Latin. I had taken one of the gowns that had been sent in for the Countess, the most modest I could find, a dark blue silk, and covered my hair decently with a mantle. I hoped I did not look too odd. I stood behind the chair she had been offered before the fire and cast my eyes at my folded hands in the long silence.

I saw how the Frenchman watched her, how his curiosity to see the legendary lady of Forli was overcoming even his good manners.

'There is some doubt, madam, as to whom, that is, where . . .'

He coughed and tried again.

'His Majesty of France is of the opinion that you, my lady . . .'

Caterina turned her face up to him, her eyes alive for the first

260

time in so long. Her voice was hoarse, ugly.

'You are uncertain, sir, as to who owns me? Whose trophy I am, no?'

'The French king does not take women as prisoners, madam. Honour requires us to protect and release any ladies who are, ahem, that is.'

'But I am not a lady, am I, sir? I am Countess of Forli. Or, at least,' her hand went to her throat, her fingers seeking her lost ruby, 'at least I was. Which means I am valuable to you. Though I very much doubt that there will be any in Italy who will step forward to ransom me. I am rich in admirers, I believe, but no longer in friends.'

'I think it best, lady, if the matter of your-ah-peculiar case be left to my master, His Majesty, to decide.'

'My uncle of Milan—'

'There is no ruler in Milan, madam, but the King of France. I wish only to know whether you prefer to remain here, as my guest, naturally, until this matter has been decided, or whether you wish to continue under the-ah-the protection of Monsieur le Duc de Valentinois.'

'I may choose?'

'Of course, madam. We are not barbarians.'

My lady rose. She was graceful again, haughty. 'Of course not, sir. Merely minions. Very well, you may inform your master that until he makes his pleasure known, I prefer to remain with my countryman, Monsieur le Duc. I wish you good evening. Come, Mora.'

And in the flick she gave to the train of her gown as she left the Frenchman staring, I saw the girl who had held a castle in Rome with nothing but her will, the woman who had chosen Ser Giovanni as her husband, who had defied the Pope himself. I knew that my lady was come to herself again, and that she would fight once more, if only for her freedom, which I dearly hoped would also be mine.

So we returned to the Palazzo Numai, where the Countess immediately set about tumbling the bundle of silks on the bed.

'What age is the Duke, Mora, would you say?'

'Four or five and twenty, madam, I should think.'

'Hmmm. Have we a looking glass?'

'The Duke has thought of everything. Look, here, madam. And brushes, and creams.'

'Was anything saved from the *farmacia*?'

'I believe not.'

My lady regarded her face ruefully in the glass, a beautiful little thing with a silver handle set with lapis lazuli.

'Then this is all I have, little witch. We must make the best of it.'

'I could have some things sent, madam, from the kitchens. Perhaps the receipt for the face, with the chicken broth and the borage? We need only boil it.' I was almost laughing, I was so relieved to have her back.

'My face can shift for itself. I had in mind—'

I understood.

'*Uxare de luxsuria*?' It was one of my invented names, we had used it before. ' I could make that . . . I need the blood of a wild boar, though. Cantharidin, strong wine.'

She giggled. 'Oh, but you are bold, little witch! You would be conjuring, even now?'

'I will be careful, very careful.' I would do anything to help her.

'Hurry then. And water for my bath, olive oil. And salt and rosemary for my teeth, be quick. What is the time?'

'About six, madam.'

'Then have the things sent and make it quickly, look there's a basin, you can do it here. And tell the maid that I accept Monsieur le Duc's offer to sup with him, in an hour or so.'

*

I accompanied the Countess to Valentino's rooms, still dressed in my dark gown. When we came to the door I was shaking, breathless. How could I tell my lady that I was come to the end of my dreams? I could not help the feeling that it was not the Countess of Forli Valentino was waiting for, but me.

The sala of the old palazzo was empty. It was less fine than I had known at the Rocca, but it had been prepared carefully, with the Duke's own furnishings. I heard that when he travelled he even took his own privy with him, made from solid silver, in a curtained litter, and the Countess giggled again like a girl when I told her that and said she hoped we would not be seeing that this evening. She was beautiful again, her thinness making her seem younger than her thirty-seven years, and I had arranged her hair loosely in a gold-looped filet so that it hung away from her temples, over her back, showing warmly against the white of her skin in a low cut mantle the colour of flame. I wondered whether she had picked that out on purpose, to remind Valentino of what he had brought her to. The room smelled of spiced incense, warm and soothing; the fire was built up with sweet cherry wood. My lady arranged herself carefully on a settle, spreading out her gown.

'Monsieur le Duc would keep me waiting, Mora?'

'Not at all, madam.'

I started. The deep shadow beside the fireplace resolved itself into a figure, a tall man, and as he stepped forward into the light I saw that his own clothes were black again, exquisite Spanish velvet, even his hands encased in fine gloves. When he raised the Countess's hand to his lips I caught the glint of a jewel over the leather on his right hand, a huge ring in plain gold, set with the great Riario ruby.

'It looks very well, Monsieur le Duc, I must admit,' remarked my lady composedly.

'The spoils of war, madam.' For the first time I heard the sibilant hiss of Castilian beneath his Italian.

He nodded for the servants to leave, but my lady caught at my sleeve.

'I prefer that my slave remain here with me, sir.'

'As a chaperone, madam?'

'Indeed.'

'Then the girl may serve us.'

I had the philtre in my sleeve. The dishes were set along the table, the same plate I had seen in the days of our captivity, chased with the flames of the Borgia sun. I took the lids from a serving of partridge with raisins and another of hare in wine. I filled a plate for the Countess and set it before her, and took up another, curling my hand back to pull out the phial. The Countess was speaking of Rome, of the changes in the city since she had lived there, as smoothly and casually as if she were entertaining in her own rooms at the Rocca. I had the cork out and was set to tip the mixture into the juices and wine on the plate when I felt the grip of leather on my wrist. I had not even seen his hand move.

'You mistake me, Countess? Or perhaps this is some sort of joke. You would seek to poison a Borgia? Disappointingly amateur.'

He pronounced it the French way, sardonically drawling, but the vice on my wrist was crushing the bone and I recalled the speed with which his blade had found the throat of the bounty hunter. I tried to control the trembling that began again in me, knowing he had the right of it if he put his dagger in my breast. I dared not glance at the Countess, but I spoke to him quickly in Castilian.

'Forgive me, sir, my lady knows nothing of this. I made it myself, it's harmless, sir.'

My lady was counterfeiting shock and confusion, perhaps a little too much.

There was a slight, a very slight, loosening of the tension on my arm.

'You are Spanish?'

'From Toledo, sir. This is nothing, I swear to you.'

My lady adjusted her expression to the placidity of perfect innocence.

265

'You would have me believe that? I could slit your throat.'

I was desperate to pull away, but he could have killed us both before I was halfway to the door. And I knew he would do it.

'I'll swallow it myself, sir, look.'

The fingers relaxed, drawing caressingly over the underside of my wrist. I felt a contraction deep inside me, for a moment the room lurched and the flames of the fire rose high in his black eyes. He was looking into my face. I saw only him.

'Do it then.'

I took it down neat in one burning swallow.

'And its purpose?'

'To make you kind, sir. To make you look well on my poor lady.'

'Stay over there. I will watch you as we dine. If you are ill, you will die, you know that?'

'I understand, sir. Thank you, thank you.'

'And we will see if your lady can make me kind nonetheless, shall we?'

I watched an hour in the shadows while the drug worked on me. Or perhaps it did nothing, perhaps it was that slight, lazy touch of his fingers that made my heart pound and my lips moisten. I could not tear my eyes from his face, from his throat as he swallowed his wine, from the blood that came in stars to his high cheekbones, from his mouth, his beautiful, beautiful mouth. When the Countess rose to her feet and made him a curtsey, I stepped forward to assist her from the room, but my body had become a stream, I could get no purchase on the floor.

'Your slave sickens.'

266

'I believe not, sir. She is a good girl, but she knows nothing of medicines. She was only foolish, and I will leave you to teach her better.'

The doors closed behind her. She had left me to him. She knew what I had done, she knew what was in the phial, and she had left me to him. It was not I, but she, who knew how things would come out.

'Come.'

I staggered and he held out an arm to help me.

'You see, you sicken. I should call my men. Or cut your hand off myself.' But the danger had gone from his voice.

'I am not sick, sir,' I managed to whisper.

'I have seen you before.'

My head swam with visions, of that night of fire, his hand on my arm, the red gleam of the ruby, of all the nights I had woken to him. I saw two forgotten bundles of blood and rags, my useless charms. My red dress, my mother's stitching above my heart, wish, desire. *Iron, to bind a demon.*

'The night you took the Rocca, sir. I gave you that.'

'You were not dressed as a maid.'

'My lady insisted. She thought I might escape, but I would not leave her.'

'Pity.'

His hand strayed at my throat now, the leather tracing the length of my collarbone. I felt my breath still inside my chest, the frantic pumping of my heart slowing, slowing, until all the blood in my body seemed to flow where his fingers travelled, red as a comet's tail.

'You are a maid, then.'

'Yes, sir.'

'As I said, a pity. I had thought of that boy. But you will do.'

My neck was held in his palm, he turned me until my back was against him and I clutched at the chair to keep myself from falling. I felt the silk of the blue dress rising against my thighs. There was nothing to protect me. His mouth was warm against my skin.

'Yes. You will do very well.'

CHAPTER EIGHTEEN

THAT NUBBY-BONED LITTLE CLERK WHO HAD COME TO Forli to treat for an alliance with Florence told me that he had warned the Countess. The best fortress in the world, he told her, was nothing without loyalty. No stronghold could withstand the force of a people's hatred. Caterina had learned this, that the respect and love she believed her people to bear for her was no more than craven fear. The cruelties her vengeance had inflicted on Forli when her husbands had been murdered had never been forgotten, and when the moment came for the people to forgive her, that forgiveness was withheld, and the gates of Imola and Forli were opened to Valentino. She believed that her Sforza sword and her Sforza will were stronger than fortune, but she could not hold the Rocca. It burned because love and loyalty were nothing to her against her pride. Perhaps I should have warned him too, Machiavelli, that he would have dealings with Valentino, and that in the end princes lost the love of their people because they did not see us as people at all.

So when everything else was taken from Caterina, her lovers and her children, her titles and her jewels, her home and her state, she laid me out for Valentino as casually as a gambler throwing down a card in a tavern. She took my love and my loyalty to her and she used them as she would, caring nothing for me, seeing only the slave who existed to serve her. I saw all this as I stumbled back along the passages of the Palazzo Numai. I saw it as I clutched my blue gown around me to stanch the ruby of blood that slid between my thighs. She had known exactly how it would come out.

I remembered the scandalised reports we had heard from her spies in Rome about Valentino's debaucheries, how his banquets were served by naked courtesans, how he had taken his own sister to his bed, how as his power increased he became ever more shameless about his tastes and ever more voracious in his desires. I thought of the love charms we had brewed at the Rocca, of the noises I had heard from her bedroom at night. Had the door been left ajar, even then, to goad me or to teach me? Her body was her last weapon, and when she saw it would no longer serve, she made use of me. She had seen so far ahead, and I, fool, had followed her blindly. The boy's clothes, the presentation of the ruby, the bungled pouring of the philtre, all this she had seen and planned, and it came out as she wished it. She thought that good little Mora, poor half-finished thing, would serve in her place, because she knew, as I did not, that sometimes more pleasure can be found in the broken will of ugliness than the willing submission of even great beauty. But Caterina, unlike me, was not accustomed to losing. I was glad now that I had not told her the worst of Adara's treachery. She did not know that her little slave had spent the last weeks of her childhood in a brothel. She knew nothing of my dreams of the man in black. I had thought, in those frenzied moments before the battle for Ravaldino began, that we were alike, she and I; but now I saw that the call I had felt through the shadows of my blood was the call of his coming.

I did not cry. I had no more tears for Caterina. My lady was lost to me. When I saw how she planned to use and discard me, to barter me for her freedom, all my love and hope and trust were sliced away, swift as a butcher's knife on the throat of a screaming pig. It was a child's plan, hers; she had not the measure of her man. But I did, now. And I saw as clear as my lost dreams how I would destroy her.

*

That first night, she was all gentleness and sympathy. She sent away the maid and lifted the blue gown from me with her own hands. She sponged the blood from my back and thighs as tenderly as if she were my mother, and my heart was raw that the softness of her attention, which just an hour ago would have made me rejoice in the certainty that my love was returned, was now merely the last act of a shameful masquerade. But she mistook my tears for those of any maid who has lost her maidenhead, and held me to her breast and soothed me, and took me to sleep in her bed, where I was sure to lie as calm as a child who has sobbed its grief into dreams. She was even a little ashamed, as Adara had been shamed, that she had sold me. When Valentino's man came for me after supper the next day, she held me tightly to her and whispered that I had to be brave, that if I could endure I should save us both. And I answered my lady stoutly that she need not fear for my courage and that I should see us both safe, for had I not promised that I should never leave her? The next night, she suggested that perhaps I might wear my boy's breeches when I was summoned, and the next she rouged my lips as eager as a bawd. And then I followed the man to Valentino's chamber, where the fire was banked high, and waited for the soft click of the closing door.

It was never love, what happened between us. Even I was not so starved as to mistake the slaking of his hunger for that. It seemed that all my life, since I left my papa's house in Toledo, I had been waiting and dissembling. First in the kitchens of the Medici palazzo, then in the porch with poor Margherita, in Maestro Ficino's study, in the *farmacia* at the Rocca. I had protected myself by becoming what people believed me to be, by performing the role they believed themselves to have chosen for me – and it had brought me to this. This was my fate, this is what I was cursed to become. I did not mourn for myself any longer, instead I felt at last that I knew what I was and I would no longer be ashamed of it. So I set myself to study what Valentino wanted of me, and whilst I made certain to keep fearful and modest before Caterina, I cannot deny that it gave me pleasure.

For he was lovely, Cesare, as beautiful as all the stories had claimed, as purely and cleanly made as that snow statue I had seen once in a Florentine courtyard. The skin of his face and neck was tan from his season's campaigning, but the flesh beneath his collar was pale as milk. He liked me to bite him, to draw a thin skein of blood down his chest and follow it with my tongue. There could be sweetness in pain, he showed me, even as his flesh tore at mine and I turned my mouth to fill it with the leather of his gauntlet to keep myself from crying out, even as his pleasure flowed into my wounds. He left me a virgin, though that too I kept from Caterina. How could he leave me anything else? Those few days, I was drunk with him, drunk with his scent in my mouth and the echoing throb of his touch on all the secret places of my body, and though I feared him still, it was soothing to make myself his creature, to feel that, at last, I was where I belonged. Under his hands, I no longer felt ugly. The copper smoothness of my slight body and the slenderness of my thighs were no longer a source of shame. He desired me. And as I watched Caterina, the lines in her face, the slackness of her childbearing belly, I felt a stab of ugly jealous pride that it was I and not she who he took to his bed.

When I woke in the mornings, stunned from the black sleep into which I always fell after I left him, I could believe that I was in a labyrinth, a nightmarish harem from some Eastern tale. I had to trick my way out or feel the softness of a silk sack enclose me before I was thrown helpless into the dark waters forever. I knew that I must not lose my head. Caterina had allowed her passion for her low-born husband to drive her to the vengeance and her state had paid the price. I was determined not to do the same. I had only days to turn his caprice for me to account.

I should make a whore of her as she had made of me. It was not difficult to leave a few of her possessions in his rooms for the servants to find and allow kitchen gossip to do the rest. Soon they were saying in the palazzo that the Countess had not defended her virtue so well as her fortress, that it was she, not I, who had succumbed to Cesare's lust. What else would they believe of a woman who had been so notoriously free with her lovers? I was a nothing, merely her odd-looking slave. No one would suspect that the soon-to-be Duke of the Romagna might indulge himself with a freak when he had one of the most famous beauties of Italy in his power. I thought that the French might not be so gallant in their protection of her if they thought her shamed, and I was right.

And then, I had to make Cesare believe in me, to need me. I needed to find what it was that made him afraid. For all of his splendour and magnificence, for all that glory seemed to follow him like stardust in a comet's tail, for all that men believed he moved so swift and silent as to be invisible, for all that his cruelty made him beloved for his mercy, I knew that Cesare was fearful. His Spanish blood ran hot with superstition, with distrust at the magnitude of his fortune. I of all people knew well enough that Spaniards answered to older gods than the one who ruled in Rome. He was careless with his papers, for why should he think an *esclava* could read? He received letters from the astrologers his father kept at the Vatican in defiance of his state, filled with the kinds of occult signs and predictions I had not seen since my days with Maestro Ficino. If his sleep was fretful, he reported his dreams; he was as suspicious of omens as an old peasant woman. They had played so high, he and his holy father, they believed that they could tame chance to their will, yet Cesare was shackled by the incomprehensibility of his future. Somewhere, he believed that he would die alone, as poor and hunted as he had rendered so many others. Fate tormented him like a courtesan, and he followed her with all the desperate expectation of an apprentice boy clutching at the robe of his first whore in a Trastevere *bagnio*. I had to make myself strong where he was weak, to convert chance to certainty, to convince him that I could conjure Fortune as clear as a Venetian balance sheet. I could comfort him, I saw, when he woke sweating and shaking from the nightmares that plagued him, his handsome face turned to me drawn with pleading, desperate to know if I could make his lady kind. But how? My sight was gone, if it had ever existed, and I could not risk a mistake. But in the way of the powerful, he was incurious. I existed to serve his pleasure and that was all.

Caterina's condition was not officially that of a prisoner, but a guest of the French king. She was permitted to read and write letters, to walk abroad, discreetly guarded, if she chose, though the foul winter weather and the wreck of her city dissuaded her from that. I knew that she was afraid of being sent to France, that once Valentino had installed his Spanish garrison and their governors in Forli he would move on to his planned conquests in the remainder of the Romagna. Her presence would be a hindrance in the field, she could too easily become the focus of rebellion. Better send her north, to stitch away the rest of her life in a French castle, for the King of France would never release a Sforza while he planned to hold Milan.

So one morning, Caterina asked for a candle and held it to a letter.

'It's good to be a woman, Mora,' she remarked as the heat of the flame brought out the characters crammed beneath the dispatch, which Valentino's spies would already have seen. Lemon juice, I thought rather contemptuously. Not sophisticated.

'They think us such fools, you see. Incapable. It's coming now, look.'

She read the message and turned to me, her eyes bright.

'Oh, it is too cruel, and too wonderful. A month ago and my standard would still be flying over Ravaldino. My uncle has an army, twenty-five thousand men, and he will move on Milan.'

I feigned to share her delight, my mind working desperately.

'Is this known, yet, Madonna? Could Valentino know of it?'

'My man writes from Chiavenna. They will not learn of it for several days.'

'My lady, you wish to remain in Italy? To see your children and fight for your state?'

'Of course. But there will be no need for fighting. My uncle will take Milan and Valentino will be forced north.'

'Then it is wonderful indeed.'

She was so happy then that she embraced me, and I endured her touch with more disgust than I had ever felt at Cesare's vicious caresses. She had trusted me, as once I had trusted her. Now, though, I saw that she had given me all that I needed.

*

'Monsieur le Duc will have peaches to his supper this evening.'

'Peaches!' screeched the cook. 'And where am I to get peaches this season?'

'I know not nor care not,' I answered pertly, 'bottled peaches is what he wishes. Find some.'

I left him, muttering about what you expected from the manners of a whore's maid, and took a turn in the city. In the ravaged cathedral of San Mercuriale I found something that would serve me and I buried it at the threshold of the palazzo, breaking my fingernails as I prised up a flag. Caterina was tense, pacing her room, sitting down occasionally to scribble at a letter, then up and pacing again, looking to the window, alert for the prospect of news. The coded message from Chiavenna she would not find, since I had taken the trouble to burn it. Slaves had no use for reading, after all.

'Please, Madonna, be patient. You will exhaust yourself. All will be well, you'll see.'

'Of course. I should rest.'

'I will have the bed warmed, and send for your supper, Madonna.'

I kept my voice as quiet and soothing as I could, moving softly about her, making as if to tidy her things so that she did not see me filching a gown and hiding it under a pile of linens, sliding a ribbon into my pocket. When she was settled, I put on my boy's clothes, looking at her submissively as I did so.

'Poor Mora.'

'I do not think I suffer worse than you, Madonna.'

The knock came and I went meekly into the passage where I told the attendant to turn his back and wait. It seemed to take forever to fasten the gown and arrange my hair as I had planned, I could not allow Valentino's impatience to spoil his temper. If

277

the guard was surprised at my metamorphosis he said nothing, I supposed he had seen stranger things. I dismissed him as we reached the door.

'My, but we are fine, this evening, Mora. I am flattered.'

'I am not Mora. I am a lady, a Roman lady.'

And then I said something in Castilian that I thought might get me whipped, or worse, something I had practised over and over so as to get the shocking words out smooth. He took a long breath, and then I feared that he might laugh, but he simply took me and turned me, his hands playing in my loose hair as I raised my gown. I could see the dish of peaches set on the table by the fire. He followed my eyes.

'A pretty touch, the peaches. Elegant, as I would expect from my sister.'

This time, I did not allow either the pain or the pleasure of his touch to send me away into that half-swoon where I knew nothing but the quiver of my hurt and my longing for release. I bit my lip and made the sounds he expected of me, I moved just so in his arms, enough for him to hurry on through my suffering until he collapsed on top of me, his face buried in the silver of my hair. I let him rest a moment, then turned beneath him, shaking out my gown and fetching the plate from the fireside. I poured wine calmly, allowing him time to order himself. When I turned, it seemed he had already forgotten me, would not even hear the sound of the latch that marked my going.

'Would you take some wine, sir?'

'Would you poison me again? You may leave me.'

'Sir, I have discovered something. Something you would wish to know.'

'Very well. Quickly.'

'I worked in the *scrittoio* of Maestro Ficino before I came here from Florence. I saw much of his art, sir. He said I had . . . a gift.'

He was curious now, curious and fearful, I could see it in the change of his face as he looked on me.

'Ficino, you say?'

'If you will come with me, sir. We will need a torch, and a guard, if you wish.'

He bridled at the idea that he might fear to be alone with me. I took him down through the sleeping house and as he held the flare with his own hands I prized up the paving slab and reached inside. I thought on my mummings with Margherita's customers, and when that didn't work, I thought on my papa, to keep myself from laughing. It was really so very easy.

'To speak with angels, sir,' I whispered, making my voice as quiet and mysterious as I could. 'My master taught me this. It is from the Kabbalah, sir, from the lands of the East before Our Lord even walked there.' I sounded just like Margherita, I had to turn a giggle into a cough. 'To speak with angels, one says a message over the image – thus.' I held up the icon I had filched from the cathedral to the light. 'And then it must be buried at the threshold, so, with the name of the person who is to receive it, and a piece of parchment for the angels to leave their answer. And then, if the calculations are correct, the answer will come within a day. And here it is.'

I had made it myself, written in wine which I hoped would look like blood in the flickering light of a torch. It was a poor charm, in truth. Maestro Ficino had never made it work, he said that he had never made the calculations correctly, but then Valentino was not to know that. I held out the paper to him with a puzzled look, appealing to his wisdom to interpret these strange scratchings.

'I asked the angels, sir, I asked them what would happen to my lady. When I saw the writing, I knew they had answered, so I came to you.'

'And I am to believe this, this Moorish nonsense?'

But his eyes were scanning the paper. It told him just what the coded letter had told Caterina, of Il Moro and his great army, raised by his relative the Archduke Maximilian of Austria, of how they had massed in the frozen fastness of the Alps and were even now descending on the lake country in their pursuit of Milan. I could see his mind, working quickly, calculating how this would affect his plans, his pact with the French, but also his suspicion, his inability to believe that this could be anything other than another slave's trick.

'How can you know this? Have you spoken with the Countess? Seen a letter? You can read?'

'No, sir, but there are many ways of reading. And there is no letter. My lady knows nothing of this.'

'Mind to whom you are speaking! Be clear.'

'As I said, sir, I assisted Maestro Ficino at the Medici palace in Florence. You might send your couriers, sir, to see if I am correct. But perhaps it will be Monsieur d'Allegre who wishes to ride north.' I made my voice servile, wheedling. 'I thought you might be glad, sir.'

'D'Allegre. Yes. I will send at once. Return to your mistress.'

'I await your pleasure, sir,' I answered, allowing just a hint of insolence in my voice as I bobbed him a curtsey and skittered out of the range of his hand.

He screwed the scrap of parchment into his palm and turned into the house. In moments I could hear his voice rousing the guard, summoning his horse. I could have run then, if I had wished it, slipped through the streets of Forli before I was missed, yet, meekly, I waited his bidding.

The key was turned in the lock after me as I entered our chamber, and the door remained locked as two short winter days crawled past. Caterina was mad with anxiety, craving to know what was happening, where Valentino was and why she was being treated as a prisoner again. I said the words she expected to hear, that we must be calm and simply wait, for would not her uncle of Milan send his men south as soon as he had recovered his duchy? So intent was she on her own plight that she missed the mechanical hum in my voice and the dullness in my eyes. For myself, I no longer cared. If I had failed, Valentino would kill me and I should be glad to be quit of my wretched life. I knew, though, that my dreams were not done with me, for had I not seen him there, in the Holy City? I trusted calmly that I should live that long, at least.

On the third day, Valentino returned. We heard the shouts in the *cortile*, the noise of hooves. Caterina was at the window, she turned as the men entered, but not quickly enough to move before they clapped a pair of iron cuffs on her wrists.

'What is this? How dare you use me so? You will answer to the King of France for this.'

'No, madam. There are no Frenchmen left in Forli. You, girl, pack your mistress's things and look sharp about it. You're moving.'

Caterina sank on the bed, her hands twitching uselessly in their fastenings.

'You must do as you are bid, Mora,' she sneered wearily. 'It seems once more we are betrayed.'

'Take courage, Madonna. We will go to the coast, no? To Pesaro? You have your kinsman there.'

'No,' she said slowly. 'If the French are gone against my uncle, Valentino will not continue his campaign in the Romagna without their lances. He will cut his losses. And my cousin of Pesaro has been burned by the Borgia once. Rome. He will take us to Rome.'

PART THREE

ROME

1500

CHAPTER NINETEEN

ON THE FIFTH DAY OF THE SECOND MONTH LUDOVICO Il Moro made himself once more Duke of Milan, while Cesare Borgia was proclaimed Duke of the Romagna. We were long gone from Forli, then, even had he troubled to send his men against Valentino to deliver his troublesome niece. Caterina was placed in a litter, its leather curtains laced tight, concealing, at least, the ignominy of her fastened hands. For three weeks we crawled through the filthy February weather, to Cesena, towards Urbino, cross-country to Spoleto, then Vicovaro. Caterina's litter was carried on the middle of the train, behind the company of five hundred horse that remained of Valentino's cavalry; I travelled further back in the baggage train, where I heard my own Spanish tongue and the strange, guttural speech of the Gascon and German mercenaries. We entered no cities, at night we bivouacked wherever we were ordered and I was permitted to attend Caterina and make her what poor toilette I could. We might have been passing through Hades, so thick was the grey mist that surrounded us, so silent the villages we passed. Even their church bells stopped at the approach of Valentino, all the peasants hiding in their huts or run away.

I did not expect to see him until he had use for me again. The news from the north had proved that the little Spanish slave was serviceable in more ways than one. Caterina was kept under the guard of twelve Spaniards at all times, who searched me before I was permitted to enter the litter, mussing my mud-splattered gown and making bawdy remarks, until I silenced them with a few of my own. After that they treated me cautiously and then, as the journey wore on, began to speak a little to me of the news from the couriers who occasionally passed us like spirits, the sweat on their horses discernible in the still, icy air, long before they came in sight, riding for the head of the train. Il Moro was at Novarra, the French were closing in. The Sforza, it seemed, would not hold Milan for long, and Monsieur d'Allegre, it appeared, had forgotten his French gallantry. We were served the same poor rations as the men, hard black bread, thin greasy soup and a few handfuls of dried fruit, no plate or napkins, not even wine. Caterina was permitted to leave the litter only to squat and relieve herself, where I did what I could to shelter her with my skirts. She was weak and grey faced and her unwashed hair dulled to a greasy bronze. Nothing in her treatment indicated what she had been, no courtesy was paid to her rank or her state. When I heard the men talking of the use she had accepted at Valentino's hands when he had kept her in his rooms at Forli night and day, I did nothing to check them. She was of no more account than a discarded alehouse trull, and though I was sure to keep my countenance about her, I rejoiced inside that she too now knew what it was to be nothing.

It was as we descended the spine of Italy into the softer lands of Lazio that I saw the troupe. We had seen very few travellers thus far, but as we came upon the route to the Holy City we began to meet pilgrims, some on foot, with stout walking staves, worn and weary with walking and fasting, others fine people with litters or even carriages, all bound for the jubilee celebrations in the Borgia city. Caterina barely glanced at them, though even the sight of a new face made for a little diversion in the grim tramp of our journey, and they often stopped to exchange news or share their provisions with the men, who were kept in good order, bound by Valentino's discipline and the promise of reward when we arrived. Their wagons came out of the mist as we broke camp one morning, plodding slowly along the crowded track. I felt a little flutter of happiness as I recognised their colours, fresh-painted since they had taken leave of my master and me at Careggi, in another life, and Addio's bright cap, blue this time, perched above the straining rump of the horse. I clambered down from the cart and trotted along the line to where Caterina's guards surrounded her litter. I would speak with these people, I explained in Castilian, they might have news from Florence.

Without waiting for permission I ran back to the wagons, letting down my hood, and as they recognised me a flurry of hands reached down to haul me in. I rode with them all that day, reliving our escape from the palazzo, eager for news of their travels. They had been south to Naples, the most beautiful city you had ever seen, set in a horseshoe of blue water with islands like jewels, and then further, to Palermo, where there had been storms and a shipwreck, and where they had spent a sweltering season eating oranges and fish that swam into your hands if you dipped them from a rock. I could see the colours, feel the brightness of that southern sun, and I wished a little that I had gone with them when they had offered, to a life with its own ever changing rhythms, secure in nothing but the pace of the horses and the uncertainty of tomorrow.

Chellus told me that my old friend was still with them, grizzled and fat, but good enough to frighten the children, and I wondered at that; perhaps he could sense me, and bring them to me when I had need. It was fanciful and I did not share my thoughts. Of Caterina I spoke little, though of course they had heard of the siege of the Rocca and the defeat of the Countess of Forli. All Italy, they said, was talking of it. I told them only that I was following the path that had been set for me – Ser Giovanni was gone and I had seen his son go safe to Florence; I followed my lady as a good maid should. In truth, I was a little ashamed to expose them to what had become of me since they left me in Tuscany. As dusk fell I left them, with promises that I should seek them out in Rome and a cloth of provisions that I had begged from the guards. They could not move so quickly, they explained. They would move back down the line and perhaps make a few coins from a show for the men, who would pay well for a little entertainment.

I was warmed by their acceptance of me, their lack of curiosity as to how they came upon me always in such odd ways. This must be the lesson of the life they led on the road, I thought – that everything comes around, in a while, and that it is best to accept what joy there is in it, and not ask too many questions.

I thought of him, though, my old wolf, as I lay tight in my cloak that night at Caterina's side. It meant something, I was sure, that he had come to me again, and I could not sleep for waiting for it. A day passed, then another, and on the third a gentleman came for me, one of the captains of whom the men whispered at night, and said that I should get up on his horse before him, and come with him to Valentino. The column was settling for the evening, we passed between little glow-worm fires in the twilight, the men easing off their stinking boots, passing skins of wine, arranging their packs as pillows. I kept my head down, avoiding curious eyes. My heart was fluttering at the thought that I should see him again, trepidatious, thrilled. We came to a clump of tents, I was set down and the gentleman led me inside, withdrawing behind me so that we were alone.

'Well, Mora.'

I started. I had never grown accustomed to it, how his voice could come from the shadows where moments before the space seemed empty. The tent was canopied in cloth of silver, burnished in the light of several glass lamps. I smelled beeswax and lavender and good wine. There was a bed, a real bed with a crimson silk tester. I wondered about the silver privy, and for a tiny second I was sad. It was the last time we had truly laughed together, Caterina and I. I took a step forward.

'No. Here. Bring the light.'

His black cloak was still smudged with the dust of the day, his head tipped back to reveal his beautiful, savage profile.

He wore a mask, the black velvet mask I had seen so often in my dreams.

'Lift it. Look.'

I stood over him and he closed his eyes. The skin was the rich creamy colour of parchment, a few lines around the eyes just beginning to betray the wear of years of summer campaigning, but lovely still. A bubbling porridge of sores marred the smooth plane of his cheek.

'The French disease. Or so they called it, in Naples. It has returned.'

'Since when, sir?'

'It came as we left Forli. I cannot, that is, my father.'

For the first time since I had known him, there was a softness in his face. He was pleading with me, to make him whole, that he should not be shamed with poxed blisters when he made his entry into Rome.

'Can you heal it?'

You are mine, I thought. All this time, and you were waiting for me. I knew now why my wolf had come to me, he knew that I would have need of him once more.

'I can try, Your Grace. I need to send a message. And I need space, and a light, I will show you. It will take a little time.'

He replaced the mask and spoke some words to the attendant outside. A quill was brought, ink, parchment. I did not think that any of the troupe could read, and nor, of course, could I, so I drew what they needed.

'A coin, sir. Gold.' I smiled to myself as I closed the paper over it. I could do that for them, at least.

'I need sandalwood. There is a small chest, where the Countess is. Have it brought. Then we will wait a little.'

The pointed almonds of his eyes caught at me.

'Indeed? Then come here, Mora.'

'Your Grace?'

With his knuckle, he traced the length of my jaw. His hands.

'A pity that you're not a boy, Mora. You would make such a pretty boy. My brother Juan would have admired you.'

I sighed, a little in sadness, a little in the anticipation of that once familiar pain. The moment would come when he soothed it. Beyond the pain, what hurt me more was how I craved the balm of him.

'No, sir, not a boy. But I will do very well.'

I turned and dropped my cloak to the floor, bracing my hands against the bedpost.

'Yes. You will do very well.'

I told him to keep from sight when Gherardus brought the wolf to me. Close, though: I wanted to be sure he could watch me. We went a little way from the camp into the trees, where it smelled clean, away from the fug of leather and horse dung and men. There was a space where an oak had fallen, a few slight saplings straining to fill its place. I looked around for a stick and scrabbled a little hollow near the roots of the upended tree, where the earth was softer. Wiping my hands on my cloak, I unpinned my hair and used the pin to scratch a few signs on the sliver of bark I held before me. With the lamp, I set it alight. In the flame of the lamp, the sweet, powerful smoke drew a plum-coloured path into the canopy of trees. I had drawn the smoke as the sign for them to come. I knew they were there, I could smell him.

Gherardus would slip his chain so that he would come to me like a wild creature, at least to one who was fearful and had his eyes obscured with velvet and could not look too closely. It was full night. I heard him first, the slight flattening of the web between his forepaws on the desiccated leaf-mould, the quickness of his curious heart, drawn by the scent. He paused on the edge of the clearing and I turned my head slowly, mindful of those eyes upon me. He trotted towards me, his black pelt silver tipped, thick with winter fat. He brought his muzzle into my palm and I knew that he smelt no fear. For a moment I almost swooned with it, the touch of his wet nose, carrying me back through my dreams, back beyond Forli and Florence to my bed in Toledo and my father's voice and the magic of the *seid*. For a moment, I believed it once again, for all that this was a masque got up to bind Valentino to me. I believed it as I had done at the Rocca, that I could conjure wolves, that they were my creatures, and I of them, that we could run together between the winds and that I was not a cursed thing. I gulped at it like strong wine, and almost turned from my purpose; I wanted to put my arms about his neck and have him carry me away, far away from everything, where the old sound would be the rush of the forest around us and the fierce joy of the hunt. I breathed deep and opened my eyes. I had a task to do.

I had brought a chunk of sausage, I pushed it gently between his teeth. I felt them grind down, his eyes holding mine. I took a clean muslin from my pocket and soaked it in his eager drool.

He licked my palm. I patted his hindquarters to send him back, listened for the clink of the chain and the man's tread, then walked backwards, to where Valentino was waiting. I cleaned the sores with wine, then I unfolded the wetted cloth, squeezing it against the pustules so the rot ran out yellow-white, working the wolf's saliva into the pits.

'There will be no need for the mask, sir, when we come to Rome. In a few days the marks will fade, I promise.'

'I shall not forget. You may go.'

The gentleman was waiting to carry me back in the darkness along the sleeping column of men. I hoped Gherardus was back safe with the troupe. I was trembling a little, less from the hurt of him than from the audacity of what I had done. Could it really be so easy? That one as great as Valentino, with all the power of men and gold that he held in the palm of his hand, could be so bedazzled by a fairground stunt, something to make children whimper and their grateful parents fling coins? The infection in the wounds would clear, his skin would heal and knit together again, but had I merely brought him a cure he would have valued it less, though the result was the same. It was conjuring he wanted from me, *seid*-magic, summoning. It was this, then, that I was meant for, but I wished, as I clambered into the litter and curled my body around Caterina's back, that I could have been for love, instead. For all that it was chilled and poisoned, I had loved her, and I wished I could love her still.

CHAPTER TWENTY

N A JOLTING TRAIN OF BROKEN CARTWHEELS AND oaths, of mud and filth and raw frost, we came to Rome on the twenty-sixth day of the month. The men were in great spirits, talking of the pleasures that awaited them once Valentino had made his triumphal procession through the city. The Duke's steward rode along the lines to oversee the unpacking of trunks and the hanging of liveries, the distribution of black batons and hangings for the mules in the crimson and gold Borgia colours. For Caterina, a black velvet gown was provided, her chafed wrists were unbound, and she was set upon one of Valentino's own wonderful Mantua horses. I could not help but admire how erect and haughty she sat, her eyes far on the horizon, for all that Valentino was displaying her in his train of booty like a conquered pagan queen. Valentino had also sent a chain, a pretty delicate thing of gilt links, which passed from the bridle of Caterina's mount to that of one of his captains. And then it was looped around mine, for I too was to be mounted, as the Countess of Forli's only attendant, with a set of breeches and a hood and doublet of crimson, with 'Cesar' chased in silver across the breast. I braided up my hair tightly and slipped on the clothes.

'It seems that Monsieur le Duc has thought of everything, Mora,' said Caterina dryly. 'How attentive he is.'

'I suppose we cannot help it, Madonna.'

'And such a charming toilette.'

For a moment I felt a thin quiver of fear that she had guessed what I had done, but there was nothing she could hurt me with now. And besides, the gift showed me that I was not forgotten.

I saw him once more as we walked our horses up the line to take up a position near its head. The mules and the baggage wagons came first. I imagined that Caterina must be wondering if any of her remaining possessions from the Paradiso were contained inside. Behind the wagons were two heralds, one in Valentino's colours, the other in those of France. Then came the infantry, a thousand strong, their sallets polished up with sand, then two columns of grooms, dressed as I was, the word 'Cesar' gleaming over the bright cloth. Valentino's gentlemen came next, peacocking in court finery, and then Valentino himself, flanked by a cardinal in scarlet on either side. The mask was gone, his skin was bright and fresh. He wore a knee length robe of his customary black velvet, its deep shadows drawing the eyes amongst the rainbow of his attendants like a cavern's mouth in a meadow of flowers. The only brightness about him was the rich dull gold of the Order of St Michael at his collar and the Riario ruby, which gleamed on his hand. He brought his horse up to Caterina, the lights in his hair shining as he politely removed his black plumed cap.

'Come, madam. You will be glad to see your old home.'

'Indeed, sir. Even with the Pope's bastard as my escort.'

I thought for a moment he might strike her. No one dared to smile. But he kept his face easy and pleasant, even a little pitying.

'You wound me, Countess. Still, with God's grace we may both live to strike another lance together, some day.' So he had heard the gossip, too, and relished it.

The men around us erupted eagerly into coarse guffaws. Caterina went white, her jaw trembling with rage, but she set her gaze in front as he tapped his spurs to his mount, and we passed into the city.

It seemed that the whole of Rome had turned out to gaze at Valentino. We rode first between the columns of a massive gate, into a broad street lined with palaces whose windows and loggias were crowded with women, craning precariously to catch a glimpse of him. In the street, the press of gentlemen and priests, pilgrims, soldiers, beggars, grooms, working folk in their aprons and capering dwarves in fine livery was so great that the horses could barely walk on. Here I saw a fantastically dressed group of Turks, there a gaggle of sober ambassadors, ragged children and insolent strolling whores, all of them crying his name until I was dizzy with it. We were swept along past a huge fortress by the river, banners bearing his name tumbling from the round tower, cannon shattered our ears in a salute as violent as the last assault on the Rocca. As we arrived at the Vatican, we came upon eleven chariots decorated with conqueror's laurels, in the last of them a tableau of Caesar victorious, crowned as an emperor, draped in a cloth of gold tapestry on which was figured the motto *Aut Caesar aut nihil*. 'Either Caesar or nothing.' He was come as a hero, as a prince, with the ravaged wealth of the Romagna behind him, trailing across Italy in a long scar of gold.

We came into an inner courtyard, the crowds still surging behind us, and Valentino dismounted, accompanied by his gentleman, to pass inside for the blessing of his father the Pope. The guard made a knot around Caterina, who, if she recalled that this place had once been her home, that here she had reigned as the favourite of the Holy Father, did nothing to reveal it. I could hear the mutterings of the people, scrambling to get a glimpse of the famed Countess of Forli. I kept my eyes low beneath my hood, but as I glanced across the crowd I caught a face I recognised, a little figure brave in a brass buttoned coat. Addio. So they were here, they had made it. I dared not signal to him, but I watched his face, praying that perhaps he would glance at me, forgetting that in my livery I was just another anonymous lackey. In a moment he was lost in the swell of the mob, but my heart was singing inside me. My friends were come and surely I could find them out.

Twenty guards were assigned to escort the Countess of Forli to her new lodging. It appeared that His Holiness planned to treat her with courtesy, for we were led uphill behind the Vatican to a small palazzo which gave views over the basilica of St Peter and the meadows behind the Castello, thronged today with stalls and cooking fires, a camp to serve the viewers of Valentino's triumph. Here, I thought, I would find my friends. I was eager to seek them out, to see something of this wondrous city, but

Caterina's grim face showed me better than to ask her leave. It was a delightful place, the Belvedere, I could imagine how pleasant it would be here on the heights in the fierce Roman summer, though the gardens through which we rode were stripped and lifeless in the dull February light. We found the house well prepared, and Caterina bade me at once draw her a bath and look about for fresh linens. I poured the water for her, the splash in the copper tub echoing against the joyous cries of the crowds below us. I kept my eyes low, could not help seeing her wasted body nor catching the stench of it after our weeks of travelling. Bathed, she was restored and called for food to be served.

'Taste it for me, Mora,' she said carelessly, 'in honour of our hosts.'

I swallowed a morsel of chicken in lemon sauce, sipped at her wine, chewed some soft bread, all delicious after the coarse scraps we had been given on our journey.

'I think it is safe, Madonna.'

I wondered if she would help me if the food was tainted, or whether she would watch me writhe and retch on the floor, now that her scheme had failed and I was no more use to her. She ate and drank a little, then turned to me, the lines visible in her wearied brow.

'I think you may dispense with those things, Mora. I dislike seeing you dressed so. It reminds me of what you have endured, for my sake. I am sorry for it.'

Before, I should have been glad of her care for me, proud that she would notice my feelings, but now I was wary. I was still useful then. No more than that.

'We will rest soon. Tomorrow or the next day we shall have visitors, I suspect. I have some commissions. You may send to the Palazzo Riario and have them told that I am come. They will bring what is fitting. Sleep, then come to me tonight.'

So she was still plotting. Even here, a politely treated prisoner, she would not give up.

'Change your clothes. Your old gown will do. I still have friends here, who I can call upon. You shall go to them.'

'Yes, Madonna.'

I saw nothing of the marvels of Rome, that night. It was raining as I left the palazzo. In moments my skirts and cloak were sodden with it, it trickled inside my hood and ran down my breast. I was to find a place near the Piazza Santa Maria, in the Trastevere quarter south of the Vatican. The unpaved streets were foul with mud and worse, I held up my soaked gown and tried not to think what I walked across. The streets were as narrow as those of Florence, the façades of fine houses jostling against swaying hovels. I passed a few pigs rootling at a bundle of rags and felt my gorge rise as I saw a naked foot crunched in a probing snout. It was an evil place, beside the river there. I expected every moment to feel a hand on my cloak, a knife against my throat, but I went on, past the sagging doors of taverns, which emitted a fug of sweat and wine into the close frozen air, starting at every cry that blew from the shadows. A hand shot from a broken barrel, scrabbling crabwise towards my leg, a hissed request for a coin. I shuddered and kicked out, sending up a splatter of filth. For all the city was crammed with rejoicing souls, this place seemed to me the refuge of the damned.

I was a long while walking. The streets twisted on themselves like a knot of wool, here bright with lamplight and liveried servants waiting with litters, here as black as the tomb, so I had to hold my hands before me, sliding along the slimed walls and dreading a warm clutch of flesh. Sometimes I smelled incense, drifting down from high balconies, and saw a woman's shape pass before a lighted window, so I could almost hear the swish of a silk sack on a waxed floor. I stepped over abandoned reeking creatures pooled in spirits and their own vomit. I wondered where Valentino lay, whether he slept in the soft arms of a priceless whore, or if he sat, his black sleeve trailing on a lintel, looking out over this place of nightmares. I longed for the wagons, the clean smoke of a campground and familiar faces, I was weary, so weary, and I cried a little at it, but I went on, for something in me impelled me to see it out. Eventually I saw the sign Caterina had told me of, a relief over a doorway lit by a guttering stump of tallow. A lion's head, crudely done in wood with a painted red flame about its neck. I gathered my hood over my face and pushed open the door.

'Good evening,' I called hesitantly.

'Filthy, if you ask me.'

The space was no bigger than a closet, piled like a bazaar with all manner of objects, from brocade curtains to cooking pots, crammed in anywise in tottering heaps. Crouched on a settle, his knees drawn up to his chin, was an old man, his hooked nose and reddish beard recalling the cruel drawings I had seen in my childhood, when the burnings began in Toledo. He was busy at a candlestick, rubbing at it with a cloth to bring out a gleam that caught the sparks from the stove and made his eyes shine yellow.

'I am come from the Countess of Forli. She is at the Belvedere. She said to remind you of her service and that I am to wait for what she requires.'

He chuckled. 'La Leonessa? So she is come at last, with the Pope's son? The whole of Rome has been talking of it. Come, warm yourself a little.'

He hunched his spindly legs further and I wedged myself gratefully into the space next to the stove. My hood began to steam, the smell of the drenched wool was rancid around my face. Cautiously, I lowered it a little.

'You're a good servant, to come along to a place such as this for your lady.' His eyes moved over my face, caught my own, but he said nothing, and I was grateful to him for that.

'She said you have something of hers, something she sent here some months ago. She has need of it.'

'Maybe, maybe not. If she had, why should I give it to you, then? You might be anybody.'

'I am the Countess's own maid.'

'And I'm the Pope's uncle.' He brandished the candlestick at me. 'True, you don't look much in the way of a thief. But all the same—'

'She said I was to remember her to you, good Signor Moise. To remind you that you have dealt together before, when she lived here at Rome. You have the collar, she says, that she sent from Forli, and you may keep it now, if you will furnish her with money and . . . something else.'

'Your proof?'

'I have no proof, sir. They have taken everything from her. She has not even a ring to set a seal with. But the collar is marked on the clasp with the Sforza wyvern.'

He considered this a while, his hands rubbing, rubbing at the silverwork in his lap.

'So it is, so it is. And I may have it, you say?'

'Indeed, if you will do as she requires.'

'She is fallen very low.'

I tried for sadness, a loyal look of resignation. 'Indeed, sir. It is a terrible thing.'

'Those men of hers sent from the Romagna. The poisoners? They can still hear them screaming, over to the Castello.'

'I have never been here, sir. I do not know you.'

'Very well. Will you see it?'

'I should like to.'

I waited in the lulling heat of the stove. I could hear him moving in an upper room, then he returned with a square casket, a cheap-looking wooden thing.

'Come here, to the light.'

It poured across my hands like water, a stream of emeralds set in gold filigree, a princess's dowry in fine mesh.

'A fishing net, see. His last Holiness's little joke. Will you wear it?'

'I?'

'Come. I'll find you a glass.'

I pushed back my trailing hair. Before he fastened it around my neck, he showed me the fastening, two serpents with pale figures in lapis lazuli waving from their mouths, captured mermaids.

'That's it, the wyvern. Here now, have a look.'

He held the stinking candle to a flat silver disc. It was cool on my skin and heavy, though it had not felt so in my hand. I looked, and saw a face I did not recognise staring back at me. The stove's heat after the night air had brought up a flush on my cheeks, the stones' rich green was darker than my eyes, making them flare in the dimness. A few silver strands curled along my cheekbone and lost themselves in the golden netting. I was not ugly. What had Caterina said, when she saw me first at Forli? *Rare*. I stared and stared. In the dancing lines of the glass his face was visible behind me, we looked a long time until I felt a current pass between us, a snap of understanding. He had known cruel words, and faces turned away, and hateful eyes which saw nothing beyond their own fear of strangeness.

'Thank you.'

Signor Moise became businesslike, unsnapping the collar and stowing it away, handing me a dense little sack and bidding me to bind it close in my gown that it should not chink as I made my way back. 'Please to tell the Countess it's what I have. I dare not go out for more.'

'She will be glad of it, now.'

'And the other thing?'

'Poppy.'

He turned his face away. 'She shall have it, but I know nothing of this, nothing. Get you gone now.'

All the strange sweet kindness between us had dissolved. He

was pushing me towards the doorway, shoving a little flask into my curled hand.

'Be safe. Keep your hand to the walls on the right, you'll come out in the Piazza Santa Maria. I have not seen you.'

When once I had come to a lighted place and felt less terror at the thought of the money I carried under my cloak, I wondered at what it would be to wear such things, to be accustomed to them, to feel that you deserved them. I wondered if she remembered it, in all that she had lost, sitting at her throat, fastened there by the very hands of a Pope. I thought I understood a little, now I had felt it against my own skin, of how she could never let go, how she could lose everything rather than abandon her pride in those two serpents, consuming, ravenous.

CHAPTER TWENTY-ONE

I KNEW THE LEGATE WHO CAME TO CALL UPON Caterina the next day, I remembered him from the garden at Forli. A greasy man, with wisps of grey hair protruding from his cap, a sheen on his sallow skin like new cheese. I stood quiet behind her chair while he explained the Pope's plans for Imola and Forli. She might retire to Florence, or wherever else in Italy she might choose, there would be a generous pension, commissions for her sons, preferment in the church. Her treasures would be returned, she could live quiet, and rich and respected. All she had to do was sign her name to a paper waiving the rights of her ruined city.

'You waste your time, sir. I will not sign.'

He spent an hour in wheedling and persuading, she smiled on him calmly, and offered him wine, and pushed away the proffered pen. He came again, the next day, this time accompanied by one of Valentino's captains, and the discussion was not so civil. The captain stood there twisting his hand over his sword-hilt, and it was in all our minds, the story of how Valentino had sent his men into the bedchamber of his sister Lucrezia's husband and how they had cut him down before her very eyes. I wondered that Caterina had not the image of the blazing Rocca before her, how she could be deaf to all those remembered screams, but she would not sign.

'You may kill me here, sir,' she spat contemptuously at the captain. 'You may cut down a defenceless woman if you choose, but I will not give away my rights, or my son's. It will be a proud day's work for you, no?' In fact,' she rose to her feet, 'you may tell Monsieur le Duc that he had better have me murdered, for I will die before I see a Borgia bastard on my lands. Tell him that, sir, with my compliments.'

It continued for a week. Each day the legate came, and each day Caterina refused him.

'I must play for time, Mora,' she told me. 'I have written to my son Ottaviano and he will get word to Monsieur d'Allegre. The French will not see their honour besmirched. They will give him men, and he shall free me.'

How could I say that it was I who had seen to it that the French would give no thought to her honour, that all Rome knew she had been Valentino's whore? There would be no troops, and her son would be ashamed to call her his mother. I could not help it, she was becoming my lady again. As I saw her, so proud, so immoveable, I could not help it, I began to pity her and feel for her as I had done before her last stand at Forli. My hands grew gentle once more as I combed her hair and pinned it up; she felt it, I think, in my touch, my sorrow that she was alone and defeated and that her bright hope would come to nothing. For she still dreamed, Caterina. Her uncle still held

Milan against the French and from there in the north, when the first apple blossom began to appear on the trees in the park, came a priest, Fra Lauro, sent by Il Moro to give succour to the Countess.

'His Holiness can hardly refuse me a confessor,' she observed gleefully. 'We will be in Milan by the end of the spring, Mora.'

She talked much of Milan then, which she had not seen since she was a child. How it stood within its circlet of canals on the Lombardy plain, where the air was so clear you could see the snow on the peaks of the Alps, of the huge red fortress of the Sforza; how, in the spring time, the city sang with the rush of meltwater which fetched down rainbows from the peaks and spun them through the streets. It was as lovely as Venice, lovelier, she said, for in Venice there was nothing to see but water, but in Milan, there were mountains which seemed to reach to Heaven. Her eyes lit up as she spoke of it, while I thought of another city, a magical place where a crystal river ran beneath the ground, and I wanted to weep at how long it had been since I, too, had believed that there was a place where I might go home.

Fra Lauro was a priest, true, but he was no confessor. The money I had fetched from Signor Moise's shop was to be disbursed by him, to bribe the guards and hire the horses who would carry the Countess from the city, to where she might join her son and his men in the countryside and there ride north. They spent hours closeted together, writing, planning, the letters went out under his surplice, but I did not trust him. There was that blindness in Caterina, that belief that the Sforza

307

name would carry all before it, yet when I thought on Ottaviano, that dull, indolent youth who had rode out with Ser Giovanni, I could not believe that he cared enough for his mother to come to her side. Had he not watched from the square in Forli as she defied the rebels to cut her own child's throat? Had she not imprisoned the boy when she suspected him of conspiring with the nobles of Forli to murder her second husband? And had she not betrayed his father's memory with the man who had taken their state? How far did she think he would heed the call of his Sforza blood?

The sun rose a little earlier each day, and its warmth called out the scent of the pine trees on the terraces below the Belvedere, and we waited. The poppy, of course, was to be my part. Fra Lauro told me that when the word came from Milan I was to administer it to the Countess's bodyguard, those twenty Spaniards picked by Valentino himself to surround her, that they should sleep away her going. They trusted me, he observed, I was one of their own. So much of Caterina's life had been this, I thought – confined, impatient, pacing before a window with a view from a painting, awaiting the arrival of letters, of men, of swords to release her only to be confined once more, tighter and tighter, so that from the Vatican itself she had come here, full circle, like a doll in a Chinese box, watching out her life in a series of littler and littler rooms.

I walked in the park and tried to make sense of it. My loyalty was creeping back on me. Somewhere, in the dark streets of Trastevere, I had lost my hatred. Caterina would make use of me, but then who was there that she would not make use of to obey the call within her that held her enslaved, as powerless in the end as I had been on the merchant ship to Genova? *Mind and be nice to the gentleman.* She had been, as I had, a bride before she was a woman, shivering in her shift before a man who owned her, and I saw it then, why she might never bow, never submit. The wolves ran in both of us. Had I too not tasted the pleasures of cruelty? I would not betray her a second time. I would see her safe, I thought, and find my way to the troupe, and go with them, as I was meant to, to my place outside the world. I had never been much for the God of churches and priests, but I knew what I had done was sinful, and in this way I might atone. Besides, I did not think I could face another season of riding and running. I was sickening, I felt it. Sometimes I was gripped by a pain in my belly so sharp I bent with it like a scythe, trying to cram it down inside me. My stomach was tender and sore, I shook as if with fever and thought longingly of the little phial of poppy tincture that would take it away. I made a tisane of camomile, which soothed it some, and hoped it was an ague that would leave me when the heat came to Rome.

But in loving her thus again, even just a little, I had forgot the curse that was on me. In April, Fra Lauro came with a sorrowful face and a letter to show that Il Moro was once more fled from Milan, locked up at Loches, the prisoner of the French. My lady refused to be discomfited, she would join her son still, she said, and then they would work from Florence to retake their city together.

'Perhaps you should sign, Madonna? It is no disgrace now, with Milan lost.'

309

'I tell you, Mora, I will not sign, I will never sign.'

'But then you would be free, and in time—'

'I will not sign. Do not press me, little witch. I would not think you a traitor, too.' I keened inside, to hear that.

Fra Lauro agreed, and reassured her, and took his leave. Just a little longer, he said, and he would send word where the horses waited, and I should pour out the poppy and we would fly. I knew that we should not see him again, that he would melt into the chaos of Rome with the last of my lady's money, lost like a snowflake in a Lombardy spring. Though it was not he who betrayed her, at the end. Valentino's men came and searched the Belvedere and found the letters and the promises of money, but it was not this alone that sealed her fortune. It was that parchment I had worked over a corpse in Forli, that the plague might fall upon the Pope. They had kept the Forlivese prisoners alive, saving them in case they were needed to testify that the Countess of Forli had tried to murder the Holy Father. They waited until she was friendless, until they were sure of her stubbornness, and then they pounced, running down the thread of her fate to bind her and bleed her for the last time. No chivalrous French gentleman would ride out for her now, the poisoner, the whore. There was no name for it even, no name for such a crime. It was beyond treason, it was blasphemy, and she would be lucky if she did not burn.

She was to be tried at once, they told her. The oily legate was with them, his rancid mouth grinning in triumph. She wore a blue gown, that day, Caterina, with scarlet strings in the sleeves where her shift showed white. Quite calm, her hair drawn off her face, her long hands arranging a little posy of snowdrops, behind her the darkening gloss of the trees and the hills of Rome, she sat and listened to the legate as he read the charges. *Witch*, he called her, and the soldiers spat upon the floor. I saw her eyes move swiftly across them, and I feared that she would try to run, that she would provoke them to cut her down there, in sight of St Peter's, and stain the floor with her blood. I could not be still.

'It was I,' I yelled at the legate, 'my lady knew nothing, nothing! Look!' I pulled the phial of poppy where it had lain safe in my gown all these long days. 'This is poison, see. I did it all.'

I made my eyes as wide as they could. *Maligno, demonio.*

'I did it,' I hissed, 'I summoned the plague on the Pope, I made the corpse walk to the Rocca that night that I might drain it of poison. I had the devil to help me, do you hear? Ask your master,' I yelled, muffled now by the arms that moved to grab me while the legate stared and crossed himself, 'ask Valentino if I am not a witch!'

I was panting, my hair was undone, I twisted and writhed like a mad thing as they fastened ropes around my wrists and stuffed a rag in my mouth until all I could move was my eyes. I was beyond myself, gulping for air between my screams. I tried for the fear then, I tried to fetch the *seid* from my blood and ensorcel them with it, but even then my sickness came upon me and I groaned and clutched at my belly, and fainted away.

The rooms in the Vatican were just as I had dreamed them. Painted all over with the double crown of Aragon, its blazing rays streaming over the walls and ceilings, the rampant Borgia bull, a *putto* astride. It was all here, why Valentino had wanted to believe in my conjuring. These were not Christian rooms, they flamed all over with the power of the old gods. Here the Egyptian Apis, black and virile, there a lunette of spinning planets, all set in multicoloured gemstones that recalled the intricate abstractions of Toledo stonework. Perhaps this was what Maestro Ficino had sought, and failed to understand. Here were the symbols and stories he had pored over all his life, here was the potent, humming heart of the strange power that had beguiled the Holy City, and triumphed. Wisdom and knowledge, the philosopher's kingdom on earth, all laid out by a painter's hand, the true reflection of the mysteries the Borgias had summoned and controlled. They were all there, the unholy family, disguised as saints. The Pope himself, on his knees, in a gold mantle worked with signs far less subtle than my papa's rendition of the *Almandal*. The Madonna he worshipped was a portrait of his young lover, a cardinal's sister. Here was black magic, and it was the only proof I had ever seen that it could work.

Valentino waited for us at the end of the long enfilade, the doors so perfectly aligned that they seemed like mirrors, that they would project hundreds of him, black clad, surrounding us in a Borgia labyrinth. Before him were the prisoners, Tommasino of Forli and his servant. A third man, I saw to my horror, was good Signor Moise. The Forlivese were grub-white, blinking dumbly at this sudden and luminous world, the poor old Jew twisting his hands and babbling. His beard was wet with spit, his eyes strayed back again and again to the bound wrists of his fellows. Each of them, I saw, was missing a thumb, though the Forli men had healed stumps on their hands, whilst Signor Moise cradled a sodden red rag. The legate approached Valentino, bowing so low I thought his nose would leave an oily mark upon the floor. The guards were closing the shutters, plunging us into night, there were no clerks waiting with quills to make a record. This was Valentino's way, to move in secrecy and darkness.

'Read the charges.'

Caterina had refused a chair. He came close to her, their heights were matched, and he flinched a little at the look of her.

'I will hear no charges. I am in the keeping of the King of France, I will answer to no one else.'

'Recall, madam, that you revoked that trust in Forli. You chose to answer to me.'

'I will not.'

'Come, madam, we both grow weary of this. Read them.'

'I will not.'

Slowly, delicately, he removed his glove, drawing each finger from its casing of velvet. The Riario ruby burned on his finger, as quietly, casually as he might swat a fly, he brought the back of his hand abruptly against her cheek. There was no other sound except the sharp tug of her breath. He left a tear of blood on her face.

'Be silent, madam. Try my patience no further.'

The legate read the charges. That Caterina, Countess of Forli had sought by means diabolical to poison the sacred person of

His Holiness the Pope. That she had conspired with the enemies of the Holy See. That she had dealt with heretics and made use of magic arts. The Forlivese were questioned as witnesses, and they swore what they had been harried and tormented into swearing in their cracked prison voices. Then they called on Signor Moise to confess that the Countess had bribed him to furnish her with poison. I wriggled and spat the rag from my mouth and called out that it was I who had done it, that I had stolen it from his shop, that he had never set eyes on me, that it was no poison, but merely a tincture of poppy seed such as helped women with their monthly pains. I gasped it out, for the sickness was so strong in me that I almost swooned with it, there were throbbing blows of pain striking through my body.

Signor Moise looked at me sadly. 'They have the collar,' he said, and I knew that he was lost.

It was no trial, I knew that. Caterina would not sign and Valentino wanted no trouble in his newly taken lands. The poison plot was a sop to the French that they need concern themselves no more with her. He would lock her up and he would rule the Romagna, and I could not let it happen. I tried again. I wept and raged and confessed with the pain tunnelling through me, and they heard me out, and I was too stupid to see that each one of my stupid brave words was another turn of the key in the cells of Sant'Angelo. They would take her there, Valentino said when I had done. They would take her as a captive where once she had reigned. I could not save any of them. Not my father, not Cecco, not Ser Giovanni, not poor Signor Moise, not my lady the Countess, for she would not save

314

herself. It was quickly done, for that too was Valentino's way, to move so swift and silent that his enemies barely felt the blade between their shoulders. In moments, it seemed, the testimonies were done and my lady was to be escorted from the room.

'My slave is not in her wits,' she said quietly. 'Look at her. She is unwell. She lost her mind in Forli, poor thing, and I was permitted no better servant. Have a care for her.'

She leaned towards me, and brushed a lock from my brow, as once she had done before.

'Let me go with you, Madonna,' I whispered. 'Let me stay with you. I will go with you anywhere.'

'No, good Mora,' she answered very quietly. 'It is done, now. It is finished. I thank you, for all that you have done for me.'

'But I—'

'No. It is finished.'

She leaned forward and I felt the brush of her lips on my cheek. As she straightened, I could see her leaving me, going far away across the years, past the Belvedere and the litter and the road, past the Numai palazzo and the walls of the Rocca, past Ser Giovanni, past her son reaching out his tiny fists in the starlight, past the *farmacia* and the park and a game we played on All Hallows Eve, until she was back in the courtyard of the Paradiso, the most beautiful lady I had ever seen, and I no more than a gift, unacknowledged amongst so many others. We were strangers again. When she spoke her voice was cold and haughty, and she would not meet my eyes.

'I will come, now.' And she walked from the room where

once she had danced with her bridegroom, her back as straight as a Sforza sword.

'And the other one, Your Grace?' asked the legate cautiously. 'The witch?' I could see him salivating at the prospect of a pyre and a screaming, living coal at its centre. I did not care.

'She is no witch. I have seen her at Forli. As the Countess said, she is out of her wits. Leave us.'

'Have a care, Your Grace. I will see that the men are without.'

'Leave us.'

I was glad of the pain, though my legs were all weak and swimmy. The thump of it kept my head up, so I could look into his eyes.

'Clever girl, Mora,' he said in Castilian. ' A remarkable masquerade. It comes out well for you, I think.'

'There was no feigning, Your Grace. I loved my lady truly.'

There was something in his hands, streaming between them, green and gold. I saw the serpents on the clasp.

'Are you a woman then, to talk to me of love? I thought better of you. Now, shall I give you this, for my pleasure, or shall I burn you? Should you like to burn, little witch? Or would you shift into smoke and fly away from me? As once you did in Toledo, so they say?'

'Toledo.'

All the time. All the time, over and over. I had thought to seem true and play false and he had been one step ahead of me. I had thought myself so clever with my conjuring trick, I had thought him so easy to deceive.

'I was a student once, at Pisa. We had a master there, a

famous scholar. One Ficino? You reminded me yourself of your good old master.'

'You knew – what I am?'

'And greatly enjoyed its confirmation. You have been very useful to me, yet as you know I have a great deal of business. Now, which is it to be? The collar or the fire?'

'All along, you waited for me. I dreamed of you.'

'As your mistress said, it is finished. Choose.'

Those wolf's eyes moved away from me, toward the shuttered windows. His city was beyond, framed in the blazing Spanish sun.

Awkwardly, my hand on my belly, I sank to my knees. I reached for his hand, the bared hand and its twice-bloodied ruby. He did not resist as I pulled it towards my mouth and set a kiss upon the ring.

'I will have the collar, sir. And I will be silent.'

A doubly soft touch on my nape, flesh and velvet, the hard weight of the gold.

'You will find me out, sir, if you have need of me? I shall come to you.'

I was craven, I could not bear to relinquish the last of his touch. His shadow shifted impatiently, he was bored, I was already gone from him.

'Do not doubt it. Perhaps I shall. Take your payment and go.'

I had walked alone in Toledo, where they had cursed me, and through the streets of Florence in my slave's motley, through Forli and Trastevere on my lady's business. No one had thought, or dared perhaps, to take the poppy from me. So before the goggling eyes of the legate and the Spanish guard, the witch of Forli walked free from Valentino's chamber, paused for a swig of poison in the stairwell and stepped out into the streets of Rome with a Pope's ransom in emeralds brazen round her throat.

CHAPTER TWENTY-TWO

VALENTINO WAS RIGHT. IT WAS FINISHED. FINISHED for the man in black, for the Countess, for me. The opiate smoothed away the pain, fractured the sunlight around me, so all I could think of was the tread of my feet, one after the other. It should not be long. I had seen the streets of the Holy City. The drug bound my head in the silken sack, the dark water waited for me. So many others waited in the rolling shroud of the Tiber, it would not be long. I walked and walked. I floated past them all with my white hair and ice eyes and my mermaid's treasure, the thieves and cutpurses and beggars, the starveling street rats, the poxed and pleading whores, yet not one of them came to do me harm. They stared and whispered, made horns of their fingers to warn me off, shrank from my passing. The poppy was sweet and warm in my veins, my tongue sought the traces of Valentino's skin. For the first time in all my scrabbling, hiding life, I walked with my head held high, displaying a life-time of unimaginable wealth for all Rome to see, yet I stayed untouchable.

I walked until the frail spring sunshine died behind the

crumbling heap of the basilica. I circled the Castello, thinking of my lady there, so that the pain came on me again, as though my swelling heart needed to burst from my breast. The waning trance of the drug spun me westwards to the rosy glow of the sky, I thought I saw his jewel burning there and reached out for it like a mad thing, that I might bring him back, for I was his creature now, bound like a dog in his gift, fit only for the cruelties and treachery of my master. Maimed, crooked thing that I was, I had often wished that my life would be done, but never had I yearned for it as now. I would see my papa again, he would be waiting for me with my mother, I had only to sink through the black mud of the river and they would be there, swathed in drifts of almond blossom, she would hold me tight against her and her love would be safe, for was she not already dead? Only to the dead could I do no harm. The pain that ailed me so returned then, deep and nauseating within me, I staggered with it and fell to the oozing ground. Something gripped me from behind, pulling me up by the flesh at my nape like a drowned kitten, hands searched at my neck, feeling for the collar. I laughed with pleasure. It was come. I was not afraid. I would forgive him, I would look him in the eyes and forgive my deliverer. I could barely turn my head in his grip but I twisted until I might catch his face, but saw only a knife's blade, the supple sheen of it alight with the last of the sunset, dazzling me. It was finished. I closed my eyes and waited for the crystal streams of my Toledo river to open their radiant arms.

*

I dream I am in the palazzo. The beautiful boy is gone from the cortile, the walnut intarsia of the benches in the loggia is dusty and scarred. My feet are loud on the cracked marble, I look down and see a pair of clogs beneath the hem of my woollen servant's dress. The heavy shoes clatter as I mount the staircase. My master's scrittoio is wrecked, the walls charred, the cabinets smashed and tumbled. I pass on. The huge fireplace in the sala is cold, the yellow silk cushions of the antecamera are hacked and moulding, oozing their down noiselessly to the wine-soaked floor. I am looking for something, what? All the luminous treasures of this house are dulled and vanished, buried beneath Florence like the weapons of some ancient sleeping giant. I turn towards the chapel. The magi stare solemnly still from the walls, familiar, but the chalices and furnishings are gone. A single candle burns on the altar, its light falling on the white headcloth of a woman who kneels before a simple silver crucifix, her plain dress dark against the linen. She turns. My lady, Caterina. Her face is gentle, she smiles.

'Good Mora. You are come.'

Something heavy lies in my palm. I have been carrying what I sought all along. I step towards her and open my hand. There it lies, the Riario ruby, the crimson flame at its heart streaming over my skin in the glow of the candle, staining it, blood-coloured. I hold out my hand, she reaches for it.

*

'She stirs.'

'Mora, Mora. Can you hear us?'

'Do not be afraid. You are safe.'

'Mora!'

There was a cloth at my lips, I felt a trickle of warm wine in my cracked mouth. My hands moved to my throat – I had become a Florentine true, it seemed – but there were only my bare bones.

'It is safe. See, we have it here for you.' A glitter of green and gold before my eyes. My eyes were open, so I was not dead. I was lying in the wagon, wrapped in something warm, a little brazier of coals glowed at my feet. I sought about for the pain, but found it gone. Annunziata's face wavered into sight, I tried to smile and lift myself up, but there was something wadded between my legs and I flinched.

'I am hurt?'

'No, Mora. We came to find you. There was news – of the lady Caterina and how she was sent to Sant'Angelo to be tried for a witch, and we feared for you, so the men went out to search, and they brought you here, to us.'

'I'm bleeding.'

Her eyes dipped, I could almost feel the heat from her cheeks.

'You were ill. When they brought you back you were too sick to walk and we washed you and saw what it was. Forgive us, Mora. We cut you. Immaculata did it. She boiled the knife in wine and she cut you, to let out the blood. But you will be well, now. You will grow accustomed to it.'

The colour deepened in her cheeks. She was plumper, and as she moved in the light of the coals I could see the new mound of her belly shift beneath her gown. I pushed my hand beneath the blanket and felt for the new tender place they had made in me. When I brought my finger to my lips it was bright and streaming.

'I don't understand. Thank you for your goodness, but I do not understand.'

'It happens like that, sometimes. Old Margherita in Florence helped a girl in this way, she told us of it. The thing, the part that keeps a woman a maid, was grown too strong, that is all. Like a lock. It can be mended, if it is done kindly, but if not the black blood builds, it is very dangerous. We feared to lose you.'

'It is what I wished.'

If I had found her, that misted day in Florence. Margherita might have made me a woman after all. My poor papa had been wrong, so very wrong, and Maestro Ficino too. It was too much. I lay back and watched the ribs of the wagon, the canvas between them bucking a little in the wind outside.

'Sleep again now, you will be stronger.'

'Take it, the collar,' I asked her. 'The men will know how to break up the stones. Please to take one of them to Trastevere, and ask for the family of a Jew named Moise. If they can find someone, give them a stone. And take another. Buy meat, wine, anything you wish. We will have a feast.'

Her quiet face was all concern, she thought me raving.

'We will have a feast, to honour my old master Ficino. A wedding feast, for you and your babe, and we will take a cup of wine and spill it.' I giggled. 'To Hymen.'

The girls whispered amongst themselves. There was something delighting them, something more than the prospect of a party.

'She is still weak,' I heard.

'The shock might be too much for her.'

'What?' I asked. 'What could shock me?'

Annunziata and Immaculata shrugged, their faces a mixture of anxiety and glee. Then the curtain of the wagon was pulled aside and a face peered in, a face covered by a tumbling mass of bronze hair, the skin as warm and speckled as a new brown egg.

Cecco.

Then I realized that I was dead, after all. I didn't mind it. I thought I would go back to sleep, and closed my eyes, laughing. I was glad to be dead. In fact, I was so happy that my last thought wondered if the dead could run mad.

CHAPTER TWENTY-THREE

'HOW DID YOU FIND ME?'

We were propped on the stoop of the wagon, cosy in a blanket and the first lemony sunbeams of the Roman spring. I was still too weak to walk more than a few steps, when I tried the pain still sliced at me, but the taint of the poppy had bled out and I knew I should get well. I could not stop looking at him, it was all I could do to stop myself reaching out to touch his face, over and over. He had not been killed. I had seen what I wanted to see, what something in me thought I deserved to see. But he had been badly injured, so badly he had lain ill a whole year. There was a hollow in his skull that fitted my thumb. That at least I could ask to touch, nestled under the thick cap of his hair.

'I tried to find you, as soon as I was well. I thought you would write to me.'

I remembered the letter of condolence Maestro Ficino had asked me to finish, which I could not bear to touch. I had moved my room at Careggi when the roof began to leak, it was perhaps still there, a soaked lump that could have saved me so much suffering, though I could not care about it now. It had taken a long time for Cecco to learn that Maestro Ficino was at Careggi, his father was afraid that Medici servants would be victimised and had taken his family to relatives at Pistoia.

'And then, for a while, I thought *you* were dead.'

His father had returned to the palazzo to look for me, that first awful day. Some of the Medici slaves had been killed, one of them a fair haired girl. I thought on my trio of enemies, and was sad for whichever of them had not deserved to die that way. Then Cecco heard that Ser Giovanni was returned, and was dealing grain for the Medici under the name of Popolano. He had heard the rumours of witchcraft at the villa and knew it could only mean that I lived. Eventually he walked all the way to Careggi, sleeping in hedges.

'For a while, my poor father had nothing. I hated to burden him.'

When he arrived, he found me gone to Forli, and wrote to me there, but by then the plague had come, and no correspondence was permitted into the town.

'I tried again, I wrote, but the French were on the move, it was chaos. Nowhere seemed safe, the roads were jammed with people leaving. Ser Giovanni was dead . . .'

'He was a good man, you know,' I said. 'Good enough. What happened in Florence was not his fault.'

And then he heard of the siege of Ravaldino, and feared again for my life. He had stayed at Careggi, doing his best to take care of our old master, who was frail and forgetful now. Maestro Ficino told him of the troupe, of our own extraordinary escape

326

from Florence, and when Cecco decided to follow me down to Forli after it fell, to try for news, he had come upon them on the road and recognised them.

'So you were there? That night on the road, with the wolf?'

'I hadn't mentioned you then. I wasn't sure I could trust them, there were so many rumours of poisoning, and unholy goings on. Then they found you on the road and I tried to get close, I was desperate, but there were guards around you all the time. I came on after you to Rome, I thought I could find you, we asked about you and the Countess all over the city.'

I didn't want to speak about Caterina. There would be time for that, one day. I wanted this happiness to last a little longer.

'So why did you follow me?' I was not flirting. I was fearful of his answer.

He looked at me. He was a man now, not a boy, and I had been right. He had grown up handsome. His hair was bronze, not carroty, his shoulders had widened, his skin was clear and tanned from the months of travel. It darkened, blood flushing up into his cheeks.

'Maybe I like trouble.'

We both looked at the ground. My throat felt as though I had swallowed a melon.

'Here, I brought you something – I've had them all this time. My father found them.'

He bounded away and returned with a rolled flour sack. He tipped out my old doll and a bundle of red cloth into my lap. I

unfolded my dress and turned it in my hands, looking for the
place where my heart had lain.

'I brought them,' he said again. 'You seemed keen on
them.'

'See this, Cecco?' I asked softly. 'This is my name.'

They were the only things I had ever truly owned, I thought.
A broken doll and a child's worn dress. Those, and a ready fortune in emeralds.

*

The twins went into the city as I asked and found a goldsmith
who did not ask questions. They brought me back a leather
pouch of stones, and the clasp with the Sforza wyvern on a
plain cord, which now I wore about my neck. I wanted to give
them as many as they would take – there was money there to
buy them a palace apiece if they cared for it, but they settled on
just three. One for now for new clothes and shoes for the horses
and a better wagon and provisions, one to keep if times went
hard and one for the child, that when it was grown it might
be whatever it wanted in this world that money could buy.
Johannes the blind musician was the father of Annunziata's
babe. He had been made in my master's sign, Aquarius, in the
coldest month of the year, when I had thought myself a prisoner
in Valentino's rooms at Forli. At first it seemed sad to me that
Johannes should never look upon her lovely face, or gaze into
the new eyes of his child, then I thought on how lucky
Annunziata was to have someone who loved her for what she
was, for whom her beauty would never fade, for whom the

sound of her voice and the touch of her hands were sufficient.

I lay another month with the bleeding, mostly in the darkness of the wagon. Cecco had shown himself surprisingly handy for one who claimed to have been bred for a scholar, and he had made himself useful fixing the axles on the wagons, mending and painting the props, but he did his work where I could see him through the curtain. I never wanted to stop seeing him. Annunziata and Immaculata brought me broth, and food when I could take it, and a length of red tabby silk for a dress that they would sew for me. They brought me something else, too. I asked after my old friend. Still with them, they said, though his eyes were glaucous now and he was tired-out by the coming heat. I asked them to help me out of the wagon one evening. I climbed gingerly to the ground, which shifted a little beneath me, but holding their shoulders I could stand firm for the first time. Addio was there, gleeful, and Casinus, with new wheels to his trolley and a silver-topped stick with a lion carved into its head to steer him along.

I had dreamed so long of wolves. They had been with me ever since I was taken from Toledo, their wildness had kept me company and comforted me, and it had been in me, somewhere. *Mind and be nice to the gentleman.* I saw it all, now.

My mother had the sight. She had left that to me, along with her protection stitched against my heart, her gift, her gift to me. My father, concerned for my odd looks, my smallness and slightness and, perhaps, a little fetched away by his own desire to commune with the old knowledge that scholars sought, had seen what was not there. I was no half-creature, no alchemist's chalice. I was made a little differently, that was all. His desire to protect me and his own faith had done the rest – convinced Ficino, convinced the bookseller, convinced me. For how else could I make sense of my strangeness? Adara and that old Toledo bawd had believed it, and tried to turn a profit on me. What that old man had done had turned something in me, but in my rage and confusion I had summoned not wolves, not the magic of the *seid*, but another self, one which could not be bound and used but which ran free, a spirit-self, which succoured me through all I had endured. I was grateful to it, in a way. Without it, I might have ended like those poor girls at the palazzo, or those in Forli, splayed out for the pleasure of a hired soldier and left to die. Or else my knowledge of herbs and cures would have condemned me and I might be counting out my last hours in a cell in the Castello, listening as they stacked the faggots outside. I had been strong enough to convince Valentino because I believed it myself. But then he wanted to believe, because he thought he knew all about me.

Through those long days in the wagon, as I healed, I sorted my thoughts once again, telling them out. I was weaving a new pattern, separating the threads of my old life to make a new one, which had not yet come clear. Cecco was not dead, I had to learn again who I was. I had loved Caterina, and the pain of her betrayal had brought out the wolf in me, but I had been loyal to her, in the end. There was no curse on me, I could not blame myself for her, or for my papa. The evil that had come upon them was none of my doing.

Rome was full of stories of Caterina. Lioness they were

calling her, the lioness of the Romagna. She was a heroine, they made poems and ballads on her. I asked the twins to fetch me a bundle of pamphlets. *Listen to the unfortunate Caterina of Forli, Abandoned without help, Who alone has the courage to fight for Italy, Who will die with honour* . . . She chose it, I knew, she chose how she wanted it to end. I could never have saved her. I peered at the smudged sheets in the dingy light of the wagon. There is the Rocca, with Caterina on the walls, there the French soldiers climbing the walls like huge-armed apes. And there are the wolves, running between them, their jaws black with cheap ink. One pamphlet speaks only of that, of how the Countess who tried to poison the Pope made league with the devil and called his minions to her aid. She kept a witch, it said, a Spanish witch, half-girl, half-boy. It was well printed, no doubt as to its source. And another, scrawled and hand-copied, claims that they came with the Borgia, that he summoned his fellows from Hell to do his bidding. They had come because they hungered, because they scented death and could not resist its call. I was no witch, to whistle up a storm of wolves.

Which left me with Valentino, with my dreams of the man in black. For I could not deny how I had seen him, how he had called to me. Here the thread tangled, I could not unpick it. I had allowed him to use me, believing I was using him, and I had to acknowledge that there was a likeness between us. I was shamed by the pleasure I had taken in him, but he had played me fair, I thought, in the end. I would put that away then, lock it up deep inside me where it should never need show itself again. No one should ever know how he had spoiled me. In Florence, picking over the heaps of greens in the kitchens of the palazzo, I had known that I must wait, that I must wait until I could conjure the wolves out of me and become Mura again.

And now I would. I would be a girl like any other girl, in a new Mayday dress, a girl who did not think on charms or learning or the messengers of the planets. That was for scholars like Maestro Ficino, not for me. I would be Mura Benito, I would walk out on a spring morning to gather herbs to heal people, as her father had once done. I wanted no more of great people, their world of pride and power and soldiers and sieges would spin along as it had always done, without me. I could live quiet, as I had hoped to once at Careggi, before my dreams were done with me, and that would be enough.

Chellus and Gherardus led him round.

'Be careful,' they warned, 'his teeth are going, but not his temper.'

I took one small, weak step forward, another. I sought him behind his poor filmed eyes, tried to find his heart beneath his draggled shedding pelt. Nothing. No wild flights through the dark wastes of the north, no tattooed giants hailing me from the frozen mists, no forests ripe with sacrifice, no affinity of the blood. I smiled. How foolish I had been. He lifted a hindleg and scratched at a flea. I put a questing hand to his coarse fur, rubbed along the skin for the squirming louse, crushed its blood-fattened carapace between my fingers. He growled low and snapped idly, irritably, so I had to snatch it back. He had never been my friend. For one tiny, plenteous moment, I was sorry.

'It is gone, you see,' I told them. 'Quite gone. Thank you.'

CHAPTER TWENTY-FOUR

I WORE MY RED DRESS ON THE DAY THE WORLD changed. The finest tabby silk, cut close to fit me. Over my heart, inside, where no one should see, I pricked out a penta-gram and stitched my name within it. Mura. I gave new dresses to the girls, blue for Immaculata, a soft green velvet to cosset Annunziata's belly. We dressed ourselves in the wagon, I combed my hair out and put jasmine water behind my ears. At my throat I wore the Sforza wyvern on its cord, as a reminder. I would not forsake my lady. I had learned from her that courage may be taken from music and dancing and loveliness, as much as from swords and men – the things I wished to forget. I hoped the music of our feast would carry to her, deep in the heart of the Castello, and that for a moment she might forget herself, and be the woman I had known in those first years at the Paradiso, when she had Ser Giovanni, flushed with her power and her love.

I found that I could give orders like quite the fine lady. This May Eve, we would have two bonfires, and Annunziata and Johannes would jump over their embers in the old way, at dawn, and be married. I sent for juniper berry to clean the flames, and we scoured down by the riverbank for rowan boughs to hang from the wagons. I told the troupe to give word that all the pilgrims in the campground were welcome, as our guests, and Casinus handed out coins from our store for pork and wine and white bread. There would be sweetmeats, too, from the finest cook shop in Rome, marchpane and candied chestnuts and *magdalenas* in the Spanish style. There were new shirts for the men and I did not forget a paper of beefsteak for a bad tempered old wolf.

Johannes began playing as we made ourselves ready. It was an odd song, like nothing I had ever heard, sad and lingering, in a language Annunziata said shyly came from a country called Ireland, a green country far away over the sea, full of black haired men and green eyed girls. 'Beautiful, Mura,' she said. 'Like you.'

She handed me a looking glass. It was a cheap thing compared with what I had handled at Forli, and at first I did not want to look. I had never found comfort in a mirror, but they giggled and teased me and I laughed too, thinking this is what it is to be a woman, and have friends. So I looked, and there I was, my hair all blanched and frosty about my shoulders, as pale as May-blossom, my eyes their familiar startling green. I looked closer and saw Signor Moise's face again, the expression in his eyes when I had tried on the necklace. Something had changed. I thought I might look pretty. More ordinary perhaps, no changeling with savage cheekbones and a wild shadow's stare, no scrawny boy in a ragged shirt, but a girl one might look upon in the street, who was young and fresh and smooth skinned, whose face might lift a heart.

'Look at her,' laughed Immaculata, 'batting her eyes like a coquette. They'll all want to dance with you tonight, Mura!'

'But there's only one she wants to dance with,' added Annunziata. And I laughed with them, like a real girl.

They were both right. Johannes was joined by a piper and a harpist and a boy with a yellow painted drum as tall as Addio, then more and more musicians from all over the campground, until he had to borrow Casinus's stick and beat it to keep them in time. The torches were lit, and the two huge bonfires, with one of the old wagons at their heart, for the troupe should have a finer one now, kept off the chill of the spring night. I drank soft red Spanish wine, and I danced, shyly at first, with Chellus and Gherardus, showing me the steps. And then, laughing, I danced with Addio who hopped about earnestly, his funny big hands warm and tight around my own. And then with men who asked me, over and over, a lumbering butcher's apprentice with apple blossom behind his ears, a whipcord Sicilian with a dagger in his high boot and gold in his teeth, a fair haired boy from Bergamo whose accent made everyone laugh. More and more of them, until I forgot their faces, dazzled by the whirl of it and their smiles in the firelight. My shoes seemed to be tapping out my name, I told it again and again, Mura, my name is Mura. I danced until I fell down panting and then I got up and danced again. I danced with Cecco. He asked me properly, with a bow like a fine gentleman, as though we were guests back in the palazzo. I danced in his arms until the first grey light showed over the city. In a while, he whispered something to me, and I whispered something back.

We did not want to spoil their happiness with a leave-taking. I went to the wagon for my cloak and my bag of stones, which were all I owned in the world, and I was about to slip away when I felt a tug at the hem of my red dress.

'You're not going, Mura?'

'I have to leave, Addio. This is not my place.'

His knobby face was twisted with concern under the most fantastical cap I had seen him wear, all patches that glowed like jewels, with red ribbons and a brass bell on the tip.

'It doesn't matter, you know, that you can't do it any more. You're welcome to stay with us. There's the babe that will need caring for, in time, and you're a good dancer, you might learn the tumbling if you tried.'

'Thank you, Addio. But I'm not leaving alone.'

'Are you ready, Mura?'

Cecco had his things. We thought to hire horses at the city gates. Addio clapped his hands and danced a little caper.

'Oh, I see, I see! The knight errant and his fine lady!' He swept us a bow, then his face grew concerned.

'You know where you go then? You will go back to Toledo?'

'No. We go to Florence.'

We. I had never thought I would say that.

'Give us a kiss then.'

So I did, and that was three kisses, one from a dwarf, one from a dead boy, and one from a future I had never dared to dream on. Cecco took my hand.

'Are you ready, my love?'

I was still for a moment, breathing in the newness of it.

'Mura, come on.' Mura.

I dreamed a she-wolf who came to my bedside in Florence. I dreamed them singing to me along the road to Forli, along the road to Rome. Beyond the mountains, beyond their singing, a man waits at a window. Behind him a city is burning. His sleeve caresses the white stone where he rests his gloved hand, black and red, with a massive jewel that glows deeper than the flames. His face is masked, a smooth coating of velvet. He turns his face to the hills, listening. In a while, it comes, one long howl. Somewhere, out there in the forest, the wolves are running. Little witch. He touches the ruby to his lips. She comes, she comes.

I shook myself.

'Yes,' I answered. 'I'm ready.'

Turn the page for an excerpt from:

THE STOLEN QUEEN

Lisa Hilton's new novel, available from Corvus
in trade paperback and e-book in 2014.

INTRODUCTION

IN THE TIME WHEN I WAS STILL A CHILD, IT SEEMED TO ME that my father's city of Angouleme was an island, a floating city gathered in the folded waves of the Charente plain. From harvest until Easter, the fields that stretched below the ramparts were bleak, wind-scoured, pitted here and there with lonely clumps of juniper that I made believe were rocks where mermaids might sing, wriggling up from the froth of chalky soil which tipped the winter rains into a silvery net of tiny streams. I had not seen the sea, then, but on bright days when my nurse Agnes would take me to walk in the garden I would scramble up on the wall and claim I could spy it, a tinsel ribbon at the edge of the horizon, and I would make poor stout Agnes puff along after me as I played at being a pirate princess, defending my kingdom against dragons, or the wicked hordes of heathen soldiers, pulling up the beach in their black-sailed ships, vicious scimitars glinting deep through their beards, clutched in gold-tipped pointed teeth. Agnes grumbled that it was no game for a young lady, and why couldn't I sit nicely under a rose bush and attend to my needlework like a Christian child, but I argued rudely that was I not a Courtenay and a great lady besides, and that serpents and infidels were very much my business.

Agnes had nothing to say to that. My mother's people were a Crusading family, princes in Outremer, the kingdom across the sea where the bravest knights of Europe fought in the bloodstained desert to preserve Christendom from the wicked wiles of Saladin, and when I was big I was going to take ship at Italy and cross those deserts myself and live in a pink marble palace with a hundred courtyards full of fountains and a troop of monkeys with gold collars to bring me pomegranates and sherbets made with jasmine syrup and mountain ice. Agnes said monkeys were nasty beasts, she was sure, full of fleas and worse, and that she had no intention of getting on a ship and then where would I be in my pink marble palace with no one to mind me? So then I would sit quietly, to please her, and pretend to study my missal, but in a while my eyes would wander up through the wide sky above my father's house to the façade of the cathedral, alive with its tumble of stone flowers and beasts, and my sensible wool cloak would turn to mail across my back so that I could feel its dusty weight, and the sharp wind that whipped up from the river below the city would be full of the scents of saffron and incense and the cupolas at the corners of my grandfather's church would shimmer in a mirage becoming the towers of the Holy City itself . . . until the bells rang for the tenth hour and I had to snatch up my book and run to wash my hands as Agnes called me to dinner.

I was playing there, up on the walls, the day the silk merchant came. It was April, and the waters of the ocean beneath me were turning from grey to the palest gold-green.

'Look, Agnes, he's here, he's here!'

Childhood has a different calendar, I think, not marked by the feasts of the Church or the regular shift of the seasons, but by the smaller, more personal rhythms of a world of which we are still the centre. For me, the New Year began when the new sunlight softened merciless Poitou wind and I began to watch for the silk merchant on the road from the south. He was Venetian, from that city which really did float on water, where all the wealth of the East was gathered to be floated along canals the colour of the silk man's strange aqua eyes. I loved to hear my mother tell me of Venice, the Crusader's gateway, from where the men of my own family had set out to fight the heathen, where mysterious ladies waited in gold-panelled rooms, combing out their hair in pearl looking-glasses, with silk sleeves to their gowns that trailed all the way to the ground. My mother had a looking glass, and if I was very careful she might sometimes allow me to peep at myself in it, but she said that in Venice the light was conjured into so much glass that the whole city shimmered like a vast mirror, a vision of Heaven at the edge of the world.

Even Agnes was excited to see him, looking carefully round to see that none of my father's grooms were nearby before hoisting her skirts, showing a glimpse of blue cloth stocking, to climb up beside me. She put her arm about me as we watched, and I remember her smell, the lavender in her linen under the darker odour of her winter gown, mixed with the olive oil of the Castile soap she used to scrub us both in the bath house.

I pointed along the road to where the silk man's mule laboured like a fat bluebottle through the swampy hollows left by the winter floods. 'Look, there he is!'

'I see him, Isabelle, yes. I see him, little one.'

If I had listened, perhaps I would have caught something different in her tone, then, but I was too excited to care.

'But there's someone else, Agnes, look!'

I felt her stiffen beside me, a sudden tension in her gentle arm, and she looked round wildly for a moment until her eyes dropped back to the road, and seeing that the second rider was alone, she let out her breath and hugged me closer.

'What's the matter, Agnes?'

'Nothing, my treasure. I wonder who that is?'

The Poitou roads are almost impassable in the wintertime. Our supplies and messages came up the river on barges; it was not until the world dried out that the time came for the men to move out for the campaigning season. It was too early for there to be anything to fear from the road, even I knew that. Agnes was always worrying. I peered as far as I dared over the worn stone, my feet dangling in the air behind me. The horseman was gaining on the mule, I could see the red and gold of his surcoat through its splattering of road-mud. He was riding crazily, paying no mind to the treacherous ground, his body hunched high over the straining shoulders of his mount, so that I could imagine the poor beast's sides slick with sweat and blood from the cruel spurs. He came up behind the silk man and the mule skittered clumsily from his path;

I heard a shout of protest as the packs were pelted with dirt. I wanted to giggle, but Agnes would not have liked me to laugh at another's misfortune, so I made my face solemn and said that I hoped the poor silk man's wares were not spoiled.

'Still, he must be important. He will have come for my father.' I felt proud as I said that, knowing that my father was the most important man in his county of Angouleme and La Marche.

'Come away now, Isabelle.'

'No! I want to see.'

'The silk man will be here soon,' she coaxed. 'We can go to the kitchens and see about some food for him. And then you can choose your gown.'

I struggled out from under her arm. 'No, I want to stay here. Look, they're opening the gates!'

'You'll fall, you foolish child! Come back, now.'

Reluctantly, I let her lead me down to the kitchen buildings, but not before I had jumped three times from the wall into her waiting arms. And then we were in the kitchens, where I was rarely allowed to go, and all the cooks and scullions bowed through the smoke and steam and said 'My lady,' which I liked very much, and we picked out a cold duck and some soft manchet bread for the silk man, and I grandly ordered some spiced wine for my visitor and was given a piece of pink marchpane to suck, so that altogether I forgot about the messenger, so eager was I to see the silk that Agnes would sew into my birthday gown.

We waited and waited in my mother's room, where we would always look at the fabrics together, but even after the silk man had unloaded his wares and washed and eaten and prayed, she did not come. I fidgeted with the hangings on her big carved bed and poked in the rushes with my toes and made a nuisance of myself until Agnes snapped at me and told me to sit quiet.

'But *maman* said she would come! She always comes. Why is she late?'

'I don't know.'

'Well send to find out then,' I said imperiously, so Agnes spoke to one of my mother's maids, who had gaggled in the doorway, as eager as

343

I to see the cloths and slippers and ribbons, and in a while she slipped back and whispered in Agnes's ear.

'*Maman* says you can start without her, Isabelle. She's very busy, and you're a big girl now. Old enough to choose your own gown.'

I thought about crying. It wasn't fair. My mother always looked at the silks with me, and told me stories about where they came from, and it wouldn't be the same without her. Still, the maids were watching, and Agnes's face was tight with something I didn't recognize, and I knew that she minded for me and that I should behave graciously.

'Very well.' I took a deep breath and motioned my hand to the silk man as I had seen my mother do. 'You may show us what you have brought. We will see if it pleases us.'

I caught a giggle from one of the maids and glared at her. She bobbed a curtsey and said 'Excuse me, my lady.' I felt better. I clapped my hands, trying to feel as happy as I had last year, and the year before.

'Come along then!'

For a moment the girls hung back, but then they fell upon the opened packs like a flock of pigeons, pecking and exclaiming, running rainbows through their fingers and holding up the jewel-coloured cloths to their faces. I pointed to a heavy red as it slithered to the floor.

'Where does this come from?'

The silk man's skin was dark like old leather, but I thought I could see that city of sparkling water and glass in his curious eyes. I liked the long lilt in his voice when he spoke, the slim suppleness of his vowels, poking through our language like the slender prow of a boat.

'From Venice, my lady. My city.'

All the same, the red was too weighty and sombre, like something a priest would wear.

'Show me another.'

He pulled out a length of golden orange, holding it up to the light so that the colours danced, then spreading it across my knees so I could make out delicate blue embroidery, a shadowy pattern of foliage.

'This is from the meadows of Anatolia, my lady. The women there labour for years on a single piece of cloth. It will be as though your skirts are a field of flowers.'

344

Agnes looked disapproving. 'You may set that aside for my mistress. It is too fine for a child.'

I didn't mind. It was beautiful, but it was not my birthday gown. The maids had gathered beneath the casement, exclaiming over a piece they held between them, but when I looked again I was puzzled, for it seemed there was nothing in their hands.

'That one.'

Agnes often reprimanded me for my eagerness, for poking and snatching, breaking things or making them grubby, but when I saw the silk the maids were carrying I held myself back, afraid to touch it. I had never seen anything so beautiful. The tissue was so fine it might have been a lady's skin; the veins on the girls' hands were visible beneath it. It was not quite white and not quite silver, densely woven like damask, but it seemed as light as a cloud. It was definitely something that a mermaid would wear.

'Please, where does this come from?'

'Oh this, my lady? This is not for sale.'

I thought I knew all his merchant's tricks, like when Agnes took me to the fair on Lady Day and the stallholders pretended they had nothing to spare because they knew we were rich. I thought I would pretend to be patient.

'But please, tell me where it is from.'

'This silk is from Persia, my lady. There is nothing like it for sale from Naples to Paris. And it is a gift, a gift for the Queen of France herself.'

'Really? For the Queen?'

'For Queen Agnes, yes. She was a princess of Dalmatia, you know, which is a Venetian territory. Her Majesty will value this greatly, so you see I cannot sell it, even to such a pretty little lady as you.'

'Is that so?' It was my mother's voice. The silk man folded himself into a bow so tight I thought he would spring back like a spinning top, and the maids' gowns rustled as they bent deep curtseys, but I rushed into her arms.

'*Maman*, *Maman*, here you are! I knew you'd come! Look at this, *Maman*, he says it's for the Queen!'

My mother squeezed me so tightly that I was lifted off the floor and she buried her lips in my neck, kissing me until it tickled while I rubbed my nose into her shoulder.

'How much?'

'But *Maman*, it really is for the Queen, we can't buy it!'

'Do you like it, little one? Shall you have it for your birthday gift from me?'

I hesitated. I wanted it, of course I wanted it, but there was something about it that made me afraid. It was a costume for a pink marble palace, like something from a story that I didn't quite want to come true. When I looked at it, it made me feel lonely.

'Won't the Queen be angry, *Maman*?' I hesitated.

My mother smiled. 'I daresay the Queen has plenty of Eastern silks to choose from. And this is white, the colour the queens of France wear for mourning, you know. Perhaps she will not like it, just now.'

As my mother spoke I saw Agnes's eyes seek her face. She raised her eyebrows, questioning. My mother replied with a barely perceptible nod.

'So you would have it, then, my darling?'

'Of course, thank you *Maman*, oh, thank you!' I tried to hop with happiness, to show my mother I was delighted, but there was a strange cold feeling inside me, and as the silk man moved to lay the cloth on my mother's bed I hated how its lightness stirred in the breeze from the casement, like a living thing. A shroud, I thought, a creeping shroud that would swallow me up and suffocate me. I wanted him gone, I wanted to choose another gown, anything, yellow or blush or green, I didn't care, but I smiled and held my mother's arm as the silk man bowed his way out to the strongroom where my father's clerk would mark the silk on the tally sticks, and the maids fluttered out, exclaiming over their ribbons and kerchiefs.

And then, when we were alone, my mother told me slowly and sadly that King Richard of England was dead, and that I was to be married. I was nine years old.